STAKED

BY KEVIN HEARNE

STAKED

kevin hearne

DEL REY • NEW YORK

2016 Del Rey Mass Market Edition

Copyright © 2016 by Kevin Hearne
Excerpt from *A Plague of Giants* by Kevin Hearne copyright © 2016 by Kevin Hearne

Published in the United States by Del Rey, an imprint of Random House, a division of Penguin Random House LLC, New York.

DEL REY and the HOUSE colophon are registered trademarks of Penguin Random House LLC.

Originally published in hardcover in the United States by Del Rey, an imprint of Random House, a division of Penguin Random House LLC, in 2016.

This book contains an excerpt from the forthcoming book *A Plague of Giants* by Kevin Hearne. This excerpt has been set for this edition only and may not reflect the final content of the forthcoming edition.

ISBN 978-0-345-54853-5
Ebook ISBN 978-0-345-54852-8

Illustrations by Phil Balsman

Printed in the United States of America

randomhousebooks.com

9 8 7 6 5 4 3 2 1

Del Rey mass market edition: November 2016

for Nigel in toronto

pRONUNCiATiON Guide

Some o' the words in this book might not be immediately pronounceable for some readers because they have foreign origins. Heck, I needed help myself. But I like learning new words and how to say them, so I'm providing a wee guide here for a few names and such in case you're of a like mind and want to know how to say them out loud. No one is going to confiscate your cake if you say them wrong, but you might score a piece of cake if you say them right. You know what? You should just have a piece of cake anyway. You deserve cake.

CZECH

Celetná = TSELL et NAH (A street in Prague)

Králodvorská = KRAH loh DVOR skah (A street in Prague)

Petřín = PET shreen (A hill on the castle side of Prague)

Ulice = oo LEE tse (Means *street*, basically. Interesting fact: The word is the same in Polish but they place it in front of the name and the Czechs put it afterward. So if you were speaking of Main Street, in Polish that would be *Ulice Main* and in Czech it's *Main Ulice*.)

Vltava = Vl TAH vah (Big ol' river that runs through Prague)

POLISH

Agnieszka = ag nee ESH ka (One of the Polish coven)

Bydgoszcz = bid GOSH-CH (City in Poland. I straight up admit to choosing it just to cause panic in my audiobook narrator. To English-speaking eyes those four consonants at the end look alarming. But they are actually two distinct digraphs that linguistically represent a fricative followed by an affricative: *sz* and *cz*. The *sz* is going to get you something like *sh* and the *cz* gives you *ch*. But when you pronounce that it's all one syllable. Try it! GOSH-CH. Seriously fun.)

Ewelina = ev eh LEE na (One of the Polish coven. The letter *w* is pronounced like *v* in Polish.)

Miłosz = ME wash (The white horse of Świętowit. That spiffy *ł* is pronounced as a *w* in Polish. And that *o* is pronounced like the *a* in *wash*, so there you have it.)

Nocnica = nohts NEETS uh (Slavic nightmare creature; nocnice, pl.)

Patrycja = pa TREES ya (One of the Polish coven. Basically as in *Patricia* but with a long *e* sound and no *sh*.)

Pole Mokotowskie = PO leh Mo ko TOV ski-eh (An expansive park in the city of Warsaw.)

Radość = Rah DOHSH-CH (Translates to *joy*. A neighborhood in one of Warsaw's districts, on the east side of the Wisła River.)

Świętowit = SHVEN toe veet (That cool little *ę* indicates an *n* sound at the end of the vowel. Slavic god with four heads.)

Weles = VEH les (Spelled as *Veles* in most other Slavic countries but the pronunciation is nearly universal. Slavic deity of the earth, enemy of Perun.)

Wisła = Vee SWAH (River that runs right through the
    center of Warsaw.)
Wisława Szymborska = Vee SWAH vah Shim BOR ska
    (Polish Nobel Prize winner for literature. Great
    poetry.)

author's note

This book begins in a very different place from where *Shattered* left off; if you missed the novella *A Prelude to War*, you might wish to read it first to understand why the initial chapters are set where they are and some of the references to Loki and Mekera. You can find it in the mini-anthology *Three Slices*, available in ebook or audio. Or if you can't wait, you can just dive in to *Staked*!

I have many people to thank abroad for their help in getting the details right. Any mistakes you find are of course mine and not theirs.

Thanks to Jakob and Simon of Otherland Buchhandlung for the German bits and to Florian Specht for his help navigating Berlin; I'm grateful to Rob Durdle for helping me with French; turbo thanks to Grzegorz Zielinski for showing me around Warsaw and pinpointing the location of Malina Sokołowska's house, as well as the black poplar tree in Pole Mokotowskie; much gratitude to Adrian Tomczyk for his companionship and translation help in Poznań and then helping with further language questions once I got home; cheers to my amazing Polish readers who greeted me at Pyrkon and were so very gracious; thanks to Tomáš Jirkovský and Martin Šust for good times in Prague and Brno; and I'm very grateful to Ester Scoditti for her guidance in Rome. Megaturbo-gonzo thanks go to Nadine Kharabian for the tour of spooky places in her great city, where I finally figured out why you never want to be Nigel in Toronto. And gratitude to the fine people at the Royal Conservatory of Music on Bloor Street for enduring my questions about the Lady in Red.

Tricia Narwani continues to be an editing genius and I'm astoundingly fortunate to work with her and the entire Del Rey team.

And deepest thanks to my readers for saying hi online and in person, having fun with Iron Druid cosplay, naming their puppies Oberon and Orlaith, and all the other unbearably awesome things you do. You all deserve a sausage. With gravy.

In a Denver coffee shop, August 2015

iron druid chronicles

the story so far

Atticus O'Sullivan, born in 83 B.C.E. as Siodhachan Ó Suileabháin, has spent much of his long life as a Druid on the run from Aenghus Óg, one of the Tuatha Dé Danann. Aenghus Óg seeks the return of Fragarach, a magical sword that Atticus stole in the second century, and the fact that Atticus has learned how to keep himself young and won't simply die annoys the heck out of Aenghus Óg.

When Aenghus Óg finds Atticus hiding in Tempe, Arizona, Atticus makes the fateful decision to fight instead of run, unwittingly setting off a chain of consequences that snowball on him despite his efforts to lie low.

In *Hounded,* he gains an apprentice, Granuaile MacTiernan, retrieves a necklace that serves as a focus for Laksha Kulasekaran, an Indian witch, and discovers that his cold iron aura is proof against hellfire. He defeats Aenghus Óg with an assist from the Morrigan, Brighid, and the local pack of werewolves. However, he also severely cripples a witches' coven that wasn't exactly benevolent but was protecting the Phoenix metro area from more-menacing groups of predators.

Hexed, book two, forces Atticus to deal with that, as a rival and much more deadly coven tries to take over the territory of the Sisters of the Three Auroras, and a group of Bacchants tries to establish a foothold in

Scottsdale. Atticus cuts deals with Laksha Kulasekaran and Leif Helgarson, a vampire, to earn their help and rid the city of the threats.

In book three, *Hammered,* the bills come due for those deals. Both Laksha and Leif want Atticus to go to Asgard and beard the Norse in their mead halls. Putting together a team of badasses, Atticus raids Asgard twice, despite warnings from the Morrigan and Jesus Christ that this would be a terrible idea and it might be best not to keep his word. The carnage is epic, with heavy losses among the Æsir, including the Norns, Thor, and a crippled Odin. The death of the Norns, an aspect of Fate, means the old prophecies regarding Ragnarok are now unchained, and Hel can begin to work with very little opposition from the Æsir. However, a strange coincidence with the Finnish hero Väinämöinen reminds Atticus of a different prophecy, one spoken by the sirens to Odysseus long ago, and he worries that thirteen years hence, the world will burn—perhaps in some altered form of Ragnarok.

Feeling the heat for his shenanigans and needing time to train his apprentice, Atticus fakes his own death with the help of Coyote in book four, *Tricked.* Hel does indeed make an appearance, thinking Atticus might like to join her on the dark side since he'd killed so many Æsir, but she is brutally rebuffed. Atticus is betrayed by Leif Helgarson and narrowly escapes death at the hands of an ancient vampire named Zdenik but ends the book with a modicum of assurance that he will be able to train Granuaile in anonymity.

In the novella *Two Ravens and One Crow,* Odin awakens from his long sleep and forges a truce of sorts with Atticus, enlisting the Druid to take on Thor's role in Ragnarok, should it come to pass, and perhaps take care of another few things along the way.

After twelve years of training, Granuaile is ready to be

bound to the earth, but in book five, *Trapped*, it seems as if the Druid's enemies have been waiting for him to emerge. Atticus must deal with vampires, dark elves, faeries, and the Roman god Bacchus, and messing with one of the Olympians draws the attention of one of the world's oldest and most powerful pantheons.

Once Granuaile is a full Druid, Atticus must run across Europe to avoid the bows of Diana and Artemis, who took exception to his treatment of Bacchus and the dryads of Olympus in book five. The Morrigan sacrifices herself to give Atticus a head start, and he is *Hunted* in book six. Running and fighting his way past a coordinated attempt to bring him down, he makes it to England, where he can enlist the help of Herne the Hunter and Flidais, the Irish goddess of the hunt. There he is able to defeat the Olympians and negotiate a fragile alliance against Hel and Loki. At the end of this volume he discovers that his archdruid was frozen in time in Tír na nÓg, and when he retrieves him, his old mentor is in as foul a mood as ever.

In *Shattered*, book seven, archdruid Owen Kennedy finds a place among the Tempe Pack and assists Atticus and Granuaile in thwarting a coup attempt in Tír na nÓg against Brighid. Granuaile is sorely tested by Loki in India and is forever changed, and an emissary of the ancient vampire Theophilus strikes down one of Atticus's oldest friends.

In the novella *A Prelude to War*, Atticus consults a tyromancer in Ethiopia to discover how best to strike back at the vampires, while Granuaile meets Loki for the second time—but this time she's the one laying the ambush.

Also, along the way, there may have been some talk of poodles and sausages.

STAKED

CHAPTER 1

I didn't have time to pull off the heist with a proper sense of theatre. I didn't even have a cool pair of shades. All I had was a soundtrack curated by Tarantino playing in my head, one of those songs with horns and a fat bass track and a guitar going *waka-chaka-waka-chaka* as I padded on asphalt with the uncomfortable feeling that someone was enjoying a voyeuristic close-up of my feet.

My plan wasn't masterful either. I was just going to wing it with an iron elemental named Ferris who was ready to do anything I asked, because he knew I'd feed him magic for it down the road. A faery snack, perhaps, or an enchanted doodad of some kind. Ferris thought such things were sweet—magic might even give him something akin to a sugar rush. Before making my run, I contacted him through the earth in a park and filled him in on the plan. He'd have to filter through the dead foundations of Toronto to follow me until it was time for him to act, but this was easier for him than it would be for most elementals. Lots of concrete got reinforced with iron rebar these days, and he's so strong at this point that he can afford to push through the lifeless underbelly of modern cities.

I dropped off Oberon and my shoes in a shaded alley and cast camouflage on myself before emerging into the busy intersection of Front and York Streets in Toronto, where cameras from many sources might otherwise track me, not only the ones from the Royal Bank of Canada. But into the bank I strode at opening time, ducking in the doors behind someone else. Ferris followed underneath the street; I felt him buzzing through the sole of my bare right foot.

Security dudes were present in the lobby but utterly unarmed. They were not there so much to stop people from committing a crime as to witness those crimes and provide polite but damning testimony later. The Canadians would rather track down and confront robbers when they were all alone than endanger citizens in a bank lobby. Some people might suggest you didn't need security if they were just going to stand there, but that's not the case. Cameras didn't catch everything. In memories they sometimes didn't work at all, because you were clever and had a snarky anarchist hacker in your crew with some kind of oral fixation on lollipops or whatever. But even if the cameras stayed on and recorded the whole crime, security guards would notice things the cameras might not—voices, eye color, details about clothing, and so on.

Off to the right of the teller windows, the vault door remained closed. No one had asked to visit the safety deposit boxes yet. I'd wait and sneak in with someone except that I could be waiting for far longer than my camouflage would hold out. And the clock was ticking on my target's usefulness; the sooner I got hold of it, the more damage I'd be able to do. So I showed Ferris that vault door and asked him to take it apart. Let the alarms begin.

It's magnificent, watching a vault door disintegrate and people lose their shit over it in real time. The soundtrack in my head kicked into high gear as I stepped over the melted slag to tackle the next obstacle: a locked glass door that showed me the safety deposit boxes beyond. It was bulletproof to small arms but lacked the thickness to stop heavy-caliber rounds. Ferris couldn't help in taking apart the entire door like the vault, but that wasn't necessary; the locking mechanism was metal and he could melt that quickly, and he did. I pushed open the door and began searching for Box 517, the number I'd been given. I found it on the left and near the floor. It was a wide, shallow, flat one, with one lock for the customer's key and one lock for the bank's. With another assist from Ferris, both locks were dispatched and I opened it, snatched out the slim three-ring binder inside, and shoved it into my camouflaged pack before anyone even stepped inside the vault. I kicked the box closed just as a couple of guards finally appeared at the melted vault door, peeking through and seeing the open glass door. One of them was a doughy dude, tall and pillowy, and the other was a hard, cut Latino.

"Hello?" the puffy one said. "Anyone in there?"

The fit guard assumed that someone was. "You're on camera wherever you go in here. You can't hide."

Wrong.

"Why would he care about that?" Doughboy said. "Are you telling him to stop because he's being surveilled?"

Hardbody scowled and hissed at his co-worker, "I've got to say something, don't I? What would *you* say?"

"If you surrender to us now," Doughboy called into the vault, "we won't shoot you. Run away and they send the guys with guns."

"You're a twat, Gary," Hardbody muttered.

Gary—a much better name than Doughboy—blinked. "I'm sorry, what was that?"

"I said you're right, Gary. That's what I should have

said to the robber we can't see." Gary didn't look convinced that he'd heard him incorrectly the first time, but the cut guard didn't give him time to pursue it. He stepped past the threshold of the vault and said, "Maybe he's in the private room in the back."

I turned around to see what he was talking about and spotted another door in the rear of the vault. Normally when customers removed their safety deposit boxes, they would step into that private room and fondle their deposits in safety until they were ready to return them. Hardbody was heading for that door, and I pressed myself against the row of boxes to let him pass by. Gary followed only to the glass doorway. He stood there, blocking my exit, and frowned at the dissolved lock.

"Somebody's got to be here," he said. "This doesn't just happen by itself."

Hardbody tried the door to the private room and found it secure. He punched in a code on a mounted keypad and peered inside once it opened.

"Anything there, Chuy?" Gary asked, finally giving me a better name for him.

"Nah."

"Well, what the hell is going on? Is this guy a ninja or something?"

Oberon would have loved to hear that, and I nearly made a noise that would have given me away had they the sense to turn off the alarm and listen. As it was, the electronic shriek gave me cover to sneak right up to Gary. Since I was fueling my camouflage on the limited battery of my bear charm, I couldn't stick around for much longer and wait for him to clear out of my way. Proper police would be around soon, and I didn't want to have to deal with them too.

I reached out with both hands and shoved Gary hard

through the threshold and to the left, leaving me a clear path to the vault door.

"Chuy called you a twat, Gary," I said as I ran past. "I heard him." It made me laugh, because Gary would have to report what Chuy called him since the perpetrator had said it.

Much cursing and outrage followed in my wake from both of the guards. A manager type was just outside the vault on a cell phone, talking to police. "Yes, sorry. There's something a bit odd going on here at the bank. Our door has been melted. Sorry."

The front doors to the bank had been automatically locked as part of the security protocols once the alarm went off, but Ferris gave me one more assist and I was out in the street. Whatever movement the cameras caught was fine; they would never get enough to identify me.

I thanked Ferris for his help and asked him to remain in the area for his reward. I'd have to scrounge up something suitably delicious for him before leaving.

<That was fast,> Oberon said through our mental link when I dropped my camouflage in the alley and chucked him under the chin. <I didn't even get started on a nap.>

"Only way to do it. Every second at the scene increases chances of capture. Ready for a spot of breakfast?" Oberon's last meal had been on the plains of Ethiopia, during the episode that revealed to me the existence of the binder I'd just stolen. A tyromancer friend of mine named Mekera had pointed the way here after we'd hunted up some rennet for her, but she didn't offer any snacks to us in the hours afterward.

<Of course I'm ready! When have I ever been unprepared to eat, Atticus?>

"Fair enough."

I knew that it's standard procedure to hole up in a nondescript warehouse or garage after robbing a bank, but I walked to Tim Hortons instead—affectionately known as Timmie's—because I felt like having something hot and coffee-like and I didn't have a big bag of money in a burlap sack to mark me as a dastardly villain. Instead, I had a backpack and an Irish wolfhound on a leash, so I looked like a local student instead of the mysterious thief who slipped past the security of the Royal Bank of Canada in downtown Toronto.

The Timmie's on York Street sported a garish green-and-yellow-striped awning, a fire hydrant out front in case of donut grease fire, and a convenient signpost pointing the way to public parking. "What kind of ungodly breakfast meat do you want from here?" I asked Oberon as I tied him up to the sign.

<The religion of the meat doesn't affect its taste,> my hound replied, a pedantic note creeping into his voice.

"What?"

<Godly bacon and ungodly bacon taste the same, Atticus.>

"Bacon it is. Now be nice to people who look scared of you while I'm inside. Do not pee on the hydrant, and no barking."

<Awww. I like to watch them jump. Sometimes they make squeaky noises.>

"I know, but we can't draw attention to ourselves right now." Sirens wailed in the glass and steel canyons of downtown as police converged on the bank. The cars would get there eventually, but the two bicycle cops I saw pedaling the wrong way down York Street would get there first. "I'll be back soon and we'll eat."

The teenager working the register judged me for ordering five bacon and egg sandwiches and a donut frosted in colors normally reserved for biohazard warnings. I could see it in her eyes: "Nice looking for a ginger, but shame about the diet."

Well, as Oberon might say, I deserved a treat. Taking my maroon cup of coffee and a bag of greasy sandwiches outside, I sat next to my hound on the curb of York Street and unboxed breakfast for him as people emerged from the shop and wondered aloud what had the police in such an uproar.

"Whadda yanno, Ed," a man said behind me. He hadn't been there when I entered, but a quick glance over my shoulder revealed him standing next to a friend in front of the window, both of them holding maroon cups like mine, both dressed in jeans and work boots and wearing light jackets. "Sirens! That means crime. In Trahno." I smiled at the local tendency to reduce their three-syllable city to two.

"Yep," Ed replied. I waited for more, but Ed seemed to have exhausted his thoughts on the subject.

<Hey!> Oberon said, his tone accusatory as he gulped down the first sandwich. <This is bacon, Atticus!>

Didn't you say you wanted bacon? I answered him mentally since I didn't want Ed or his friend to worry about my sanity if they saw me talking out loud to my hound.

<But I thought it would be Canadian bacon! Aren't we in Canada?>

Yes, but maybe you were trying to be too clever there. People in Canada do not call that kind of meat Canadian bacon, the same way people in Belgium do not call their waffles Belgian waffles.

<Well, it's still good. Thanks.>

I snarfed the donut and slurped up some coffee and then pulled out the cause of all the trouble: a binder full of names and addresses, many of them international. There was no handy title page announcing their significance, but they were alphabetized, and I flipped to the

H's. There I found an entry for Leif Helgarson, providing his former location in Arizona. It told me two things: This was, as I'd hoped, a directory of every vampire in the world, stored offline and therefore unhackable. But it was also months out of date at the very least. Leif had still nominally been the vampire lord of Arizona's sun-kissed humans around the time of Granuaile's binding to the earth, but he'd shown up twice in Europe since then—once in Greece and once in France. Germany too, if I counted a handwritten note. He was clearly on the move, and I had to assume the same would hold true for many other names on the list since I had started to pick off vampires via Fae mercenaries. Once word got out that this binder had been stolen, they would move for sure. So if it were to be of any use, I would have to move quickly, before they knew I had this. A USB drive with a file on it would have been more convenient, but since I was sure the idea was to make everything inconvenient for hackers and keep the speed of technology on their side, they had saved a hard copy only.

The two who would hear about it first and perhaps spread the word were the safety deposit box's owners: the ancient vampire Theophilus and the arcane lifeleech, Werner Drasche. The latter was most likely in Ethiopia where I'd left him, swearing in German and arranging a flight to Toronto. Theophilus, I knew, wouldn't be traveling across an ocean to chase me.

I flipped to the *T*'s but found no entry there for Theophilus. Damn. Either he was using a different name or wasn't listed here at all.

"May I join you, Mr. O'Sullivan?" a voice with a Russian accent asked. I whipped my head around to find the speaker, because no one should be calling me by that name anymore. A Hasidic Jew dressed all in black stood there, cup of coffee in one hand and a small paper bag in the other. His beard had been black the last time I saw him, but now it was shot with streaks of gray that fell from either side of his chin.

"Rabbi Yosef Bialik," I said. "What are you doing here?"

"Sharing breakfast, I hope," he replied. "I assure you that I have no wish to fight. Our past quarrels can remain in the past."

"You're alone?" I asked, scanning my surroundings for other figures in black with weaponized beards. The last time I'd seen him, more than a decade ago, he had ganged up on me with the rest of the Hammers of God.

"I'm alone."

"Well, sit down then, and tell me what you want."

He tossed the bag down next to me and then used his free hand to steady himself as he half-sat, half-collapsed to the curb with a grunt. "Getting old is no fun," he said. "You look very well. Unchanged, in fact. How do you do it?"

"I'll tell you if you tell me how you knew where to find me. I've only been in town a few hours."

"Ah! Easy. The Hammers of God are witch hunters, yes?"

"Yes."

"We are sensitive to the use of magic. Any kind. So while we cannot track you, whenever you use magic nearby, we can feel it. And your magic I have felt before. It has a particular flavor. You used quite a lot of it a couple blocks away."

"And you just happened to be in Toronto?"

"Yes. I live here now. Retirement."

"Retirement? Here?"

He shrugged. "Toronto is great city. Many kinds of peoples, many kinds of food, few evils outside of the local government. The hockey team is bad, but you cannot ask for everything. And I am married now. My wife is from here."

"Oh! Congratulations."

"Thank you."

"Don't get me wrong, Rabbi, it's great to see you when you're not trying to kill me, but . . . what do you want?"

He picked up his bag and fished out an everything bagel with cream cheese. The bag crackled loudly, and he didn't speak until he had crumpled it into a ball and set it beside him. "I suppose what I want is fair warning if something horrible is going to happen here. You and horrible go together like pickle spears and sandwiches."

I could say the same for him, but instead I said, "Nothing will happen. Nothing I'm planning anyway. I'll be gone in a few days."

"Then I wish to deliver an apology."

"You do? For what?"

<For never giving me a snack.>

He hasn't even met you yet, Oberon.

<That doesn't matter. It's only polite.>

We'll review manners later.

"For my behavior years ago," the rabbi said. "I did many things for which I may not be forgiven."

"Like killing the youngest, weakest member of the Sisters of the Three Auroras with your fucking Cthulhu beard tentacles there—sorry, I didn't mean to get so intense. It's just that I still have nightmares about that."

"Understandable. And deserved. It was that episode and the next one, with that man who claimed to be Jesus—"

"Uh, that really was Jesus."

"As you say."

"Well, I'm pretty sure he would say it too. And to be clear, Rabbi, his existence doesn't negate or invalidate—much less eradicate—the existence of your god. Or any of my gods, or anyone else's. He just is. As is Yahweh and Brighid and Odin and the rest."

He nodded, and his beard, thankfully, did not move of its own volition. "I can accept that now. I couldn't back then. It requires a flexibility of thought, yes? A certain openness to the idea that people must walk their own road to salvation and not necessarily follow me on mine. I had taken my faith too far." He shook his head. "It is difficult for me, now, to think of my younger self. I wince at the memories. I was filled with so much anger and had lost the contemplative peace of Kabbalism. But those encounters with you—and watching, from afar, how the Sisters of the Three Auroras conducted themselves afterward, among other things—caused me to re-evaluate. I saw that I was wrong to judge them. I should *not* have judged them. That is the business of a perfect being, yes?"

"I suppose it is. Does that mean the Hammers of God don't hunt witches anymore, despite that line in Exodus about not suffering a witch to live?"

He sipped his coffee before answering. "Some still do. I personally do not. But I have convinced many of them that focusing on clear evil—demons walking this plane, for example—is much more morally defensible than pursuing witches who may yet be redeemed."

"That's good to hear."

"Yes, I think it is good. I do not know if it will ever be enough to pay for what I did—guilt is a heavy burden. When a man leaps into the fire, how many steps must he take to walk out of it? Have you ever overstepped yourself, Mr. O'Sullivan?"

"Oh, gods below, yes. Horribly. Still paying for some of my missteps. I think there are some I haven't paid for yet. Trying to make it right, though."

"What's the difficulty, if I may ask?"

I made a raspberry noise at the enormity of the question. "I have plenty of difficulties, but right now I'm worried most about the vampires. They all want to kill me, and I don't think I can talk them out of it. They're actively pursuing me now."

The hedge of hair above the rabbi's eyes dipped, and his mustache drooped in a frown. "There are vampires here? Is this why you are in town?"

"I'm sure there are some here, but I'm in town for this," I said, pointing to the binder. "The names and addresses of vampires around the world."

The rabbi froze except for his beard, which began to stir even though there was no wind. I was beginning to recognize that as an emotional tell and I had to suppress a shudder, because semi-sentient facial hair is viscerally disturbing.

"How did you acquire that?" the rabbi asked.

"Using the magic you sensed. I stole this from the bank on Front and York. There are thousands of names here. Maybe tens of thousands—the type is small. I'm not sure which ones are the leaders, though. And I'm also unsure how I'll make much of a dent in the list before it becomes moot. The leadership will soon know that I have this list and alert everyone to move. But maybe some of them will be stupid enough to keep the same names. I can at least use that to track some of them."

"Extraordinary." Keeping his eyes on the binder, his hands moved that sad, smooshed everything bagel to his mouth. The schmear of cream cheese drooped out from the edges and some of it fell, ignored, onto the precipice of his beard, hanging. It bobbed up and down as he ate mechanically, thinking.

<Look at that, Atticus. Totally rude. Didn't even offer me a bite.>

You just had five bacon sandwiches for breakfast.

<Yes, but what about second breakfast?>

I doubted the rabbi was a Tolkien fan, so I said to my hound, *I don't think he knows about that.*

"Perhaps . . . well. Mr. O'Sullivan, I would like to offer my assistance if you would accept it."

"You'd come out of retirement for this?"

"Absolutely. Vampires are one of the clear evils that the Hammers of God still fight. We would relish the chance to take advantage of this."

"We? You're speaking for all of them?"

"I believe I can safely say they will join us with enthusiasm. They have been finding more vampires recently in any case. Something has been disturbing them, making them move in the open."

"That would be my doing. I've had mercenaries hunting them, and some are trying to hide while others are trying to fill the power vacuum left by those we already staked."

"Admirable. We are on the same side, then." He grinned at me, a brief flash of white underneath the hair. "Is refreshing, yes?" He nodded as he spoke, and the cream cheese fell onto his coat. I wanted to point it out to him but also didn't want to let slip this moment of accord.

"Yes, it is," I said. "How many of your friends might join in?"

"There are hundreds of us scattered around the world."

"All right," I said. "Rabbi Yosef, I'll make you a deal. We'll go scan this and you can send the file to your associates. For every thousand vampires the Hammers of God eliminate, I'll give *you* five years of youth."

"How?"

"Immortali-Tea. It's just natural herbs and some bindings, nothing diabolical about it. You see the results before you."

"Hmm. We would stake a thousand vampires if we could in any case. It's our duty."

"Great, so it's win-win. I guess you're not able to sense vampires the way you can sense me?"

"No. Our power comes from the Kabbalistic Tree of Life, so they are invisible to us as dead things. And I should stress that we cannot sense you personally, only the use of your magic, which is very attuned to life."

"Yeah," I said, smiling at him, "being bound to Gaia will do that. Hey, uh, you got a little schmear there—"

"Oh! Thanks for telling me."

We set about the scheme immediately. It would take us hours to scan and get the files out, and before the day was through, Werner Drasche would definitely know I had them. The Hammers of God would have a short window in which to act.

"If you move to catch the ones in this hemisphere before sundown," I said, "that will be your best chance. The ones in Europe—the really old and powerful ones—are going to hear about the security breach while they're awake and have a chance to move tonight."

"We must take what the Almighty offers us, then."

"Well, caution your people too," I warned him. "There may be traps waiting at these addresses instead of vampires. I would vastly prefer this strike to be an unequivocal win for the good guys. Just once."

"May it prove so," the rabbi said, a quirk in his beard indicating that he might be happy. "Even if we fail to slay a single one, I am glad we met today, Mr. O'Sullivan. It confirms that I have done right to choose a calmer, quieter path. This great good we are about to do would not have been possible had I clung to my zealotry."

I supposed that was a polite way of saying we couldn't kill vampires together today if he had killed me twelve years ago, but I wasn't about to say anything to make him feel more guilty about his past than he already did. I couldn't judge him; the gods knew I had more to atone for in my long life than he did. We parted amiably and traded phone numbers like old friends.

With the vampires suitably placed in tumult by my actions and perhaps some of them facing a final mortality very soon thanks to the Hammers of God, I went shopping. There was an arcane lifeleech doubtless on the way, and I had preparations to make. Though you never want to be Nigel in Toronto, I would have to become him one last time if I wanted to take care of Werner Drasche. And, with luck, I would never be haunted by that chapter of my past again.

First I visited the Herbal Clinic and Dispensary on Roncesvalles for a few things and then traveled to Jerome's on Yonge Street for a suitable costume—well, formal wear, which felt like a costume every time I crawled into it and cinched a tie around my neck. I was advised by the haberdasher that ascots were making a comeback, and I said, no, no, they weren't, he'd been terribly misinformed. I did manage to pick up a gold pocket watch and a shaving kit while I was there—both essential to reprising my role as Nigel.

We took all to a hotel downtown, where in my room, under the glare of a white bulb attacking yellow wallpaper and a sulfurous curdled granite countertop, wearing an expression of acute chagrin, I shaved off my goatee while Oberon tried to comfort me with his improvised singing.

<*In a beefless hotel! Where a man's got a beard to lose!*

Ain't no gravy nowhere! 'Cause he's got the Nigel blues!>

"Oberon, I appreciate the thought, but you're not helping me feel any better about this."

<I was just about to start in on my howling cat solo. That always makes me feel better.>

"Please don't. Have mercy on me." I washed and

toweled off my naked chin and began step two, using my purchases from the Herbal Clinic, one of the hotel's plastic cups, a few drops of Everclear, and a stir stick intended for coffee.

<Whoa, hey, what's that you're doing there? That's not something nasty I have to drink, is it?>

"No, it's not a tea. It's a tincture. Remember when the Herbal Clinic let me use their mortar and pestle?"

<Yeah. They asked you a lot of questions.>

Yes, they'd been quite curious and I'd lied and told them it was for a salve, but in truth the blend of herbs would spur my beard growth for a short time. When I needed to age rapidly or grow something ridiculously ursine in a few days instead of waiting a few months, I used this mixture, which I altered with a little bit of alcohol and Gaia's magic—much in the same way that Immortali-Tea was a blend of fairly common herbs with a little help. Taking an eyedropper and being very careful about where the drops fell, I applied the tincture to my cheek halfway down my jaw on either side. I'd have a few weeks' growth of hair there in the morning, muttonchops straight out of the nineteenth century. Once I got all dressed up in my formal costume, pocket watch in my gray pinstriped vest, and slicked-down hair—I would look like the lad I'd been in 1953 who got into so much trouble.

"It's just something to help me get into character. It's a role I haven't played for seventy years."

<What's this Nigel thing all about anyway? You still haven't told me the whole story.>

"Oh, you want a story, do you? Well, we *are* in the bathroom and you *are* quite dirty from all that mud you picked up in Ethiopia . . ."

Oberon's tail began to wag. <Do I get a bath-time story about historical Atticus?>

"Go on, hop in, and I will tell you why you never want to be Nigel in Toronto."

<Okay!> Oberon's entire back half began to sway back and forth, and he accidentally tore down the shower curtain in his haste to get into the tub. <Uh, that thing was ugly,> he explained. <And in the way.>

CHAPTER 2

Asgard is an alien place, nothing like you see in the movies or comics or fantasy paintings. Except maybe it has a watercolor feel to it, pigments splashed on stark white paper with sharp defined edges and everything blending in the middle. Atticus described it a bit like that—the light is strained and cold and sere, unlike Tír na nÓg, which has the visual warmth and richness of a John William Waterhouse painting. I really don't belong here and I cannot wait to leave.

Orlaith and I are stuck, however, until I can remove Loki's mark from my arm, and Odin represents my best chance of making that happen.

He told me the mark is a sort of cloak keyed to Loki's genetic signature—but the god of lies can see through that cloak if he wishes. Hel and Jörmungandr have the mark, too, and that's what's keeping them hidden from the gods, frustrating Odin and Manannan Mac Lir and everyone else trying to divine their locations. But Loki knows where they are at all times, just like he knows I'm in Asgard now. He would dearly love to know what I'm doing here—he said as much and threatened Orlaith in an attempt to get me to explain my first trip, when I'd come to ask for Odin's help.

The allfather said at that time that he would need Loki's genetic material to dissolve the mark and it was my task to procure some. That's when I returned to the cabin in Colorado, to find Loki waiting for me. He thought to surprise me, but our cabin was well warded against fire and I was able to surprise him instead. I gave Loki a tomahawk in his back and a swift blow to the jaw, and he gave me blood and teeth and a measure of vengeance for what he did to me.

The unfortunate upshot is that our cabin in Colorado is not safe anymore; Loki knows about it now, and the new place in Oregon won't be ready for days or possibly weeks. I suppose it's working out as it should: Atticus is hunting down the man who killed his friend in Alaska, and I have much to occupy me here. Not in terms of active tasks, since there is little to do but wait for Odin to craft a solution, but rather in terms of personal growth: I need to construct a new headspace, and I must decide whether to erect a literary scaffolding in a language where I already have some fluency, such as Russian, or to learn something entirely new. Frigg was kind enough to grab a selection of works for me from "some library on Midgard," and I am reading a copy of Dostoevsky's *Notes from Underground* now. I find myself agreeing with a passage here and there: *Nature doesn't ask your permission; it doesn't care about your wishes, or whether you like its laws or not. You're obliged to accept it as it is, and consequently all its results as well.* That isn't bad at all, but after the ecstatic optimism of Walt Whitman, he's a bit like plain oatmeal to my taste—fiber-rich and good for you, but lacking a certain joy. That may be true of almost everyone, though, compared to Whitman. Regardless, I will have to read more extensively in the language before I make my decision. If I'm going to take the trouble to memorize something, I want it to be transcendent and worthy of echoes in my head.

What truly echoes in my head continuously, though

I'd much rather it would be silent, is the voice of my younger self, crying out to deliver a long-deserved come-uppance to my stepfather. For he is a man, like Dostoevsky's vision of nature, who does not ask permission or care about your wishes or whether you like him. He plunders and pollutes the world at the same time and sneers at everyone who doesn't have the guts to just take everything they can while they can.

I confessed to Atticus once that I wanted to become a Druid partly to reach my stepfather, since human laws wouldn't. Atticus pointed out that going after individual polluters wasn't rational, and I see that. He's right. But this need isn't rational. It's emotional, and I have to do something about it. I can't simply let it go and walk away. He's more than a mere polluter. He's a dick who laughs at animals dying in his oil spills.

Yet I fear that in my own private revenge fantasies I'm missing giant signs along the road that say FATAL MISTAKE AHEAD and DO NOT ENTER, FOR DEATH AWAITS YOU WITH NASTY BIG SHARP POINTY TEETH. I'm acutely aware that I should free my mind of his poison and just outlive him. But sometimes we do things that make no sense except in some arcane calculus hidden in our emotions. And we can seek therapy or religion to provide us relief like balm on chafed skin, but that's denying our own power to heal ourselves and trying to silence old pain with new opiates. Somehow I will need to deal with him, knowing it won't work out just the way I want but emerging from it feeling purged of his lingering gloom.

It's a measure of his enduring power over me that I could think of him in such surroundings. Despite the alien feel of Asgard, I could not wish for a couch more magnificent for my studies; my guest quarters are liberally supplied with flowers and fruit and ample light, and there is a warm thermal spring for bathing when I want to forsake one luxury for another.

It's a couple of days of such isolated decadence before I'm summoned to Odin's hall. He believes he's found a solution, and the dwarf Runeskald, Fjalar, is with him, as is his wife, Frigg.

Odin holds up a stone chop that looks distressingly familiar and speaks in a smoky whiskey voice. "If we're going to free you from Loki's mark, we're going to have to fight fire with fire. Fjalar has lent his aid in crafting a Rune of Ashes that will burn away that which has been burned into you. It is infused with Loki's genetic code, thanks to the teeth you provided, and that will unlock the seal and allow transformation."

That sounds like more than I want. "Uh . . . transformation into what?"

"Into a free human. But also into a defeat for Loki." Odin displays the briefest of smiles, but he isn't properly keeping score, in my view. Loki didn't just brand me down in that pit outside Thanjavur—he took two very powerful magical weapons with him: the Lost Arrows of Vayu, and Fuilteach, my whirling blade crafted by the yeti. To even the score, someone would have to steal them back.

Odin hands the stone chop to Fjalar, who places it in the grip of a pair of iron tongs and thrusts it into the coals burning in Odin's hearth. Scenes from several movies flash through my head, where the bad guy does something similar to stimulate dread in the restrained protagonist, but I am looking forward to it. I would endure any pain to get rid of Loki's mark. Pain fades, but freedom is an enduring joy. Admittedly, the freedom I'm seeking is a mental thing—I mostly want my privacy back. Knowing you're being watched by a creep isn't like any physical restraint, but it *is* a shackle on your conscience.

We stare at the fire together for perhaps ten seconds and then become aware that waiting in silence for the entire time it takes to heat the chop would be uncomfortable. Frigg clears her throat and says to Fjalar, "Do you leave for Svartálfheim soon?"

"Very soon," he says, but before I can inquire why he might be going to visit the dark elves, Odin chimes in with the perceptible air of one who wishes desperately to talk of something else.

"Tell me, Granuaile, did Loki reveal anything else that might allow us to guess when he will act?" he asks.

"No, I did most of the talking. Told him I would kill him the next time I saw him. He didn't reply, but I assume the reverse is true."

I shift my eyes back to the dwarf, considering. The last time I saw him, the Runeskald was working on axes that would cut dark elves in their smoke forms and force them to take physical shape again. If he is going to visit Svartálfheim, it might not be an innocuous trip.

Fjalar forestalls any more conversation by saying, "It's ready." The stone is glowing faintly red when he plucks it out of the fire. It's not bright orange like Loki's was, but I have no doubt I'll feel the heat just fine. "Your arm, please, quickly."

Orlaith, I'm going to be in pain and yell a bit, but don't get upset. I need this.

<Okay, if you say so.>

I roll up my left sleeve, exposing my biceps where Loki branded me. Fjalar's gloved left hand reaches out and guides my hand under his left armpit, bracing me there and using his palm to lock my elbow and keep the arm straight.

"Do your best not to move. Fight the instinct."

"I will," I say, nodding to him and tucking my tongue firmly behind my teeth. I don't want to bite it off when the pain hits—and I'm quite sure it will hit regardless of what I do to block it. I'd been blocking all the pain I could when Loki branded me and I still felt it; his chop did more than burn the skin—it seared the aura, if I understood Odin correctly, marked me on a level beyond mere flesh. Fjalar's Rune of Ashes will presumably do the same. At least I hope it will; multiple tries at this would not be fun.

I can feel the heat radiating from the stone on my cheeks and arm as Fjalar positions the chop above my biceps.

"Do it," I tell him through clenched teeth, and he doesn't hesitate. He clutches my elbow tightly and brings down the chop directly on top of Loki's mark, and the sizzling pain is nothing I could have prepared for. It burns everywhere, not just on my arm, and my muscles seize up and even my throat is unable to scream past an initial cry of shock. But that first, quick gasp opens my mouth and then, despite trying to prepare for it, I bite my tongue anyway. I taste coppery blood in my mouth, and sweat pops out on my skin all over.

"Gah!" Blood spurts out of my mouth and sprays Fjalar in the face. He's keeping the rune on my arm much longer than Loki did. Or maybe it only seems that way.

Orlaith's voice cries out in my mind. <Hey! Granuaile, that's blood! He should stop! He's hurting too much!>

I agree heartily but tell her, *It won't be much longer. I'll heal.*

"We have to make sure we burn it all away," Fjalar says.

"It's through . . . my skin!"

"Ah! So it is."

He yanks the rune away and some additional strips of skin come away with it. He releases my arm and calls to a pair of Valkyries. "Bring the water."

I miss where they come from or how long it takes for them to get there—an eternity of pain—but two Valkyries arrive with a large vase sloshing with cold water. I thrust my arm into it, and the lancing fire abates somewhat. Then I'm able to shut off the nerves, pull it out in relief, and examine the hole in my biceps. There's not a trace of Loki's mark left—just crispy Granuaile. I can't flex my arm, but I laugh in delirium anyway. The god of lies used some dark unholy thing to break most of my bones and then branded me, thinking it would break my mind too, turn me into his meek servant. Well, it hadn't quite worked.

"Haha. Hahahahaha. Fuck Loki." I turn to Odin and grin broadly, not caring if it looks as unhinged as it feels to my own muscles. "Am I right?"

CHAPTER 3

While the bathwater ran, I unwrapped one of those laughably small hotel soaps and then looked at the mud caked on Oberon's fur, especially his belly. It was a David and Goliath situation, but I had little choice except to proceed and hope the wee bar of soap would win.

"All right, buddy, here we go," I said, starting out by splashing him underneath and then pouring cups of water on his back. "No shaking yourself until we're through."

‹Hee hee! It tickles, Atticus! Hurry up and distract me.›

"Okay, let's begin," I said.

To understand what happened to me, you have to know a little bit of Toronto history first.

I had come to Toronto in the fall of 1953 as a pre-med student. The world had learned a lot about surgery and patching up bodies after shooting the hell out of everything in two world wars and another war in Korea, and I thought I might be able to pick up something useful, so I enrolled in the University of Toronto under the name of Nigel Hargrave, with every intention of staying a few years as an earnest wanna-be doctor. I wound up staying only a few months, and the reason for that is a spooky old building and a tragedy in the nineteenth century.

The University of Toronto was actually a collection of old colleges, many of which were religiously affiliated, and one such college—now the Royal Conservatory of Music on Bloor Street—used to be a Baptist seminary long ago. It's a red stone Gothic marvel built in 1881, the kind of building where you're sure the architect was laughing maniacally to himself as he huffed a lungful of lead-based paint fumes. Pointy spires and sharply sloped roofs and large windows. Wood floors that echo and creak when you step on them. And attending the seminary in the late nineteenth century was a young man named Nigel, betrothed to Gwendolyn from Winnipeg, dark of hair and possessed of a jealous eye.

Oberon interrupted my narrative with a question. <Hey, isn't there a monster named Jealousy, Atticus? You told me about it once, and I remember because it didn't treat meat well.>

"Oh, yes, that was a Shakespeare thing, from *Othello*. Jealousy is *the green-eyed monster which doth mock the meat it feeds on*."

<Not a sensible monster then.>

"No."

One summer day way back when—these were the days before automobiles, when people rode around in horse-drawn carriages or else they walked—Gwendolyn was crossing the hard-packed dirt of Bloor Street to pay a visit to her Nigel. She had baked a cake specially, and she had a red dress on with a thin matching shawl about her shoulders. Nigel had bought the dress for her, and she knew he was wearing a gray pinstriped suit she had bought him, and she probably thought privately that the two of them made a very smart couple with excellent taste. But because she was worried about dropping her cake, she didn't cross the street to the seminary college as quickly as perhaps she should have. And she wasn't paying attention to her surroundings. That's why she didn't even try to get out of the way of the horse and carriage that ran her down—she didn't see it.

Knocked over and trampled by a quarter-ton animal, then run over by the weighted carriage wheels, ribs broken and bleeding internally inside a restrictive corset, all poor Gwendolyn could think of was getting to see Nigel one more time. She first dragged herself and then got some help to make it to the flat stone steps of the seminary, where she died mere seconds before Nigel emerged to investigate the cries for help. Seeing his fiancée's pale dead face there and the callous driver of the carriage continuing down Bloor Street as if nothing had happened, he was filled with a rage unbecoming a minister. Everything he cared about had been ripped from him, and he wanted an eye for an eye. Or at least a chance to deliver a good punch to the jaw, or maybe three. So he rashly chased after the man who had run down his girl and eventually caught him. And then he got himself killed, for the driver of that carriage was armed with a revolver and ill-disposed to fisticuffs with a mutton-chopped ginger man wearing a gray pinstripe and gold pocket watch.

Nigel's spirit quite sensibly moved on wherever it was he thought he should go, no doubt missing that he had just been given an object lesson on why it's better sometimes to turn the other cheek. Gwendolyn, however— she had unfinished business. The horribly mangled cake didn't matter except as a visible symbol of her undying love. She couldn't move on until she told Nigel she loved him and heard him say it in return, just one more time.

So her spirit moved into the seminary building, where she searched for him and haunted the building as the Lady in Red for decades afterward.

<Oh, no, this is going to be bad for you,> my hound said as I soaped him up.

"You think?"

<Oh, yeah, you're doomed.>

"Yes, I am."

No one had warned me about the Lady in Red before I entered that building in 1953. No reason why they would, really. She was a shy and retiring sort of spirit, looking for a ginger man named Nigel with muttonchops and wearing a gray suit. If you didn't meet the criteria or catch her feeling sorry for herself, you'd probably never see her. During that time the building was in a sort of limbo, used by the university as an administrative dump and also to proctor certain exams. The Royal Conservatory of Music didn't take over the building until the 1970s. I had to go there to take exams and on my first visit noticed that many of the rooms were unused and might make ideal rendezvous spots. Such spots were prized by college students because dorms were very closely monitored to prevent "lewd and immoral acts."

Well, opportunity eventually presented itself and I met a coed who had a strange thing not for muttonchops or gingers but for guys named Nigel. Being fit was just a bonus to her; somehow there was nothing so attractive to her as the name of Nigel Hargrave—she told me it sounded rich and aristocratic. Maybe that's what she was actually into—aristocracy, I mean, not my name; I never really figured her out. But I was lonely and not particularly principled, so I arranged a meeting at one of those rooms in the old building. The scheduled exams were listed on a bulletin board in the entrance hall, so we chose a room on the second floor, I picked the lock, and we entered to take consensual delight in each other on top of a desk.

And while we were in the middle of those delights, half dressed but fully enthusiastic, Gwendolyn, the Lady in Red, finally discovered a man who bore a striking resemblance to her fiancé, Nigel. That he was in sexual congress with another woman displeased her mightily, and she could not be mistaken—she knew it was her Nigel, because my partner kept shouting that name, and I had the ginger muttonchops and the same gray suit she'd expected him to be wearing that day she came to deliver the lovey-dovey cake. It was at that point that the shy, retiring ghost became a completely unhinged poltergeist. Desks began moving in the room, including the one we were on. Chairs left the floor—wildly inaccurate at first, like the Imperial stormtroopers in Cloud City, but growing closer as a cry of betrayal built and built and effectively killed the mood dead.

My partner stopped calling out my name and appropriately freaked out, dashing half-clothed from the room. I never saw her again.

"NNNNNigel! Hhhhhow could youuuuuu!" a breathy, ethereal voice raged at me.

"I, uh . . . think there's been a mistake. Who are you?"

A red apparition swirled into form, very proper and charming and allowing me to note details of the dress, which helped me place her origins later. The illusion of propriety broke down around the mouth: It gaped unnaturally wide as it shouted at me. "I'm your fiancée! Gwendolyn!"

"What? Hey, I'm not the guy you're looking for. My name's not really Nigel either."

"Liaaaaarr!"

The furniture got really aggressive at that point and clocked me pretty good, and there was very little I could do but run. There's nothing a Druid can do about a ghost, honestly. Nothing physical about them to bind or unbind, and my cold iron amulet is just a hunk of metal to them.

That does not mean, however, that ghosts are not subject to being bound—they are typically bound to a space near where they died, albeit by intangible spiritual tethers rather than anything tied to the earth. For me to escape her, all I had to do was escape the building. Or so I thought.

As I pelted through the hall and then down the grand staircase leading to the exit, all manner of papers and books and dust devils followed me along with her screams. I got a textbook to the temple at one point and fell down but scrambled back up again, staggering a bit. She chased me right out the door in a rather shockingly immodest display and then, much to my horror, kept going. Now that she'd found her Nigel, she had moored herself to me and unchained herself from the building. I had to skedaddle, which I think is the best possible word for getting the hell out when a poltergeist thinks you've jilted her. Where the university's law library is now, there used to be a giant old oak that I had tethered to Tír na nÓg, and I used that to shift away to safety and do some research on who or what she was.

Later on, I shifted back in and waited to be attacked, but Gwendolyn the poltergeist wasn't lurking by the oak. She had probably returned to the building she had haunted before, but there was no way I was returning to check. I picked up what few things I had at my lodgings and took off before she could locate me again, never to return to Toronto until today.

* * *

<So that Gwendolyn Lady in Red could still be out there right now?> Oberon said as I rinsed him off.

"Yep."

<And she could still be very mad at Nigel?>

"Yep. She appears to have quite the impressive memory for a ghost."

<And you're going to dress up as Nigel Hargrave again on purpose?>

"That's right. Except this time I will try to be her Nigel instead of the pre-med student she mistook for him. She's capable of talking—she has things she desperately wants to say to Nigel, you see—and I have something I need to say too."

<You should sing her a love song. Music soothes the savage ghost.>

"Uh, that's *breast,* Oberon, savage breast, not savage ghost. William Congreve wrote the original line, and he gets misquoted a lot."

<Well, it's no wonder. I've never met a savage breast. Tasty ones, yeah, fried up and covered in gravy, but never savage.>

"You've been a good hound in the bath. Let's get you dried off and feed you a sausage or two."

CHAPTER 4

Few things chap me tits worse than big cities. Smelly things, choked with cars, and the horizon choked with big rectangular signs telling people to buy newer cars. I says to Greta, "I love it when ye kick me arse, but this city is doing it in a way I can't fight back. This Paradise Valley of yours is no paradise to me, love. I simply can't live here in this fecking wasteland of concrete and cactus. I need me trees." And gods bless her, she says she'll move to the country with me. Sort of.

"How would Flagstaff be?" she says. "We'll live on the San Francisco Peaks, with all those pines and aspens, and we can go into town when necessary."

That sounds dodgy to me. "When would it ever be necessary?" I asks her.

"Well, we'd have to get food once in a while."

"Why go to the city for that? We can hunt and grow our own. Get some sheep and goats and chickens."

"All right, Owen, if you want to do that, I suppose it's possible."

"It's more than possible. It's the only way to live."

She smiles at me and I feel hope again. "Then I'll transfer myself over to the Flagstaff Pack," she says. "It's far past time for me to pick up and move on, and Sam and Ty are good guys."

"Aye, good sparring partners," I says. The leaders of

the Flagstaff Pack are younger wolves than Hal Hauk and much of his crew in Tempe, but they're a happy couple, share their beer, and don't mind going a few rounds with a bear every so often. Truth be told, I'd rather go back to Ireland, but I can't ask Greta to do that. She needs a pack to run with when the moon is full, and I'm not sure they have one over there.

A lot of business with something called a Realtor happens after that—they have people these days who do nothing but sell houses, and they aren't even the ones who built them. Makes no fecking sense. "Here," says I to Greta, "here's this field full of prairie dogs I found and it has a shack to shite in. I will sell it to ye for stupid money. Is that how this Realtor thing works?"

"More or less. Except it's the owner of the shack who puts it up for sale, not the Realtor."

"Well, then, why do you need the Realtor person?"

"Lots of legal reasons. And it prevents the buyer and the seller from getting into fights."

"Oh, well, I can understand that, then. I bought some bad venison once from a man who lived in a bog, and I wanted to pound the piss out of him. Should have had a Realtor do it for me; that would have been handy."

"No, Owen, that's not what Realtors do—"

"Well, they fecking should! There's all manner of men living in bogs who need a good thrashing, and I bet there's people who would pay. Could be a full-time job. Maybe it should be *my* job. Siodhachan says I'm supposed to have one."

Greta gives up trying to explain Realtors after that, and I stop asking and just let her handle the modern horror of it all. She finds a place outside city limits, which suits me fine, with plenty of tree-dotted land attached to it and a house that's way too big but she says will come in handy.

"Handy for what?" I asks. "I don't need a fecking castle."

"You might," she replies.

I have no earthly idea what she means and she says to wait, she wants to sit me down with Hal and Sam and Ty and talk through something.

The sit-down comes a couple days later at Sam and Ty's house when Hal drives up special from Tempe. They give me fancy beer and smile a bit too wide. They have cheese you can spread on crackers and clearly expect me ancient mind to be destroyed by the sheer cleverness of the idea. They must want to ask me to do them a favor and they're afraid I'll say no.

"All right, what is it, then?" I says. "If you're going to try to convince me to get one of those cell phones, ye might as well give up now."

"No, nothing like that, Owen," Greta says. "As far as we know this is something you actually want."

"All right, I'm listening." I sink into a brown leather couch, and it sucks away at me backside like it will never let me rise again.

"From things you've said to me, I believe it's your wish to train additional Druids."

"Right, right. Not sure where I'll find parents to let me do that, though. These people don't believe in magic, and if they do they don't want their kids involved in it."

"Well, there are some parents who *do* believe in magic and would like their kids to be Druids very much."

"There are?"

"Yes. Parents who are werewolves."

"What's that, now? I thought ye couldn't have kids. The transformation would kill the baby every time."

"That's correct, but there are a few recently turned wolves around the world who had children before they were bitten. And of course they're worried about them. They don't want their kids to become wolves, but neither do they want their kids to feel excluded from their lives. They see Druidry as a perfect compromise. Their kids can remain in the magical world and even run with packs once they can shape-shift, but they never have to live with the curse of lycanthropy."

"How young are we talking?"

"Let me ask instead, what would be the ideal age?"

"Six to eight. They absorb languages easier when they're young, and I can shape their minds to handle headspaces much better than if you start later. That way they would be bound to the earth when they're eighteen to twenty," I says.

The wolves exchange a glance, and it's Hal Hauk who speaks next. "We know of six children who fit that range. If you're agreeable, we'll have their parents transferred to the Flagstaff Pack and then you can be in charge of their instruction going forward."

"Well, hold on a minute now." I try to sit forward on the couch and it fights me. I have to paw at the damn armrest to pull meself up. "You're suggesting I start a grove here in Flagstaff? On Greta's land?"

"Why not, Owen?" Greta says. "We have the space. We have privacy. We have lots of trees on the property. And you can build what structures you want in addition to what's already there. A greenhouse, maybe, for herbs and vegetables."

Six apprentices at once. With the full support and resources of the werewolves. It sounds suspiciously good.

"These kids haven't been bitten, right? You can't bind 'em to Gaia if they've been bitten."

"No, no, they're perfectly normal in every way," Hal assures me. "It's just their parents who are different."

"Once they're bound, you know, they can't ever be affected by a bite. Gaia won't let them turn into werewolves. It's why I can spar with ye without fear."

"That's a definite plus as far as we're concerned," Greta says.

"They'll be vulnerable until then, mind."

"We understand. Strict safety measures will be in effect. They already are."

"Well, then," I says, "I'm not opposed." Smiles break out and I hold up a hand to stop them. "But don't get too excited and don't do anything yet. We don't want to start something like this if Siodhachan is going to come along and cock it all up. I haven't heard from him or Granuaile in a while, and I should make sure they know to leave me alone from now on."

Hal's face suddenly looks tired, but he nods. "Probably best, you're right. I know he's worried about vampires right now—I am too, I suppose. One that used to work with us claimed the entire state as his territory. I don't think he would mess with us, but should he decide to turn nasty it could be quite disastrous."

"Aye. So we'll be cautious. I'll check in with Tír na nÓg. Brighid has already given me her blessing in general to start training Druids, but I would like to get her specific blessing on this. We may enjoy the protection of the Fae as well as that of the pack."

Greta leaps up from her seat and pounces on me, pressing her mouth to mine and returning me to the clutches of the leather couch. "Thank you for considering it, Owen. It means a lot to us."

She's warm and her hair smells like berries and vanilla and her breath comes quicker as we kiss, and then she rears back and twists me nipple hard before backing away to the door, a wicked smile on her face. "Run with me, Teddy Bear," she says, using that nickname she thinks is cute but still confuses me. I am nothing like a teddy bear.

"If I can ever get out of this thrice-damned couch, I will," I says. But before Greta can bolt out the door, someone knocks on it. She opens it and a voice asks for me.

"Who would be asking for me here?" I wonder aloud, and struggle to get up. "Damn this fecking couch, Sam; take an axe to it and set it on fire already!"

Laughing, he extends an arm to me and says, "I can't do that. It's Ty's favorite."

Ty looks wounded, and I feel like an ox box for making it happen. "Sorry, Ty, never mind me. I'm an ornery shite. Take it out of me hide next time we spar. Defend the honor of your arse-munching couch."

The man at the door is Creidhne, one of the Tuatha Dé Danann. He has a couple of flat wooden boxes under his arm, and he smiles when he sees me.

"Ah, Owen, I'm glad I caught you. Brighid said this would be a likely place to look."

"She did? Well, I guess she's been watching me more carefully than I thought. What can I do for ye?"

"Just accept these. I've finished your knuckles, and I have some gifts from Luchta as well."

"Me knuckles?" I'd forgotten all about them. Creidhne had taken measurements of me fists and promised to fashion some kind of weapon for me, as a personal test of his skill. I hadn't asked for them—he volunteered. I suppose that the Tuatha Dé Danann are longing for glory again now that there are Druids in the world once more—I mean, more Druids than Siodhachan, who was in hiding for two thousand years.

"Aye. Can't wait to see you try them on. Have you a minute to spare or have I come at a terrible time?"

Greta catches my eye. "We can run later, Owen," she says. "But expect a rough one."

"I'm looking forward to it," I reply, then I tell Creidhne he's welcome and introduce him to all the wolves. Ty fetches him a beer and I raise my bottle. "To Goibhniu and his craft," I says, remembering his brother, killed by a spriggan during Fand's attempted coup on Brighid. "Not a day goes by I don't miss him." We drink to his memory and then, at Sam's invitation, Creidhne sets down his boxes on their dining room table. One is larger than the other, but both are custom varnished maple. Creidhne opens the smaller of the two, and the interior is lined with red felt. A set of brass knuckles rests inside, etched with bindings that the god of craft cannot wait to explain.

"They haven't been named yet, but these are weapons worthy of a name," he says. "Unbreakable, amplifies your strength, and serves as a power reservoir for Gaia's energy."

"What do ye mean by that?"

"Well, Siodhachan and Granuaile both have something similar. Ye may find yourself cut off from the earth at times in this modern world and need some juice for a binding. Ye can store some in these knuckles and draw on it as needed. Siodhachan has his silver bear charm, and Granuaile stores hers in the silver end of Scáthmhaide. They chose silver in case they had reason to worry about werewolves." His eyes dart to his hosts, suddenly aware that he might be giving offense. He hurries on, "Well, bronze can store that energy too. These knuckles can each store more than both of those combined."

"Well, that makes me happier than a swim in a pool of porter. What happens when I shape-shift, though?"

"That's the best part! They shift with you and adapt to your forms. When you're a bear they encase your claws; when you're a ram they cover your horns; when you're a walrus they coat your tusks; and when you're a kite they move to your talons."

"Aw, you're just showin' off for your brother now, aren't ye?"

"Perhaps a little," he says, proud and pleased. "The great drawback to Scáthmhaide is that Granuaile has to find a way to carry it no matter what her form is. Tremendously powerful weapon otherwise—the invisibility binding is incredible—but she can't shape-shift efficiently with it. In practical terms she's tied to her human form. I didn't want you to have to worry about that. These will morph with you and always be useful."

"May I try them?"

"Please do! I would love to see them in action."

I pluck them out of the felt and slip them on over me fingers. They are cool against the skin and fit perfectly. I note that they are thin but wide, covering the space between first and second knuckles. I don't feel any different while wearing them, but I expect that will change once I get outside and charge them up.

"Very nice. Let's go outside and give a boulder a bad day."

Flagstaff's at seven thousand feet, and it lets you know it in December. It hadn't snowed yet but it is certainly cold enough for it. That doesn't matter; I strip to me skin as soon as I get outside and feel the rush of energy flow up from the tattoo on the sole of me foot. I don't draw too much—it isn't necessary. I'm just taking the knuckles out for a test punch. An innocent chunk of rust-colored stone that had never done anything to me is my first target, sticking up out of the pine needles about thirty yards away from Sam and Ty's house.

"Will I scratch these or damage them by hitting rocks and walls and things?"

"They should be fine," Creidhne says.

"And me hands?"

"Should also be fine."

Normally I wouldn't bother punching a stone. Your fingers would break long before the stone would, and rock doesn't make any noises to let you know it's hurt. But if you're going to test a weapon you have to do it right.

I cock me right fist, half expecting to shatter me hand, and let one fly at the rock. It doesn't split and turn to dust, but neither does me hand. Instead, the blow turns the top layer underneath the knuckles into a fine webwork of crazed lines. And I feel nothing but fine and powerful.

Encouraged, I follow up with a combo, more muscle behind the punches this time, and chips fly from the stone.

"Holy shit, Owen," Greta says. "Are your hands okay?"

I show them to her. No blood. No redness signaling an oncoming bruise. "Perfectly fine."

I shift to a bear with the knuckles on to see what happens. The brass flows, stretching and shaping itself to me claws. I have brass bear claws! I swipe at the ground with one of them, expecting resistance from the half-frozen, dried-up clay soil, but it scoops away like cottage cheese. Incredible. I shift to a walrus next, just to see the brass on me tusks. I can feel the brass move and flow up me hands to me face as I shift, and then there they are, gleaming brass-coated tusks. I bellow at Creidhne and the wolves to make them laugh, and then I skip the ram form and shift to a red kite. The metal moves from face to feet, and me talons are still very sharp and covered in the brass. Curious as to how the extra weight will affect me flight, I take wing and note that lifting off the ground requires just a bit more effort, but once airborne I don't perceive a difference; additional strength flows from the brass into me wing muscles and there is no strain. To test the talons, I light on a ponderosa tree branch and nearly snap it off. They will require a light touch, then, when I'm wearing them, or else I'll damage trees unintentionally.

It's a fine gift, far beyond anything I deserve, and I glide to another branch and land gently on it to get control of meself. Kites' tear ducts aren't easily triggered by emotions, so it's a good form for me to have some feelings without leaking them everywhere. It's been a fine day, what with the possibility of having shiny new apprentices and some knuckles to beat the shite out of a deserving man in a bog somewhere, plus the promise of a run with Greta later. It's more bounty than I could reasonably expect—more than I ever enjoyed in me old life. I really owe Siodhachan for days like this, damn his eyes.

When I fly down and shift to me human form again, I take off the knuckles and bury Creidhne in praise.

"You are the finest craftsman alive! They're wonderful! Perfect!"

The son of Brighid bows in thanks. "I trust you'll do something properly legendary with them. If ye don't make yourself famous with those, the effort's entirely wasted."

"I'm sure something will come along," I says, grinning at him.

"When ye name them, you'll let me know, won't ye?"

"Of course, of course."

"I have one more thing for you, and then I'll take me leave."

"Oh, right, there's another box!"

We pile inside and I put me clothes back on to warm up. The larger box from Luchta holds three wooden stakes, hardwood beauties carved with bindings.

"Luchta heard that Siodhachan has yewmen going after vampires and is trying to make the world safe for Druids. So he made these for the three of you."

"Hold on a moment now," I says. "Siodhachan's doing what?"

"My understanding is that the vampires have declared open season on Druids again—all three of you. They were the ones who spurred the Romans to wipe ye out, ye know, back in the old days that I guess you missed, and only Siodhachan survived. And you, o' course, by skipping past it all."

"I didn't know that. He never told me that."

Greta breaks in and says, "I thought he told you everything while you were touching up his tattoo."

"No, no, he must have left out that part. Mostly he talked about cocking up with the gods, and there was only one vampire he talked about—no, two. One almost killed him because the first one betrayed him."

"Right, that was Leif Helgarson who betrayed him," Hal says. "He betrayed us as well."

"But it's this old vampire named Theophilus who's out for your blood now," Creidhne says. "Or anyway he's the one who's giving the orders."

I turn to Greta. "Well, this changes things a bit, love. We can't start a grove here when we might have bloodsuckers coming after us. It wouldn't be safe."

Her eyes flash at me and she shakes her head. "They'll be perfectly safe and you know it. They'll be inside a warded house at sundown and up at sunrise, all of them protected by us and their parents, and none of us easy to kill."

"I don't know what grove you mean, but look at these stakes, Owen," Creidhne says. "They can't be splintered or snapped, just like Scáthmhaide, and they have the unbinding for vampires carved right into them. Stab a vampire anywhere—left hand, right big toe—and they'll be unbound. You don't have to hit them in the heart with these."

"I didn't know such a thing was possible."

"Neither did Luchta until he tried. Look, Brighid wants the Druids to win this time. These stakes were *her* idea, and Luchta made it happen."

"Brighid's idea, eh? Well, I need to pay a visit to your

mother in any case. I have to talk to her about starting a grove here, and maybe she knows where Siodhachan is."

"I don't think she does. I brought all the stakes to you because we thought you would know where to find him."

"I can try calling him," Hal says, pulling out his cell phone. We watch in silence as he taps at the screen. He uses the speaker function so we can all hear, but the call goes straight to voice mail. "Nope. Either his phone's off, or it's dead, or he's not on this plane," he says.

"Oh, I'll bet you he's on this plane," I growl, feeling the old ire swelling inside when I know Siodhachan's up to his shenanigans again. "He's out there somewhere right now with his cheeky hound, doing something dumber than eating a bowl full of llama shite, I guarantee it."

CHAPTER 5

Purposefully seeking out a poltergeist might be one of the dumbest things I've ever done. Well, that and growing muttonchops.

When I woke and checked the man in the mirror, the areas where I'd applied O'Sullivan's Patented Miracle Beard Tonic had outgrown the top half of my sideburns by about half an inch. That required some trimming. Then I had to flatten my hair down with some greasy goo, part it on the left, and plaster a curl of it on my forehead.

<Well, *that's* different,> Oberon commented when I emerged from the bathroom. <I sure hope that style doesn't catch on with the world's poodles.>

"Can't believe it ever caught on with humans," I said, fetching my gray suit from the closet. It took me a couple of tries to get the tie looking right—it had been a lifetime since I wore one.

I took Oberon out for breakfast and a walk, during which he got admiring stares and I got furtive, uncertain glances. The morning's newspaper declared that a strange rash of ritualistic murders had been carried out yesterday in America and Mexico, mostly in the Pacific time zone, where an alarming number of rich one-percenters had been stabbed in the heart and then beheaded. The Hammers of God had managed to score a few for the good guys, I saw.

I set Oberon up in the room afterward with the DO NOT DISTURB sign and a food channel on the television, his favorite babysitter. He was currently into a show about strange foods from around the world—strange, that is, to American tastes. He would tell me all about them and then demand to be taken to various destinations to try the live squid or the roasted locusts or whatever.

I was careful to keep from him how worried I was about this operation. There were so many things that could go wrong, and I probably hadn't thought of them all. My hound was happy when I left him, though, highly amused by Americans trying the Korean dish called *hongeo,* or skate, which is quite possibly the nastiest food in the world.

My first stop was a used bookstore, where I found an old edition of the King James Bible with a red ribbon for a bookmark. I brought that with me instead of my sword, Fragarach. Gwendolyn's fiancé knew nothing of swords but had a thing for gospels.

Then there was no more time to waste: Werner Drasche was doubtless in Toronto by now and looking for me, so it was time to visit the Royal Conservatory of Music on Bloor Street, specifically Ihnatowycz Hall, the modern, sponsored name of the old building where Gwendolyn had died in the nineteenth century and become the Lady in Red, and where, some seventy years later, she had mistaken me for her fiancé, Nigel.

Once I walked into the building, a funny thing happened: People stopped staring at me as if I were a walking fashion faux pas and smiled at me instead. In the music world, eccentric dress was a marker of genius. Or something.

"Must be a pianist," I heard one student whisper to another as they passed me on the grand staircase.

"No, he's gotta be a cellist," the other whispered back. "They're all bugfuck."

The building had far fewer unoccupied rooms than in the fall of 1953. People were practicing in them or taking in musical theory lectures and living a blissful life of art and chair politics in whatever orchestra or symphony they belonged to. And many of the smaller rooms were faculty offices now.

There was nothing available on the second floor, where Gwendolyn originally found me, so I climbed the stairs to the third floor and found an unoccupied classroom. The number of desks that could be tossed at me was unsettling, but I chose one near the door and knelt down next to it, Bible in hand, and spoke aloud.

"Gwendolyn? It's me, Nigel. I would like to speak with you, please." I kept going on in that vein for a long while, repeating my name and hers and my wish to speak. My knees began to throb after an hour, and I considered that perhaps Gwendolyn had moved on. It would hardly be surprising—what would keep her lingering here after the supposed betrayal she'd suffered?

"Well," I said, getting to my feet. "I just wanted to say I'm sorry."

"Sssssorry for what?" an ethereal voice whispered, and there, across the room, a red vision floated above the professor's lectern.

"Sorry I wasn't there for you when you needed me. When you were trampled by that horse in the street."

"That is alllll?"

"I've never forgiven myself for that. Your death could have been prevented if I had only come out to meet you."

"Annnd what about the other womannnn?"

"What? There is no other woman. There never has been and never will be."

"*I ssssaw you, Nigel! I ssssaw you with herrr!*" Furniture shifted around, scraping against the tile. I was going to be bombarded with flying desks soon. Before that became too much to bear, I had to convince her that she hadn't seen her Nigel with another woman—for she truly hadn't. He'd been faithful to her, as far as I could discover from my historical research.

My plan relied on the idea that ghosts have one thing in common with hounds—they're not too clear on the passage of time. As far as Gwendolyn was concerned, Nigel was not only still alive, he was still attending his Baptist seminary in the nineteenth century. Things like cars driving on paved roads outside and electricity inside—those simply didn't penetrate whatever consciousness she had. The only thing that mattered to her was her relationship with Nigel, which was probably why she ignored or simply did not see minor differences in our appearance and voice. If she was ever to have a chance of moving on, she needed to repair that relationship with Nigel and get a sense of closure.

So now I had to be the man himself.

"I don't know what you saw, Gwendolyn, but whoever it was, it wasn't me! I would never do that to you. There is a lad here at the college who looks a lot like me, though. Maybe you mistook him for me."

"*Nnno! It was you! You were wearing that suit! Sssshe kept saying your naaame. Ssssshe called you Nigel!*"

Desks levitated off the floor, twitching and spinning, and one of them rocketed at my head as I shouted a desperate response and ducked. It still clipped me painfully on the forearm I had raised to protect my head. "Gray suits are common as corn, Gwendolyn! And whoever the woman was that you saw called *him* Nigel, not me. Did he say his name was Nigel?"

That made her pause and she forgot about the desks, allowing gravity to pull them down to the floor again with a crash. *"Nnnooo."*

"What did he say his name was?"

"Hhhee didn't. Just that it wasn't Nigel."

"Well, there you have it."

"Then whyyyy did sssshe call him that?"

"I haven't the slightest notion. People do strange things, Gwen. I have heard—I wouldn't know, of course—that some people enjoy role-playing. Perhaps that was what you stumbled across."

"Rrrole-playing?"

That was a rabbit hole I didn't want to explore, especially since I was playing a role at that very moment, so I hurried past it. "Yes. I am so very sorry that you have been plagued with doubts, but it gives me so much joy to see you again."

"Joy sssseeing me like thisss? Do you nnnot think me damned?" she said.

"Not at all," I replied, which I knew had to be the right answer—one hardly tells one's fiancée that she's damned—but then I had to think of why that would be so. Traditionally a ghost would be at minimum cursed if not damned in the eyes of a Protestant minister, provided that a minister believed his eyes. But then I recalled that Spiritualism was quite popular in the Victorian era and was bound to have some influence on the Nigel of the past—the idea that spirits not only could communicate with the living but were predisposed to do so. Nigel hadn't been a black-clad Puritan and he wasn't some modern Fundamentalist. He'd been a product of his time. "You're just waiting before you move on. You still have something to do here—something to teach me, or to teach us all. And I want to help you, Gwendolyn."

"Hhhow?"

"The man who ran you down—I know where to find

him. He needs to be stopped before he hurts anyone else with his carelessness."

"I don't want revennnge."

"No, no, me neither. This is simple justice. And peace of mind. I worry about who else he might hurt. You can leave this place, right?"

"Yess, but I don't want to leave. I want to talk to you."

"And I want to talk to you. But I think it's important to stop this man first, and then we can talk all you want." She nodded her agreement, and then I held up a finger. "Just one moment while I make arrangements? Wait here for me for a small while?"

"I willlll wait. I have been waiting allllready."

"I'll be right outside the door and return for you as soon as possible."

I grinned at her as I climbed to my feet and scooted for the door. Once in the hallway I turned on my cell phone and immediately got pinged with missed calls. One of them was from Hal Hauk, my attorney, with whom I wished to speak anyway, so I thumbed the callback button.

"Atticus, where are you?" he said.

"Toronto. Look, Hal, I need you to get ahold of Leif and ask him for Werner Drasche's number."

"What?"

"You can still get in touch with Leif, can't you?"

"Yes, but who's this Werner Drasche?"

"Long story. I just need his number right away, okay?"

"Okay, but we've been trying to get hold of you regarding something else. Your archdruid wants to start a grove up near Flagstaff, take on six apprentices."

"Apprentices? Where'd he find them?"

"I found them. They're the children of pack members, born before their parents were turned."

"Sounds perfect! Except that things are going to be

warming up on the vampire front. You all should look out, take precautions."

"Were you responsible for this morning's headlines?"

"Yeah, that was me. Or sort of me. Remember that guy in my shop with the beard who tried to throw a silver knife at you that one time?"

"Oh, yes, that odd rabbi."

"He's much more calm now. It was his organization that did all that last night, using information I gave them. I'm moving fast and ambushing them as much as possible, but they're going to catch up with me eventually. There could be blowback, especially after today, so you guys should watch out."

"Thanks for the warning."

A familiar growly voice shouted in the background of the call. Hal said, "Your archdruid says to meet him in Tír na nÓg at the Fae Court. He has something for you."

"All right, I will, but I have things to do here first. Werner Drasche's number."

"Call you back soon."

It was only five minutes of agonizing waiting in the old chapel before Hal called back with Drasche's number and gave me Leif's as well for future reference.

"Leif was only too glad to cooperate," he said. "Said to tell you to carry on, you're doing well."

"Gods below, he's a smug bastard."

"What's he talking about?"

"I'll have to tell you later. Clock's ticking."

We rang off and I dialed the number for the arcane life-leech. He picked up immediately and answered in German. I replied in English.

"Hello, Werner. It's your favorite Druid."

"O'Sullivan! Where are you?"

"Probably not that far from you if you're in Toronto."

"I am. Your little stunt will not do you any more good. I've sent notice that everyone should move."

"You must be very popular among the vampires right now, what with compromising their security and making them lug their coffins around. And all those staked vampires on the West Coast. Your people will be scrambling around to keep the reports on all those autopsies secret."

He cursed in German. "That witch in Africa said you'd never return to Toronto!"

Mekera was a tyromancer, not a witch, but Drasche probably would not care about the distinction. "She told you the truth as best she could see it. I'm just unpredictable. We have that in common, Werner. When you killed my friend Kodiak Black, you left a note that said you wanted to talk, yet all you did in Ethiopia was spray bullets at me. That's uncommon rudeness, Werner, especially when I spared your life the first time we met."

"You want to talk? We're talking now."

"It's not good enough somehow. Let's do it in person. I have something to say to your face, and I bet you're wearing a fabulous ascot today. Meet me in Massey Hall on the corner of Victoria and Shuter in a half hour. I'll be inside."

I disconnected before he could reply. Whether he came alone or with a bunch of hired muscle, the people of Toronto would be safe. He couldn't leech anything from an empty theatre. I ducked my head back into the classroom and saw Gwendolyn still hovering there, a vision in red.

"Everything's settled. Shall we go?" I extended a hand to her and she floated toward me, something approaching a smile curving the slash of a mouth on her face. We descended the grand staircase together, and the single person we saw on the way froze for a second and then hurried up past us without saying a word. When we stepped outside into the sunlight on the steps where she died, I paused to look at her.

"Ready?"

"*I'm ready, Nigel,*" she said, though her voice was a faint whisper in the daylight and she looked like someone had gotten too enthusiastic with the transparency slider.

"Excellent. Please don't trouble yourself about these roads and the strange carriages and clothing people wear. There have been a few changes since you passed. Progress."

She made no answer, and it was just as well. I had to worry instead about other people troubling themselves about the red apparition floating next to me. Perhaps I would get lucky, I thought, and I'd be the only one who could see her.

That didn't happen. I was hailed twice on the brisk walk to Massey Hall, once by a pedestrian and once by someone in a car, and asked what was that red smudge next to me.

"What?" I asked. "I don't see anything." That got rid of them. They would no doubt make optometrist appointments soon.

Massey Hall was a dirty brick lump of a building on the outside, covered in soot and grime reminiscent of buildings from the Industrial Revolution. Fire-escape stairwells on the front of the building, intended to give people on the balcony a fleeting chance in case of disaster, sloped down to the left and right, bracketing the front doors in an iron triangle. Three double doors with small windows above them were painted candy-apple red to reassure everyone that the building wasn't derelict and promised all kinds of fun inside. The inside was a beautiful theatre with excellent acoustics, which was why everyone put up with the ugly outside. And like most theatres, it's spectacularly empty during the day, making it an excellent place for a tête-à-tête in the middle of a huge city. Drasche would appreciate that I'd be cut off from the earth. It would be a fair fight—or appear so to him as he walked into an ambush. And it was fine if he suspected an ambush: Short of demolishing the building with me inside, there would be nothing he could do, and I hoped the half-hour window to act would prevent him from orchestrating something like that.

"The man who ran you down," I said to Gwendolyn, "is bald and has strange tattoos all over his head. I want to talk to him alone inside this building. If anyone else tries to enter the building—from any door on any side— please keep them out as best you can. Close and lock the doors. Toss them across the street. Whatever it takes. Just get the bald tattooed man in and keep everyone else out."

"Vvvvery well."

"Can you lock and unlock these doors?" I asked, pointing to the first pair. Best to make sure.

"Yess."

"Would you please unlock one for me?" She could do it faster than I could by flipping the tumblers, and I didn't want to use any of my stored energy if I didn't have to. Once they clacked, I pulled open the door.

"Thanks, Gwendolyn. You can leave this one open until the bald man comes inside. He shouldn't be long."

If he was the punctual sort, anyway. It had taken most of a half hour to walk from the conservatory to the concert hall, and that was a nervous speed-walk.

"Beeee careful, Nigel," she said.

"Thank you, I will."

I had to cast night vision once inside and find the light board. It took me a couple of minutes to figure out how to bring up the house lights, but once I did I returned to the main seating area and shuffled sideways down the twelfth row of seats. In the middle of it I crouched down on the floor, which was a bit cramped but kept my head out of sight. I took off my confining shoes with a sigh of relief.

Drasche burst through the doors in the back of the theatre moments later, shouting my name. "Where are you? Let's have that talk!"

Casting camouflage and beginning the drain of my bear charm, I peeked above the chair backs to locate him. His suit was a somber slim-cut black for a change, but he'd come through on the ascot, with a glowing shade of teal that qualified as optic assault. Hands clasped behind his back, he scanned the theatre for me, and his eyes flicked up to the low ceiling directly above him, which was the floor of the balcony. He probably wondered if I was up there, and he hesitated before stepping out from under it, not wishing to give me a free shot at him if I was waiting above.

"Talk to me, Druid. What is it you wish to say?"

I whispered a simple binding to see if he'd learned anything from our first meeting on the beach in France and discovered that he had; all his clothing was synthetic fiber now. Nothing natural for me to bind.

"You're an abomination and a threat to all life," I called, and his head swiveled in the direction of my voice, trying in vain to spy me. "And since you did nothing positive with your life once I spared it, I need to rethink my mercy."

I put the sole of my foot on a metal seat back, which was bolted to the floor and under which I knew Ferris, the iron elemental, lurked. I didn't feel the buzz of him immediately underneath me, but he had to be nearby. He was still waiting for his treat after yesterday's heist.

//Man with magic in his skin / I sent to him through the metal / It is yours now//

"Here's my mercy," Drasche said, and he brought his hands forward with automatic weapons in each hand, little machine guns with huge clips curving down from the handle. He pointed them in my general direction, and his fingers held down the triggers.

Steel-jacketed bullets zinged and popped off the theatre seats and I ducked down, lying flat in the aisle and maintaining my camouflage. Lots of bullets was Drasche's answer to Druidry, and it was why I hadn't bothered bringing Fragarach: You don't bring a sword to a gunfight.

Unfortunately, Drasche didn't need to see me to hit me. With all the ordnance he was throwing around, it was only a matter of time—seconds, in fact—until one of them ricocheted off the metal seats and nailed me. I felt it plunge into my back and perforate my liver. I grunted involuntarily, dropped my camouflage, and triggered the healing charm instead, hoping a single bullet would be all I had to deal with. But I heard him run out, reload, and start up again, and he must have heard me grunt, because this time he zeroed in on my row and the next one down. One burst got me four times when it hit the chairs behind me. Two in the same area of my back, one ripping low through my guts, another that missed my spleen and got my pancreas instead, and two more that tore through the hamstrings of my right leg. When he ran out of ammunition for the second time and I heard him reload once more, I dug into my pocket for my phone. I was rapidly running out of juice dealing with my wounds and wouldn't make it without help. It was all I could do to stop the internal bleeding and knit my stomach back up before the acids leaked out and dissolved my intestines. If I died here, cut off from Gaia, there'd be no save from my soulcatcher.

Drasche got off perhaps ten rounds from his fresh clips before Ferris finally emerged from the floor, much later than I would have wished but very hungry. *"Was ist das?"* he said in German. *"Nein!"* I had to see this, so

I risked levering myself up on my left arm and poking
my head out in plain sight, gasping in pain as I did so.
Drasche didn't put a bullet in my head, because he
wasn't looking in my direction anymore. He was staring
at his pointy-toed boots and dancing around as a furry
black collection of iron shavings crawled up his legs and
torso, traveling up to his head. "O'Sullivan!" he shouted,
dropping his guns and frantically brushing at the flowing
iron, which ignored his efforts and continued upward.
"What is this?"

"That's Ferris," I said. "Never bring a gun to an elemental fight, Drasche."

Ferris reached the alchemical tattoos on Drasche's
scalp and cheeks—arcane sigils that gave him the power
to leech energy directly from living things as long as he
had line of sight—and then the iron elemental began to
feed on the raw magic imbued in the symbols.

Judging by the sounds Drasche made, it was not
a painless process. His attempts to repel Ferris were
fruitless—the furry iron flowed like water around and
under his fingers. I smiled faintly as I sank back to the
floor and dialed 911. The screaming in the background
would provide some urgency, I hoped, to the ambulance
and the police. The operator tried to ask questions about
what she was hearing, but I thumbed off the connection
once she knew the location and that I'd been shot.

A dull thud suggested that the lifeleech had collapsed
to the ground, but I didn't worry about his health. Ferris
wouldn't kill him—he couldn't, because that would be
breaking the rules Gaia set down for elementals. He'd
merely turn Werner Drasche from a monster to a human
with monstrous proclivities.

I was far more worried about myself. The energy in
my bear charm ran dry—overtaxed by the demands of
healing and further evidence that I should really make
another ten or so—leaving me with five gunshot wounds,

a wave of pain, and a fine start on a case of shock. When my vision turned red, I thought I was on the verge of blacking out, but it turned out to be Gwendolyn floating above me.

"NNNNigel? You're hurt?" her whispery voice breathed.

"Yes. The blackguard shot me. But paramedics—I mean, a doctor is on the way." She wouldn't know what a paramedic was. "Though I'm not sure he'll be in time."

Her pale smudged face turned to where Drasche writhed and screamed in the aisle.

"What is happening to himmm?" she asked.

I didn't know how to explain Ferris to her, so I said, "Justice. Are there any more men outside?"

"Nnno. He came alooone. He shhhhould die." Her fists clenched at her sides and her eyes lit up with rage.

"No, no. Gwendolyn, listen to me," I said, realizing that this was my chance to set her free. "He is getting what he deserves now and will get more when he arrives in hell. Do not tarnish your soul with violence. It is time for you to move on, as it is time for me. Go on and wait for me, Gwendolyn. I'll be there soon and we can be together again."

Her head turned back to regard me, and the signs of anger fell away. All her edges softened and she made a noise somewhere between a sigh and a coo. The ghost swooped down until she was a mere inch above me, and I shivered from the chill of her proximity. *"I love youuuu, Nigel."*

"I love you too, Gwendolyn," I said, hoping it would be enough to soothe her restless spirit. "Always. Go on now, and I'll join you. Very soon."

"Sooooon," she said, slowly rising and then dissipating in wisps of red until all I could see was the ceiling of the theatre.

"Farewell," I whispered, hoping that wherever she went she would find the real Nigel waiting for her.

Werner Drasche's screams wound down to moans and eventually whimpers in German, and I might have let loose a moan or two of my own. When Ferris finished with the lifeleech, he thanked me before leaving.

//Delicious// he said.

//Thanks for your help earlier// I replied, since he could do nothing else for me, and he melted away, leaving me to shiver in silent pain and hope I didn't bleed out before help arrived. Or that Drasche wouldn't summon the strength to grab one of his guns and crawl down here to finish me off. Apart from getting shot, it had been a couple of good days in Toronto—though to be truthful almost any day would be good in comparison to getting shot. Still, I had enlisted the Hammers of God in the world's biggest vampire hunt, stripped Werner Drasche of his powers, and sent a long-suffering ghost to her rest. It would be a good story to tell Oberon—oh, gods below, Oberon! He was still in the hotel room, and I wouldn't be getting back to him anytime soon. He was also much too far away for me to reach via our mental bond, so he'd be worried. I thought of calling Hal, since I didn't know where Granuaile was, but didn't want to remind Drasche that I was still alive. I silenced the phone and texted him instead:

Shot in Toronto. Need someone to take care of Oberon in hotel. Send Owen maybe?

I added the hotel info and sent it. In a few seconds I got a glorious if terse reply:

On it.

"O'Sullivan," Drasche's voice grated. "What did you do to me?"

I made no answer and tried to breathe as quietly as possible. The lack of damage to my lungs kept me from coughing, at least.

The acoustics of the theatre allowed me to hear the rasping of cloth on carpet as Drasche dragged himself down the aisle and a wet hand slapping against the metal of a gun. "Going to make *verdammt* sure you are dead," he growled.

There was nothing I could do. I had all the mobility and martial capability of a soggy sponge and the same magical ability as he did—that is, none whatsoever. He must have picked up only one of his guns, because I heard him begin to crawl in my direction and the gun made a clacking noise at odd intervals when his hand came down. He grew closer and closer, and the sound reminded me of that final sequence of *The Terminator* where the robot dragged itself after Sarah Connor. Except that she could move a little bit and had some handy machinery around to crush her pursuer.

"Ahh, there you are!" I stretched my neck, looked to the end of the aisle, and saw Werner Drasche peering back at me. His eyeballs gleamed abnormally white and mad in a puffy red face with little pinpricks of blood dotting it and plenty more smeared around where he had tried to shoo Ferris away. The ink of the alchemical tattoos still remained, but the magic infused with them was gone and he still didn't realize it. He knew from experience that he couldn't leech any energy from me, so he truly didn't know what had been done to him except that it had hurt. "Lying defenseless in a pool of your own blood. I kept telling Theophilus that gunning you down was the simplest solution. How delightful to be proven right."

"That's not his real name, is it?" I asked. "Theophilus. That's some kind of nickname he thinks is clever."

Werner Drasche laughed at me. "You think I would ever tell you that? I would—"

He cut off abruptly as a squad of shouty, armed men burst into the theatre and demanded that he drop the gun *now*. He looked back over his left shoulder, but since he was flat on the floor the result was that I saw the very top of his head for the first time. He had a Rose Cross there instead of an alchemical symbol. Strange.

"Ah, sustenance!" Drasche said, grinning as he twisted to face the officers. He didn't move his right hand with the gun but rolled a bit onto his right side so that he could stretch his empty left hand back at them, clutching at the air. He was trying to leech energy from the officers, first to heal and then to pump himself up to finish me off, but it didn't work, and the shouts got more insistent. Every second he held on to that gun increased the chances that he would be shot himself. But Drasche was stubborn and perhaps a bit slow to realize his predicament and just remained still, straining to do something he no longer had the power to do. The police converged, pointing their weapons at him, fingers on triggers, and eventually kicked away his gun. It skittered down the aisle as they grabbed his arms and yanked them behind him. Drasche finally realized he was a regular, powerless human, and his carefully cultivated arrogance evaporated. Being manhandled like the criminal he was caused him to lose his shit. He shouted curses in a mixture of German and English and struggled to free himself, but they had him cuffed in short order.

That's when I called for help and got it. "He shot me," I said weakly, and that's all I had to do. Drasche would go to prison after some cursory medical treatment, unless one of his vampire friends came to bust him out in the night. Regardless, he was simply human now, and I knew that would be a fate worse than death for him after centuries of preying on people.

Saying "he shot me" was all I *could* do, anyway—I was fading fast. I had been able to take care of single bullets on a couple of other occasions, but I'd also been able to access the earth's power when I did so. Five rounds and no juice meant I was completely dependent on modern medicine. Paramedics probed me and asked me questions that I tried to answer but succeeded only in spewing out an unintelligible verbal slurry. They gave me plasma as I was trundled into the ambulance and whisked away to a hospital somewhere.

The ride was almost absurdly short—a block away, it seemed—but during the ride it occurred to me that I'd certainly be staying the night in the hospital, most likely sedated, and if Drasche knew where I was and managed to make a call, he could summon his vampire buddies not only to spring him but to take me out. Even if the police posted a guard on my room for some reason, a vampire would simply charm him or her and walk on past, ripping out my throat while I slept.

As I slipped into unconsciousness before reaching a surgeon, I mouthed a prayer to the Morrigan that I'd get to wake up.

CHAPTER 6

With Loki's mark dissolved, I feel simultaneously free but hunted—like prey, in other words. I can go wherever I want, with the proviso that someone could be (and probably is) watching. Surveillance-state London, in other words, but instead of the government tracking my movements, it's anyone with a talent for divination.

Loki is not particularly adept at that himself, but he knows people who are. He could still find me and set me aflame anywhere outside my warded cabin. That's the trouble with earth-based wards: They don't travel well. It's what caused Atticus to bind cold iron to his aura—he couldn't think of any other effective way to ward against magic on his person.

It's going to be a long process, doing that to myself, but after seeing how much the Fae hate it, I'm wondering if I should. Still, I think hiding from divination is a necessary safety measure and something I should pursue now, considering my current enemy: Loki can't kill me if he can't find me. I don't want to ask Odin or any of his pantheon for help, though. The price they'd want me to pay would probably have something to do with their apocalypse, and the exchange of services would not be in my favor.

The same would hold true of the Tuatha Dé Danann. Scáthmhaide was a gift, but any further favors would come at a price, and they would be sure to ask for a heavy one. Atticus might have a decent suggestion for me, but I doubt he'd encourage anything beyond cold iron. I don't relish rehashing that conversation and I don't know where he is right now anyway. That's the way I'd like to keep it for a while: I have things I want to do besides hide myself from the gods. I have old business to conclude with my stepfather.

Orlaith and I are somewhere in Sweden now, deposited here by request via the Bifrost Bridge after saying our farewells to Odin and Frigg. We're on a lakeshore near some bound trees and we can go wherever we want, but we pause to appreciate the view. There's some kind of hawk or perhaps an eagle hunting for fish—distance makes identification impossible. It's chilly and the sky is overcast; it looks like it will snow soon. Orlaith's tail wags when I point out the raptor hunting for its lunch. It dives down abruptly and comes up with a squirming pike in its talons.

<Food looks good,> my hound observes, her tongue lolling out to one side.

"Very subtle, Orlaith," I reply. "Let's go find some in India. I have someone I need to see there."

I shift us to a familiar banana grove outside of Thanjavur, India, where it's much warmer than Sweden and the sun is shining. They often enjoy highs in the eighties during December.

<Remember this place,> Orlaith says. <Mostly vegetables here. But Oberon brought me a ham bone. Oberon coming soon?>

"No, we won't see Oberon and Atticus for a while. But the market in town should be hopping, and I bet we'll find some chicken, at least."

We do indeed find some, and with basic needs met I pull out my phone and launch a browser, spending a few futile minutes trying to find a current address for one

Mhathini Palanichamy, whose body Laksha currently inhabits. Time to act like the lost tourist I really am. I ask people who look friendly and willing to speak English how I might find a friend in town, feeling underdressed in my dull jeans and T-shirt in the midst of so many colorful saris.

A Tamil University student sets me straight by telling me that the local search engines work fine but are mostly in the Hindi or Tamil languages, neither of which I speak. I offer her my phone, and in moments she has found the most likely address and sets me up with a walking navigation map.

I feel the eyes on me from men and women alike as I make my way to the Palanichamy residence, and it's just as well that I don't speak the languages or else I would probably have to open a can of whup-ass on some men who catcall me. None of them approach, though, either owing to the presence of Orlaith at my side or the tomahawk at my belt.

When I reach the address, my patience is tested further by the man who answers the door. He doesn't speak English and dismisses me rudely, slamming the door in my face without making any serious effort to understand why I'm there. I pound on the door with one end of Scáthmhaide until he yanks it back open and shouts at me.

"Mhathini," I say, and repeat her name until it penetrates and he gives up his intimidation game. He shouts for her in the house and eventually she appears at the door, both wary and weary.

Her sari is blue and green and her ruby necklace shines brightly against it, but her face is wan, even though the pallor of the hospital has improved to a healthier color. At least she brightens perceptibly when she sees me and says my name. A rapid argument with her brother or cousin or whoever the male is ensues, until he finally storms off, leaving us alone.

"Sorry about that," she says, stepping outside and closing the door behind her. "Mhathini's family is quite conservative."

"Hey, you sound good!" I say, giving her a hug. When I last saw Laksha she had a severe speech impediment due to her host body's brain injuries, but she had assured me she could work around it and she had.

"Thanks. It took a few days, but I have her rewired now. Had to work fast if I wanted to have any kind of say in my life."

"Ugh. Who was that? Your brother? He had the distinct whiff of an asshole about him."

"Yes, he's the brother, but they all have that attitude, unfortunately. Let's talk out of earshot. The father speaks English and is not above eavesdropping. The brother has gone to fetch him. He'll be out shortly to berate me for going outside alone, no doubt."

"Alone? I'm here."

"Alone with a stranger is worse than being actually alone."

"We'll convince him that we're friends somehow."

Laksha smiles, a bit crooked but relieved. "I'm so glad you've come to visit." She greets Orlaith and gives her a scratch behind the ears. Without waiting for anyone's permission, we walk two blocks to a tea shop, and Laksha tells me on the way that Mhathini's mother works in the silk industry, her father is an IT consultant who works from home serving clients in the UK, and her brother is a computer science major at the university.

"And what about you?"

"Mhathini was about to get married, which was apparently to be the sum of her future. But then she got in that car accident that landed her in the hospital. I am fairly certain from what I could glean of her remaining memories that it was not an accident but rather a suicide attempt."

"What?"

"Her family is so very abusive. Not physically—I mean verbally. Lots of assertions that Mhathini is stupid and ugly and things of that nature. She didn't think the marriage would improve matters. And of course the marriage is off now—the man married someone else while she was in a coma—so at this point I am reminded daily of how useless I am."

"Well, that's bullshit and you should move on."

"I think Mhathini tried to do just that."

"That's not what I meant."

"I know what you meant, Granuaile, but you are speaking from a place of tremendous privilege."

"What? I am not—"

"Hold that thought, please," Laksha says as we arrive at the tea shop. They have three outside tables and we sit at one, where Orlaith can join us. After we place an order, Laksha picks up the thread of our conversation. "Think about it, please: You have money and the ability to go anywhere you wish on the earth without spending that money. Plus significant physical abilities. These assets make you think it is simple for women to leave abusive situations."

"I never said it would be simple—just that you should do it. And you have significant abilities too, Laksha. There's nothing keeping you here except your own will. If the situation is unbearable, then why have you decided to bear it?"

Laksha shrugs noncommittally and looks down at her lap. "This is my karma."

I snort in disbelief. "How do you figure that?"

"I don't know what happened to you that night with the rakshasas and your father and Durga . . ."

That's not a night I wish to relive, so I say, "The short version is that I'm here and all the rest are not."

"Yes. I'm sorry about your father."

"Thank you."

"Well, after my austerities and prayers, after all of my efforts to battle the rakshasas, during the moment I was likely to do the most good, my help was firmly rejected."

"Rejected how?"

"I left my host body's mind, you see, to do battle with the raksoyuj in the ether, as I promised you I would. And while I was in the ether, the woman died—I don't know how, for she was alive when I left. And Durga told me—not verbally; these were words I heard in the ether itself—that it was not my place to help, that my place was in my necklace, and then she forced me to return there."

"Durga said that exactly? You're not paraphrasing?"

"She said that. And then my next memory is of you telling me to inhabit this body or you would leave my necklace behind to be found by whoever walked by. So this is where I am supposed to be."

I shook my head. "That doesn't follow. I told you to inhabit that body because it was the only one I could find on short notice. I was in a hurry, and that is all. I was not acting at Durga's instruction and this was never intended to be a prison sentence for you—and I remind you that it's not a prison of any kind. You can leave that body right now and you know it."

"No. I am stained by my past, and regardless of your intent in the hospital, I know that this is where I belong."

"You *belong* in an abusive household for trying to help me? I'm sorry, Laksha, but I must reject that premise completely. Durga could not have meant that you are never to help anyone again. Why would she want that? Her words applied only to that situation—because you truly couldn't have helped with my father. That raksoyuj was formidable, to say the least. I mean, Durga had to make an effort to kill him. He was a challenge. I'm sure she didn't mean for you to sit here and submit passively to some patriarchal toad for trying to help."

Laksha bobs her head to either side, a noncommittal gesture, and our tea and biscuits arrive. We spend a minute with the rituals involved in serving it—milk and honey, the clink of spoons on porcelain—and then Laksha speaks again.

"You have given me new information and I'm grateful. I will consider it, I promise you, and act should I feel the need. You are right that I can leave at any time. But you are completely dismissing why I am staying."

I shake my head, uncomprehending. "No, I don't mean to be dismissive. I guess I don't understand."

Laksha flashes a smile at me over her teacup. "That is both likely and easily forgiven."

"Help me out a little bit?"

She sips, savors the tea, and puts down her cup. "This is not my meek acceptance of systemic misogyny. I am not in need of your rescue. What I need is to atone for centuries—*centuries*, Granuaile!—of my own cruelty and arrogance. So whether Durga meant for me to be here or not is immaterial. *I* feel I need to be here, to feel what it's like to be at the mercy of an arbitrary, power-mad individual like I used to be. I am learning. I am becoming empathetic and understanding the horror of how I used to behave. This is where I am on my spiritual journey. Where are you on yours?"

I flinch because the tone of her voice feels like a slap. "I'm not really on one. Gaia is my jam, and she's in favor of life on earth. That's about it. Journey's over, I'm at my destination."

"You haven't told me everything. You're different. Something else has happened to you besides the death of your father. What am I missing? Is it something to do with why you're holding your arm awkwardly?"

Yes. She's missing what Loki did to me, and my determination to never let something like that happen again. Being at the mercy of an arbitrary, power-mad individual has very little to recommend it—I knew from experience with both Loki and my stepfather—but if she feels that it's necessary for her own personal growth, then my opinion doesn't matter. Still, her question and its answer shift my vision a little, allowing me to glimpse what she must be seeing: I'm much angrier and more aggressive than I used to be. And, yes, I have cause—but the tragedy is that I've lost that giddy wonder I had when I first became bound to Gaia. There was peace too, which I felt even while being pursued across Europe by Artemis and Diana. It's all gone now.

"You're missing why I came to see you," I say, knowing that she would recognize I wished to change the subject. "I need a way to hide myself from divination and wondered if you knew how I could make it happen."

Laksha grimaces at me, sucks at her bared teeth, and squints her eyes. "You think I can help you with that? I have absolutely no talent in that kind of magic. If I did, I wouldn't have been so surprised to see you."

"But . . . oh. I guess you're just my go-to for advice. I had a problem and I came to you first."

Laksha affects a Southern accent, which she must have picked up while living in Asheville, North Carolina. "Well, ain't you just sweeter than peaches?" She drops it and continues more seriously, "Advice is easy enough. Go see those Polish witches we dealt with in Arizona, if you know where they are. They put a cloak on your boyfriend's sword. I was able to remove it, because I'm quite good at destruction, but I could never create something like that."

"Oh! Duh, I should have thought of them. Yeah,

they're actually in Poland now. Atticus convinced them to get out while they could."

"And where are you now? Still in Colorado?"

"In transition to Oregon." I let her know that the most reliable way to contact us is through the Tempe or Flagstaff packs, since we have ties to both.

"I'll remember that," she says. "If I leave here I will let you know. But if I do it will be for Mhathini's benefit, not mine."

"I beg your pardon?"

"She's still in here," Laksha says, pointing to her temple.

"She is?"

Laksha nods, a wan smile on her face. "I'm hoping to convince her to stay rather than move on."

I'm intensely curious—how much of Mhathini is left after the trauma? Is Laksha capable of rebuilding what's lost? Is she talking to Mhathini regularly inside her head, like she used to do with me? But before I can ask any of these questions, a man shouts and rushes over to our table. Orlaith stands up and growls at him and he pauses, but he doesn't back away. When Orlaith does nothing more, he spews a stream of annoyed Tamil at Laksha—or Mhathini—and I guess that this must be her father, who has left the house in such a hurry that he forgot to zip up his pants. He also hasn't shaven or perhaps even showered for a couple of days, yet he is doubtless telling Mhathini how wrong *she* is to be out in public without a proper escort.

It sets my teeth on edge and I want to growl at him too, but it's not my place to intervene. Laksha shoots a mute apology at me with her eyes and I wave back in silence. As she rises from the table to leave, I glare at him, daring him to say or do anything that would allow me to give him a proper retort, but he just stares back and then drapes a protective arm around the person he thinks is his daughter, steering her back to his house, where he can belittle her in private.

Though I don't have anything but American money on me, it worked fine in the market and I give the waitress everything I have, which is enough to pay for a month's rent or maybe two. I figure somebody here should have a good day.

CHAPTER 7

Damn Siodhachan to a dark and juicy hell for making me shift to an unfamiliar city to tend his perverted hound. I can't even bring Greta with me as a guide, because he told me once what happened to her old leader, Gunnar Magnusson, when he shifted planes: The poor lad was sick all over his shoes. Werewolves don't handle plane-shifting well, and I can't ask her to suffer through that just to let a hound outside for a dump.

Hal Hauk pointed out that I didn't have to go; he could have called some pack that lived outside the city limits and one of them could have driven into town to take care of Oberon. But Siodhachan asked for me specifically, and, besides, I'm curious about who could have put his bony arse in the hospital. Maybe I'll get to try out me new brass knuckles on him or her—or it.

So I shift into Queen's Park in Toronto with a sheaf of printed papers that Hal calls "Google Maps," whatever the feck that means, and they're all marked up with arrows telling me where to go to get to the hotel and then a bunch of numbers to call to figure out which hospital Siodhachan is in. Once I find him—Greta says he's officially using the name Sean Flanagan these days—I have another stack of maps telling me how to get there. I also have a handful of small pieces of paper with the number 20 on them and a picture of an old woman wearing a necklace of white beads. Greta says to me, "These are Canadian," and that if I give them to people in this country they'll do what I want. When I asks her if that will work on Siodhachan, she says probably not.

It's midafternoon and the walk from the park to the hotel takes me a half hour or so. I keep asking strangers if I'm heading in the right direction. They're a friendly and helpful lot, and I wonder if it has anything to do with the old lady on the small pieces of paper.

The hotel is a tall building, which means a lot of stairs for me. Greta says the elevator is faster, but I don't trust them, because I don't know how they work. I know how stairs work and that will be good enough.

Siodhachan's room is on the sixth floor, Hal told me. Room 633. When I reach it, I can hear the television blaring inside and there's a sign on the doorknob that says DO NOT DISTURB. I figure that has to be a joke, since Siodhachan asked me to come here, but I don't think it's very funny.

I try the handle, only to discover that it's locked. I pound on the door and call out to the hound. "Oberon. Open the door if ye can. It's Owen." His voice filters into me head.

<What are *you* doing here? Where's Atticus? Wait—how do I know you're really Owen?>

"Because I can hear ye talk and answer back. I'm here at Siodhachan's request. He's been hurt and I'm to take care of ye until he's well."

<Atticus is hurt? How bad?>

"I don't know yet, I just got here. Would ye let me in so I don't have to keep shouting through this fecking door?"

<Hold on. I can move the handle down but you'll have to push it open, because I can't pull. No thumbs.>

True to his word, the lock disengages and the handle, a short horizontal bar, moves down. I push it open and the giant wolfhound bombards me with questions before I'm even in the room.

<Where is he? Who hurt him? Are they dead yet or will they be dead soon? Can I help them die?>

"I don't have details. All he did was text Hal Hauk in Arizona that he's in a hospital somewhere in this city. So we have to call around to find him. Is there a phone here?"

<Yes. Next to the bed.>

"Good. When we find which hospital he's in, we'll go straight there and get some answers."

The television is on and showing pictures of people eating way too damn loud. The hound shows me how to turn it off and then we can concentrate in peace.

The phone is an intimidating device and it's full of instructions on the front, unlike cell phones. But it doesn't work like it should. Greta said when you use landlines like this, you get a dial tone first and then you dial the number. Except when I start dialing, the fecking thing starts ringing as soon as I punch the first number.

"Room service," a voice says in me ear.

"What? I'm trying to dial the hospital."

"Pardon, sir? Is this an emergency?"

"No, not for me. I just need to make a call, and when I started dialing, you answered."

"Oh, I understand. You need an outside line. Hang up, then dial nine, wait for the dial tone, then dial your number."

"I hate this fecking century."

"I beg your pardon?"

I slam the phone down on the voice and pick it up again. There's a dial tone, but I do what the man said and punch 9. The tone skips a beat, then continues. I try the number for the first hospital again, and this time it works.

Unfortunately, there's no one registered under the

name Sean Flanagan at Mount Sinai Hospital, so the call is a waste of time. I move on to the next number, St. Michael's. The lady on the phone says, yes, Sean Flanagan is a patient there, but she can't give me any more information unless I'm a family member. I hang up on her rather than argue. I'll just go down there and see with me own eyes how he's doing.

"Right, he's at St. Michael's." Consulting the Google map, I notice it will take us a while to get there. "Looks like a bit of a walk. You need a walk anyway, don't ye?" I ask the hound.

<Yes, a walk would be good right about now.>

"Anything ye need to bring? We won't be coming back here, because I don't have the key."

<I'm supposed to be on a leash in the city, but that's it. Everything else is Atticus's stuff. Oh, wait! He left his sword here. It's under the mattress. He's going to want that.>

"I should imagine so." I retrieve it, strap it to me back, leash the hound, and leave the rest. Down the stairs we go, past some rather shocked people in the lobby who didn't know they made dogs in Oberon's size.

Once he's outside, Oberon informs me that he's going to need to do some "urban fertilization."

"Is that what ye call it?"

<Atticus says my waste helps plants. It's science! Which is great, because I like peeing on them. I like to pee on streetlights and fire hydrants too, but it turns out that doesn't help them like it helps plants.>

"And what do ye do when ye have to shite in the big city?"

<Well, you are never supposed to do that on the sidewalk, Owen. That's rude.>

"Hey, I know that already, ye don't have to tell me!"

<You hardly know how to use a phone or turn off a television, so obviously I can't assume you know these

things. Since you didn't have sidewalks in your day, I thought maybe you weren't aware that they are not for shitting.>

"Gods blast it, I was asking ye where *you* shite in the city, not where I should do it!" I might have said that a bit too loudly, because people on the sidewalk look at me out of the corners of their eyes and swerve away from the man talking to a giant dog about where to drop a pound. Maybe I should talk to him the way Siodhachan does, with me mind instead of me mouth. I can do it, but it doesn't come naturally. I never bound myself to an animal this way.

<It depends on the city and the degree of my fecal urgency.>

"Fecal urgency? This is the strangest conversation I've ever had, and I've had some bloody strange ones lately."

The hound eventually takes care of his business behind a hedge we're passing and then brags about his discretion.

<Nobody will step in it there, and it will break down in a few weeks.>

"Well done," says I, thinking for two whole seconds that I'm going to have some peace before the hound speaks again.

<I'm hungry, Owen.>

"That's too bad. I don't have any food on me."

<But we're passing all these restaurants and I can smell the good things inside. You can go in and buy something. Please?>

I start to object that I don't have one of those credit cards that people always use to pay for things but then remember that Greta gave me the paper with the old lady on it, and something clicks. I pull it out and show it to the hound. "Hey, do you know if this is cash money?"

<Yeah, those are Canadian dollars! And you have a lot! You can buy plenty of food!>

"Who's this lady with the beads, then?"

<I think that's the queen. She was in *The Naked Gun*. Which means those aren't beads. Those are pearls.>

I don't understand all of that, but at least I learn that Canada is ruled by a queen.

"All right, where should I go to get food?"

<This place up ahead. I can smell the gravy.>

He stops in front of a small shop with a large glass window painted with red and white letters. POUTINERIE, it says.

"What is a *poutinerie*?" I asks him. It's an unfamiliar word.

<I don't know, but they have gravy. Just get something with gravy on it. I'll wait here like I'm supposed to.>

There's a small line inside and a menu posted near the ceiling. I can't make any sense of it except that it sells all different kinds of whatever poutine is.

"Give me whatever's most popular here," I says to the merchant when I get to the front of the line. "As long as it has gravy on it."

"Everything has gravy on it," the young man says. He has dull eyes and red spots on his face, but his tone sounds like he thinks I'm stupid.

"Good. Two of your popular things, then."

He asks me if I want a drink; I says water, then he pronounces a number and looks at me like I'm supposed to do something. I give him Canadian money and he gives me some back—it has a number 5 on it and no queen; it has a dodgy man with a bald pate and a stiff white collar instead. Maybe he's the king of Canada. He also gives me a small white piece of paper and calls it a receipt. I have just completed me first modern trade.

There's a short wait and then I'm given two brown boxes with folding flaps on top and a bottle of water. I take this outside to the hound, open one box and set it down for him. Poutine turns out to be fried potatoes with cheese curds all covered in gravy.

<Oh, man, this is my new favorite thing,> Oberon says as he gulps it down. I have to admit that once I try my own, it's not bad. Hunger slain, we proceed to the hospital, where the hound suggests that I camouflage him so that he can go inside with me. I figure I have plenty of juice in me knuckles, so I put them on, cast the spell, and we go inside together.

I pretend to be Siodhachan's father when I inquire at the front desk about him. The nice lady informs me that he's in something called the Intensive Care Ward, recovering from surgery, but says I can't go any further wearing a sword.

Well, balls to that. I tell her I'll go put it in my car, find a corner to duck around, and cast camouflage on meself, telling the hound to stay out of the way and I'll return soon with Siodhachan. I walk back in, follow the signs to Intensive Care, and eventually find Siodhachan's room. He's unconscious or asleep, in a bed with metal rails on the sides, and he's got all manner of tubes and things in his nose and his arm. There are beeping noises and loud breathing, and none of it sounds natural. He's wearing a flimsy piece of cloth, and I don't see his regular clothes around. It's like they dressed him to look fragile. I don't think I should throw him over me shoulder in his condition. Somebody really did kick his arse.

I reach out to Oberon with me mind. He might know what to do better than I.

Oberon? Can ye hear me?

<Yeah. Did you find him?>

Aye, but he's unconscious and has all these tubes in him. He's not walking out with me right now.

<You need to get a wheelchair. Pull the tubes out if it won't make him bleed, get him in the wheelchair, and push him right out.>

What's a wheelchair?

<As you might expect, it's a chair with wheels on it. Helps you move people who can't walk. Look around in some of the rooms or the halls; you'll see one eventually.>

That takes a bit more time than I would like, but the hound is right; one eventually comes along. A nurse wheels an old man into a room near Siodhachan's and helps him into bed. He looks like he's about the age I was before I drank that tea Siodhachan made for me, and his skin is dry and papery. He's asleep before the nurse is finished pulling up the sheets over his thin frame. I wait for her to leave and then I cast camouflage on the wheelchair and steal it. A few minutes after that, I've stolen me a Druid and I'm out of the hospital with a camouflaged Siodhachan in the chair. I drop the camouflage on meself and the hound as we walk away but keep it going on me old apprentice. The hound gets more and more worried when Siodhachan doesn't respond to him—apparently he's never had his food reviews ignored before, and the discovery of poutine should have roused Siodhachan right away.

Eventually I get Siodhachan to Queen's Park and stop the chair right next to the bound tree I used to shift in. Looking around to make sure no one's watching, I drop his camouflage, then I squat down and pull his right foot off the little metal shelf so that his heel can touch the earth again. Oberon thinks he should wake up immediately on contact.

<Why isn't he talking now?> he asks. <If he can touch the earth he should be able to heal, right?>

"Well, yes, but there's no telling how bad he is or what they did to him in there. Greta was telling me about modern medicine. Lots of drugs involved, and lots of it is synthetic shite they cook up somewhere. They may have knocked him out on purpose."

<Oh, yeah, they do that. I've seen it on TV loads of times.>

"What he needs is a good long soak in the healing pools of Mag Mell. But I don't think I can shift ye there meself."

<Why not?>

"I don't know either of ye well enough to carry you along. I used to know Siodhachan, but he's got two thousand years on me. I'd worry about containing him. And, besides, I don't have the headspaces for it. I only have one extra, and Siodhachan has, what, three?"

<Five extra, I think.>

"See, that's one fecking impressive brain there. We get him awake, and he can shift both of us."

The corner of Siodhachan's mouth tugs upward and his eyelids twitch a wee bit. "Aw, Owen," he says, though his voice is slow and slurred. "You're sho shweet."

"You're awake?"

"Just in time to hear you shay shumthing nice about me."

"Well, don't let it go to your head! The truth is, your smarts are better hidden than a pair of snake nuts."

<Atticus! I'm so glad you're okay! I have to tell you about this new thing I ate! It's called poutine, and it's mostly gravy!>

"I'm deffy . . . definitely not okay, Oberon. Sho tired. Groggy."

"They have you pumped full of drugs, lad," I says.

<Oh! Oh! There's a better word for drugs, and it's *pharmaceuticals*. That's five syllables, so I deserve some more poutine.>

"We need to get you to Mag Mell," I says. "When do you think you'll be clear enough to shift?"

"Need to break down kam . . . chemical. Sss. Chemicals first."

It's a long couple of hours of the hound talking about food and his favorite entertainments after that. People passing by give us curious stares every so often, but they mind their own business and I admire them for it. I shift away quickly to get the fancy stake Luchta made for Siodhachan, and he doesn't even notice. When the sun goes down, it starts to get cold quickly, and that, along with the cleansing he's been doing, finally allows Siodhachan to announce that he's ready.

I have to help him up and he winces—his right leg is shredded—but he shifts us all to Tír na nÓg, leaving a mystery wheelchair behind, and then to the plane of Mag Mell, where I carry most of his weight over to the healing pools and he sinks into one with a happy sigh, tossing away that cloth he calls a hospital gown.

"What day is it?" he asks, all the slurring gone from his voice.

"Same day, lad. What happened?"

We trade stories, and it makes me cringe to think of what these modern weapons can do to a body. It's a problem I'll have to consider, because he's right—his sword is no use against weapons like that, and neither are me shiny new knuckles.

"Those are impressive, though," he says. "If you can shatter rock with them I wonder if they'd stop a bullet. Wouldn't want to try catching one, though. What are you going to name them?"

"I don't know yet."

I take off his sword and place it next to his hand by the side of the pool, then give him the stake from Luchta as well.

"Look, lad, keep that vampire war as far away from me and Flagstaff as possible. I'll have a bunch of wee kids to look after soon."

"Hal said as much. I'll try, but you should be aware that they may come after you to get to me. Or to retaliate against something I do. Just ward and be wary."

"I will."

"And . . . Owen?" His face is all scrunched up as if he's expecting a beating for what he's going to say next.

"What is it?"

"Maybe go a bit easier on them than you did on me."

It feels like ice water in me pants to hear him say that. I gasp and everything retracts. But then I say, "Aye, lad, I will." There's silence for a few beats and then I add, "Greta would tear me up if I said a rude word to those kids. And their parents would join in, no doubt. I'll try not to repeat me cock-ups."

His face relaxes and he smiles. "Fair enough. I'll try to keep mine to a minimum as well."

"Good, good. Speaking of Greta, I'd best be getting back to her. Going to visit Brighid for a moment and then head home. You'll be all right now?"

"Yes. I appreciate you taking the trouble to bring me here." He says farewell and the hound thanks me for the poutine. I can tell he won't shut up about it for days, but it's Siodhachan who will have to listen to it, so I figure that stopping for food was a win for me in every way.

The Fae Court in Tír na nÓg doesn't operate on Canadian time, so it's hopping like a rabbit warren during humping season when I get there. There are quite a few of the dodgy sorts of Fae around, far more than I had seen before, and I wonder why that is. I hang back and listen, ask a couple questions, and learn that Brighid has granted amnesty to a lot of Fae and other old creatures that had either been imprisoned or exiled for a long time.

"She's being more accommodating," a winged faery explains, "after Fand's attempted coup. We may have lost our queen, but at least the First among the Fae is listening to us now. And Fand may return someday, just as these others have."

She's probably right about that. Fand won't remain imprisoned forever. The Fae will start asking soon when she might be released, and eventually their questions will turn into demands. And the same goes for her husband, Manannan Mac Lir. Brighid can delay only so long before this temporary goodwill turns to ashes. But I'm not sure letting a bunch of prisoners free will do anything to keep the peace. Some of them are going to be grateful, sure, and be a grand addition to society. But some are going to be resentful and start throwing shite at things. She'd better be ready to duck.

But perhaps Brighid's thinking that she can simply imprison them again and say, "Well, I gave them a chance, didn't I? Not my fault if they're stupid gits."

I find a chamberlain figure near the front of the crush of beings, dressed all fancy and doused in perfume. I tell him I'd like a brief audience with Brighid, and his eyes stray down to me tattoos. They widen as he recognizes I'm bound to Gaia. "You're a Druid?" he says.

"Aye. Eoghan Ó Cinnéide."

"She's left instructions to bring you before her immediately should you appear. Please come with me."

That's a pleasant surprise, and I ignore the scowls I get from a group of pixie widows as the chamberlain interrupts their audience to introduce me—not just to Brighid but to everyone, since he shouts my name. I notice Brighid's wearing a new kit. It's a set of lighter armor instead of the heavy stuff she wore during the coup attempt, painted a metallic blue. It leaves her arms and legs largely unprotected, but her vital organs are under wraps. And the area around her throne is warded tighter than a hedgehog's rolled-up arse anyway; I can feel the bindings warning me away from it.

"Welcome," she says. "What news?"

"I'm starting a grove, taking on six apprentices to be

Druids. Wanted ye to know. Whatever protection ye can afford would be grand."

"Ah! This pleases me very much, Eoghan. Give the details to my chamberlain and I will see it done. I would speak longer, but I have much to do. Is there anything else?"

I think of how Siodhachan is trying to wipe out vampires and it's going to be all blood and exploding organs until he's done, but she probably already knows that since she had Luchta make those stakes and I don't need to announce it where everyone can hear. So I says, "No, that is all."

She bids me farewell, and I bow to her and chat off to one side with the chamberlain while the pixies resume their audience. I tell him about the property in Flagstaff and how it needs to be warded and after a few seconds become aware that something huge looms over us and smells like sweaty feet.

A gray-skinned hulk, probably twice me size, stares down at me with tiny black eyes and big tusk-like teeth sticking up out of its mouth. There's a bit of drool leaking out the side, and there are also patches of lichen or fungus attached to its skin with either mud or shite or both used as an adhesive. It has a cloth wrapped inexpertly around its hips, and it's doing a terrible job covering up the huge thing it's supposed to be hiding from view. It's a great fecking bog troll, the kind that doesn't care if you see his cheesy dangly dong. The worst kind of troll, in other words.

"I know you," it rumbles, and its breath is a visible cloud of decay. "You're a Druid."

"Ye have a keen eye," I say. "Would ye excuse us, please?"

"No, we have business. I remember."

"I don't think we do."

"I was on a Time Island. Released with many others. So were you. And you owe me gold."

"You're mistaken. I don't owe you shite."

"No mistake. You crossed my bridge in the bog and didn't pay the toll. You look younger now, but I remember. You owe me gold."

When he says that, it triggers me own memory. He's right. In the old days I'd been crossing a bog on me way to visit a cousin when this troll pops up in the middle of it and demands that I pay him to cross the rest of the way or it's over the edge for me. I had no gold and no intention of paying if I did, so I cast camouflage and snuck past him. The troll had cursed me and promised someday he'd make me pay, and I'd told him from a distance that no one's bollocks should ever smell that bad.

Why Brighid thought releasing trolls would make anything better I cannot fathom. It would only lead to situations like this—bullying people going about their business. This one's attention had no doubt been drawn when the chamberlain announced me as a Druid of Gaia. Now he knew me name and quite possibly where I lived, if he'd been listening in to our conversation.

To make him go away, I pull out the Canadian money Greta gave me and thrust it at him. "There," I says. "Take it."

His eyes shift to me hand, his mind churns like thick pudding, and he finally says, "That's not gold."

"It's better than gold, lad. It's got the queen of Canada on it, and she walks around wearing pearls, see? It's like her neck is sweating wealth. And look here: This one has the king of Canada on it. Serious man there, ye can tell by his collar, and this is serious money. Ye can buy anything with this, and it's a good deal more than any toll I've ever heard of."

"It's only paper. Worth nothing. You owe me gold."

"I don't have any fecking gold, do I? This is all the money I have, so you'll have to take this or nothing."

"You bring me gold tomorrow."

"You take a bath first," I says, and walk away, shoving the money back in me pocket. The troll won't throw any punches in the Fae Court. But I see as I push through the crowd that there are several other trolls present, and their eyes all follow me as I edge to the perimeter of the Court's meadow, where there are bound trees that I can use to get out of there. I recognize some of those trolls—ugly is hard to forget sometimes—and they no doubt recognize me. I'm the guy who never pays to cross a bridge.

Why are there trolls at the Fae Court anyway? They're not creatures given to courts of any kind. They must have a problem and are hoping for an audience of their own. Their bogs and rivers and bridges are probably all gone by now, and they can't make the same living that they did in the old days. But I represent that old living to them, and they want to hold on to it more than anything, I expect.

People do that—cling to their past because it's the only thing they consider safe. Trying something new or just accepting it turns their livers into jelly. But that's a load of bollocks. Ye take the new and appreciate it if it's good, like whiskey or poutine or girlfriends who bite, or ye dismiss it as shite if it's bad, like cell phones and cars, and move on.

O' course, there's people like Siodhachan too: He does everything he can to escape his past but can't seem to do it. He has a lot more past than the average lad, though. Maybe that's why he looks so fecking haunted all the time.

When I reach the trees, I look back and see the trolls

are still watching me. I smile and wave to them before I shift away. They couldn't come after me that way—they have to use the Old Ways to get to earth, and there aren't any of those in North America. They'd never get any gold out of me. Time to leave the past in the past, boys.

CHAPTER 8

I nodded off in the healing pool—fairly safe, since the attending faeries come to the rescue if your head slips underwater. But I wasn't safe from getting splashed in the face, and neither was Oberon, who drifted into slumber behind me. Both of us got a rude awakening.

<Hey!> Oberon said. <What the—oh. Shutting up now.>

When I blinked away the water, I saw that I wasn't alone in the pool anymore. A woman with jet-black hair and marble-white skin sat across from me. "Hello, Siodhachan," she said in a throaty rasp.

"Morrigan? You're alive?"

"Quite dead, yet I cling to a different kind of existence thanks to those who still worship me. Far easier for me to manifest and visit you on this plane."

"Is something wrong? Am I . . . Is this the end?"

"No, it's not the Chooser of the Slain visiting you at this time. It's a reminder that you have work to do that you haven't been doing."

"Ah. Is this visitation but to whet my almost blunted purpose?"

"An odd way to put it, but I suppose so," she replied, completely missing the allusion to *Hamlet*. "You must visit the Svartálfs, and do it soon."

"How soon? I'm getting better, but I'm still a little messed up here."

"Tomorrow they will be attacked. You must prevent it."

"Attacked by whom?"

"Dwarfs. Æsir."

"Æsir as in Odin and Freyja?"

"No, none of the gods. But they have full knowledge of what's to be done."

"So by intervening I'll be contradicting the will of Odin?"

"Yes, but that's never bothered you before."

"It's just that we're supposed to be working together now. I gave him whiskey and Girl Scout cookies. We're practically . . . bros."

"That shouldn't change, Siodhachan. The point is to get the Svartálfs working with you as well."

I shook my head at the enormity of the task. "There's centuries of prejudice there on both sides, lots of mistrust. It would be like asking the Fir Bolgs or the Fomorians to work with the Tuatha Dé Danann on a friendly basis. Turning enemies into allies in a day sounds impossible."

"It is fortunate then that you don't have to do that in a day. Merely prevent genocide so that trust can begin to build."

"Did you say 'merely' prevent genocide?"

"That's something you can do in a day, Siodhachan." She slid forward through the water and planted a cold kiss on my cheek while her sharp, frigid fingernails rested on my throat. "Don't disappoint me."

"Morrigan, the dark elves have tried to kill me recently on multiple occasions. I don't think they'll accept me as a diplomatic envoy."

"Go anyway." And her fingers tightened on my throat, drawing blood under her fingernails. "Unless you'd like me to visit you again as the Battle Crow."

"Well, no, I can't imagine why I'd want that—"

She sank into the water and melted away in it, the visitation abruptly ended. I checked. No one in the pool but me.

"She's gone," I said, mostly to myself, but Oberon thought I was talking to him.

<I'm glad. I know she gave me food once, but she still scares me.>

"That's okay. She scares me too." I needed to get moving but realized that, while I had a sword and a stake and a hound, I had no clothes. The faeries attending the healing pools had taken my hospital gown. I called one over and asked if she might do a couple of things for me.

"Please tell Brighid I'm here," I said, "and need to speak with her on an urgent matter regarding the Morrigan." That should bring her running. "And then if you could find me some clothes, I would appreciate it."

"Very well, but how are you feeling?" the faery asked. "Are you ready to leave?"

"Well enough," I said. After she departed, I hauled myself out and checked a bit more thoroughly. Most of the internal organ damage was mended, because that was always a priority of healing, but my muscle tissue in my back and right leg was still tight at best and remained torn in places. I would have to limp for a while and eat some protein to repair that more quickly, and in truth I could use some more time in the pool, but time I didn't have.

I also didn't have any idea of what happened to Werner Drasche after his arrest. Was he still locked up or did he escape? And where was . . . ?

"Oberon, did you remember to get that binder out of the hotel room in Toronto?"

<Uh, no. Was that important? I told Owen to bring the sword.>

"Thank you for that, sincerely. You deserve a snack."

<Heck yes I do!>

"But the binder was important too. I wonder if it's still there. I mean, I didn't check out, so it should be."

<I will go with you and you can lean on me as you limp.>

"Thanks, buddy."

<And I'll show you where the poutine is.>

"Excellent."

The faery appeared to say that Brighid would arrive soon and gave me a white fluffy robe that had obviously been stolen from a hotel on earth—the logo was still embroidered on the breast. I'd been hoping for something like pants and a shirt, but I guessed I could suffer the stares I would get walking through Toronto in a robe. I would go to the front desk, ask for a key to my room because I'd lost it, and then they would ask me— oh, no.

"My ID was in my clothes. Which Owen left at the hospital."

<Oops.>

It wasn't an insurmountable problem. I could still get into the room by unbinding the lock. But the identity of Sean Flanagan would have to be retired permanently. There would be plenty of questions for the gunshot victim who disappeared.

I mentally reviewed what else I had to do before I took off to Svartálfheim, perhaps never to return. I wished I could check in with Granuaile—I hadn't heard from her since I left for Ethiopia. All I knew was that she was in Asgard and therefore very difficult to reach at the moment. I hoped she was well. But since reconnecting with her would be impossible, there was one other matter to see to in England.

Brighid arrived before I could make plans, looking annoyed. It turned out not to be annoyance with me, however—she had loads on her mind after Fand's revolt.

And, much to my surprise, she had no problem whatsoever with me going to Svartálfheim at the Morrigan's
urging. "She gave me the same message," she said.

"She did?"

"Via Eoghan, yes. He relayed the message. And I'll go
with you. Tomorrow, then, at dawn?"

"Uh . . . yeah," I said. Her quick agreement knocked
me off balance. "But you'll want to wear the super-tough
armor."

"Oh, I will. Would you like some for yourself?"

I hadn't worn armor in centuries, but against dwarfs it
might be handy, especially in my condition. "Do you
have any that would fit me?"

"I can get you something that will serve," she said, a
tiny smile on her face.

"Great. At dawn."

Brighid departed, and Oberon and I left soon afterward. For the record, Toronto is a wonderfully diverse
city and people are used to seeing all types, but a limp-
ing man wearing nothing but a robe and a sword *will*
draw attention. Oberon carried the stake in his mouth,
because it looked innocent there. If I carried it, I might
look like I planned to stab someone, and the sword was
already giving that impression.

I was unclear on just how much time I had spent in the
healing pools, but it was morning again in Toronto
and we passed by the same Timmie's we had before. Ed
and his companion were there, sipping their coffee and
watching the world go by, though I didn't realize it was
them until the first man spoke up as we passed. "Boy, ya
never know what you're gonna see in Trahno, Ed."

"Yep." Ed was the best color commentator in the
business.

We took the elevator to the sixth floor, where I took
the time to bypass the lock on my room. It turned out to
be gloriously undisturbed. The binder was there and so

was my backpack and a very welcome change of clothes. Open-ended stays with a reliable credit card on file can be wonderful.

If the police were monitoring the financial records of Sean Flanagan, checking out would let the police know that I was still alive. That was fine; they'd never hear from him again, because I'd be getting a new identity from Hal. The hospital could have my old ID.

Once outside and walking back to Queen's Park, I had to break the news to Oberon that the poutinerie wasn't open yet and I didn't have any money anyway. We would have to snaffle something to eat elsewhere.

"Let's head over to the UK. It's midafternoon there, that dead time of the day in pubs when cooks are either cleaning the kitchen or taking breaks. They're not hovering over the food, in other words. Should be able to lift a few bangers without any trouble."

<Can we get a haggis in Scotland?>

"Ugh. We can try."

We shifted across the Atlantic to a wee place north of Dumfries, where I found one of those small country hotels that doubles as a pub near the bound grove of trees we used. They did not have haggis—a small mercy—but they did have some lamb ready to go, and a camouflaged sneak into the kitchen gave us a much-needed repast. They had an herb garden in a greenhouse out back, and it was doing all right but could be better. I spent some time mending the soil there as payment for our food. They would never recognize that they'd been paid, but it was a salve for my conscience: I already had enough evils clinging to my back and didn't need to carry around petty theft as well.

Bellies full, we shifted south to a grove near Windsor Castle, where I followed the instructions Hermes had given me to summon the West Wind if I wanted to get in touch with Olympus. The globetrotting was wearying, especially when I needed a few days more to heal, but I felt that neglecting this duty before traveling to Svartálfheim would be an egregious error.

Little Lord Ankle Wings himself streaked out of the southern sky after about an hour, coming to a halt some five feet off the ground.

"Hermes," I said, nodding to him.

"Druid. What do you want?"

"I'd love to set Diana free if she will agree to terms," I said. The Roman goddess of the hunt had been cut into sections and imprisoned in rock because she had vowed never to rest before she killed both Granuaile and me. Artemis had agreed to live and let live, but Diana held on to one hell of a grudge. "But I would like Jupiter to be present. We agreed we'd visit her monthly, and at this point I'm a bit late and don't want to let it go any longer. I know Mercury usually delivers such messages to Jupiter, but would you mind relaying the request? I'm about to leave the plane tomorrow, and I would hate for Diana to miss her chance at freedom."

"Wait here. I'll deliver your message." He flew away without any further pleasantries.

In another hour, as the sun was sinking red into the west, Jupiter struck the earth as a thunderbolt nearby and startled Oberon and me out of our skins.

<He didn't have to make his entrance like that, right, Atticus?>

No.

<So he's kind of like one of those cats that walks up and takes a swipe at your nose with his claws just because he can?>

Yes.

<I don't like those cats.>

Jupiter was fully armored—or at least armored by Roman standards, which left the legs somewhat vulnerable, though he did have greaves. His dark oiled beard jutted out below his helmet like a column of basalt, and lightning sparked in his eyes and in his fists. I thought we might be in trouble.

"Don't worry, this show isn't for you," he said. "It's for Diana. I want her to see how very displeased I am."

"An excellent idea." In my Latin headspace I called to the elemental of England, Albion, and requested that he bring Diana's various parts up out of the earth so that we may talk to her. I continued to speak to Jupiter in the other. "May I offer a suggestion that might also urge her to accept a truce?"

The Roman god of the sky nodded, and I continued: "I'll remain out of sight and you talk to her. Please relay my offer that the Druids will speak to Gaia and take special care of the grove in which the dryads live—we will be sure the trees flourish, in other words, and their dryads along with them. I sincerely regret the unpleasantness and want to make it right, so long as I secure her pledge not to hunt me or have others seek my death."

"Understood." He nodded once and then asked, "What news regarding this Ragnarok business?"

"We are still in the opening moves of the chess match. I'm leaving tomorrow to try to secure a new ally—the dark elves of Svartálfheim. It's why I wished to do this now—I'm not sure when or even if I'll be back."

The earth parted between us and Diana emerged, severally. I stepped back behind her head—or, I suppose, at the top of her head, where she couldn't see me. She had an excellent view of Jupiter, though, which must have been very intimidating.

"Welcome back to the light, Diana," he said. "I hope it will be permanent. The Druids are offering concessions and I hope you will consider carefully, because it specifically addresses the injury you claim to be fighting for."

Diana's confident voice contained a bite of scorn. She

had not been cowed by nearly two months of solitary confinement in the darkness. Mortals would have broken in mere days, but not an Olympian. "Go on, then," she said.

"They will protect the dryads and their groves and make sure that they flourish with the strength of Gaia. And they sincerely regret inspiring your anger. All that they ask is that you allow them to live and do not conspire against them."

The goddess of the hunt did not answer, and Jupiter eventually had to prompt her, eyes flashing.

"Well? What say you? You go free and the dryads will be better off."

"I . . . accept."

The thunder god's expression softened and the lightning in his eyes faded. "This pleases me. Swear to me that you will abide by the conditions of your release. You will no longer hunt the Druids and will not seek to bring them harm by any other means."

"I swear all this in your name."

"Good." His eyes flicked up in my direction and I asked Albion to set Diana free. The chalky soil native to the area crumbled away, allowing Jupiter to reattach Diana's limbs and head to her torso. From there the divine healing abilities of the Olympian immortals took over, and in minutes she was whole again. Jupiter helped her up, she brushed some dirt and dust off her arms and clothes, and then turned to see me standing there with Oberon.

She clenched her jaw and then her fists, and I immediately regretted not casting camouflage, as the mere sight of me was a clear provocation to her. Such a provocation that a cry of rage ripped loose from her throat, and she charged me barehanded. I drew Fragarach, which set off spasms of pain all down my back, tried to set myself on a gammy leg, and warned Oberon to stay out of the way.

"Diana!" Jupiter shouted. "You swore!"

She kept coming. I readied a low swing at her mid-section, something she couldn't duck. And then Diana exploded into golden ichor and organ chunks, and Oberon and I both got covered in her viscera and cut up with little pieces of bone shrapnel. A crack of thunder accompanied the explosion and explained what happened: Jupiter had obliterated her with a thunderbolt rather than see her break her word.

<Ow! Auughh! Dang it, I just had a bath!>

Oberon, do not lick any of that off! Ichor is poison to us. Let it sit and we'll wash you as soon as we can.

Jupiter growled a few choice curses in Latin and then apologized in English. "Sorry about that. I thought she would keep to her word."

"Blech. I thought so too."

"I'll deal with her on Olympus," he said, for she would re-spawn there after a while. The Olympians had a pretty sweet immortality deal compared to most other pantheons: They really couldn't die. Get rid of their bodies and they'd come back in new ones. Most other pantheons just got a long life in one body, and after they shuffled off their original mortal coil they could manifest every so often for short periods of time, like the Morrigan did, depending on the power they derived from their believers.

"How exactly will you do that, if I may ask?" I said, wiping golden gunk off my face. "She obviously can't be trusted. Her word means nothing."

"No, but she can be watched and dealt with, as you just saw."

"And if you're too late? If she slips past your guard? If she employs someone else to assassinate me?"

"You will be safe," he assured me. "It's a matter of personal honor now. She's given me insult."

"I'll leave it in your hands, then," I said, for there was very little else I could do. Though I didn't give voice to them, I already had serious doubts that I would ever be safe from Diana. Whether by design or accident, I'd been outmaneuvered. Jupiter had turned all my leverage to goo. Diana or one of her proxies could strike at any time in the future and then Jupiter's assurances would be meaningless, because I'd be dead. And what would he do if someone were to confront him, anyway? Shrug his shoulders and say, "My bad"? As Manannan Mac Lir had already discovered, while "working" with Poseidon and Neptune to search for Jörmungandr in the ocean—an entirely fruitless endeavor so far—the Olympians were unreliable allies at best.

"Farewell, Druid," Jupiter said.

I chucked my chin at him and braced myself for his exit—it came a split second later in a thunderbolt that made my hair stand on end and burned the air, leaving us alone in the English countryside.

Oberon's charged fur stuck out all over and he shook himself, which got rid of some of Diana's gore but did nothing to improve his appearance. <I would be okay with never meeting that guy again,> he said.

I agreed and decided my best move would be to impose on Sam and Ty's hospitality until it was time to meet up with Brighid. Besides, I needed to leave Oberon somewhere safe. There was no way I'd risk taking him with me to Svartálfheim.

Ty's jaw dropped open when he answered the door and saw us standing there in slimy, golden glory.

"May we use your bathroom, sir?" I asked.

"My God, Atticus, you look like you had an orgy with egg yolks and orange juice."

"We might need a loofah," I admitted.

"Dare I ask what happened?"

"An Olympian exploded on us and it was yucky."

"Damn. Why can't you get your kicks by BASE jumping or parasailing, like regular folks?"

<See, Atticus? I keep telling you we should go parasailing.>

Ty opened the door wider and stepped aside to let us pass. "Well, you know where the bathroom is."

"Thanks."

Get in the tub, I told Oberon privately, *but don't you dare wreck the shower curtain this time. I don't care how ugly it is.*

<What story are you going to tell me, Atticus?>

I'm going to tell you about someone who burned down a convent for love.

<Yay! A love story! But I guess not for the love of God.>

That would be an excellent guess.

chapter 9

Contrary to my expectations, I have absolutely no trouble finding the Sisters of the Three Auroras when I get to Warsaw. When I shift into the city with Orlaith, using a tethered black poplar tree in an expansive park called Pole Mokotowskie, they are waiting for me, having a picnic. All around the tree, in fact, doing it properly with blankets on the grass and baskets full of bread and cheese and pierogies. A few of them have glasses of wine in their hands, which is the sort of thing that is widely practiced but truly only permissible until the police arrive to issue citations.

<Hey! Food!> Orlaith says, just as Malina Sokołowska raises a half-eaten baguette to hail me around a mouthful of sandwich.

"Ah, Granuaile! Welcome!"

Thirteen pairs of eyes fix on Orlaith and me and it's pretty uncomfortable, because I'm acutely aware of being targeted. I don't really know them that well, except by reputation and a brief meeting. When we were first introduced—I mean the ones that never messed with Atticus and the Tempe Pack at Tony Cabin and died for it—Atticus and I had been naked in an onion field near Jasło, running from Artemis and Diana. The coven had been waiting for us there because they'd seen something big coming in advance, which turned out to be Loki rocketing out of the sky to confront us. Pulling the same I-knew-you'd-be-here trick again, except specifically applied to me, only emphasizes why I need shielding from divination.

The new coven members had never been introduced to us. And now that I'm possibly at the receiving end of whatever they want to throw my way, I realize I don't know what to expect. Do they use wands to direct their spells? Flailing jazz hands and eyes rolled back in their heads? I remember Atticus saying they're quite fast and skilled in physical combat but recall very little information in the way of offensive magical attacks. Atticus claims that Malina can summon a hellwhip out of the air, but surely I don't need to worry about that in such a public place. Especially since I'm not actually from hell, just Kansas.

"You're in no danger, I assure you," Malina continues in her mild Polish accent when I do not reply. "We saw that you wished to talk and so here we are, enjoying the day. No one will bother us. Please, sit."

Orlaith, I say privately, *I know these people but do not trust them yet. Do not accept any food from them.*

<Aww. Okay, but I hope you trust them soon.>

Out loud, I say, "Thank you," and then mutter a binding in Old Irish to keep all my hairs on my head, a precaution that Atticus recommends when dealing with them. I move to take a spot on a blanket to the coven leader's left but with a basket between us. The nearby witches make minute adjustments so that they can see me better, while the ones on the opposite side of the trunk move so that they have a clear view. They're not dressed alike, to suggest that they're anything but friends, or in any fashion that might suggest they're into the occult. They're wearing clothing appropriate for a sunny but chilly late autumn day. Some wear jeans, others leggings under skirts with their feet shoved into

boots and purple scarves around their necks. Light jackets of varying materials and colors, and a couple of
cute knit hats on their heads. Besides Malina, whose
long straight blond hair instantly identifies her, I think
I recognize four other original members by Atticus's
shorthand descriptions: Owl-Eyed Roksana, Bedhead
Klaudia, Kazimiera Who's Damn Tall, and Cherubic
Berta.

"Would you like a cucumber sandwich or something
to drink?" Berta asks. She has rosy cheeks and I suspect
she might be a bit sloshed, judging by the besotted grin
on her face and the nearly empty glass of wine in her
hand with an even emptier bottle nearby.

"No, thank you," I say. "I ate recently and I'm not
hungry."

"I'd introduce you to everyone, but I expect you're
here for business rather than pleasure," Malina says.
When I nod and grimace by way of apology, she smiles
in understanding. "We appreciate you being direct and
forthright with us. What did you wish to talk about,
then?"

"Your predecessor placed a cloak around Atticus's
sword that shielded it from divination. I wonder if you
can do the same thing to me?"

"Yes. We can provide you with a divination cloak. But
it's not the sort of thing for which we accept coin."

"That's good, because I don't have a single, uh . . . I
was going to say penny, but you probably don't use
those in Poland."

"No, we use the grosz for small coins," one of the
witches says—since her legs appear longer than some
people are tall, I think she is Kazimiera.

"Don't have a single grosz on me either."

"Then you can earn your cloak," Malina says, "by
helping us find the white horse of Świętowit."

"I beg your pardon?" She's moving quite fast—she

probably already knew what I was going to ask and what she would ask in return.

"Świętowit is an old Slavic god of war and divination. There are slightly different spellings and pronunciations of his name depending on which Slavic country you're in, but he was—or is—important to Polish pagans like ourselves."

"And he had a white horse. Did he lose it or did somebody steal it?"

"We're not sure."

"Why is the horse important? Why isn't Świętowit looking for him?"

"We are not sure Świętowit is still alive, actually. But we believe that the horse is."

It appears that there are no quick answers to my questions, since I'm missing context. "You'd better start at the beginning."

Malina turns to one of her coven with overlarge glasses and a thicket of frizzy, dirty blond hair tamed into a thick ponytail. "Roksana, you're better at this sort of thing. Will you give her the condensed version?"

"With pleasure." She smiles primly and swings her giant peepers in my direction. "To the northwest, off the coast of Germany in the Baltic Sea, there is an island called Rügen."

"Really? Named after Count Rugen, the six-fingered man?"

"What? No. Named after the Rujani people, a Slavic tribe that occupied it from the ninth to twelfth centuries. The current name is a German corruption."

"Oh."

"On the northeastern tip of the island, at Cape Arkona, there was a fortified cult site called Jaromarsburg. They had a temple there to the god Świętowit. It was the last outpost of Slavic paganism before the Danish king laid siege to it in 1168 and defeated the Rujani. The Danes burned down the temple and the carved idol of Świętowit and forced everyone into Christianity afterward. The Rujani were eventually assimilated into the Germanic tribes nearby, and their language died out in a couple of centuries. But what happened to Świętowit and his horse is what we wish to find out. They disappeared."

"You mean they were physically present at Jaromarsburg?"

"Perhaps not Świętowit himself. But his horse was, until—we are guessing—immediately before the Danish invasion."

"And how do you know this if it was almost a thousand years ago?"

"The priests of Świętowit were using the horse to divine victory or defeat in battle. Had the horse been present before the invasion, they would have known about their imminent defeat and abandoned the site."

"Forgive me, but I'm not sure that follows. Men have been known to be stupid on occasion and not listen to sense when their pride is on the line. That's pretty much the history of every war ever."

The witches stare at me until Klaudia snorts in amusement. She's the sleepy-eyed sensual one with short, wild hair and a coppery tan. Her lips, soft and poufy like pillows, quirk upward, and they are so beguiling and infinitely kissable that I cannot look away until Malina says, "Klaudia! Stop that."

"Sorry," she says, as I blink and shake my head, free of the charm. "But it's fun to play with the Druids."

I remember Atticus warning me about their charms and telling me that something very similar had happened to him. I see the pattern: Malina wants me to know that her coven could kick my ass if they wanted, but she doesn't want to communicate that herself. She has Klaudia do it with those movie-star lips of hers and then disciplines her—very mildly—to give me the impression that she's the fair one who looks out for my well-being. It's the friendliest of threats, brandishing a pair of delicious lips instead of a weapon, but it's still a threat.

"Apologies, Granuaile," Malina says, and then hurries on before I can escalate her message into a confrontation. "The reason we believe the horse is still around has something to do with Loki, which we thought you might find interesting."

"Yes, you're right about that."

"We haven't confirmed any of this, but it's a mysterious pattern of absences, and we think you might be able to confirm it one way or another. After Loki escaped us, thanks to the strange interference of that Finnish god, we began a series of rituals to try to divine his connections to other pantheons. Do you know of the Slavic god Weles?"

"No, sorry."

"How about Perun?"

"Him I know."

"Weles is Perun's nemesis, a sneaky trickster type. The parallel with Thor and Loki is quite clear, in fact. We are fairly certain that Perun is alive but not on this earth."

"That's correct. He's a guest on the Fae planes."

"Interesting. Thank you. We are less certain about Świętowit. He may be alive but, if so, he's on a distant plane. He might also be dead. Difficult for us to tell either way from what we're sensing. But of Weles we get absolutely nothing. He has been hidden somehow so we cannot confirm whether he lives or not, much less his whereabouts."

"Wait. The Slavic plane was burned by Loki," I say. "Perun wondered how Loki could have gained access to it."

Malina nods. "You see what we are thinking. Weles is working with Loki."

"Loki has a kind of divination shield."

"We thought as much. We cannot find him either. We are making guesses based on a series of holes where there should be something present."

"So why would—oh! Maybe a quid pro quo kind of thing is going on. Weles wanted Loki to burn the Slavic plane and almost certainly wanted him to kill Perun. Partially successful there. And Loki hides Weles so that Perun and everyone else will assume he's dead. But what would Loki want from Weles in return?"

"Świętowit and the white horse, of course."

"Hold on. Are you saying Loki wants the white horse because . . . ?"

"You can ask the white horse if you will win or lose a battle you begin today and it will tell you."

"Oh, shit!" I cry, as understanding dawns. "He's using the horse to know when to start Ragnarok!"

"That was our conclusion also. It would be more accurate on matters of war than any other seer. So we want the white horse."

"Yeah, I think we have the same interests here. We can't have him endlessly bribing allies until he finds the right combination for victory. If Loki's going to start something, let him be uncertain about it. Can you not find the horse in your divination?"

"Unfortunately not. It was a long shot to begin with since we didn't know its name, but we assume Loki has shielded it also. Our best guess is that if you find Świętowit alive, he may be able to tell you where to find his horse. And if they are both dead, then Weles must owe Loki some other service."

"Where would I begin looking for Świętowit? When was the last time you saw him?"

Malina's eyes flick to Roksana, and I turn to her for my answer. "We have never seen him," she says, "nor has anyone in living memory. He has either four heads or four faces on one head, depending on how he manifests. Pretty sure he'd get into the news if he'd been around recently."

Her dry comment earns a laugh from the coven, but it is marvelous news to my hound. <Wow! He could eat four steaks at one time!>

But he only has one stomach, Orlaith. I'd be worried about four sets of teeth to brush. Or what if he got sick? Four stuffed noses. Ew.

Roksana continues, "I would suggest looking around Jaromarsburg, or speaking with Perun, if you have access to him. He may be able to provide you with some clues." I nod, thinking I should talk to him in any case. He'd surely be interested to know Weles is likely allied with Loki. It makes more sense than Loki's assertion that he went after Perun so hard simply because he despises thunder gods. There are a buttload of thunder gods in the world's pantheons. Why single out Perun? He must have had cause. And thinking of causes, I had to question why they were so interested in this horse.

"This is more about giving the finger to Loki than finding the horse, isn't it?"

The witches all looked to Malina to answer that one. She nodded once. "Both him and Weles. The Zoryas do not often spend much of their time on the Slavic plane but had they been there when Loki set fire to it, they would have been burned. It gives me nightmares. And to think we already had Loki in our power once . . ." She shook her head. "Well. I would like another chance at that. Or if I can't have him, at least deny him whatever he desires."

"All right, then," I say, and look at Malina. "I find Świętowit or his horse, but preferably the horse, and either bring it to you or confirm it's dead, and in return you give me a divination cloak."

"Agreed, but with an amendment: If you find Świętowit dead or alive, we would like to know where he is."

I extend my hand to her and say, "I accept your proposal." She shakes it and I smile, because I have a bona fide quest. "If he's on another plane, I wouldn't be able to bring him here anyway. Bringing back the horse will be tough enough."

Malina's brows draw together. "Why is that?"

"I only have one other headspace in which to carry someone else when I travel the planes. Right now I've been using that for Orlaith. I need to memorize a body of work in another language before I can bring someone else along for the ride—it provides structure for the shift because people are put together in specific sequences like words are in literature. I learned how to speak Russian, but so far their literature is pretty dire and gloomy and I haven't felt like memorizing any of it."

"Szymborska!" Berta blurts out, and the faces of the other witches light up.

"Yes!" Roksana says, more excited than I've seen her. She nods so enthusiastically that I fear for her neck. "You should learn Polish and read Szymborska!"

"I'm sorry, who?"

"Wisława Szymborksa was a Polish poet, and a Nobel Prize winner," Klaudia explains. "She wrote about small things, details in life that carry great significance. The English translation I saw in America was a good one. Maybe you should try that, and then, if you like her work, learn to read it in Polish."

"That's an excellent idea," Malina says. "Szymborska isn't a dire nihilist."

"Thanks for the tip. I'll definitely look into it." I rise to my feet, eager to get on with it. "I'll meet you back here when I have something. I'm sure I won't have to tell you when—you'll probably know that before I do, haha."

They laugh politely, but Malina stops me after a couple of steps. "Before you go, Granuaile, might you have any idea about when Mr. O'Sullivan plans to make good on his promise to rid Poland of vampires?"

"Oh, he's working on it," I say. "That's for sure."

"We know he's been eliminating vampires elsewhere," she replies. "But he's not doing it here, where he said he would."

"I haven't seen or spoken to him for a while, but I'm sure he hasn't forgotten and I'm sure he has a plan."

"Do remind him for us the next time you speak, won't you?"

"I will," I promise. "See you later, Sisters. Enjoy your picnic."

<Where are we going now?> Orlaith asks as we return to the tree.

Germany. You know they have sausages in vending machines there?

<They do? Germany sounds like a very smart country.>

CHAPTER 10

I didn't tell Oberon how worried I was about him as I ran the bathwater. I just reminded him not to lick his chops until I said it was safe and to let me know if he felt any pain. I'd had to trigger my healing charm already to combat ichor poisoning; a couple of Diana's bone splinters had cut my skin, and the insidious stuff had entered my bloodstream. Trace amounts like that I could take care of, but if Oberon ingested a mouthful I'd be hard pressed to deal with that.

Sam and Ty had one of those detachable showerheads with a ringed metal hose that visually suggested a steel caterpillar. Turning the water on full blast to get the most pressure I could, I told Oberon to close his eyes so I could focus on his snout first.

<Hey! Suffering cats, Atticus, what are you doing?> he protested, and squirmed as the water assaulted his snout and began to sluice the ichor away.

"Keep still, buddy. We have to get this off you quickly."

<You're acting like it's nuclear waste.>

"It's worse than that."

<It is? Then get it off me!>

"I'm working on it, Oberon."

<Tell me that story so I can think about something else.>

"All right, we're heading back in time to seventeenth-century France, at the court of Louis the Fourteenth."

<Did he ever get mad about his name?>

"What?"

<Did he ever say, "Geez, all the names in the world out there and my family picked Louis *fourteen times*?">

"I don't think he was embarrassed about it. He was the king."

<Oh. Yeah, I guess that would take the sting out of it.>

The court of a king is littered with pages waiting to do small errands for the nobility. You're tripping over them quite often, and someone has to train them how to get out of the way and conduct themselves properly. That task fell to the father of our heroine, who trained his daughter with all the pages of the court to fence and take insult and give it right back. Her name was Julie d'Aubigny, and she was married very young to a man named Maupin, who was sent to the south of France for work while she remained in Paris. She was known as Mademoiselle Maupin after that, a famous opera singer, lover, and duelist.

She often dressed as a man but did not disguise her face or do anything else to pretend she was actually male; she sang for her supper in local taverns and participated in fencing exhibitions with a man she traveled with for a while. But when she tired of him, she began a torrid affair with a young woman, and eventually her lover's family found out and decided to solve what they saw as a problem by sending the young woman to a convent. Mademoiselle Maupin did not give up, however—she was in love. She applied to this convent in Avignon herself, taking her vows and reuniting with the young woman. She immediately began plotting their escape and came up with a simple plan: Set something on fire. What she set on fire was the body of another nun—already dead—in the bed of her young lover, thereby covering their escape. They had another three months of passion together before their own flame flickered out and the girl returned to her family. Mademoiselle Maupin, in the meantime, was charged with arson and body snatching, the penalty for which was to be burned alive. She never faced those charges, though—she got pardoned by Louis XIV later, thanks to her connections at court.

Mademoiselle Maupin hit the road again, singing, taking a series of male lovers, and occasionally kicking someone's ass in a duel, until she arrived in Paris and joined the opera there. Her life was only mildly tempestuous for a while—she had to beat the hell out of a misogynistic actor once and her landlord on another occasion—but then she landed in serious trouble again when she attended a fancy ball dressed as a man and kissed a young woman there in front of nobility. This was quite offensive according to the social customs of the time, and she was promptly challenged to a duel by three different men. She went outside and beat them all, one after the other; while they bled in the street, she went back inside and kissed the girl again.

Kissing the girl wasn't the true problem: The problem was that she had very publicly broken the king's law against dueling within the limits of Paris and had to leave the country for a time. She relocated to Brussels, sang in the opera there, had several more affairs, and then returned to France, where she sang in the Paris Opera until 1705. Her final affair was with a woman who died in an untimely fashion, and she took her lover's death quite hard and retired from the opera altogether. She entered a convent, in fact, and died a couple of years later at the young age of thirty-three. It was a short, violent, but passionate life she led. She didn't give a damn about gender roles, and she kissed and fought whomever she felt like kissing or fighting, and she sang beautifully and snatched bodies when she needed to. That was Julie d'Aubigny, or Mademoiselle Maupin.

<Wow, Atticus. She was awesome! Did you ever meet her?>

"I did not meet her personally, but I did see her perform *Tancrède* at the Paris Opera in 1702."

<Was she good?>

"Oh, she was very good. And you are very good. We almost have all this gunk off you. How are you feeling?"

<Something stings pretty bad on my right shoulder. The front, I mean.>

I examined the area, parting the fur with my fingers, and found a shallow scratch from a bone splinter there. I'd taken the brunt of it, but Oberon hadn't escaped completely. There was some yellow discoloration around the scratch, which meant that it had indeed been ichor-covered and some of it had managed to get into Oberon. I would have to directly heal him or else it would get worse. Ichor poisoning functioned like cancer in that it turned a mortal body against itself, and even small amounts could be fatal eventually. There wasn't an herbal remedy for it that I knew of, so I'd have to break it down inside him, as I'd done to myself.

"Okay, you're cut up here. Don't shake yourself off or talk or anything. I need to concentrate to deal with this. Just let me know when it stops stinging."

Directly healing another creature by the old laying-on-of-hands is always a tricky business. The Hippocratic maxim of "First, do no harm" is especially true when it comes to using Gaia's energy, since she frowns rather severely on using the earth's magic to do any direct injury. But finding what was *not* Oberon and was clearly invasive wasn't that difficult—it simply required patience and thorough attention. It turned out there were only a few milligrams of ichor inside him, nothing to send him into shock or seizures now, but enough to do the job eventually if I didn't stop it. Unbinding the molecular chains of the ichor into their components left a few random proteins coursing through him—they would eventually get flushed out—and rendered the rest of it inert. Oberon was shivering by the time I was finished.

<It stopped stinging, Atticus, but I'm cold and wet now.>

"Okay, buddy, sorry that it took so long. You can shake off now and roll around on a towel. I have to trade places with you and wash myself."

Once I scoured myself several times and my skin stung all over with the raw thrill of exfoliation, we emerged damp but refreshed from the bathroom. I borrowed Ty's phone to call Hal Hauk and tell him my Sean Flanagan identity was toast. "I'm going to need a new set of papers," I told him.

"I'm going to need money for that, and you can't afford it anymore," he said. "Your accounts are drier than a high-desert well since Drasche got access through Kodiak Black and emptied them. You're going to owe me."

"Understood. I'm good for it, Hal. It's this war with the vampires. It's so very draining, hahaha."

"Gods." Hal's voice was weary. "I sentence you to three centuries in pun prison for that."

"You are the very best of attorneys."

"Yeah, yeah."

"How's the Oregon deal progressing?" Kodiak Black hadn't managed quite everything of mine, and that's where most of my remaining funds had gone—a cabin property in the Willamette National Forest. For me, the entire point of building up multiple accounts had always been for precisely this purpose: to pay for a new hiding place the next time I had to run. I couldn't flip houses; I had to abandon them along with my identity every time I ran, and that took cash. Once we had our new safe house settled, I wouldn't need to impose on anyone else.

"Almost finished. Few more days. I'll bring your ID up to Flagstaff when it's ready."

"Thanks, Hal."

We rang off and I turned to find Sam and Ty standing behind me, arms crossed and staring as if I'd trespassed somehow.

"What did I do?" I asked.

"You tell us," Sam said. "Which Olympian's ichor did you just wash down our drain?"

"Diana's."

Sam's eyebrows shot up. "The huntress Diana? You have her on your trail—a trail that leads to our door?"

"I certainly hope not. Jupiter said he'd take care of it."

"Jupiter can't even control his own urges," Ty pointed out. "What makes you think he'll be able to rein in Diana's?"

He echoed my own worries about the situation, but I didn't want to openly agree. "Look, fellas, I'm leaving in a few minutes. I have this thing to do with Brighid on one of the Norse planes. If Diana shows up—and that's a *big* if—you're welcome to tell her I'm in Svartálfheim."

Sam's jaw dropped in disbelief. "You're seriously going to visit the dark elves?"

"It's either that or displease the Morrigan. I really don't want to annoy the Chooser of the Slain. But I can't take Oberon with me. It's too dangerous." I clasped my hands together and gave them my best pleading, hopeful expression.

<Hey, wait, what? You're leaving me here?>

I have to. Svartálfheim is no place for a hound. It's no place for a Druid either.

Sam shook his head and Ty sighed. "You really are a giant pain in the arse, like Owen says."

"I'll find a way to make it up to you," I promised.

"Oh, no, we'll think up something ourselves," Ty countered.

"Thank you very sincerely for watching him. But I gotta warn you guys: After the bathtime story I just told him, Oberon may try to hump your leg and then challenge you to a duel. Or vice versa."

CHAPTER 11

I've had a few days to prepare, but me palms are sweaty when I see the families approaching from the house. I hope I look competent to their modern eyes and not like some wild cock-up of a man. I'm in a robe, since I plan to be shape-shifting, and me bare feet are chilled while the rest of me feels overheated. Sam and Greta are with the group and they smile at me, happy over what is to begin here, but the families and the children look as nervous as I feel. Or maybe they're just tired; they all had long trips to get here on short notice.

Not a one of them looks Irish or anything close to it, and I think that's grand. It's best, methinks, to have Druids from all over Gaia; that way they'll each have a special stretch of the earth calling to their hearts. It's what we should have done back in the old days, if we'd been thinking properly, but instead of actively trying to spread Druidry everywhere, we just assumed it would grow outward from Ireland and keep going. It never got out of the European continent, and that's a mistake we don't need to repeat.

I'm standing a good distance from the house in a field of bunch grass already gone dormant for the winter. Pines stand tall behind me in formations leading up the mountain, and the air is crisp. There are worse places I could start a grove. Greta presents me to them all, and

I nod once and say, "Welcome." I get a few nods and a couple of shy smiles in return. Then the introductions begin.

First is a married couple and a wee girl from someplace called Mongolia. They have a translator with them while they're learning English, but Greta assures me that she's pack also. Straight dark hair, high cheekbones, golden-brown complexions. The father, Nergüi, is the new pack member; his wife's name is Oyuunchimeg, but she wants to simply be called "Meg" in the United States. The girl is seven and her name is Enkhtuya. The parents get nods, but I squat down on me haunches so I'm not so large and intimidating and grin at the girl, who wants to be called Tuya.

"Nice to meet ye, Tuya," I says, and she relays a polite reply via the translator.

Next in line is a family from Peru. Both of the parents, Diego and Rafaela, are new pack members and are very worried about protecting their boy, Ozcar. They speak English with a charming accent and have warm-brown skin and thick black eyebrows. Ozcar is a shy lad and doesn't respond to my greeting except after prompting from his parents. He might be a bit small for his age, a bit thin. Time and oats will take care of it.

Mohammed and his son, Mehdi, hail from a village in the mountains of Morocco, a place called Chefchaouen, which is rather fun to say out loud. The boy's mother is missing, but I don't inquire about it right then; she may be in the house, or simply elsewhere, and if not, there is plenty of time to collect such stories later. They're dressed in white, and Mohammed has a little cap on his head that I suspect has some kind of religious significance. I'm not up to speed on all the religions that have sprung up since me own day, but it really doesn't matter. Gaia doesn't require worship, so Druids can pray to whomever they want.

"Thank you for doing this," Mohammed says. "I don't want to outlive my son. If Mehdi becomes a Druid, he can live longer, yes, like wolves?"

"That's right," I tell him, though I leave out that this is a recent development thanks to Siodhachan. "I know I don't look like it, but I'm in me seventies."

Mohammed clasps his hands together and says something in a language I don't recognize as he lowers his head in what I assume is a prayer of thanks. One of the monotheist religions, I'm guessing.

The religion of Sajit, however, is a serious problem for him now that he is a werewolf, as his translator explains. He's a Hindu from Nepal and this has something to do with why he's a strict vegetarian, yet when he shifts once a month his wolf won't let him shift back without eating meat, which he finds very distressing. He wants to make it very clear, therefore, that his daughter, Amita, should not be forced to eat meat as part of her apprenticeship.

"Ye both can eat what ye want," I says to him, and shrug. "It doesn't matter to me." Amita's mother is absent as well, and the wee girl is reluctant to make eye contact. Her complexion is lighter than her father's—tawny where his is a warm sepia—but I can tell she's going to be tall like him.

Luiz is an earnest six-year-old from Brazil and missing his father. His mother, Natália, greets me in broken English. They have a translator but clearly already know a few words. Luiz has a gap between his front teeth that makes me like him.

The last family is a father and daughter from Zambia, and they possess skin of a deep, rich umber; their hair is cropped very close to their skulls. The girl is by far the tallest of the children, though I'm unsure if that's simply because she's older than the rest or if she's truly above average. The father, Sonkwe, is fluent in English, and his daughter, Thandi, is learning well. I note that her eyes take in everything: When she's finished absorbing me, her eyes drift to the trees as her father speaks, volunteering why he's a single parent: "After I was bitten," he says, "my wife left us. She thinks I am a monster now."

If she truly thinks that, then I wonder why she would leave her child with a monster, but I keep me questions in reserve. Now is not the time for them.

"There isn't a one of ye that's a monster," I says, and nod to the translators to indicate that they should relay my words. "You're just bound to lycanthropy now. Fancy word for a certain kind of binding. All magic is a binding of some kind. And Druids are bound to the earth. To Gaia." I'd stood to meet the other children after Tuya, but I go ahead and squat again so that the kids would know I was speaking to them and not their parents. I pull up my right sleeve to reveal my tattoos, then speak to the apprentices, sweeping my eyes across them in turn. "This ink is not for decoration. It's my binding to the earth, and that in turn allows me to bind myself to four animal shapes and do many other things besides. When you are ready, you will be bound to the earth in the same way, and then you will be able to shape-shift into four different creatures. But a Druid's shape-shifting is different from a werewolf's. It's faster, painless, and we don't have to do it at all if we don't want to. But you're probably going to want to. Wouldn't you like to fly?" The kids nod and I smile. "Sure! Who wouldn't? One of your shapes will be a bird of some kind. I'll show you in a minute."

My eyes flick over to Greta and she nods, encouraging me to continue. She coached me on what to do next, warning me about modern cultural standards of modesty.

"The thing about shape-shifting is, ye can't do it with your clothes on. Or if ye do it's mighty painful and ye can hurt yourself. Better to get rid of your clothes first, and get rid of any shame about your body while you're at it. The shape you were born with is perfect in Gaia's eyes. That should be good enough for anybody."

I rise from me crouch and say, "I'm going to shape-shift to a red kite now, just to show ye what I'll have ye workin' for in the years ahead. All the language schooling, all the mental exercises, and all the physical training will be to get you ready for the responsibility. But make no mistake. It's fun too."

Switching to Old Irish, I bind my shape to a red kite as I turn my back and throw off my robe. They see it fall and me shrink down to a bird of prey at the same time. I screech at them and all of them gasp, but the new pack members especially—they've all endured the painful transformation to a werewolf and can't conceive of the process being fast and smooth. I take wing and circle around them a couple of times, their eyes following me, and I can see the kids are excited now. I light next to me robe and shape-shift directly to a bear, giving them a friendly grunt. They're delighted by it, and this is Greta's cue to come on over and drape the robe across me back. I turn around and shift back to human and the robe falls into place—all her idea.

"Nobody is going to mind a little ass," she said to me before they arrived, "but it's hardly necessary to show them the whole package, is it?"

I didn't see why it mattered, but she did, so I agreed to do it her way.

The kids are so juiced they can't stand still: A couple of them actually jump up and down and clap. And the parents are happy too, smiling down at their kids, because such joy is infectious.

"Gaia gives Druids these forms to help protect her better—our primary function is to protect the earth. And you do that by watching out for the elementals, and in turn they kind of watch out for you. When you're bound to the earth, you'll be able to talk to the elementals directly. But I can let ye talk to the elemental here right now. Flagstaff rests on the Colorado Plateau, so we think of this elemental as Colorado. I've already let it know you'll be here today, and it's going to give each of you a small sphere of sandstone, which I don't want you to lose. You will use it to talk to Colorado. First, take off your shoes so the earth can feel your presence."

I have never seen any group of kids so eager to be barefoot. They all plop down and start tugging at their shoes, and their parents laugh. Once they're all back on their feet and wriggling their toes in the earth, I send a message to Colorado through my tattoos that the new apprentices are ready and standing opposite me. The ground in front of the kids breaks and crumbles, and spheres of sandstone rise up out of it, each with a slightly different pattern of tans and reds.

"All right, I want ye to pick up the stone, close it in your hand, and concentrate on saying hello to the earth. It doesn't matter what language you use. It won't use language to reply back, but you'll feel it."

They all bend down to pick up their stones and then scrunch their eyes closed in concentration. I have to admit it's fecking adorable. After about ten seconds they start laughing and happy-crying when they hear Colorado in their heads, and damn if me own eyes don't get watery at the edges. It's tough to not get emotional when ye finally realize that you're not trapped on the planet with things that want to eat ye or tell ye what to do. All the earth wants ye to do is thrive, and ye feel that love whenever ye contact an elemental.

I look up at the parents and tell them we'll be at it awhile and they can let us be. "Ye can ask me any other questions ye might have later on." They say thank you by word or gesture and depart with Greta and Sam, leaving me with the kids and the three translators. I let the kids commune until the parents are out of sight, and then I interrupt them.

"Colorado doesn't speak in language, ye may have noticed. You get pictures and feelings. You can ask it simple questions, though, and it will understand what ye mean as long as ye think it really hard. Ask Colorado to show ye the places and creatures it loves the most. You will see."

Some of them whisper the question aloud in their effort to think really hard, but once Colorado begins to answer, their faces switch from awe to surprise to wide smiles and more as images filter through their heads. Whatever they're seeing, it's all new to them, since they come from very different parts of the world and would not be familiar with the native plants and animals here.

I give them a few minutes and then thank Colorado, asking it to stop.

"All right, I want ye to tell me what you saw. Tuya, you go first." One by one, down the line, they tell me about snakes and lizards and scorpions, mule deer and native trout, the blue-green waters of Havasupai Falls in the Grand Canyon, the sandstone buttes of the Navajo Nation and the canyons cut by floodwaters there. Thandi is last, and she begins to tell me about coyotes but then breaks off and her eyes pull away from me face to look at something over me right shoulder. She points and squeaks, "Big ugly man!"

I half expect it to be a joke and get a round of giggles out of them when I turn around to look, but she isn't kidding. The very definition of big and ugly is coming this way out of the pine trees. It's that fecking bog troll who says I owe him gold.

"Holy shit," one of the translators mutters.

"All of ye run back to the house now," I says. "Find Greta and your parents and tell 'em there's a troll come calling. Shoo, now, go on!"

The translators herd them away and the kids scurry toward the house with jerky little kid legs, leaving their shoes behind. It's a grim face I'm wearing when I go to meet the troll. He's lumbering in long, plodding steps, and he still hasn't figured out how to hide his dangly bits. What he *has* figured out is how to find me and get here without using one of the Old Ways, a feat I thought impossible. And it probably still is. What's really happened is that he's found someone to help him. And the bastard has also ripped up a young aspen tree to pound me with. Well, we'll see who does the pounding.

I fish me knuckles out of the robe pocket, slip them on, and charge them up as I walk, and I also mutter the bindings to increase me strength and speed. I'd like to simply go at him, but I need to know first how he got here.

There are bound trees nearby—Siodhachan saw to that—which means one of the Tuatha Dé Danann could have brought him. It certainly wasn't Granuaile or Siodhachan. It could not have been any of the lesser Fae, because most of them need oak, ash, and thorn to shift, especially if they're bringing someone else with them, and there isn't any of that growing together in this part of the country. That leaves two possibilities: He came to earth via one of the Old Ways in Europe and traveled here under a glamour—extremely unlikely— or there's an Old Way up in the San Francisco Peaks we don't know about.

I thought there weren't any Old Ways on this side of the globe, but it's possible that someone made a new one.

A shiver of dread tickles me spine at a thought and I say to the troll, all smiles, "Mornin', lad, good mornin'. How was Fand when ye spoke to her?"

"She is fine," he says without thinking, because trolls are grand at that.

"Good to hear, that is. She's very helpful, eh? Helping you find me and then arranging a path for you to get here. So kind."

"She is good, yes."

"And all that from prison!" A prison, I might add, chosen by meself and her mother, Flidais. I had acted as Brighid's proxy in that matter to make sure Fand would be secure, and Flidais had come along to make sure her daughter was well treated and the Fae would have no cause to complain on that score. "She's truly powerful."

The bog troll's gnarled gray face squishes and moves around with great effort of thinking. "Prison? She's not in prison."

That tickle o' dread becomes the uncomfortable sound o' me bowels liquefying, for he had just confirmed me worst fear. At some point Fand had quietly escaped and was now helping bog trolls hunt down Druids, in addition to whatever other shenanigans she could think of. Since starting a war in Tír na nÓg was her last great idea, I don't like to think of what else she might be up to now.

"Oh!" I says, chuckling at him. "That's right, I forgot she's out. Where is she now?"

"She's at—wait." The horrible accident of his face turns suspicious. "I'm not supposed to say."

Damn. So close. At least I'd learned more than Fand would have liked.

"I'm here for my gold," he rumbles. "You crossed my bridge and never paid. It's time." He twitches the tree trunk at me in a not-so-subtle threat.

Greta will never get me to buy a cell phone, but she did show me the Internet and get me signed up on this thing called Twitter, under the name @ArchdruidOwen, so I could learn how people today can socialize while being separated by hundreds or thousands of miles. And she told me about Internet trolls, which are smaller and less dangerous than bog trolls but may smell just as bad. I remember her first rule regarding them, which was actually me own rule two thousand years ago, and smile up at my uninvited guest.

"Sorry, lad, but I never feed the trolls." And then I haul off and punch him hard, directly in the dong.

Troll skin is naturally tough and makes wearing armor unnecessary, and troll skin foreskin is no different. But me new brass knuckles could shatter rock, so I wasn't quite sure what would happen when I made contact. In hindsight, I should have pulled me punch a bit, but I'm so mad that he's there threatening me new Grove and that Fand's escaped that I just go for it, which means I'm abruptly in a new kind of nightmare when me fist punctures the skin and keeps going.

I'm up to me elbow in spongy troll cock, and we're both profoundly unhappy about it and yelling fit to beat a *ban sidhe*. He crumples inward by reflex, grabs with his massive left hand, and yanks me out of there and tosses me through the air a good thirty yards or so. I land on the exposed face of a half-buried boulder and it crunches me left shoulder blade, shooting pain through the whole arm before it goes numb and useless. I roll onto me right side in the bunch grass and lever my body up, staggering to me feet as the troll realizes he's not going to die but just be permanently disfigured in his dank and smelly junk. He gets powerful angry about it and forgets all about getting his gold out of me. All he wants now is to stomp me to a smear in the mud. Or bash me on the head with that tree of his. He picks the latter option, bellowing and charging with the tree, though due to his injury he's kind of lurching more than running.

The day I passively wait for a charge to arrive is the day you can dip me in a lake of salted whale shite. Speaking quickly, I throw off me robe and shape-shift to a ram. I charge him right back, lame left front leg and all—I'm still faster than he is by a far stretch. He's a right-handed lad, so he'll be planting his left foot to take his swing. That's the leg I aim for as I lower me head, horns covered in the brass. He tries to adjust and take me out with his aspen trunk but whiffs over me head as I get inside his guard. I plow into his left shin and don't completely take off his leg but it's a near thing. The bones audibly fracture in a few places, and I stumble sideways, rocked by the collision. He goes down loud and heavy and won't be charging me again: The bones have erupted through the back of his leg and stick up like spires.

Thing is that there's no easy way to finish him off—and I will be finishing him off out of necessity. You can't put your fist through a man's wood and expect him to forgive and forget. He had gone too far in coming after me, and I had gone too far in my response. It's a death match now, and it's not going to be easy for either of us to survive.

Climb up on his back and he can roll over and crush me. Try to get to any of his organs, and his perfectly functioning arms and hands can get to me first. He's already looking for me and, damn it, while I'm looking at his face he kicks out blindly with his right foot, a trick move where he's bending it over his left while lying face-down, and it knocks me over and I land on that lame left shoulder. Bone grinds against bone and I bleat, which is a fecking awful noise. The ram form isn't useful any-more, so I shape-shift to a bear as he rolls over to his back, pivots on his hips, and raises that log of a leg in an attempt to heel-kick me into paste. Me left arm still isn't working of course, but I'm counting on the right one to win this. I dart in a bit closer, raise up on my back feet, and meet that troll's leg with my claws, gouging deep grooves across the tendons at the back of his ankle and effectively halting his descent. After the reflexive recoil, he brings it down again, pain be damned, and I'm still there. I'm clubbed to the ground by the back of his calf and see spots in me vision, but I just keep lashing out with me claws until the pressure disappears and he's rolled away to escape me. I struggle up and am unsteady on me paws, forget I'm injured, and try to put weight on my left front foot, which crashes me to the ground again. When I manage to lift myself off the ground once more, I see through blurred vision that the troll is grabbing for that tree trunk with giant fingers. He's also spinning around somehow in the sky, but I know that can't be really happening—he's clocked me upside the head right well. Might as well be dead already, because I don't have the wits left to dodge another blow, even if I can accurately judge where it's coming from in time. Three of those trees rise up in the air and hang there for an impossible time, frozen like I was on that island for all those years, and then they begin to fall in different directions. I hear them—or it—crash back to earth but am not rightly sure where it lands except that it's not on top of me. Me vision won't focus and I blink furiously, trying to locate the troll, and when I finally find him he's not moving. He's underneath the tree, and I think that's mighty strange. Then I see the stained grass and earth around us and realize that he bled to death. My claws must have opened a few arteries, and, combined with his broken leg and that other thing I did, he ran out of juice pretty fast.

I shape-shift back to human and lie on my right side so all me tattoos can soak up energy and help me heal. Moving that much makes everything spin again, and I'm sick on the grass. Greta's face appears in front of mine soon after that, and all I can think is that I probably still have vomit in me beard.

"Owen? Owen! The kids said this thing is a troll."

"Are they safe?"

"The kids? Yes. You don't look so good. Your arm's out of its socket."

"It is? Well, it's worse than that on the inside."

"Owen, your eyes aren't tracking me. Can you see me?"

"Aye, all four—no, five of you."

"You're concussed."

That's a new word for me and I tell her so. "I don't know what that means. Hope it means I'm handsome."

"Of course you are. But tell me, are you healing right now?"

"Aye. Trying to."

"Focus your efforts on your brain. It's probably swelling. And don't go to sleep."

"Funny ye should say that, because I'm quite sleepy."

"No, no, don't sleep. Talk to me. Why is there a troll here?"

"I owed him money. He didn't want Canadian money, though. Showed him the queen and the king of Canada and everything, but he wouldn't take it."

"What? You're not making sense."

"It's because of Fand. She escaped. She's free. We have to find her."

"Which one is Fand again?"

"The one who wants to kill us all because we aren't living in the past."

"Is this because of something your apprentice did?" Her expression darkens just referring to him like that, and I think sometimes she would blame Siodhachan for bad weather if she could.

"No, love, not this time. This time it's me own fault. My fault I never fed the trolls. My fault that Fand escaped and sent him here. I'm sorry."

"How is it your fault that Fand escaped?"

"I was responsible for keeping her locked up. However she managed to spring free, I should have thought of it first."

"Pfft. I hate that shoulda-woulda-coulda crap, Owen. You can never go back. You can only go forward. Like this arm here. You can't go back to when it was never dislocated. You can only shove it back in and hope it heals all right. I'm going to do that now," she says, grabbing me near the elbow.

"Easy, now. I'm handsome and concussed."

Maybe she tries to go easy and maybe she doesn't. It fecking hurts regardless, and I howl about it when it pops back in. She doesn't apologize, though, because there's simply no help for some pain: Sometimes ye just have to clench your teeth and endure it.

"What are we going to do about this body?" she says. "We can't leave it here."

"I'll have the earth take it in," I answer. "The kids don't need to see it all torn up like that. And they don't need to see me like this either. You'll keep 'em away until I'm healed, won't ye, love?"

"Yes, I will. Or their parents will. They're all at the house now. Except for Mohammed, I guess, because here he comes."

Mohammed's a lad of Greta's mind about the past: He doesn't ask what happened but rather asks what needs to be done next. Greta requests a new set of clothes for me and some water, and he dashes away to fetch them.

But in doing so—moving forward, in Greta's mind— he's still dealing with the past. It's always strung out behind us, innit, attached to our arses like a roll of toilet paper we trail out of the bathroom, pointing the way to the giant shite we just took. It doesn't matter if we flushed it down: Everyone still knows what we did there. So it's fine to *say* it's all done and you have no connection with the past, that you're a new person every second, but silly in my view to pretend that person isn't made of the old one.

I know I can't feed meself that plate of bollocks and swallow it. I can go forward and maybe put Fand back in prison before she does any more harm, but I can't pretend I'm not at least partially responsible for her escaping in the first place.

And I can't pretend that I don't understand Siodhachan anymore. The lad's got himself mired in a bog far worse than the one this troll used to live in and he doesn't know how or even if he's going to get out of it. I have to tell Brighid that her enemy is loose, and I don't know how I'll manage that without dying of shame, but it's nothing compared to what me old apprentice is facing.

Times were a whole lot simpler back when they were frozen for me.

CHAPTER 12

Fand had recently set the dark elves after me as part of her effort to rid the Fae of one Iron Druid, and I had barely escaped my encounters with them. Had they not relied on their magical weapons, against which my cold iron aura proved to be excellent armor, they would have ended me for sure. They were strong and fast and, unlike the average Bond villain, not given to conversation; rather, they were silent and implacable, like the nameless thing you used to fear was hiding in your closet or under your bed, childhood nightmares made of flesh and smoke.

I had never been to Svartálfheim but knew in theory where it was—Manannan Mac Lir had given me a map of the nine realms, which placed the entrance in Niflheim between the Vir and Ylgr rivers. It wasn't to scale, however, and I doubted very much that the entrance would be as plainly visible as it was on the map. And since we would have no luck putting Svartálfheim into a GPS app, I was somewhat worried that we might spend significant time just figuring out how to get there.

Brighid was waiting for me at her throne in the Fae Court when I arrived, already dressed for battle and leaning on the sort of massive oversize sword one saw in anime. Unlike the diminutive protagonists of those dramas, she had the muscle to swing such a massive weapon. She also had a set of armor and a shield ready for me—Goibhniu's old kit, in fact, which fit me well and assured me instantly of its quality. She helped me into it, since none of her Fae attendants could get close to me without turning to ash. As she did so, I noticed that there appeared to be fresh etchings in the armor, laid down on top of the old decorative patterns; some of the edges were still raw.

"Is this a binding of some kind?" I asked.

"Added it last night," Brighid said. "Protection against fire. I know your aura protects you from my fire to some extent, but that won't protect the armor itself or your sword. Pointless to have your skin immune and not what you're wearing. You'll cook in this otherwise."

"Not sure I understand," I said. "Are you planning to set me on fire?"

"How do you think we're getting to Svartálfheim?" Brighid replied. "We're flying there aflame. We have to follow the roots of Yggdrasil down to Niflheim and then cross a considerable distance to get to the dark doors of Svartálfheim."

I tried my best not to geek out. I had always wanted to fly like a mutant superhero, and flying with Brighid was bound to be a smoother ride than the jerky, twitching ascent to Asgard that Perun gave me one time. I covered my excitement by saying, "You know how to get there already?"

"Aye. Scouted it soon after Eoghan told me the Morrigan's message. The entrance is guarded."

She wrapped the scabbard and handle of Fragarach in a ribbon marked with the same bindings as the armor, and then we were ready. We shifted separately to the same point on earth—or Midgard—where one of the main roots of Yggdrasil was bound. It was an idyllic stretch of Sweden with a fair blue lake that Freyja had turned into a portal when we had to visit

Hel. Brighid likewise made a portal next to the root of the Midgard tree that was bound to Yggdrasil's, albeit a much smaller one.

"Jump through," she said, "and I'll catch up as you fall. I don't want to set this tree on fire."

So I cannonballed through the portal and fell into shockingly cold air, the sky of Midgard gone and replaced by the gray dismal mist of Niflheim. I got about five seconds of free fall next to the root of Yggdrasil before I was cocooned in warmth and bright orange flame surrounded my vision. Brighid appeared on my right, gesturing that I should straighten out headfirst like her, and once I did she redirected our flight, pulling us into a horizontal trajectory a thousand feet or so above the great wyrm Niddhogg, who was stretched out fatly as he munched at the root of Yggdrasil. We banked west and Brighid pointed out two specific rivers originating from the spring of Hvergelmir.

"That one is the Vir," she said, indicating the one on the left, which threw up a curtain of steam into the air, "which borders Muspellheim. We will follow that and then turn north at a waterfall, cross a snowy plain, and find the entrance hidden on a wooded hill. Sentries watch from among the trees."

I nodded, not wanting to shout through fire, and watched the miles disappear underneath us. The lava-scorched crags of Muspellheim were occluded by the steam rising from the Vir River, and I hoped we might see a fire giant from a distance. But all too soon we had banked across the vast sea of snow, never sparkling like it does in sunlight but gray, slick, and wet, like mucus under the cloud cover. A few islands of stunted pipe-cleaner trees poked up in the distance—the hills Brighid spoke of—and off to the east was an anomalous blob of black and light blue that somehow managed to wink and gleam in the dishwater light of Niflheim.

I pointed to the blob on the snow and asked Brighid, "What's that over there?"

Her head swiveled to examine the oddity and then, when it didn't make any sense to her eyes, she altered our course to take a closer look. A minute or more revealed that we had not been seeing a single thing but many things made one by distance. What we were looking at was an army of Æsir in blue glass armor—the Glass Knights—accompanied by a battalion of stout dwarf elite infantry, the Black Axes. They were marching toward Svartálfheim. The dwarfs would have new runes on their axes that could cut a dark elf in smoke form and force him into corporeal solidity; the Glass Knights had defensive runes on their tiled armor that rendered them invulnerable to the dark elves' knives, much like my cold iron aura. It allowed them to wait in safety until the dark elves could no longer maintain their smoke form and then shoot them with fléchettes as soon as they solidified.

Once I explained this to Brighid, we pivoted in midair and shot ahead of the army to warn the dark elves.

The entrance to Svartálfheim boasted no intricately carved stone doors or huge walls, no pillars or obelisks or massive sculptures outside to celebrate and prop up the cultural ego. It was a simple pair of wooden doors set in the hillside, albeit dark like ironwood or ebony, and manned by four bored guards. High enough and wide enough to move in some fabulous furniture but far short of grandiose.

To their credit, the guards did perk up at the approach of a fireball in the sky. They dissolved into black smoke as we touched down, melting snow into a puddle beneath our feet.

"Hold!" Brighid said in Old Norse as soon as she extinguished her flame. "I am Brighid, First among the Fae, and I come in peace to bring you news."

One guard solidified and spoke, though he was nude now. Their clothes had all fallen away when their bodies turned to gases.

"You do not come dressed for peace," he said.

"My armor and sword are not for you. They are for the army of Æsir and dwarfs approaching your doors even now."

He cocked his head in disbelief. "The Æsir have come to Niflheim?"

"Yes. And we are here to fight for the Svartálfs. Please alert whoever needs to know and either allow us entry or bid them come here."

The other three Svartálfs solidified, and the guard who spoke to Brighid told one of them to fetch help. He immediately dissolved again and filtered through a gap in the doors without ever opening them for us. The remaining guards didn't speak, knowing that it wasn't really their place to question us. They'd challenged us and sent word to leaders inside, and now it was their task to watch us and wait in silence, like assassins are wont to do, until given further orders.

I sloshed out of the puddle of meltwater onto some firmer powder and checked the eastern horizon to see if the army was visible yet. A slightly darker smudge might be them or might not. Niflheim is by and large a bleak smudge of a landscape to begin with.

Brighid likewise moved out of the puddle so her feet wouldn't freeze in the ice, and eventually a muffled voice called from behind the doors, asking if it was clear. One of the guards responded with something that must have been a code phrase and the doors opened, allowing the egress of five dark elves dressed in identical shimmering white robes that were tied with sashes of varying colors. They also had circlets on their foreheads, affixed with a stone in the center matching the color of their sashes. I guessed that they represented a guild or governmental structure, though I recalled no one mentioning it before. Probably because so few people visited Svartálfheim and lived to tell about it.

The woman leading them announced herself to be Turid Einarsdottir. She had a blue stone and sash and she made introductions without stating titles. One name in particular grabbed my attention: Krókr Hrafnson.

"Krókr?" I said. "Head of the assassins?"

He wore a black sash and a piece of polished obsidian in his circlet. He tensed as if he expected me to jump at him, but he answered, "Yes. Who might you be?"

"I'm the Druid that Fand of the Tuatha Dé Danann hired you to kill. None of your assassins came back, did they?"

His expression hardened and he shook his head by way of reply.

"Well, their deaths weren't entirely my doing. Most of them were taken out by Æsir and a single dwarf Runeskald. This Runeskald has figured out how to protect against your black blades and also cut you while you're in your smoke form, making you vulnerable to a killing blow after that."

The dark elves scoffed in unison. "Impossible," Krókr said.

"I witnessed it with my own eyes. He appeared with several axes inscribed with different runes and waded right into the middle of your men. They tried to pierce his armor but could not. Meanwhile, he tested each axe in turn. I believe his fourth one worked. Tore right through smoke, and then a Svartálf took shape with a shallow gash across his chest. He couldn't go back after that, and the dwarf finished him."

"And now there's an army in similar armor," Brighid said, "no doubt with similar weapons, designed to destroy you and marching here to do just that."

"Why?" Turid asked. "We've done nothing to them."

"It's not what you have done. It's what they fear you *will* do. They believe you will fight against them when Ragnarok arrives, and they would rather fight you today, when they have an advantage, than on the day they are beset on all sides."

"We have no plans for Ragnarok other than survival," the dark elf leader protested.

"You mean you are neutral? The Æsir do not see it that way. They are assuming that since you are not actively on their side, you must be on the other side, with Hel and Loki."

"That's narrow-minded thinking. This is done with Odin's approval?"

"We do not know for certain since we have not spoken with him," Brighid replied, "but it is difficult to imagine that he is unaware of this. The fact that such a force marches at all implies his approval."

"Where is this force now?" Krókr asked.

I pointed behind me. "See that smudge on the horizon?"

Krókr squinted, then turned to a couple of the guards and asked them to scout the army, admonishing them to stay out of range and not engage.

"Assuming that truly is the army you speak of, why are you here to warn us?" Turid asked Brighid after the guards had departed. "The Tuatha Dé Danann have never shown us kindness before."

"That is true. And I am not here to be kind now either," Brighid said. "I am here because I am sworn to protect Gaia, and she would suffer greatly if the Svartálfs remain neutral or fight on the side of darkness during Ragnarok."

The Svartálfs exchanged glances with one another and shrugged, leaving Turid with no advice on how to proceed. "You seem to know more of the future than we do. Why do we matter so much?"

"That I do not know. All I know is that one of our best seers, the Morrigan, said that you must join the side of the Æsir if Gaia is to have a chance of surviving."

Turid's brows drew together and her mouth drooped in a frown. "What do we care if Midgard falls?"

"I did not speak of Midgard. I spoke of Gaia, the anchor for Yggdrasil and the nine realms and the anchor for all other planes dreamed up by human minds. If Gaia falls, then so do the nine realms, you understand? It is in everyone's interest to ensure Gaia's survival."

Krókr scoffed, "So we must join the Æsir, who are even now on their way to kill us all?"

"Exactly," I said. "But this is not insurmountable. It's a misunderstanding. If we can convince them you will fight with them at Ragnarok, there is no need for bloodshed."

"We have no wish to fight with them or against them," Turid pointed out, "or to participate in Ragnarok at all."

"So lie," I said, "and save your people today. Because I've seen their armor in action. The Æsir portion of that army call themselves the Glass Knights. They will systematically fire fléchettes once per second and make sure that they hit you when you're corporeal, and their runed tiles are impervious to your weapons. And then the Black Axes will hack you apart like so much meat once you're bound to your naked flesh. That's what happened to your assassins, and it will happen to your entire population if you don't give them a reason to stop."

"I don't see how we can change Odin's mind now."

"You can worry about changing his mind later. Right now you need to prevent them from wiping you out. They're incredibly prepared to deny you *Sigr af Reykr*— Victory from Smoke. But give them anything else and they'll fall," I said. "Use conventional weapons. Bring some archers out here and loose a few flights. Arrows will mow them down."

"And fire will burn them," Brighid said, kindling a sphere of flame in the palm of her hand.

"Good," Krókr said. "If you're so anxious to help, we'll let you stall them while we gather a force together behind the gates."

The other dark elves turned their heads and frowned at Krókr's words but did not gainsay him.

"We hoped to fight with you rather than for you," Brighid said.

"I don't care if you fight. Sing and dance for them if you want. Just give us as much time to prepare as you can." His peremptory tone struck me as the sort that would get him barbecued. Delivering orders to Brighid like that marked him as incredibly confident or simply stupid.

Brighid did not reply to him, however, or set him on fire for his insolence. Instead, she addressed the other Svartálf leaders. "Does Hrafnson speak for all of you in this matter?"

They paused, exchanged glances, and then Turid said, "He does. We will prepare and be grateful for any time you can give us."

"Unbelievable," I said as they withdrew into the gate, taking the guards with them. Brighid's mouth dropped open as the door closed in our faces, leaving us out in the literal cold to face an army by ourselves. The guards who had left earlier to scout the army streamed past us as smoke, not pausing to share their intelligence but filtering through the cracks of the doors to report their findings.

"I think I might know why the dark elves have few allies," she said.

"Yep," I said, turning around. The smudge on the horizon was a definite chunk of something solid now. "Shall we go down to meet them or wait here?"

"Let's go down. Quick flight. Are you ready?"

"I'm still not in great fighting shape, but I'm as ready as I'll be today, I suppose."

We may have looked to the Æsir like the descending wrath of Loki as we approached in a ball of fire—that was my guess judging by their relieved expressions once we landed in front of them and the dissipating flames revealed our figures. But for my money they should not have looked relieved at the appearance of Brighid.

Leading the army, marching in front, was the red-bearded Runeskald, Fjalar. He didn't recognize either of us except as people who were not Loki, since we wore armor. He peered at it rather than at our helmeted faces, trying to discern the nature of the etchings. Brighid's bindings looked nothing like runes, however, so all he could learn from them was that we weren't Norse. He called a halt to the march and shifted his axe down from his shoulder to a two-handed grip.

"Who are you?" he said, and I was a bit disappointed that he didn't go epic with it and give the moment its proper weight. I'd hoped for a "Verily" or a "Tell me in sooth" or something like that.

Both of us had full helmets on, so we were merely armed warriors to his eyes. And, I realized, since Brighid had her hair tucked up and didn't forge her armor with the stupid mounds for breasts one sees in video games, he probably didn't realize she was female, much less a goddess.

Her head nodded once in my direction, indicating that I should speak for us.

"You know me, Fjalar. I'm Atticus O'Sullivan, Druid of Gaia."

"And who else?"

"Someone more powerful than I am."

He gazed at Brighid, who is in fact taller than I am, and might have guessed her identity if he leapt immediately to the Irish pantheon. "What are you doing here?"

"We're here to ask you to turn around. I hardly think you have a peaceful mission to the dark elves with that army behind you."

"I can't turn around. I have orders from Odin himself."

"But surely you have battlefield command. Call it a strategic withdrawal. The situation's changed and you need to reassess—as does Odin."

"And how has the situation changed?"

"The dark elves are under my protection. And the Tuatha Dé Danann's."

Again Fjalar shifted his eyes to Brighid, trying to gauge the threat level she represented. It should be radioactive.

"Why? What makes you care about them?"

"They deserve to live until Ragnarok like everyone else."

"But they're on the side of Loki and Hel!"

"They claim to be on no one's side but their own."

"Of *course* they say that! But skulking, creeping, they fill all that is not light like the darkness they are—"

"Ah, there's the skald talking now! And it's all poetic bullshit covering up the fact that you want to walk in and murder people because they *might* do something at an ill-defined point in the future and because you don't like the way they look. Go back and rethink this."

"If Odin, in his wisdom, is satisfied that this is the right course, I will not question him."

"Meaning you're not thinking for yourself. And also assuming that Odin has all the facts, when he may not. Have you tried talking to the Svartálfar?"

"It's not my place. Nor is it my place to listen to you.

There are two sides: Asgard's and theirs. On which side will you stand?"

"First, that's bullshit either-or thinking. And second, I've already told you that the Svartálfar are not on the side of Hel any more than they are on yours. They're neutral, and if you'd take the time to talk to them instead of marching on them, we could spare a lot of lives here."

"I asked where *you* stand, Druid."

"Right here in front of you, demanding that you not attempt genocide."

Fjalar paused and craned his neck to look at the gray ceiling of clouds. "So you would defy Odin?" He spied and then pointed to Hugin and Munin, circling above us. They had not been there earlier. "He's watching."

"Then he can watch me say this: I would defy anyone who wished to commit genocide, including Brighid." In fact, I was starting to wonder about Odin. Loki wanted to burn the world, and Odin wanted to just wipe out part of it. There was a difference of scale, but the sentiment was the same—denying people their right to live because you didn't like them. It gave me pause to think about what I was doing: Do vampires have a right to, uh, *unlive*? Was my situation any different? I supposed it was: Theophilus had actively sent Werner Drasche and others to kill my friends and me, and he would doubtless do so again. He intended me to be the last victim of a genocide he'd carried out centuries ago with the help of the Roman legions, marching to do his bidding much as Fjalar and company were marching to Odin's. But my rationale of an active self-defense was perilously close to Odin's, and could bear some further scrutiny later.

"I certainly hope you would defy me in such a case," Brighid said, igniting her left fist. It did much to draw Fjalar's attention, as did her three-level voice, in which

she could speak only truth and could be quite persua-
sive. "I am Brighid, First among the Fae, and I also will
protect the right of the Svartálfar to exist. Withdraw
and let us talk calmly of these matters and come to an
accord."

"No," Fjalar replied. "You underestimate the will of
Asgard. The time for talk has past. We must prepare for
Ragnarok."

I cocked my head at him and said, "When was the
time for talk, exactly? Because I must have missed it.
Seems like you haven't talked to the Svartálfar at all."

"Enough! You insert yourselves into matters that don't
concern you. Move aside."

"Be very concerned, Runeskald," Brighid warned in
her three-part voice. "If you move forward, you will be
the first to die an unnecessary death. I can read those
runes well enough to know your armor does not protect
against fire."

"You may send me to Valhalla if you wish," Fjalar
said. "Either way, I will fight in Ragnarok."

I raised my left hand in a plea for him to stop. "Fjalar,
no. Wait—"

The Runeskald lifted his axe high and shouted, "Æsir!"
As soon as he brought it down, pointing it at Brighid and
shouting, "Forward!" the goddess of fire lit him up like
a stump, just as she had promised, and I wondered why
people who believed in the next life were so anxious to
start living it instead of enjoying the one they had.

Fjalar cried out in agony and the Black Axes roared in
response, charging right through a wall of flame that
Brighid laid down between us. They went from orderly
to berserk in less than a second and didn't care how hot
she could make it for them; they were going to take a
swing at us no matter what.

Brighid unhitched that monstrous sword of hers and
swept aside the first few axes. I likewise was able to

parry a couple of swings with Fragarach, but the tide coming against us was too huge, and the third dwarf who missed kicked me in the right knee—the leg that was already uncertain thanks to Werner Drasche—and I went down. Axes clanged on my cuirass and failed to penetrate, but I still felt them like powerful punches to the ribs. I took a kick to the head, which rung the belfry pretty good, but Fragarach's enchantment allowed me to cut off at the knees the dwarf who did it, slicing clean through his armor. Brighid helped out by setting those immediately around me on fire—the pain distracted them long enough to delay a coup de grâce—and then she bowled through them, hooked her arm underneath one of mine to scoop me up, and turned on the fire jets. We only rose twenty feet or so and hovered, facing the army now unable to reach us, their front line on fire and rolling around in the snow to try to extinguish themselves. The back lines of Glass Knights fired a volley of fléchettes at us, some of which went wide or short. The darts that did hit us pinged harmlessly off our armor.

"Not my best diplomatic achievement," I told Brighid.

"They won't listen while they can choose the path of glorious battle," she replied.

"Ugh. Yeah. Maybe we can shut that path down."

"I don't wish to set them all on fire. Relations with Odin are going to be strained enough as it is."

"I don't want that either. We could immobilize them from here by binding their legs together, or whatever. I'll take the leather, you take the glass? Then we talk to Hugin and Munin."

"I like this plan."

"Then let's make it so," I said, with my best attempt at imitating Sir Patrick Stewart.

We both began to speak in Old Irish, crafting bindings that would force swaths of leather or glass to adhere to another one we targeted nearby. I started with the nearest fully bearded dwarf I could see in the second rank, zeroing in on the leather jerkin peeking through the joints of his armor and binding it to his neighbor. When they were yanked off balance by the binding and then collided, they fell down into the snow, with much cursing and confusion. I repeated the binding on two more nearby soldiers and made an ungainly grouping of four hopping-mad dwarfs, spitting at each other as they tried to win free. Then I moved on to repeat the process with four more and saw that Brighid was operating in much the same way, though a lot faster. The Glass Knights were covered all over in those runed glass tiles, whereas the leather on the dwarfs was a bit more difficult to pinpoint. It took a half hour or so, but we eventually had the entire army tied up into clusters that could still move if they cooperated but could certainly not fight. They were having some pretty epic tantrums about it too; I didn't think the spirit of cooperation was going to blossom anytime soon.

"Now," Brighid said, projecting her voice over the field as only the goddess of poetry could, "let us discuss how we can all go home alive after this."

She lowered us to the ground slowly, and it would have been awesome except that when I touched down, my right leg would not support my weight. Besides the gammy hamstring, my knee had been thrashed, so it was simply saying "nope" to helping me stay upright. Toppling over sideways did not make me look like a badass. Luckily, Brighid was commanding enough for the both of us.

Her helmet tilted back and she found the ravens circling above. "Hugin and Munin. Odin. Listen well, for I speak true." Her voice boomed in three registers. "We bear Asgard no ill will and regret the injuries and death sustained today. We acted to prevent war and save life rather than take it. We wish the Svartálfar to join us against Loki and Hel on the day that Ragnarok arrives. We believe they will play a pivotal role once they become our allies instead of a neutral third party. Bringing them to our side will require effort, but it is an effort we feel you should make, so that both they and the Æsir can continue to thrive."

Some jeers and epithets got hurled in our direction at that, but Brighid ignored them.

"Send an envoy—unarmed—to negotiate in good faith. I will guarantee safe conduct for both sides. Your army will remain here until I hear a reply. They will be released to return to Asgard once that envoy appears. That is all."

Hugin and Munin squawked and spiraled into the clouds, ascending up the root of Yggdrasil to return to Odin.

Brighid surveyed the army for potential threats, saw that they remained akimbo in the snow and supremely cheesed at us, and nodded in satisfaction before turning to check on me.

"How fare you, Druid?"

"Leg is pretty messed up, but I'll be able to limp out of here eventually. Working on it. Is Fjalar truly dead, or can we save him?"

She took in the charred remains of those she had set aflame; I could smell the cooked flesh and saw smoke rising from the corpses, but I had hope that perhaps he was merely unconscious. Brighid evaluated the bodies for a few seconds and shook her head. "Fire is unforgiving, and I did not hold back."

"Oh." I was sorry for that and wished Fjalar would have been more reasonable. Silence fell between us, except for the uncomfortable shifting of bodies in the army and the dark curses muttered at us from various quarters.

"Shall we go visit the Svartálfs while we wait?" I said.

"Sitting here in front of the army is getting awkward fast."

"Very well."

We flew back to the dark doors of Svartálfheim and called out that we had good news: The army had been halted and an envoy would arrive soon for talks.

"No one else need die today," Brighid said. "We can talk in peace of a more lasting accord." With her permission, I stood behind her right shoulder, kept my weight on my left leg, and surreptitiously leaned on her back for support. Soon the doors opened and the leaders of the Svartálfar reemerged. This time, they deigned to favor Brighid with a shallow bow, and she in turn did the same and removed her helmet. If I stopped leaning on Brighid to remove mine, I would fall over, so I kept my helmet on.

It was poetry after that. Brighid was much better at slinging words around than I was, and before long we had a pavilion set up outside with tables and chairs and hot drinks and nobody killing anybody else. I got to sit, Brighid melted some snow away so that I could put my bare foot down on the earth and draw some strained energy from Gaia to aid my healing, and then she employed that honey-throated voice of hers to convince Turid and Krókr that fighting against the hordes of Hel would be better for the Svartálfar in the long run than sitting it out—the logic being that it was quite possibly going to be the end of the world, and you didn't want that one to go the wrong way. She actually made them smile and laugh a couple of times, until the envoy from Asgard showed up an hour later.

It was not who we expected. Not that we expected anyone in particular, just that we did not expect that particular envoy. It was a man dressed entirely in gray with a beard like a cliff wall and a patch over one eye, with two ravens riding along on his shoulder: Odin himself. Everyone tried to be cool, but it's difficult not to sit up a bit straighter when Odin joins your party. Sort of like if you're relaxing with your friends and Neil deGrasse Tyson walks up, you suddenly want to talk about science: His arrival changes the subject. Two dark elves flanked him and one carried Gungnir, Odin's spear.

"I come in peace," Odin said right away, his head tilting toward the guard for a moment. "I gave up my weapon willingly."

Introductions were made all around. When attention fell on me, Odin's remaining eye narrowed but he said nothing. That was enough to communicate his displeasure with me, however.

"Excellent," Brighid said. "Before we begin, can we all agree that saving the world would be better than allowing Loki to torch Midgard and all the nine realms to bring Gaia under his and Hel's control?"

Everyone nodded or grunted assent, and Brighid beamed. "Good. That's a strong foundation to build upon. The fact that the leaders are here and we don't need to use go-betweens is also good. Let's proceed."

Hours of grievances and apologies followed, together with arguments and concessions and more than two trips into the trees to relieve bladders filled by hot spiced cocoa. I only mention those trips because they were perilous journeys for me, which I hopped at first and then gingerly limped through. At no point did we enter the doors of Svartálfheim.

Near the end I must have dozed off, lulled by the drone of carefully controlled voices, because Brighid had to shout me awake. "Siodhachan!"

"Eh? Wuzzah?"

"We are finished. I need your help unbinding the army."

"Oh, yeah? Hey, yeah! I hope they're not frozen to death. What did I miss?"

"Say your farewells and I will tell you on the way."

Odin accompanied us back to the army, and Brighid filled me in. The new accord between Asgard and Svartálfheim included trade agreements, remunerations for past trespasses, new diplomatic channels—and also a promise that no dark elves would accept a contract that would harm Granuaile, Owen, or me.

"Wow," I said, "that's impressive."

"And they will fight with us in Ragnarok," Odin added, "which is all I wanted anyway. This exercise served its purpose."

I nearly snarled but managed to merely grunt in response. Fjalar's death, all those other dwarfs set on fire, was an *exercise*? Including the crafting of that armor and those axes? That was a long and risky game to play, believing that you could maneuver someone into becoming your ally by threatening to exterminate them first.

It wouldn't have happened if Brighid and I had not become involved—which then made me wonder if she had been in collusion all along. Perhaps the Morrigan too. I would not put such scheming past any of them, even though it meant using Fjalar horribly and resulted in many other deaths besides. Would Fjalar still want to fight as one of the Einherjar, knowing that he'd been manipulated so? Would the Svartálfar wish to maintain their new alliance if they knew Odin had somehow tricked them into it?

It was all speculation, but I didn't ask for confirmation from either of them. Brighid was my ride home.

CHAPTER 13

Traveling to Cape Arkona is not as quick as much of my travel, since there are no bound trees on the island. I have to shift to the German mainland and take a ferry out to Rügen. But because Orlaith has been so patient and such a good hound, we stop at a sausage haus and order a sampling of their trade—bratwurst, knackwurst, and weisswurst.

Orlaith is happy to be petted by a couple of older women on the ferry and obligingly growls at a young man who wishes to use her as an excuse to flirt with me. My weapon, Scáthmhaide, can be mistaken for a fancy walking stick so that to some eyes I look like a hiker instead of a martial artist.

"Ach! Control your dog!" he says to me in accented English.

"My hound is quite controlled. You will notice that she growled instead of bit you. That means you should go away now."

He starts to berate me in German, an ugly sneer on his face. I don't need to listen, so I ask Orlaith to bark and lunge at him but not bite. He jumps back and leaves us alone after that, though he curses us from what he thinks is a safe distance. I smile and wave him goodbye. The older women return and pet Orlaith some more.

Rügen turns out to be a lovely place, with expansive

fields and rolling terrain. Orlaith and I stretch our legs and run across to the northeastern tip, passing hikers and campers and a shepherd with a small flock of sheep.

<Fluffy meat,> Orlaith comments.

The remains of Jaromarsburg rest precariously atop chalk cliffs that crumble into the sea a bit more every year. There are no handy signs telling me which way to go to find Świętowit, so I squat down, close my eyes, and reach out to the elemental of the region, which is associated with the lake plateau of the nearby mainland. It's called Mecklenburg.

//Greetings / Harmony / Land is beautiful// I send to the elemental, and he—I don't know why I'm assigning it a gender, but Mecklenburg just *feels* masculine—responds with joy.

//Greetings / Harmony / Welcome Fierce Druid//

I'm not sure how to proceed. I can hardly ask Mecklenburg if he saw a white horse go through here a thousand years ago. Elementals wouldn't notice what color a horse was. They do tend to notice gods, however, since gods often warp existence around them and bend the rules a bit. Their magic leaves traces and therefore can be tracked.

//Query: any gods here?//

//Sometimes. Not now//

//Query: gods with horse?//

//Sometimes//

//Query: near my position?//

//Below. In ground//

That is perplexing. Why is the horse in the ground? Maybe the horse is dead? Or else there is a space underneath Rügen. I ask Mecklenburg to show me, and through my tattoos it guides me to a spot a few hundred yards away from Jaromarsburg, in a churned-up field lying fallow for the winter, past a lighthouse. The ground opens up in a square, showing me a flight of stone steps leading down into darkness, and I shake my head from the déjà vu. "Nope, nope, nope! I'm not doing that again," I say aloud. I didn't need another encounter with a creepy trickster god in a subterranean chamber. Though this is somewhat different from that pit in India: These steps are permanent, and the chamber is already excavated. It's not an abandoned archaeological mystery but more of a secret underground lair, the entrance to which is disguised by a chunk of nondescript turf.

//Query: horse is down there?//

//Yes// Mecklenburg says.

//Query: which god visits horse?//

//Earth god Weles//

Oh. That would explain the location of the horse, at least. //Gratitude / Harmony / Will return later// I say, and urge Mecklenburg to close up the hole in the ground.

"Back to the ferry, Orlaith," I say. "Weles might not be down there now, but I don't want to face him alone if he comes back. We need backup."

<Atticus and Oberon?>

"No, I think they're busy doing something else. We need Perun. He would know best how to deal with Weles."

<I don't remember Perun.>

"He's friendly. Atticus told me he likes to play with hounds. Oberon wrestled with him."

<Did Oberon win?>

"They wrestled for fun and succeeded in having plenty of fun, so I think they both won."

<Best way to play,> Orlaith observes.

Perun is not difficult to find in Tír na nÓg. A couple of inquiries at the Fae Court and I'm told right where to go. He's with Flidais, of course, and I catch both of them partially hammered down by the river.

"Granuaile!" he says, all jubilant and hairy. He raises a bottle to the sky. "You know what time is it? Is time for vodka!"

"No, thank you," I say, and notice that the two of them are somewhat disheveled yet wearing blissful, post-coital grins. I thank fortune for not arriving much earlier or I might have caught them busy with each other. "I've come to talk to you about Weles," I explain, and his expression falters.

"Weles? What about Weles? Is dead. All my peoples dead now. Is only me and Flidais and vodka now. Have vodka. Here." He thrusts the bottle at me and I wave it away.

"No, no, he's not dead. That's what he wants you to think. He's working with Loki. He's the one who let Loki into the Slavic plane."

"What? Say this again. No: Explain." He drops the bottle, and his good cheer evaporates. The shadows underneath his brow darken, but little sparks dance in his eyes. The air begins to crackle and hum, and I realize that I am not wearing my fulgurite talisman that protects against lightning.

"All right, but easy with the electricity, okay? I'm not protected, and neither is my hound."

"Oh. Is easy fix. Here." He dips into a pouch at his belt and produces two new fulgurites, blessed by him to protect against lightning. "This way if I lose temper you no get hurt."

"Thanks." I wedge one of the fulgurites in Orlaith's collar and tell her not to scratch at it, since it's protection, then hold mine in my hand. Any skin contact will do. Safe from accidental strikes, I tell him what I pieced together with the Polish coven and that the white horse of Świętowit is hidden underground on the island of Rügen, visited on occasion by Weles. "I didn't want to go down there, since I know nothing about him."

"Is good you did not go," he says. "He would have traps there for certain. And snakes." A few stray fingers of lightning arc around his mane of hair, which is charged and standing out somewhat. His fists are clenched tightly, and I can tell he is barely maintaining his control.

"Snakes?"

"He like snakes very much. When I am eagle, I eat snakes very much. You know Weles is sometimes snake?"

"Uh—no. Are you saying you want to . . . eat him?"

"No. Am saying we are not friendly."

"Ah! That's a relief." Flidais chuckles at this, and Perun is distracted by it. The charged air dissipates and I'm grateful to Flidais for dispelling the tension, even if that was not her intention.

"Would you like me to show you where this white horse is being kept?"

"Yes. Let us go." He pats Flidais on the thigh and she shakes her head.

"I cannot go with you," she says. "I'm in charge while Brighid is away."

She does not appear to be in charge of anything except sprawling on the riverbank, and Perun guesses what I am thinking.

"Brighid and Atticus are in Svartálfheim," he says. "Flidais must be emergency person now."

I want to ask why Atticus would go to the land of the dark elves, but I refrain; I'll catch up with him later.

"Then it's you and me, Perun," I say.

<And me,> Orlaith adds.

Always, sweet hound, I tell her privately, giving her a scratch behind the ears. We move off a few paces so that Perun can say his farewells and get his weapon, but Flidais does briefly accompany us to earth, simply to shuttle Perun there—I can't bring Perun with me without another headspace, and I don't know him well enough anyway.

When we take the ferry to Rügen this time, nobody wants to pet Orlaith, despite her being just as adorable as before. I take a wild guess that the scowling thunder god holding an axe next to us has reduced our approach-ability. Perun wanted to fly at first, but I protested that Orlaith would not enjoy it.

"So," I say, "tell me what should I expect from Weles besides snakes. What does he look like?"

Perun sniffs, considers, then lifts a single buttock off the bench and farts without a shred of embarrassment. It is his first comment on Weles, perhaps, but then he elaborates: "When he is snake, he is big black snake. When he is man, he is still thin like snake. Tall. Long straight black hairs and beard, with droopy mustaches. Narrow face with cheekbones standing out. Sometimes he wear hat—no, is not right word. What is thing like crown but not crown, you wear in band around head, no top?"

"Maybe a circlet?"

"Yes, circlet! This is word I need. He has circlet with ram horns on it, and sometimes he wear this. Make peoples think horns grow on his head, but is lie. Is there to make peoples think he has many powers."

"Well, does he have many powers?"

"Yes."

"Can't blame him for his horny haberdashery, then."

"What is haber-dashing? I am not knowing this word." The rest of our ferry ride is pleasantly occupied with the rich history of haberdashers and their profession, and Perun adds "visit a London haberdasher" to his personal bucket list. But our faces set into grim lines once we hit land and lope across Rügen to the spot where Weles has hidden the white horse of Świętowit. I check with Mecklenburg to make sure Weles didn't show up while we were gone and he says no, the only god nearby is Perun. The turf parts for us, the staircase beckons, and Perun goes first, holding his axe out in front of him as he descends, perhaps thinking the axe will trigger any traps first and give him time to avoid them. But that makes little sense to me: If Weles is an earth god, he probably has deadfalls rigged or some kind of cave-in planned. You don't dodge cave-ins or obliterate them with lightning blasts.

"Perun? Hold on. Don't move."

"Okay. I am not moving."

The walls of the staircase are earth and chalk, solid for the moment but unstable, easily collapsed. I put my palm against the wall to see if it's "living" earth or cut rock by calling out to the elemental.

//Query: Mecklenburg? Can you sense me here?//

//Yes//

//Please cancel all earth magic on this island except my own bindings//

//Yes / Fierce Druid bindings only//

//Harmony / No earth-god magic here// I realize almost too late that the chambers themselves were probably created by magic and hastily add, //But keep shape of chambers//

//Harmony//

I give a small, pleased sigh and Perun looks up at me, a question in his expression. "I just canceled any earth magic on the island except mine," I explain.

"You can do this?"

"Yes. Atticus did it once to Bacchus. Certain gods work their miracles through the earth all the time and the earth allows it, but the wishes of Druids always take precedence, since we're actually bound to the earth and gods are more bound by faith."

"So his magical traps will not be working now?"

"Correct. But if he has strictly mechanical ones, those will still be operational."

"I am understanding. We go."

The light wanes to almost total darkness for a stretch, but a source of light grows below as we descend, along with a strange hum. When we reach the bottom of the stairs, we hear a click in the walls and some dust falls from above, but nothing else happens.

"I think we just triggered a trap," I say.

"And yet we still walk," Perun replies. "Is good."

"Yes."

The chamber at the bottom widens and is lined with shelves filled with glass cages. We can see them because there are Ecobulbs hung from the ceiling, powered by a generator somewhere that must be the source of the humming we hear. And inside those cages are many, many rats.

"What the hell is going on? Those aren't rigged to break on us, I hope?" I say.

"No, is not trap. Is food for *next* trap."

"What?"

"Listen. You hear it ahead?" Perun points to an arched passageway at the other end of the chamber, with a single dim light illuminating it. "Under hum you hear hissing."

"Oh. Yes, you mentioned there would be snakes."

"Rats are food for snakes."

"How thoughtful of Weles."

<Fun fact: Snakes are not very tasty,> Orlaith observes. <Probably because they eat rats.>

When did you eat a snake?

<Oberon and I found one in Colorado and tried it. We thought it was icky.>

We pad down the corridor toward the sounds of hissing, which is not typically a good survival strategy. After a short distance the corridor ends abruptly at a wide pit about thirty feet square and perhaps twenty feet deep. The bottom of the pit has helpfully been illuminated so we can see that the floor is completely covered in writhing snakes. It's much too broad to jump. There appears to be an extendable bridge mechanism on the far side, and on our side is a helpful length of chain dangling from the wall with an illustration beneath it showing a bridge over the pit.

Perun is about to pull on the chain when I stop him. "Whoa, wait. Why would Weles put a pit here and then help us to cross it?"

Perun drops his hand. "You are right. He would not do this. Is trap. We pull chain, we go into pit with many snake."

"Exactly. And I bet it's a mechanical trapdoor too. It won't require magic to work."

Perun considers the space, looks at Orlaith, then says, "Maybe I make wind and we fly across?" Orlaith is of course the trouble; Perun and I could shape-shift to winged forms and fly across with ease.

"I have a better idea," I tell him. "Let's make a real bridge we can depend on." I contact Mecklenburg again and ask him to span the pit for us with an earthen bridge three feet wide. After a brief wait, it begins to form on either side of the pit, until it meets in the middle. Elementals are awesome.

Snake pit successfully navigated. Another corridor waits on the other side, bends a bit, and the throbbing of generators becomes much louder. When we reach the end of the corridor there's a floor-to-ceiling iron gate, easily managed and unlocked, and the reason for the generators becomes obvious: We are at the edge of a large cavern and there are a ridiculous number of UV lights mounted on the ceiling, shining down on a broad pasture of lush turf. It's the finest underground grazing land I've ever seen—also the *only* underground grazing land I've ever seen. All of it built to house and hide the warhorse of Świętowit, a beautiful white stallion who has spotted us and is prancing around on the far side, shaking his head in agitation and snorting.

"Wow," I breathe. "You don't see something like this every day." It's a lot of trouble for a single horse. But that wouldn't matter to Loki: Knowing the best day to start Ragnarok would be priceless information to him. I wonder if he asks the question daily, weekly, or if he only asks when he thinks something has changed in his favor. Even if he doesn't appear daily, those generators have to be switched out, the snakes have to be fed, and the stone stable over to one side has to be mucked out every so often. We shouldn't linger here. Somebody has to be visiting this place regularly, and I begin thinking defensively in case they visit soon. "Perun, let's get over there to the stable," I say. "That horse looks pretty upset, and we need it to calm down if we're going to get it out of here."

"How will stables help?"

"I don't want to set up our operation here, where someone can come in behind us."

"What operations?"

"A quick one. You'll see." We jog over to the stable, the warhorse watching us from the far side of the pasture, and I ask Orlaith to hide inside the stable.

<Why hide?>

If someone comes in to mess with us, you will be our surprise counterattack, I say, though I truly just want her to be safe. *And I need you to guard my clothes and my staff, pretty please.*

She agrees and I begin to disrobe. Perun politely turns his back and says, "I think I understand operations now. You will be speaking horse to horse."

"You got it on the first guess. Wait here, please." He nods and I shape-shift to a chestnut mare, which I must confess is my favorite animal form. Running is so effortless, and I love the feeling of my mane and tail whipping in the wind—not that there is any wind in this cavern. Just a nervous, twitchy stallion. I figure if I approach him as a horse, he won't feel immediately threatened and will let me get close enough to make contact and soothe him before he charges at me.

He keeps bucking as I grow closer, however. The sudden appearance of another horse is not as calming as I had hoped. He is a smart horse who knows how to count, and there had not been two horses in this cavern until this very moment. He knows something odd is going on.

Gods below, he's magnificent. Milk-white hide and a coal-black mane. I switch my vision to the magical spectrum, examine his turbulent aura, and find the threads of his consciousness. I reach out with my own, bind them together, and send him feelings of peace and harmony and my unabashed admiration for him. He rears back at first, pawing at the air with his hooves, but when he returns all four legs to the earth, he snorts once and grows still, open to hearing—or feeling, or seeing— more. I send him visions of the sky above Rügen and an invitation to go there with me. He nods his head, and I also feel his great desire to go. He hates it down here. No sky. No other horses. He has been so very lonely. I respond with happiness at his decision to accompany me and am about to tell him to follow, when movement tears my attention away from him.

Someone is coming through the gate that leads to our exit. He is like a stick of charcoal, dressed all in black and topped with a drape of black hair. Only his forehead, cheeks, and nose are pale; all else is darkness. He glances at me and the horse of Świętowit, dismisses us, and then he spies Perun by the stable. His hands curl into fists, his jaw juts forward, and his teeth are bared in a snarl; Perun does the same when he sees the man in

black, who I suppose must be Weles. It's glaringly obvious that they hate each other.

Perun shouts a challenge at him and I expect to hear
Russian, but it's something older, because these gods are
much older than that language. But I do recognize the
name Świętowit, and maybe a few others; Perun is most
likely demanding to know where they are. I don't understand anything that Weles says in return. His voice is full
of spite, though—he probably told Perun off in the rud-
est possible terms—and that looks like the end of diplo-
macy. What happens next is a bit comical: Perun lifts his
axe and tries to summon lightning, but that's a non-
starter underground. Weles spreads his hands to either
side, palms up, fingers clutching as if he's holding an
invisible goblet in each, and raises them up in dramatic
gesture. When there's no response to this, he blinks and
looks down at the grass, bewildered that nothing has
happened. No earth magic for him, no thunder for
Perun. I'm thinking they're going to have to duke it out
with good ol'-fashioned fisticuffs, but they surprise me
and shape-shift instead. Perun tosses down his axe and
takes wing as the biggest damn eagle I've ever seen, while
Weles flops, twitches, stretches, and becomes a horror-
show serpent, a truly gargantuan snake that could swallow me whole as a horse. Perun screeches and the snake
hisses, and it makes me shudder.

<Orlaith,> I say, my mental voice slightly changed by
my animal form, <don't come out. Stay hidden and
guard my stuff. I'll be there in a minute.>

<Okay,> she says.

I recommend to the warhorse that he stay where he is,
and then I circle around the edge of the pasture toward
the stable. The serpent doesn't care: He only has eyes for
Perun, who's circling above, gaining speed, and looking
for an opportunity to dive. The snake coils itself to reduce the target area, forcing the eagle to go through the

fangs if it wants to get to the body. It bobs and weaves its head, trying not to lose Perun in the glare of the UV lights, but considering the trouble I'm having keeping track of him, I imagine that it's difficult.

When I'm halfway to the stable, Perun attacks, and it's so fast that I can't track what happened exactly—just that the snake is bleeding and there are some feathers left behind afterward. No clear advantage to either.

At the entrance to the stable I change back to my human shape, so that my hooves won't clop loudly on the floor and draw the snake's attention. And as soon as I do, I think maybe I *should* be drawing the snake's attention, to give Perun a free shot. Putting most of my body behind the stable entrance, I simply peek my head out and shout, "Weles!"

The snake's head swings around and spies me. It rears back, and I scramble away from the door just as the massive head plunges through, breaking the frame with the power of its strike and snapping its jaws closed on air. And then just as quickly the head is gone, hissing as Perun takes advantage of my distraction and attacks from above.

<Granuaile! Are you okay?>

Yes, I'm all right. But I need Scáthmhaide. I see it resting next to my folded clothes and snatch it up, casting the binding that will turn me invisible.

<I didn't know snakes were allowed to get that big.>

Me either. Wait here, please.

Sneaking back to the door and peeking around the shattered frame, I realize that while I might be invisible, the snake can still doubtless taste me in the air. It knows I'm around, but its attention is back on the ceiling, keeping track of Perun once more. There's more blood than there was before. I can see gashes in the snake's flesh where Perun's talons or maybe his beak did some damage. But I figure that with Scáthmhaide and an assist from Gaia, I can deliver some serious punishment and give Perun one more chance. There's no question in my mind that I'm doing the right thing: Any friend of Loki's is an enemy of mine. So I bound forward, leap up and spin to increase the force, then bring down Scáthmhaide with every ounce of power I can deliver on top of the serpent's uppermost coil. I hear the spine snap and the impact travels up my arms, and there will be no graceful landing for me. It takes all I have simply to hang on to my staff.

The snake makes a sort of gurgling hiss instead of a cry of pain. Then the light disappears, I'm punched in the gut and the back, and the light returns, all before I hit the ground. Once I'm there, flat on my ass, the agony begins. Not from the fall, but from the two huge fangs that punctured my torso when the snake lashed out on instinct. The left half of its mouth caught my left half; bottom fang into my guts, top fang into my back. There was venom in that bite, which hits a second later, burning like acid in my veins and throwing my muscles into convulsions. I gasp and struggle to reach the cool serenity of a headspace where I can focus on directing my healing while the other headspace suffers. Atticus told me it was a survival skill and had all these distracting tests during my training to make sure I could access the serenity while the chaos raged elsewhere, but there is no distraction quite like genuine, fiery pain. It demands that you give it your full attention and resists being shut out. So it takes several false starts and five to seven precious seconds before I can create that separation in my mind and let one headspace convulse while the other coolly deals with the internal bleeding and breaking down the toxins. And during those few seconds, while I gasp for air on the ground, my head turns to the left, I see the giant snake head of Weles slam to the ground right in front of me, and directly below its jaws, at the top of what could be considered one enormous neck, are a pair of eagle talons. Perun got him because of me, which, honestly, helps me slip into the headspace I need. I can't talk, since everything is either pain or the healing of it, and that worries Orlaith something awful, because she's suddenly there and licking my face and trying to say things that I can't spare the concentration to answer if I want to live.

I really shouldn't be picking fights with any more gods. I managed to do some serious damage to Loki recently but only because conditions were perfect: He'd been overconfident and attacked me where I had placed wards against his fire. If he had caught me anywhere outside the fire wards, or if he had brought any other weapons—like Fuilteach, the whirling blade he'd stolen from me, or the Lost Arrows of Vayu—he might have ended me. His simple failure to respect me as an adversary made him vulnerable, and he wouldn't make the same mistake again. It strikes me that the holes in my body and the poison in my blood are a result of the same kind of arrogance: My Druidic powers, while impressive, do not truly put me in the same weight class as gods. And neither do Atticus's. He finds a weakness, surprises them, and gets help. Going toe-to-toe will not work. Had Weles not been distracted by Perun, I don't think I ever would have gotten close to harming him, even with invisibility. And had Perun not finished Weles off, I surely would not have this slim opportunity to heal. He would have struck again and maybe even swallowed me whole.

The venom of Weles is a nasty combination of a fasciculin and a cardiotoxin. The latter is easiest to take care of; as the toxin tries to bond to the muscle of my heart tissue, I can break it down before it depolarizes the cells and prevents contraction. The fasciculin is much worse. It's causing involuntary contractions throughout my entire body, leading to painful spasms and twitching. During my apprenticeship, Atticus gave me extensive training in poisons and their chemistry, including snake venom, so that I would know where to focus my attention when and if I found myself poisoned. The fasciculin attacks a certain kind of neuron that uses acetylcholine as a transmitter of signals. It annihilates acetylcholinesterase, which functionally tells muscles to stop contracting, thereby causing those involuntary contractions. Can't fight back when your muscles won't obey you. It also causes more agony than you'd think something like that should. To combat it and restore voluntary function, I have to not only break down the toxin but rebuild acetylcholinesterase. And beyond the venom, there's the matter of two rather large puncture wounds, with significant tissue damage and bleeding.

In my quiet headspace I work on my body chemistry to save my life, while in the loud, painful arena of my other headspace I notice that Perun, as an eagle, really does eat snakes. His beak plunges repeatedly into the neck of Weles and rips out chunks of flesh and viscera, making sure that his old enemy bleeds out. He spits out some of the chunks but swallows others. The large coil of the snake doesn't move at all past the point where I broke the spine; only the top third twitches and struggles in vain to win free. It is chilling to watch the death of a god in real time at the hands—or, rather, the talons and beak—of another god.

The eagle is not unscathed, I notice. There are chunks of feathers missing, bare patches in its plumage. It has been bitten, or at least scratched, by those fangs but, curiously, is not suffering the same effects of the toxin that I am. Perhaps Perun is immune.

The great serpent's eyes go dull and the twitching ceases, while I continue to struggle on to survive. Perun steps off the snake and watches it for a full minute to make sure that it really is dead. Then he shifts back to his human form, summons his axe to his hand, and hacks away at the neck until it's severed completely, cementing the death of Weles. Only then does he look up and notice my critical condition.

"Granuaile!" he says, crossing to me and kneeling by my side, taking in my spasms and the hole underneath my ribs. "Oh, no. Is not good. But fight this! Do not die! I am owing you much. You help me defeat Weles." He stretches out fingers toward the hole in my gut and then shrinks back. "Am not healing god. Cannot help you but am wishing I could."

I cannot help him either, though he appears not to notice his bleeding puncture wounds, now clearly visible on his human form. I envy his immunity to the venom.

My limbs still shudder with involuntary spasms, but I am slowly turning the tide, and some of the violence, some of the pain, is receding. Knowing that it will at least not get any worse, I spare a few minutes to deal with internal bleeding. Perun adjusts himself so that he's in a lotus position rather than kneeling and mutters something about healing with me. He closes his eyes and I do the same. It's helpful, I find: Less incoming stimulus equals more attention that I can devote to righting the ship. And I spare a thought for Orlaith, who's still very worried.

I am not okay but I am healing, sweet hound. Need all my faculties for that. Please be patient with me.

<Okay! I will guard you. Love Granuaile.>

Love you too.

Time slips by after that and I slowly improve, until my eyes snap open at a thought.

"Loki's mark!" I croak, and then cough at the effort of speaking aloud. The coughs send spears of lightning through my torso.

"What? Loki?" Perun says, and then, more alarmed, "Where?"

I pause to catch my breath and then say in a soft voice, "Weles probably has Loki's mark on him somewhere. A circular brand of runes. Hides him from the sight of all but Loki. So Loki probably knows Weles is dead. He might come to investigate."

Perun's eyes go wide. "Is very bad news!"

"And I bet the horse of Świętowit will have the same mark on him. When we move him, Loki will know. Can you check?"

"Yes. I can do this."

Perun unfolds himself from the ground and disappears from my sight for a while. My limbs are not shaking as much anymore and I'm making progress against the toxin. Mecklenburg is helping me quite a bit, giving me his energy, and I thank him for his help.

//Gratitude for your strength// I send to him in my Latin headspace.

//Harmony// Mecklenburg says. //Fierce Druid must be well//

And it's then that the uncertainty and fear fall away and I know I *will* be well, eventually. And it's also at that moment that I appreciate the time it took me to get to this place. Had I not trained in languages and cultivated different headspaces over those twelve long years, I most certainly would have succumbed to the poison. Binding to the earth is useless without the knowledge and training to use it properly. When you're dealing with years two through ten you think, holy *hells,* this is a slog—I certainly thought that on more than one occasion—but those ancient Druids knew how to train and discipline a mind. All of that training was saving my life now.

Perun returns to inform me that the horse indeed has a small round brand on his flank. "We should be leaving," he says.

"I can't move yet," I tell him, and then explain that while prudence dictates that we should worry somewhat, we may have no cause. Loki is no more a god of healing than Perun is, and I wounded him severely when we last met not long ago.

"When can you be moving?" Perun asks.

"Soon, I hope. I don't want to stay here any longer than necessary."

"What if I carry you out?"

I blink. That possibility had not occurred to me. Perun would certainly have no trouble slinging me over his shoulder like a sack of potatoes. But I might suffer additional injury if he did so, and I'd be cut off from the earth.

"Maybe let me lean on you and get dragged out upright? I need to keep my right heel in contact with the earth."

"Yes. We do this."

"But . . . the horse."

Perun looks across the pasture at the horse, which has now pressed itself against the far wall, hoping to remain unnoticed.

"Oh. Yes. We need horse, but is afraid."

"Drag me a bit closer?" I ask. "I can talk to it, after a fashion."

With many grunts and sharp gasps on my part, I'm lifted to my feet and manage a half walk, half shamble with Perun's help toward the white horse of Świętowit. My occasional twitches and convulsions make the progress difficult and emphasize that we are both, as a result of our shape-shifting, very nude. We'll have to remember to get dressed before going upstairs.

I keep trying to reach out with my consciousness to the horse until we finally make contact.

Hello, I tell him. Or, anyway, I send him greetings. I hope my words translate into meaning in his mind somehow. We may not yet be at that level of understanding, but my patience at this point is strained, since I have so much else to worry about. *I am the chestnut mare. Human now. I take both forms. Are you ready to greet the sky once more?*

The stallion tosses his head and snorts. Not really a yes—he's still spooked. He will need some convincing, and there won't be a way to hurry through that. I sigh and force myself to take the time to do it right.

I am Granuaile. Do you have a name?

His reply is that, long ago, some humans used to call him Miłosz.

Miłosz, I would like to take you to a group of women who will protect you from the god who branded you.

The thought of the god who branded him upsets Miłosz quite a bit. He whinnies, rears up, and then bucks around.

Let us go together. We will run there under the sky. There will be apples and oats.

Apples appear to be a pleasant thought, and he settles down. I get a question from him next and an image of a grotesque four-headed man that I can only assume must be Świętowit.

No, Świętowit won't be there. We are looking for him too. We would like to reunite you. Do you know where we might find him?

Miłosz has no idea, but he walks toward us and I feel or sense the moment when he recognizes Perun as a friend of Świętowit. That reassures him and he is ready to leave with us.

I'm not positive that the Sisters of the Three Auroras will be able to withstand a concerted effort by Loki to take Miłosz back, but I do know that they won't make it easy for him and could quite possibly bring him under their power again. Getting the horse there while Loki is still wounded—and while I'm still wounded—will be the trick.

We return to the stable area and get dressed. I have to lean against the wall to put on my jeans; I'm not yet steady enough on one leg to manage it without support. Pulling on my shirt is excruciating, considering the wounds in my back and gut; the skin, ragged and oozing blood, is at least closed up at the dermis level, and the internal bleeding is all right for now, but the tissue damage will take much longer to deal with. Orlaith volunteers to carry Scáthmhaide in her mouth until we're up top, and I thank her.

I try walking by myself to the exit, but it's slow, erratic progress, since I'm never sure when my legs will obey me or decide to contract or extend on their own. I fall down twice, which is not fun, but I'm so relieved that I can walk at all that I insist on struggling the whole way to the bridge. There I ask Perun if I can hitch a ride on his back until we get to the other side. I don't trust my legs enough to risk them over a snake pit.

As we walk away on the other side, I ask Mecklenburg to raise the floor of the pit so that it functionally ceases to exist as a pit and the snakes will have a chance to get out. Likewise, we open all the rat cages as we leave, allowing them to escape or not as they wish. Perun gives me another piggyback ride up the stairs so that I don't tumble down them, and when we're finally out of there and standing on the turf of Rügen under the afternoon sun, we all smile. Or, at least, Miłosz and Orlaith demonstrate the equivalent of happiness by prancing around.

We walk to the ferry, and by the end of that walk I'm feeling confident with my muscle control. The toxin's been nullified and I have my motor control back. I still have plenty of work to do on my torso, but at least it's not preventing me from being mobile.

I charge up the silver reservoir of Scáthmhaide to continue healing during the ferry ride, and we get some looks boarding with a horse and hound—or maybe its concern over my bloody shirt—but no one gives us any trouble.

The sun has almost set when we reach the mainland and a figure separates from the shadows. Despite the chill he's bare-chested, which draws plenty of stares. The fact that he's in phenomenal shape and has a wide golden belt supporting bright red pants of a flowing material probably has something to do with it too. Or maybe it's the huge, club-like weapon he has slung over his shoulder. His skin is a dark, rich brown and his hair is cut close against his skull, as if perhaps he had shaved it a couple of weeks ago and hadn't kept up with it. Everyone's looking at him, but he's looking right back at us as we disembark.

"Perun," he says, nodding once to him. "And you must be Granuaile." His voice is a thrumming bass, and I can't place his accent but I love it.

"I'm sorry, have we met before? I think I would remember."

Brilliant teeth flash at me. "We have not met. If you were to ask Odin, he would say I am here at his request. But in truth I do not care what Odin wants. I am here because I wished to meet you. I am Shango."

"Shango? The Orisha? God of thunder?"

Lightning dances in his eyes, just as it does in Perun's every so often, and he nods at me with a tight grin. "The very same."

"Why did you want to meet me?"

"I have heard you delivered a long-overdue beating to Loki. I would like to hear the story from your own lips. And Odin tells me that this horse is rather important to Loki. You have some distance to travel to his new home, and there's a chance that Loki might show up along the way. I hope you will allow me to accompany you. If Perun and I are both with you, it may serve as a deterrent, and, failing that, I would be honored to fight him by your side."

Oh, damn. I really like to listen to him talk. I want to take him to dinner and just have him read the menu to me. And he's so polite.

"I see. And why did Odin ask you to meet me?"

"He does not want Loki to have this horse any more than you do."

"His name is Miłosz. And this is my hound, Orlaith."

He makes eye contact with both and greets them properly, calling them by name. Lots of people would not pay them that respect, and he rises another couple of notches in my regard.

"I'd be delighted for you to join us," I tell him. "Though I hope to hear more about you as well."

"We will be running all through the night, yes? Plenty of time."

It will be my second run across Poland, although we'll be crossing the northern half and from west to east rather than east to west, but at least it won't lack for sterling conversation. And every step will get me closer to the time when I can address the real reason I became a Druid. My stepfather has lurked in my mind like dishes left over from a dinner no one enjoyed and no one wants to clear away. A divination cloak will finally allow me to attend to that chore in privacy. I think it's long past time I cleaned house.

chapter 14

When Brighid and I returned to the Fae Court in Tír na nÓg—she looking regal and I looking every bit as injured as I was—we had a surprise delegation of yewmen waiting for us. It was a large one: a hundred or more. They're creepy things, as one might expect from creatures spawned by the Morrigan, and devoid of any sense of humor or indeed most human emotions except for greed and bloodlust. They were highly effective mercenaries against the vampires—they had no blood to suck and could not be charmed, and bullets that might be fired at them by thralls were mere annoyances. They were perfect vampire hunters, actually, except for the high price tag on their services.

They had come to inform me that I had overdue bills to pay. The yewmen didn't have any vocal cords, however, so they had to communicate via a spokesfaery. They must have written down in advance what they wished to say. Or used sign language or played charades. I really didn't know.

"We have staked and beheaded many vampires for you, Druid," their spokesfaery said in answer to my greeting. Her high, reedy voice, similar to a hamster on helium, didn't match the grim visages of the yewmen. "And at first you paid through Goibhniu. But now Goibhniu is dead. We have not been paid the bounty on six hundred and eighty-three vampires. We will not kill any more until you pay in full."

"I, uh, yyyyyeah. About that. The vampires have managed to degrade my ability to pay."

The faery repeated, "We will not kill any more until you pay in full." She must have exhausted her scripted speeches.

"Got it." I gave them a thumbs-up. "I'll work on that. When I have the money, who should I contact?"

"Me," Brighid said, injecting herself into the conversation. "You will pay me." She looked at the yewmen. "I will be his guarantor. I expect that will be acceptable."

"Brighid, you don't need to do that, I haven't asked—"

"I am volunteering freely and expecting no favors in return, Siodhachan. It's done."

I nodded acknowledgment, realizing that I'd have to find myself a lucrative job very soon. I'd never been much of a get-rich-quick sort of guy; a long life had allowed me the luxury of getting rich slowly through investments. I could raid the store of rare books I had buried years ago by the Salt River in Arizona as a temporary solution. Auction off a few of those and I could live comfortably for a while and maybe pay down a fraction of the debt I owed them. But even if I sold everything—a troublesome prospect since some of them were genuinely dangerous tomes—I doubted I would be able to pay their bill in full.

Since lingering would only expose me to the stares of unpaid mercenaries, I took my leave and shifted back to Flagstaff outside Sam and Ty's house, wondering how I could possibly keep the war going in the short term. The Hammers of God were a welcome addition to the cause but not nearly as efficient as the yewmen. They would not be able to ignore the bullets of thralls, for example, who protected older vampires during the daytime. And the vampires could replenish their numbers faster than we could slay them by turning new victims. Without a much greater advantage, it would be a war of attrition that we had little hope of winning.

Oberon was stretched out in the grass near the house and saw me shift in. He bounded over to see me, excited to share some news. <Atticus, guess what? I heard Sam and Ty talking about the citrus air freshener Hal keeps in his car, and they think it's stinky too!>

"Sweet vindication, eh?" I said, petting him on the neck.

<Yeah. Hey, your face looks like you're trapped at an emo concert. What's wrong?> Oberon asked.

"It's a math problem," I replied, leaving out the exhaustion and the beating I'd suffered.

<Oh. I can't help with that. If you need something peed on, though, or a cat's day ruined, I'm your hound. Or maybe you have a sausage on you that you'd like to get rid of?>

"No, sorry. I'm worried that there's no solution to the vampire problem. There are many more of them than there are of us. Thousands more."

<Thousands is more than millions, right?>

"No, it's the other way around."

<Well, are they *all* mad at you or is it just the one guy you told me about—Theo Phillip?>

"You mean Theophilus?"

<That's the one. It's just him who's really after you, right? But the other vampires all do what he says. So what if you challenge him to a duel, like Julie d'Aubigny would? Then when you defeat him you can tell all the other vampires to drop dead, heh heh.>

"That's . . . actually a good point." I hadn't heard of any specific vampires who wished to end the Druids other than Theophilus. If I could eliminate him—which was the endgame anyway—perhaps the rest of the vampires would redirect their attention to internal power struggles and leave the world's three Druids alone.

<Of course it is! We don't have to walk into Mordor. We can hop on the eagles and fly directly to Mount Doom!>

"The question is how I get to the eagles—or, rather, take the obvious shortcut you're implying. I don't even know where he is, and since he's technically dead I can't target him with divination. I know he must be moving around, and I figured he'd eventually come after me in person when he felt threatened enough. I was hoping the yewmen would either get lucky or goad him into the open, but that's not going to happen now."

<Well, who might know where to find him?>

"Maybe Leif does. I need a phone." Hal had given me Leif's number, but I had entered it into my phone in Toronto rather than memorize it, and that phone was still there, left behind when Owen kidnapped me from my hospital bed. I could call Hal again, however. "Come on, Oberon. Let's go inside. Your advice was worthy of a snack."

<Yes! You know, Atticus, I've been thinking that I should have a surname, and now that you bring it up, I think Snackworthy would be an honorable family name for a hound. What do you think?>

"Oberon Snackworthy, eh?"

<It sounds noble, doesn't it?> When I didn't answer right away, he said, <What? Is it too much?>

I knocked on the door before entering and shouted a greeting into the house, announcing myself.

"Yeah! Come on in!" a voice called, and Ty appeared shortly afterward. He was about to cook up a lunch of bison burgers, so that would serve instead of a snack for Oberon, and he loaned me his phone so that I could call Hal. But in looking through his contacts under *H*, I saw *Helgarson* there.

"Ty, you know Leif Helgarson?"

"Yeah. Not well, more like acquaintances. He was the vampire boss of Arizona, so he knew all the pack leaders and seconds. As a courtesy, he'd call to inform us when he was moving through our territory."

"Is this number for him current?"

"Should be. Updated it when Hal was here and you called."

"Fantastic." The burgers were already in the pan and frying up by the time I got a call placed to my former attorney. He picked up on the second ring, which told me he was probably in the other hemisphere at the moment—where it was nighttime. His dry, cultured voice sounded amused.

"Hello, Ty," he said, responding to the caller ID on his phone.

"This isn't Ty. It's Atticus."

"Ah, my favorite Druid. What a pleasure to hear from you."

I was in no mood to exchange pleasant banter with him and could no longer conceive of a time when I would be. "Where are you now, Leif?"

"Why do you ask? Is it time to relieve me of the burden of undeath?"

"Not yet. More interested in whether you are with Theophilus."

"Oh, no, I am cast out now. A Lucifer in the veritable heaven of vampirism."

"Excessive pride led to the original fall, I believe. That sounds about right. I hope it wasn't anything I did."

"It was, but I assure you that I am content with my place. I'm still on the coast of Normandy, near where we last met, sipping from the wine-infused blood of the French. I like to drink from the people who drink pinot noirs best. Delicious bouquet."

"I'm happy for you. But since you are so content and

unfettered by obligation, you should have no problem telling me where to find Theophilus."

"Only the problem of uncertainty. He does not keep me apprised of his movements now that I am out of favor."

"Give me a guess, or tell me who can point me to him."

"I am truly severed from reliable associates, alas. My best guess is that you will find him in Prague at the moment."

"Big city, Leif. Where in Prague?"

"The Grand Hotel Bohemia is his favorite. Heavy curtains on the windows and scrupulous attention to guest privacy."

"This had better not be a setup, Leif."

"It is, as I said, only a guess. Act on it or not, as your conscience dictates."

Oh, I would act on it, all right. I'd leave Fragarach with Ty and Sam and take the new stake with me and act on it with gusto.

"Enjoy your pinot blood," I said, and ended the call with my thumb.

CHAPTER 15

It's been too long since I've had any sleep. Greta wouldn't let me until she was sure I'd handled the concussion, so it's dark by the time me vision and thoughts clear up. She takes me to one o' those hospitals like Siodhachan was in and runs me through all these machines that can take pictures o' your insides without cutting through the outside. By that time I'd had enough help from Gaia to set me brain right, so the doctor says, nope, Mr. Kennedy is not concussed, but that left shoulder is a mite dodgy, innit?

He introduces himself as Dr. Sudarga, and he smells like he's fond of vanilla soap. Greta tells me later that his name indicates he's from a place called Indonesia, or anyway his family was generations ago. He shows me X-rays and points out all the fractures and muscle tears and whatnot, and I think it's pretty helpful. Seeing the image gives me focus on what to fix, and that will make me healing more efficient.

"Great," I says. "I'll get right on that."

"I beg your pardon? How are you getting on it?"

Apparently I've said the wrong fecking thing, and Greta hurries to explain. "He means he'll rest and follow your instructions to the letter."

"Not if it includes taking drugs," I says, and Greta sighs and puts her face in her hand. I get the idea that

I'm supposed to do whatever Dr. Sudarga says. His eyes shift back and forth between me and Greta.

"If you don't want any pain meds, that's of course your decision," he says, "but we really need to immobilize that shoulder."

"Try it and I'll immobilize you, lad."

"Owen!" Greta exclaims.

"What? We don't need instructions or anything else." I do understand that I've been rude somehow, so I turn to the doctor and try to let him down easy. "Dr. Sudarga, thank ye kindly for showing me that picture of me bones, but I don't want to take up any more of your time. All I want now is a shot of whiskey and a bed."

"If we don't immobilize that shoulder, your muscles might not reattach correctly and you could be looking at permanent damage. It's likely you'll need surgery."

"It's not likely at all. I told you I'm on it and it'll heal up just fine."

He blinks and looks at Greta. "If he leaves without treatment, I'm not responsible."

This is such an obvious statement that I don't know why he wastes breath on it.

"May harmony find ye," I says, and I leave the room. I hear Greta apologizing to him, which I don't think is necessary, and I get a fine long lecture afterward about how strange behavior like that is going to get written down and remembered and maybe invite official scrutiny. The better thing to do would have been to let him put me in a sling and then take it off as soon as we left.

"If we never go see a doctor again, then we don't have to pretend like that," I says. "Look, it's fecking dawn already. We were there all night to find out that I'm not concussed and my shoulder's rubbish, which I already knew when I went in."

"I wanted to confirm your head was all right, and that was the only way to do it. The Tempe Pack has a doctor in it and he knows about our unusual healing. With everyone else we have to make allowances."

"Maybe they can *allow* me to take care of meself," I grumble.

"So ornery! If you hadn't already had your ass kicked, I'd kick it for you."

"I know. Sorry, love. I'm just worried about Fand, and I want to see if I can find out where that troll came from."

"You have the apprentices to teach this morning."

"Aye, but I don't think it's safe to roam around the property yet until I shut down that troll's path to me Grove. Will ye take a walk with me into the woods to look for it after I focus a bit on me shoulder?"

"Sure."

Once we're back at the house I take time to reconnect with the earth, bind those tiny fractures together, and make sure the muscles are attached properly. They'll need time to rebuild before I can use the arm, but once I'm satisfied that the foundation is set, I use that trick Siodhachan taught me to ease the pain and let the healing continue on its own as I walk. I slip me knuckles on as a precaution. No telling what we might find up there in the ponderosa pines.

We don't have many evergreens in Ireland, and the smell is still something new to me nose. I like this forest and the crunch of the needles underfoot, the skittering noise of a kicked pinecone, and the chattering of squirrels. Greta's walking on me right side, her breath steaming the air, and it's a bracing winter morn—or near enough. It'll be solstice before we know it. She grins at me and feels lovey enough to grab me hand and squeeze it.

"Feeling better?" she asks.

"A bit," I have to admit. "Trees are always the cure for your modern bollocks."

"How do we find where the troll arrived?"

"We can either track it by smell, because by all the drunken gods that lad had a powerful scent, or I might get lucky and be able to spot the path in the magical spectrum."

"Smell would probably be faster," she says.

"Aye. When we find where the trail ends, that's where he emerged, and then I can either untether the tree or figure how to destroy the Old Way."

"How are they different?"

"Eh. Kind of like the difference between a private and a public road. Only Druids can use tethered trees freely, because we're bound to Gaia. Lesser Fae can use some of them but have trouble bringing other people along. Old Ways, though, built by the Tuatha Dé Danann, are like your highways. Anyone can travel them, no magical ability required except maybe having some way to see the path. That's what I think we're looking for. Trolls can't use the tethers to Tír na nÓg unless a Druid shifts with them. Good thing too. Last thing we need are trolls swinging their cocks all around the world."

"Well, you can't follow a scent trail the way you are, and if you shape-shift you're liable to mess up your shoulder even worse, aren't you? So that means I should probably play the bloodhound." She sheds her jacket and drops it to the forest floor.

"What? No, ye don't have to go through that. I'll shape-shift and it'll be fine. I'll walk on three legs, keep healing and everything."

Greta spins in a circle, scanning the area. "It's no trouble, Owen. Look, we're already deep enough into the trees that no one from the house will see anything." Her hands cross over her stomach, grab the bottom of her shirt, and pull it over her head in a fluid motion.

"I don't give a loud juicy shite if anyone sees ye." I begin to unbutton my shirt as fast as I can with one hand. "I don't want ye to have to go through the pain of the shift when ye don't have to."

"That's sweet, Owen," she says, tossing her shirt to the ground on top of her jacket and reaching for the fly of her jeans, "but I stopped fearing the pain a long time ago. It can't be avoided, so I just accept it as part of my day."

"But this *can* be avoided, Greta. I told ye I'd do it—"

"No. Shh!" She puts a finger to her lips and then points uphill, her eyes focused on something over me left shoulder. I turn and see a blue-skinned troll stepping from behind a pine onto the hill. He hasn't seen us yet; he's motioning to someone unseen, who becomes seen shortly thereafter: another troll, this one with brown leathery skin, stepping from behind a tree that's not wide enough to hide their bulk. It's the anchored end point of an Old Way. They're coming through from one of the Irish planes.

I start tearing at my clothes now. "Fecking stew me bollocks in the queen's own cup o' tea, the bastard had friends! I'll keep 'em busy while you're making the change," I say, since her shift takes much longer than mine. Two more trolls step through. "And if you can call anyone else to help through your pack link, we could probably use it."

She nods and continues undressing. As soon as I'm free of me clothes, I shift to a bear and charge up the knuckles. Greta's bones start to slide and pop, and that draws the trolls' attention. There are six of them bunched together now, and I roar as I head uphill to face them in an awkward three-legged lope. Two of them have actual weapons, and the other four scurry about to find some—which means they pull up trees. One wraps his arms around the tree anchoring the Old Way, and another slaps him in the back of the head before he can uproot it. "No, not that one! We need it!"

"Urgh. Too big anyway," he says, and by that time I am closing fast on the first blue troll. Unlike the bog troll from yesterday, he has his package securely wrapped, bless him, but has instead decided to adorn himself with the skulls of his smaller victims and the teeth of larger ones. These are strung on ropes about his neck, and so he makes hollow clacking noises when he moves. All about showing off, this one. Has a fancy club that looks carved instead of simply pulled out of the earth. I watch him hold it over his shoulder, wait for the swing, and then, when it comes around to clock me, I rear up and meet it with me brass-coated claws. They punch through the wood and shatter it into splinters, leaving the troll with a handful of toothpicks but no injuries. The leather-brown troll steps in and aims a kick at me from the left side, and of course he tags me in the lame shoulder and sends me tumbling across the hill in a new explosion of pain that pierces right through me nerve blocks and tears apart all the work I'd done to bind it together. Damn but trolls are unfairly strong. I can almost hear Dr. Sudarga saying, "I *told* you we should have immobilized it."

It would be smarter to fight in camouflage now, but Greta's not finished shifting yet. She's yelping and howling through the change, and a few of the trolls are wondering what that's all about—if they were released from Time Islands, like me, they wouldn't know anything about werewolves. They might be thinking she's a wounded animal right now—which I suppose she is—instead of an imminent threat. I don't want them paying too much attention to her, so I have to remain both visible and annoying. I lumber up on me three legs, charge back toward the blue lad, and, with an assist from Gaia, leap up far higher than should be possible—a trick that finally gets Greta to stop calling me Teddy Bear and calling me Air Bear instead. Blue Bones can't get out from underneath, and he throws up a forearm to block me attack. The brass claws shear right through his arm, rake down his chest, rip apart his skull necklaces, and then dig into his guts, pulling some of them out. He worries about putting them back in with his remaining hand after that, and I don't have to worry about him. I have five other trolls to worry about, because I have secured their undivided attention. Leather Lad has a real club; the other four have saplings. The guys with actual trees have to slam overhead if they want to hit me; they can't swing in an arc to catch me, because other trees get in the way. I can dodge them. It's Leather Lad I have to watch for. He's got a club with spikes on it, and if he connects I'll have to go to that fecking hospital again.

He moves forward, growling, and I hobble in reverse, growling back. He lunges and swings the club in a long, sweeping arc, and I have to leap away and fall on me right side to dodge it, though it still clips me with one of the spikes and leaves a deep scratch. Bears are strong but not terribly agile on the ground, so I'm vulnerable. He steps forward with a "Raahh!" to take advantage, cocking his arm back for another swing, and the lads behind him are grinning and cheering him on, anticipating the kill.

We're all surprised, but none more than Leather Lad, when Greta leaps at his unguarded neck and her teeth sink in, taking him to the ground. When he hits the ground, her momentum carries her a bit beyond, but she never lets go of that throat, so she tears it out and takes it with her. She shakes the flesh a couple of times from side to side and then flings it away, showing lots of bloody teeth to the other trolls and barking an angry challenge at them.

"That's not a normal wolf," one of them observes. Quite the scholar for a troll. "Not a normal bear either. Animals shouldn't be able to do that to us."

Ah, he's referring to the natural armor of troll skin. Well, werewolves shrug off magic, especially low-level stuff like armored hide, and Creidhne's brass knuckles represent far stronger magic than theirs.

Four against two now. They're wary, strong, and slow. It occurs to me that I'm also strong and slow as I struggle to me feet. Greta, though, is faster than a bowel movement after eating a pound of dried figs. She's also much faster than a troll can think.

She bunches her muscles and leaps forward, charging the nearest one, and he wastes precious time figuring out that he can't lift up a tree and smash her with it before she gets to him. So he lifts up the trunk end and hides behind it, effectively blocking Greta from reaching his throat. She bounces off, scurries behind him, and tears up the tendon behind his right ankle, the one that modern people named after some Greek warrior. The troll falls on his arse, and Greta makes sure she isn't underneath. The tree falls down on top of the troll, and while that doesn't do him terrible damage, it does mean his hands are busy trying to throw it off instead of protecting his throat. Greta tears it out for him and then scampers away as another troll tries to pound her to jelly with his makeshift club. He misses and smashes his friend's face instead. I'm on the move, though still slow, but the remaining three trolls are not paying attention, because Greta is now far more dangerous in their eyes. They've all raised their clubs and are just waiting for Greta to move into smashing range. I'm so hobbled that I can probably do more good as a distraction than anything else, so I position myself behind them and roar as loudly as I can. Two of them are still mighty worried about Greta, but one looks around for me, and he's the one that Greta goes for. A couple of bounds and a leap and she's flying at his throat. He catches on at the last split second, instinctively drops the tree, and just swipes at the air in front of his torso in a desperate attempt to ward off her attack. It works: His arm, almost club-like in itself, bats her aside, and she tumbles less than gracefully to the ground.

"Ha!" one of them crows. "Now we smash—" But he is so very wrong. By choice, Greta's not a pack leader, but she has all the charisma of one, and in the absence of Sam and Ty her wishes are paramount. Through the pack link she called the parents of me apprentices and their translators, and they arrive in time to swarm the last three trolls and tear them up. A couple start to come for me—they're so excited they can't tell friend from foe right now—but they pull up short and turn their heads to Greta. She has them firmly under control. They return to finish off Blue Bones and make sure all the trolls are well and truly a buffet for vultures.

It's awkward to stay in bear form with me shoulder so messed up, so I shift back to human and yell about it because the pain gets amplified—an out-o'-place bone shard can wind up somewhere tender during a shapeshift and make the problem worse. Still, that's six trolls down and the kids were never threatened. I shout, "I love it when we kick arse together!" Greta shakes herself all over and lets her tongue loll out to the side in a canine smile. "I'm going to get me clothes and check out that Old Way." She lifts her head a couple times in an approximation of a nod and I pick me way downhill, wincing, trying to figure out how to get me cocked-up shoulder bones back to playing nicely together again. It's going to bother me a good while.

Getting into me pants takes so long I don't bother with the shirt, and I just carry it with me. Greta's waiting by the tree the trolls appeared behind and shifting back to human. I wait for the process to finish before I try talking to her.

"Siodhachan says that werewolves have trouble traveling the planes. Gunnar used to get powerful sick. The theory is that your protections against magic fight against the plane-shifting and make ye queasy. So it's best if I go alone."

"Careful," she says, still shuddering from the change.

"I will be. And I'll be back as soon as I can manage."

Flipping me vision to the magical spectrum, I can see the Old Way laid out before me, lit up like a trail of fireflies at dusk. Six steps forward, turn right three steps, quick left and another left, then right, and with every step the cooling bodies and the pines fade and the lush eternal summer of Tír na nÓg gets closer.

When I reach the end, I find meself in a nondescript area of Tír na nÓg. There are no helpful signs pointing me to Fand, nor any Fae nearby that I can question about it. It's hidden perfectly because it's smack in the middle of nothing special. Cursing at the necessity to shift to a bear again, I shuck off me pants, shift, and follow the trail of troll stench down to the river. That means the trolls arrived by boat from elsewhere, then. A dead end.

But at least while I'm here I can visit Fand's prison to see if she left any clues there. And maybe figure out how she escaped.

Flidais and I put her on one of the Irish planes seldom visited by the winged Fae that adored her so much. It used to have a bonny name long ago, but now it's a lawless place they call the Badlands, where the trolls and Fir Bolgs and other assorted nasties have chosen to live. It's connected to Tír na nÓg by a well-guarded Old Way. Popular wisdom holds that you follow the rules if you use it to enter Tír na nÓg, and feck all the rules once you enter the Badlands. Lots of banditry and preying upon one another as soon as you set foot there. If you can make it through that, you tend never to come back again—too much trouble to fight through—and the various beings live as hermits as much as possible in jealously guarded territories. Flidais and I figured that if we hid Fand on that plane far from the Old Way, no one would even find her, much less engineer her escape. Flidais crafted a new Old Way in secret, accessed by hidden cave entrances on either end, and then set what we thought were incorruptible guards on her. The cell she was in was dead material—all glass—and utterly disconnected from the earth: It hung from iron chains set in the ceiling of rock. To ensure she couldn't stretch out through that tenuous link and connect to the earth, we lined the ceiling with layers of hard plastic. Deprived of energy, she couldn't unbind anything to escape. Her guards were in iron armor to further discourage binding and even had a hunk of cold iron to use as a talisman should they need it. She was to be given food, water, and anything she wanted to read, and that's all. She had a chamber pot and had to lock herself up in iron manacles if she wanted the guards to empty it.

Imagine me surprise when I arrived at her secret prison to find her still in it. I look at the guards—four of them—and they're the same ones we originally set upon her. Nothing different there. But nothing about this happy scene matches with the fact that I have an Old Way leading to me Grove and a troll who as much as admitted Fand had helped him get there.

"It's been a while since I've visited, lads. Anything to report? Anything unusual?"

The guards all tell me no. Fand stares at me from her cell, hatred burning in her eyes, and still blindingly beautiful, like ice crystals in the sun. She hasn't a stitch on her.

"When's the last time ye emptied the chamber pot?" I ask the guards.

"Few days ago. She hasn't asked."

It gets me thinking. If that isn't really Fand but an

imposter, she wouldn't want to be chained up in iron. That would mess with the glamour.

"Time to empty it, I'd say." I go to the cell and tell her to chain herself up. She's slow to comply but she does it, and there isn't a flicker of a change to her appearance.

"Huh." Either that really is her or it's an exceptional illusion to withstand the touch of iron. Still, it can be done. An extra dose of caution is warranted.

"Give me the hunk of cold iron, lads. I'm going in."

Fand's eyes widen somewhat when she sees me approach with the cold iron in me hand, but she says nothing. When I hunker down and stretch out with the iron to place it against her foot, she shrinks away.

"Come on, now. I just want to make sure you're Fand. Are ye someone who'd be killed by the touch o' cold iron?"

She shakes her head no.

"Then let me do this or I'll have the lads in here to immobilize you completely."

She nods and keeps still as I touch the cold iron to her right foot. The skin shudders, then ripples, and her appearance changes as the glamour is dispelled, flowing up from the leg, until I'm left with a human but definitely not Fand. It's a rather ordinary-looking pale woman with mussed dark hair and a large nose.

"I figured," I says. "Who are ye, then, since ye aren't Fand?"

"I'm a selkie."

"A selkie?" That would make sense, since they were one of the few kinds of lesser Fae that weren't killed by cold iron. Their human side protected them. But that pointed to a larger problem. "One of Manannan's?"

"Aye."

"He cast the seeming on ye himself?"

"Aye."

"Fecking hells."

I round on the guards. "When was Manannan Mac Lir here?"

They exchange glances and say he never was there at all. I wince. Of course not.

"Then who was the last visitor?"

"Flidais was here a few days ago," one says.

Back to the selkie: "So Manannan came here glamoured as Flidais, brought you with him, visited Fand, switched your appearances, and walked out with Fand?"

She nods. "Except I was glamoured as Perun, not my true shape." Meaning Manannan and Fand walked out together disguised as Flidais and Perun. They might still be glamoured that way and be up to all kinds of mischief.

"And you've had no visitors since?"

"No."

So Flidais doesn't know that Fand's escaped with Manannan's help, and neither does Brighid.

"Ye can stay here as ye are," I say. "I'll let someone else pass judgment." I toss the key to the shackles on the floor near enough for her to reach. "Unlock yourself after I'm out."

And who, I wonder, will pass judgment on me? I imagine Brighid might have something to say after trusting me with keeping Fand secure. But I surely did not expect Manannan to still be so in love with her that he would spring her from prison after she tried to kill him and all his selkies. And how did he find out she was here, anyway? I suppose it doesn't matter. If and when we find them, we can worry about it then.

I toss the cold iron back to the guards when I exit the cell. "You lads were suckered good with a glamour. From now on, everybody gets touched with the cold iron before they go in. Make sure ye know who you're dealing with."

It's a long shot, but I visit Manannan's estate just in

case he's foolish enough to be there. He isn't. Place is entirely empty, wards all dispelled. The pigs and sheep are all gone from the grounds. Not a selkie or a faery in sight. That means they're off somewhere, plotting together, and they either have an entourage or they killed them all to make sure no one told any secrets.

"Well, this is a sad sack of shite," I say in the silent castle kitchen, once a hub of frenzied activity. "We're all going to take it up the arse and probably won't even get our pants pulled down first." Me eyes spy some fine whiskey on the shelf, and I remember saying to Dr. Sudarga that all I wanted was a shot and a good long rest in bed. I pull out a glass and take the bottle down. Sleep will have to wait, but I might as well have that drink now.

CHAPTER 16

For the record, Shango is a really super-charming thunder god. I know only the barest sketches of his pantheon, and after he spends a couple of hours telling stories about them and the beliefs of his people, I'm simultaneously enthralled and ashamed. Enthralled for obvious reasons but ashamed that I didn't know more about the Orishas already. It's an unfortunate truth that in the Western education system—well, in the Western countries, period—we are sadly deprived of the rich variety of African traditions. So much so that many make the mistake of thinking of the entire continent of Africa as a monoculture rather than the vast collection of disparate cultures that it is. Shango's people primarily hail from Yorubaland, which spans the southwestern portion of modern-day Nigeria into a couple of neighboring countries, Benin and Togo, though he also has worshippers scattered throughout the world as a legacy of the slave trade. A consequence of that legacy is that he and the other Orishas get out of their homeland quite a bit to keep track of their people and do the odd favor here and there. And I suspect he might be more powerful than Perun, because he continues to enjoy healthy worship from around the world.

Perun, I think, begins to feel outclassed halfway across Poland, because his English is not nearly so good. He shuts up for a while, and what little expression I can see underneath his beard looks sour. I speak to him in Russian, which I am fairly certain Shango does not speak.

"Are you feeling left out, Perun?"

He lifts an eyebrow at me first, throwing some shade, perhaps, but then he dissolves into a sheepish grin. He replies in the same language, in which he has no fluency issues.

"I suppose I am. Silly of me, I know. But we gods of older, smaller pantheons have our insecurities too. My problems with English are persistent, and I have not devoted enough time to eradicate them. So it is my own fault if I am feeling inadequate. Please forgive my mood."

"Done. But do join in whenever you feel like it. I enjoy hearing from you too."

When we get to Bydgoszcz, we have to choose whether to follow the southern or northern bank of the Wisła River to get to Warsaw. I choose the south because there are a couple of large forested swaths on the way, according to the elemental, which will allow us to make good time and not have to worry about roads and people staring at the strange group of people running as fast as a horse and hound. And, besides, once in Warsaw, the Wisła River bends south, and we'll wind up on the side where I met Malina's coven before.

Apart from my aching innards, I'm starting to think it might simply be a pleasant run for us as we trek through Kampinos National Park, which is only twenty kilometers or so to the northwest of Warsaw. It's the especially dead time of night, around three in the morning, and nothing stirs to give us the feeling of an imminent attack—the attack just happens. Out of the mist clinging to the Wisła River, three grayish figures rise and float toward us with glowing white bulbous eyes. Their arms and fingers are long and sticklike, straight white hair streams back from their scalps, and I can't see much in the way of legs, but that might be because they're flying, so their legs are stretched out behind them.

"Uh, Perun, what are those?" I say.

The Slavic thunder god turns and gasps. "They are *nocnice*!"

It's an unfamiliar word and I'm not even sure what language it comes from, so I sputter, "Yeah, but *what are they*?"

He doesn't get time to explain, but in short order I figure out that they're unfriendly, because one of them floats right through my defensive swipe with Scáthmhaide and locks a cold collection of bones around my throat, bearing me to the ground with surprising strength for something so insubstantial. The same happens to Perun and Shango, and then we all try to fight back. The trouble is, my staff and fist just whiff through the thing, though it is undeniably exerting tangible force upon me. I pull out a knife and stab into it and watch my hand simply float through it. A hoarse, halting whisper that might be a laugh huffs out of its toothy mouth, and my windpipe closes as its hands constrict. I can't breathe and I can't bring any force to bear on this thing. I look to the gods for tips, but they're having the same difficulty. They're being choked to death and can't lay a finger on the *nocnice* in return. One or both of them summons winds to try to blow them away—not a bad idea considering their ephemeral nature—but all that does is kick up leaves and toss my hair around. I see a fireball in the sky above and understand what's happening: This is Loki's doing. The fireball doesn't descend; it just hovers, watching. He's arranged a second ambush for me where he lets some other creature do his fighting for him. And, as before, it's a carefully chosen creature against which I have little or no defense. I can't even begin to figure out how I would bind this intangible thing if I had breath to speak the words.

<Granuaile!> Orlaith shouts in my head as I try to think of some way to affect this strange spirit. Its bony fingers are right on top of my cold iron amulet and it doesn't care. <Let me help!>

No, wait—I project to her, but Orlaith has already pounced on top of the *nocnica*. I expect her to simply fall through it on top of me, but instead she lands palpably on its back, her teeth tear into its substance, and the whispery laugh becomes a hoarse cry of surprise and slides into a scream. Orlaith pulls it off me, teeth embedded deeply, and shakes her head back and forth like she would with a chew toy, the instinctive attempt to snap the neck. I don't think the *nocnica* has a spine in the traditional sense, but Orlaith's move shakes the creature apart into clumps of dirty vapor, and the scratchy wail fades and the bulbous eyes wink out.

Good hound! Thank you! Can you do that again, to the ones on Shango and Perun?

Orlaith hacks once and says, <Yes. But they taste horrible.>

As she bounds over to help the gods, I check the position of the fireball, which hasn't moved, and then look around for Miłosz. He's perhaps forty yards distant, pacing and snorting in nervous agitation. I wonder again why Loki doesn't use the special weapons he's acquired from me—where are Vayu's arrows or the whirling blade, Fuilteach? Perhaps neither would survive the journey in flame and he's saving them for a special target—Odin would be my guess, and perhaps Freyja.

Orlaith dispatches the two other *nocnice*, thus becoming the first wolfhound to rescue a couple of thunder gods, and as they get to their feet I say, "Eyes to the sky, guys. It's Loki."

They look up, spy the fireball, and snarl. In tandem

they raise their weapons to the sky, and the weather takes a decided turn for the worse. Loki can survive their lightning strikes, I think—he had no difficulty with Perun the first time we met him, in a field near Flagstaff. But the Asgardian decides against escalating and moves off to the north. The thunder gods don't pursue, since they're supposed to protect the horse instead of chase Loki down, but they mutter about him being a coward. I privately disagree: He's bold enough when it suits him. He simply plays the odds. Were any of us alone, he'd probably dive right in, but facing two thunder gods plus a Druid who can wink out of sight and clock him upside the head is not an ideal scenario. Maybe it's because he's still healing from the tomahawk I put in his back: I sure hope so. After he's out of sight I promise Orlaith a deer hunt soon and go to soothe Miłosz, while Shango asks Perun what the hell those things were. I listen in because I want to know as well.

"*Nocnice* are nightmares," he says in English. "Damned souls who choke peoples as they sleep, leave no trace. Not usual to attack like this."

"Why couldn't we touch them?" Shango asks.

Perun shrugs. "Is way of nightmares, yes? They get you in clutches and you cannot fight back. Only wake. Except we already awake, so no escape for us."

"Then why could Orlaith take them out?" I say.

"Any dog, even small ones, can do this to *nocnice*. They guardian against many spirits. They bark at night sometimes and you think, what you barking for? Stop that. Sometimes dogs hearing and seeing things we do not, and they scare them away, protect us. Roosters do this too, but nobody like roosters except hens. Good thing you like dogs."

Orlaith, is this true? Do you bark at spirits sometimes?

<Maybe. I never saw one before now. But sometimes I

feel something bad coming, and I bark until the bad feeling goes away. Oberon does this too.>

Well, thank you.

"That was not the kind of fight I hoped for," Shango says.

"Loki rarely gives you that," I reply. "You have to find a way to surprise him."

We continue from there, much more paranoid than before, but nothing else attacks on the way into Warsaw. I lead Miłosz and our escorts to the same bound poplar tree in Pole Mokotowskie, where I assume I'll find the coven, but it's only Malina herself.

"An hour before dawn is a hell of a time to return victorious, Granuaile," she says, shivering in the cold. "I couldn't believe the divination when I saw it. But since it *is* victory, I'll forgive you." She grins in wonder at Miłosz. "Wow. The white horse of Świętowit. Did you have any trouble? Oh!" Her eyes drop to my blood-stained shirt. "I see that you did."

"Yes, plenty. But I'll be all right eventually." Getting slammed to the ground by the *nocnica* had not done my injuries any favors. I would be an utter wreck without Gaia's continuing aid.

"And these gentlemen are?" Malina asks, looking at Shango and Perun. I'm not sure that I should introduce them as such.

"Hired muscle," I say, and hope the lie isn't utterly obvious on my face. I suppose it might be technically true in Shango's case. He'd said something about Odin wanting him to help me give Loki the finger on this one, and maybe he paid in the currency of his favor. Not that Shango would give a damn about favors from Odin. Regardless, they're keeping their distance, signaling that they feel no need to be introduced, and I respect that. "They don't talk much, and they'll leave once the horse is safe."

"Right. We should get going, then. We'll take him to my place. The house and all the land surrounding it is warded."

"Warded how, if I may ask? I mean, against what?"

"Well, fire, of course. Loki will not be burning everything around him like he did in that onion field."

"What about demons and spirits?"

Malina smirks. "No problem. If they get past our wards, we have hellwhips for those. You can relax. We channel the powers of the Zoryas and they are protective goddesses. We know how to protect our homes."

I figure that must be true. If Odin is fine with Miłosz staying with the sisters, it must be as safe as any place he could find in Asgard.

Malina had seen we'd be arriving on foot, of course, so she rode her bike to the park. "We have to cross the river, so it will be a few more kilometers. I suppose your early arrival is good for something—we'll have the streets practically to ourselves."

She leads the way, blond hair resting on a red coat, and we follow through a city getting its last few minutes of sleep. It's slower going, since so much of it is paved and I have to run without any juice from the earth. The sun isn't above the horizon, but the eastern sky has lightened from pitch to merely gloomy by the time we cross the Wisła River. There's a genuine ray of sunshine announcing the dawn when we turn onto Ulice Lipkowksa in the Radość neighborhood of Warsaw. It's quite nearly bucolic—fenced properties on an acre or two, mixed in with wooded areas. Pines grow there, since the soil is somewhat sandy on that side of the river and the pines send their roots deep enough to hold on. Once in the canopy of the neighborhood, the urban hum fades and you don't think that you're only five minutes away from a city of two million people getting ready for Christmas or assorted pagan good times.

Perun and Shango take their leave at the gate to Malina's property. They summon winds and lift up into the skies, and once they're clear of trees, Shango flies south and Perun heads north. It blows their cover pretty spectacularly.

"Hired muscle, eh?" Malina says, her tone drier than a week-old bagel.

"Yeah! But also thunder gods. Forgot to mention it, sorry. I thought you would know already."

"I only divined your arrival with the horse," she says, opening the padlock on the gate. It looks like a perfectly normal lock, but a quick flip to the magical spectrum confirms that there is a whole bunch of hoodoo surrounding it. There are also layers of protections ringing the entire fence and arcing over the property in various shades of purple, from lavender to deep violet. I'm sure that while I lived in the same building as the sisters in Tempe, their floor of the tower looked like this, pulsing with warning.

Malina Sokołowska's funky white house sits behind a brown slatted wood fence that encloses the whole acre and a half, and the architecture is old school—I can tell by the popped-out windows with triangular tiled hats on the second story, and the giant casements for the first-floor windows are a giveaway too. I'm guessing it was built in the 1930s. There's moss growing on the wide stone steps leading up to the main house, and a smaller set leads to the door of what must be either attached servants' or guest quarters. Most of the coven is outside waiting for us on the steps, bundled up in coats and purple scarves, sipping thermos cups of tea or coffee held in their gloved hands. Their smiles are wide and genuine when they see Orlaith and me. Berta bounces up and gives me a hug and then asks if I would like some cake. "I knew you were coming," she says, "so I baked you one."

"That would be great," I tell her, "but I'd like to make sure that Świętowit's horse is happy first." To the wider group, I announce, "His name is Miłosz."

A couple more witches emerge from the house and then the entire coven steps forward, grins on their faces, for introductions to the horse. He shies a tiny bit at the crowding, but I send soothing thoughts to him and explain that these women will be taking care of him now and protecting him from the god who branded him. There will be apples and oats and he'll be able to take walks in the woods and enjoy the sky from now on.

He already knows Malina, and introductions to the other four witches I know proceed quickly. I point out Roksana, Berta, Klaudia, and Kazimiera, and they say hello to Miłosz. Malina darts inside the house to get me a fresh shirt and light jacket for the chill.

I have to slow down and take my time after that, switching my head into recording mode. Formally meeting the rest of the coven will be news for Atticus when I catch up with him. He signed a nonaggression treaty with the original five shortly after he took me on as an apprentice, and these new coven members are not technically bound by it; he'll want to know who the free agents are. And I have to remind myself that I am not bound by that agreement either—and neither are any of the sisters when it comes to me. When they are smiling and welcoming like this, it's difficult to remember that we aren't really friends. Maybe they would like to be, though. I think Malina is a very different leader than the old one, Radomiła. Her new witches all appear to be in their twenties, but that doesn't mean anything; I'm thirty-four now but still look like I'm in my twenties.

Martyna is a brunette with bangs and has the rest of her hair tied back in a ponytail. She has piercing blue eyes rimmed in thick mascara and sharp, thin lips she's painted blood red. "If you'd rather not have that heavy cake," she confides to me, "I made some delightful cookies." Her eyes dart to Berta and her lips turn up on one side. Berta's eyes are narrowed, and it's evident that there's a friendly competition going on to see who can first foist her baked goods on the Druid.

"Hiiiiii," the next witch says, bobbing her head once and smiling at me. "I'm Ewelina." Her bubbly greeting is a stark contrast to the Swedish death-metal T-shirt I see peeking out underneath her jacket. She has hot-pink streaks in her black hair, multiple piercings in her eyebrows, a ring in her nose, and a stainless-steel stud underneath her bottom lip. Unlike the others, she has no purple scarf, but she wears dark-purple eye shadow instead. She throws up some horns with her fingers as if she's at a Dio concert and nods once. "Rock on." I think that might be all the English she knows, and that's fine—her smile goes a long way, and her few words of English are more than I know in Polish.

Agnieszka looks somewhat colder and more nervous than everyone else. Her violet scarf is wrapped around her to such heights that her mouth is completely hidden. I see only her prominent nose and eyes above it, like an old Kilroy graffiti from World War II. She has purple mittens on her hands, which I notice when she extends one to shake mine. "I'm not very good at baking—or anything normal, really," she says, apologies in her tone, "but I'm quite good at wards if you need anything like that."

"That's very kind. Thank you."

Next, a blond witch who's spent a lot of time in the sun introduces herself as Dominika. She's shaven the right side of her head down to her ear but let the top and left side grow straight and long, in a sort of homage to New Wave styles of the 1980s. Her exposed, perfectly shaped right ear has eight different piercings with beautiful rings and studs, and when I begin to stare at it I realize that it's what she uses to charm people. Wow, an ear witch. I blink furiously and look at her eyes, which are shining with excitement.

"I love horses," she says. "Will you tell Miłosz I'm so glad he's come to stay with us? He is magnificent!"

I relay these sentiments to Miłosz, and he nickers in response to the flattery. Dominika pulls an apple out of her coat pocket and asks, "May I give this to him?"

"Of course." She moves it under his nose, presenting it on top of her palm, and he nabs it with his lips and then crunches down with evident satisfaction.

Magdalena has a giant mane of dark hair that frames her head and hides her neck so that her very pale face appears to float in black waters. Her complexion combined with that hair remind me uncomfortably of the Morrigan. But it's not her hair that she's using to charm people: She uses her eyebrows, shaped into graceful arches, and an uncanny ability to raise either of them independently or waggle them around.

Casting eyes sideways at Berta and Martyna, she says to me, "You should not be eating cakes or cookies. Scones are best."

"Oh. You've made scones, then?"

Her right eyebrow lifts heavenward. "No. I can't bake for shit, as you Americans say. I just have strong opinions about breakfast. We should not be feeding you cake and cookies as the sun is rising. You need meat and cheese, and if there must be bread, then a scone."

<Oh, I like this one,> Orlaith says.

Zofia is the definition of petite: I'm not sure she's fully five feet tall. Her hood is up, fringed in white fur, and a thick braid of auburn hair spills out of it and falls down to her chest. She nods and says only, "Pleased to meet you," in a thick accent. I think, like Ewelina, she is reserved because of language rather than because she has nothing more to say.

Patrycja is either the daughter of immigrants to Poland or one parent is not ethnically Polish. Her complexion is russet brown and I'm sure she's asked constantly about her heritage, so I don't ask—it doesn't matter anyway. She's dressed in winter running clothes and wearing a pair of those abnormally bright running shoes, so I'm guessing she likes her exercise.

"Did you really run all the way here from Germany?" she asks.

"I did. I had help, though. Gaia provided most of the speed and energy."

The last witch, with deep-set eyes, a narrow nose, and brown hair chopped evenly at her shoulders, approaches with a gift-wrapped rectangle in her hand. "I'm Anna," she says. "This is for you."

"Oh! Thanks, Anna," I say, taking it from her and unwrapping the package. It's a collection of poems by Wisława Szymborska, both in Polish and English, side by side. "This is perfect! Thank you!"

"We thought it would be a nudge in the right direction," she says. "We will help you all you want with the language, you know."

"I'm genuinely looking forward to it."

With introductions complete and a few more apples offered to Miłosz, we lead him around the side of the house, which is a strip of property wide enough to drive a car through—and that's by design, I see, since there's a garage tucked in the back, out of sight from the street. There's also plenty of room for Miłosz in the rear of the property, easily a full acre if you subtract the house, though I notice that the fences are further screened with cedars and evergreens.

Malina returns with a shirt and jacket for me, sees where I'm looking, and says, "Yes, we have privacy around the perimeter, and a little farther on you'll see that the canopy of that oak and willow provide an aerial screen as well. That's where we do all the outdoor rituals."

I spy a fire pit, a bona fide cauldron hanging above it, and a makeshift altar underneath the trees. "What kind of rituals would those be?"

"Like your divination cloak. We'll get started as soon as you're ready. You've certainly held up your end."

"Oh, I'm ready. Let's do it. But let me ask Miłosz first if he needs anything."

Sending images along with my words, I ask him, <Do you need water or food?>

I get the sense that he wouldn't mind some of both, and I turn to Dominika. "He'd like something to eat and drink."

"Great! If he'll follow me I'll show him where we'll be keeping him."

<Follow Dominika. Tan person with blond mane,> I tell him, pointing to her. He obligingly clops after her and she giggles a bit.

"It's so cool that you can talk to him. Druids are awesome."

"Thanks. So are witches."

"Save me a spot in the circle, Sisters," Dominika says. "I'll be there as soon as I finish with our handsome guest."

Agnieszka guides me over to the fire pit, where there are some glowing coals from earlier. She instructs me to sit in a very specific spot between the fire and the altar, facing north. After checking my position, she coaches me to scoot over a minute amount, then tells me not to move once the ritual begins. "The more still you are, the better the cloak will adhere."

Patrycja throws some kindling on top of the coals and coaxes the fire to life again. Berta and Martyna stand next to the altar and begin chopping up bundles of herbs they had already laid out for the purpose.

Ewelina hauls over a bucket of water and pours it carefully into the cauldron. When she finishes, she looks up and catches me watching her. Her teeth flash at me and she throws up the horns. "Rock on."

The rest of the witches stand around me in a circle, with gaps for the others to take their places later. Malina kneels down next to me to explain what will happen.

"The true nature of our divination cloak is really a blessing bestowed upon you by the Zoryas. With their help, we are going to hide you from the second sight, the third eye, the fourth horseman, the fifth element, the sixth sense, the seventh son, and all other seers, deities, and methods of extrasensory perception."

I have so many questions after hearing that list, but the one thing I really want to ask about is the fifth element. I keep my mouth shut, though, because I don't want to lose any Druid Wisdom Points and it already sounds like they are giving me the equivalent of a Multi-pass.

"Once this blessing is bestowed," Malina continues, "it *can* be removed, as your Indian friend removed the cloak from Mr. O'Sullivan's sword. But it will require a skilled practitioner of the magical arts and ritual. It's not something you can cancel easily."

"Understood. But what about cold iron?"

"Mr. O'Sullivan's cold iron aura never affected the sword's cloak, and he handled it often. You have that talisman," she says, pointing to my amulet, "and you can wear it all you want afterward. But I need you to remove it now so that we can target you for the ritual."

"Oh. All right." I take off my necklace and put it over Orlaith's head, asking her to keep it safe for me.

"Your hound will need to remain outside the circle, by the way."

I ask Orlaith to wait for me outside the circle, with my amulet and Scáthmhaide, and once she does I feel acutely vulnerable, because the Sisters of the Three Auroras could target me with something else now and this might be the end of a long con on the gullible young Druid. I don't know whether to be proud of my paranoia or saddened that I think so poorly of these women who have done nothing but be kind to me so far. I mean, except for that time Klaudia snared me with those charmed lips of hers.

The question, I suppose, is whether getting a divination cloak is worth possibly dying for. Considering all I have already gone through to get it—getting bitten by a snake-god—I think I have to answer yes. I certainly can't continue to be the method by which Atticus's many enemies track him down. And until I get this cloak, I can't even begin to free myself from all his entanglements. This god or that Fae monstrosity or the other evil wizard bro will continue to use me to get to him, unless I do something about it. And fuck that. I'm not going to be their stepping stone or hostage or anything else. I want myself removed from the picture. In practical terms, *not* getting the cloak would probably be just as deadly as letting the sisters have their free shot at me now.

"This will take about an hour, and all you'll hear is Polish from now on," Malina says, rising and taking her place in the circle.

"Oh, and one more thing," Berta says. When I turn around, she waves at the chopped-up plants on the altar. "We have to throw some of this stuff in the pot there, and it might smell bad. We have to sprinkle some of this on you too."

"But you won't smell bad!" Martyna hastens to reassure me. "Only the boiling stuff smells bad. We need you to have some of the raw stuff on you for focusing."

"Oh . . . okay," I say. "You did all this for Fragarach?"

"We sure did," Malina replies. "It's only an hour of work. Mr. O'Sullivan had to do much more than that to earn it. And you had to do much more as well."

That is certainly the truth, but as Martyna dumps a load of yarrow and some other herbs I can't immediately identify into my hair and on my shoulders, I say, "No, I mean this." I jerk a thumb at my beflowered hair. "You sprinkled herbs on the scabbard and had the cauldron and everything? In Tempe?"

"Yes. We had a secluded spot in the desert for our outdoor rituals."

I cough, then sneeze from the pollen. "Maybe I can use your shower afterward."

"Of course."

They begin in earnest after reminding me once more to remain still, and it's a slow, peaceful time listening to the language and absorbing its rhythms. The longer it continues, the more relaxed I feel, because building takes longer than destroying. If they meant me harm, I would have felt it much sooner. Orlaith falls asleep, lulled by their voices. Planes fly overhead on occasion and birds chirp, but otherwise it's just thirteen witches chanting in Polish and an awful stench rising from the boiling cauldron. Near the very end I feel a gentle pressure all over, and my eardrums pop in and then pop out again. All of the coven raise their arms at that point and smile at the sky, a familiar ecstasy written on their faces: Goddesses have worked their will through them. When Gaia speaks through me, I feel the same way.

"That's it," Malina says. "You're blessed, or cloaked, whatever you want to call it."

I change my vision over to the magical spectrum and look at my hand, not knowing quite what to look for. I never got to see the cloak on Fragarach.

"Feel free to test it with any seer or deity you wish," Malina goes on. "We guarantee our work."

There, floating above my aura, the sheerest layer of lilac gossamer tells me that the Zoryas have indeed blessed me. Or, pending confirmation, I should say: That lilac bit wasn't there before, and *something* has been done to me.

I will definitely confirm it, but I am already confident that they have dealt straight with me. The cold iron test would be prudent, however.

"Congratulations," a couple of the witches say, and I smile in response but don't say anything yet.

Orlaith, will you bring me my amulet, please? I ask as I get to my feet and brush flowers and pollen dust off my shoulders and shake out my hair. She wakes and ambles over, tail wagging.

<Is it time for breakfast yet?>

I think it might be. Thank you, I tell her, retrieving my necklace. I drape it over my head and let it take its accustomed place just below the hollow of my throat. I watch my aura, examining that lavender layer closely on one arm and then the other. It remains strong and doesn't flicker.

"My thanks to the Zoryas," I finally say to Malina, shoulders sagging with relief. "And my thanks to you all!"

"Our pleasure. Fulfilling a contract always feels good."

<What are we doing after breakfast?> Orlaith asks, and I suspect she's not really interested in the answer but rather wishes to keep me focused on breakfast.

We're going on a secret mission, because now we can keep secrets, I tell her.

CHAPTER 17

Prague is one of the most beautiful cities in the world—for my money it's in the top five. The architecture is goth as fuck, pointy bits at the top and stone curlicues underneath, and the squares are full of bronze sculptures that celebrate ideas more than military conquest. It's a setting that whispers of magic and mystic euphoria and bloody danger too. It was where Leif Helgarson had been turned to a vampire a thousand years ago.

Oberon and I arrived via the tethered trees of Petřín Hill, which is situated on the west side of the Vltava River, after nightfall—and also after I had taken some time to catch up on sleep and healing. It was overcast and some mist had rolled in, clinging to the trees, and we both took a moment to appreciate the smell.

<Have we ever been here before?> Oberon asked.

"I've been here many times, but this is a first for you."

<Then I must ask you what I always ask when we go someplace new: What kind of food do they have here that I would like?>

"I think you'd like the beef goulash. Slow-roasted, tender beef in a thick, spicy gravy." I began to pick my way downhill toward the Charles Bridge, and Oberon trotted alongside.

<That sounds great! Goulash me, Atticus! Uh, is that right? Is goulash a verb?>

"Not normally, but now that you say it, I think it should be."

<Yes! I am looking forward to goulashing for as long as I can.>

"We'll see if we can arrange it. We have to be vampire hunters first."

We crossed the river by way of the Charles Bridge, a wonderful structure graced on both sides by baroque sculptures and handy lights for night walks, and I paused at the statue of St. John of Nepomuk to point out something to Oberon.

"See these plaques at the base?" I said, where there were bronze bas-reliefs of St. John's death. "Notice how parts of them are shiny?"

<Yeah! Why are those parts so clean?>

"Because people keep touching them, and all those hands have polished those parts to a golden glow. The legend is that if you touch the image on the right side— the one depicting the priest being thrown into the river— you'll have good luck and return to Prague soon."

<Oh! So what's going on with the left—hey! That shiny part on the left is a hound!>

"Yep! People touch the image on the right for luck, but then they also pet the hound on the left, because hounds are so awesome. That hound has been petted by millions of people over the centuries. That's why he's so shiny."

<Wow! That's a pretty lucky hound. This is now my favorite statue.>

I leaned forward and gave the hound on the statue a quick scratch behind the ears. Then I touched the priest on the right. I'm not a Catholic, but I could use all the luck I could get, and in theory, at least, the Big Guy in the Sky was rooting for me, along with the gods of several other pantheons, thanks to Rebecca Dane. The least he deserved from me was a courtesy greeting.

"All right, let's move on. But keep your nose open for dead guys instead of goulash. I'm counting on you to give me a heads-up before they attack."

Once we got to the eastern shore we plowed down the cobbled Karlova Ulice, past innumerable shops hawking expensive crystal, amber necklaces, or cheap souvenirs, and barkers trying to get us to eat at one of the many restaurants or take in a theatre show. I admired the astronomical clock in the Old Town Square, lit up at night, and people either admired or shied away from Oberon as we passed. Tourists enjoyed beers or dinner at one of the many outdoor seating areas there, and the locals enjoyed the money the tourists spent.

After crossing the square we continued down Celetná Ulice, and once we reached the Grand Café Orient we took a left up Králodvorská Ulice, which would bring us to the Grand Hotel Bohemia from behind. It loomed above us on the narrow street, six stories of yellow cream, its façade curved around the corner it occupied.

We stopped before rounding the corner to the entrance.

"All right, Oberon, *Star Wars* pop quiz: Which phrase is used most often in the movies?"

<Oh! I know! "I've got a bad feeling about this," or some variation of that.>

"Correct! And that's my feeling right now. I don't trust Leif. Or any vampire, really. So I'd like you to be my ace in the hole here in case something goes sideways."

<Well, you should have a bad feeling. I smell dead people now.>

"That's somewhat encouraging. If the vampires are here, maybe one of them is Theophilus. I can pull a Julie d'Aubigny and end it."

<Heck yes! Be like Julie!>

"But in case something goes wrong, I'm going to camouflage you and leave you here. If I have to retreat I will come back this way, and I want you to knock down the first person who's following me. Don't bite or engage them, just knock them over, and then catch up with me."

<Got it. I can do that! And then you can goulash me.>

With Oberon kept safe—which was truly my intention in leaving him there, not that he protect my retreat—I proceeded to the double doors of the Grand Bohemia and cast camouflage to give me some time to scope out the place, unobserved.

The outer doors opened into an unusual glass-enclosed foyer, with five angled panels, two of which were doors leading to the left and right of the center panel. The reception desk and staircase waited straight ahead across a tiled floor, and flush with the front of the building to either side were carpeted sitting areas with little cocktail tables. The furniture was upholstered in rich red and gold frilly patterns, with matching heavy drapes framing the large arched windows. A huge portrait of Karl IV, the fourteenth-century Holy Roman Emperor who ruled from Bohemia, gazed benevolently upon the hotel guests and reminded them that Prague had once been the capital of the Western world. In the back of the room, to the left of reception and the staircase, a doorway with CAFÉ/BAR emblazoned above it announced that potables could be had, and I glimpsed a bored bartender behind the taps.

The seating areas on either side of the lobby were occupied by six individuals each, and once I switched my vision to the magical spectrum, I saw that every single one of them was a vampire. I pulled out the stake and wondered where to begin. Which, if any of them, was Theophilus?

I didn't get a chance to find out. One of the vampires

on the right was wearing slightly odd glasses that I first dismissed as pretentious fashion, but they were modern infrared goggles. He couldn't see through my camouflage binding, but he could sure see my heat signature standing there and not actually entering the lobby. He could no doubt smell me too. I caught this as he pulled out a phone, thumbed a speed-dial number, and then said in German, *"Er ist am Eingang. Ja. Machen wir."* He rang off, nodded at the others on his right, and they rose together. A quick glance at the left side of the lobby confirmed that the vampires there were doing the same, and my bad feeling got infinitely worse. German Goggle Vamp shouted, *"Schießt auf die Tür!"* and the guns came out from under jackets and I ducked just in time to avoid the worst of the fire. They wound up shooting each other more than me, but I still took a bullet in the left hamstring as I threw myself at the door and crawled out to the sidewalk. Once there, I realized I couldn't stand up—not only because of the bullet in my leg but because if I did, the goggles guy would see me in infrared and have a clear shot as I ran by the front windows to where Oberon was. My scent would help them find me too, so the best option was to stop being human for a bit until I could ditch them. I triggered the charm that changed my shape to a sea otter and wriggled out of my clothes on three limbs instead of four, leaving them on the sidewalk for the vampires to smell, then I scampered as quickly as I could manage, hobbled as I was, along the base of the building so that my heat signature could not be seen through the windows, carrying the stake in my mouth. I hoped no one but vampires had been hurt. Just as I reached the corner, vampires burst out of the hotel entrance accompanied by a human—one whose voice I knew too well.

"O'Sullivan!" he called, and I peeked back around the corner to confirm it was him. Werner Drasche stood

among his vampire entourage, looking up and down the
intersection, plainly not in custody in Toronto anymore.
And while he was no longer an arcane lifeleech, he was
still a gigantic thorn in my side and showed a disturbing
talent for outfoxing me. He must have been waiting out
of sight, perhaps in the bar somewhere, and that was
who the goggled vampire had called when he spotted
me. I really should have killed him when I had the
chance.

Well, Drasche could have this round; I was so extremely outgunned that there was no use in trying to tilt
a lopsided battleground in my favor. I should count
avoiding the ambush as a win.

Oberon, let's go, I said to him through our mental
link. *Don't wait to stop anyone. I'm going to fly out of
here, and you follow along on the streets, okay? Try not
to knock any tourists over.*

<Okay.>

I shifted directly from otter to owl, since my arms
were in good shape and I wouldn't have to depend on
that damaged left leg. I'd worry about healing it later. As
I took wing in the direction of the Vltava River, I heard
Drasche launch into a series of taunts.

"You can't win this war, O'Sullivan! One way or another, we'll get to you!"

He made a good point: My goal was still a good one,
but I couldn't win using current methods. I'd have to try
another way to get to Theophilus, because they had
been waiting for me at the Grand Hotel Bohemia with
guns and infrared and Drasche's personal force of undead Austrian muscle. Which meant that Leif had betrayed me again.

CHAPTER 18

There is a certain freedom granted in privacy—a sense of fulfillment and ease that comes with the simple knowledge that no one is watching. It's why we feel all right about singing in the shower. And in this modern world, where we are constantly under surveillance of one kind or another, I suppose a compelling argument could be made that both our privacy and our freedom are illusions. Atticus and I don't worry about conventional surveillance too much; stay off the Internet, use burner phones, and pay cash for everything you can, and that will at least make them *work* to find you. Using assumed identities is a huge help as well. But I haven't had true privacy—true freedom—until now, with a divination cloak shielding me from the prying eyes of gods and seers of all kinds. And I know just how I want to celebrate that freedom.

I want to pluck out the metaphorical thorn that's been embedded in my psyche for years and then see if I can't find my way back to a happy place. Laksha's question about where I am on my own spiritual journey has lingered in my mind, and I've been thinking about it—there was a rebuke there, and a well-deserved one. It put me in mind of Whitman's rhetorical question about judgment in *I Sing the Body Electric: Do you know so much yourself that you call the meanest ignorant?*

Nope. I certainly do not. And the primary problem is that I do not know enough *of* myself. I have old wounds that have never fully healed, and I need to address them before I can move to help others. And in truth there is no balance that I can achieve but my own.

I have long delayed seeking that balance, in favor of more pressing business, but I feel that it's finally time to take care of it. Being able to take care of it was one of the primary reasons I became a Druid, but I have purposely waited since becoming bound to Gaia, to ensure that I would not act rashly. Instead, I have coolly planned a course of action that will serve Gaia and also serve my personal need to give my stepfather the finger.

As a child, when I came to live at his place in Kansas—the slightly smaller one, not the sprawling monstrosity he bought my senior year—I quickly saw that my mother was a prize instead of a person to him, and I was a burden he had to tolerate if he wanted the prize. He never laid a finger on me—I'm more fortunate than so many others in that regard—but the most love I was able to ever wring out of his face was a look of mild disgust. Never a kind word. Maybe it was because I was a tangible reminder that he had not always possessed my mother. Any interest he gave me was feigned, and that was only in the presence of others. I know my mom must have seen something good in him besides his bank account; her regard for him, at least, wasn't feigned. I think she admires single-minded determination. My real dad had it and so does Beau—and I suppose I possess a fair measure of it myself.

The only time I think I ever saw him smile at me was when he was waving goodbye as I left Kansas for Arizona State.

So, yes: I have hurt feelings, which I probably should have sought to address long ago. His aggressive disdain, heaped on my real father's distracted abandonment, did nothing good for my psyche. It's why I took to playing alone outside as much as possible, enjoying an area that wasn't so firmly under Beau's control. Later it wasn't playing but reading in a tree house that my mother had hired someone to build for me—Beau certainly wouldn't do it. I stayed out past dark and burned through a whole lot of batteries for my flashlight. I felt more at home there than in the bedroom he allowed me to sleep in.

But there again, Beau Thatcher found a way to be hurtful. He has long regarded the whole world, including the people on it, as resources that exist for him and his cronies to exploit so that they may have their sprawling estates and luxury cars and congressmen in their pockets. His moral compass always points to himself; he is his own true north. He helped fund three or four corrupt scientists who denied the reality of climate change, giving his company a thin shield of shady science to protect his short-term profits.

And now that the world is racked by freakish storms, convulsing from drought and floods and rising sea levels, with massive die-offs in the oceans and extinctions continuing on land, he still refuses to own up to his share of the responsibility for it, and his money gives him the privilege to ignore the troubles that most people face. The world will never make him pay for his company's oil spills and carbon pollution, because American laws are written to protect men like him. But Druidic law allows the punishment of despoilers, and I'm a Druid. The application of those laws is up to me.

Atticus feels that pursuing despoilers of the earth is futile, since there are so many of them and so few Druids, and when I look at cold numbers on paper I see the sense of that. But my heart cannot meekly accept criminal pollution as inevitable. That would mean accepting that Beau Thatcher is a force of nature instead of a single shitty human being. And I suppose that is where Atticus and I disagree.

"Ready for a bunch of running around, Orlaith?" I ask my hound.

<Sure! Run where? Trees?>

"Probably not so many trees. Lots of plains with prairie dogs."

<Name for those things is so strange. They aren't really dogs.>

"Human language is funny that way. What kind of beef jerky should we pack?" I ask. I need lots of protein to aid in rebuilding my torn tissues. "What's your favorite flavor?"

<Any beef flavor is good. Except no horseradish or mustard.>

"Great. Beef for you, turkey jerky for me." I fill up a pack with water and jerky at a convenience store and then we shift to Kansas, following a prearranged operating procedure.

I have memorized the locations of every well and refinery owned by Thatcher Oil & Gas. I contact Amber, the elemental of the Great Plains, and let her know what I'm planning. I'm going to sabotage all the drills by unbinding their inner workings and then, with Amber's help, I'll cap the wells with a very hard stone. If they try to drill more, they'll ruin a few bits in the process and Amber will let me know. I'll sabotage the refineries and heavy equipment as well so that all the machinery they own becomes useless hunks of metal. Production will shut down and stay that way until the company completely replaces its infrastructure. No one gets hurt. Everything will simply stop and cause the company to spend a huge amount of capital to get going again. But Thatcher Oil & Gas bought that equipment over many years instead of all at once and I'm hoping it'll be too expensive to refit one of the last remnants of a dying industry. If they do pony up, I'll cripple everything again and again until they go bankrupt and shut down or else figure out that it's wiser to invest in solar or wind.

It is exciting at the beginning to shut down the wells, but after a few hours it turns into drudgery. The iron horses aren't guarded; they're just doing their monotonous work on the plains, and in most cases we don't even have to sneak up on them. I'm not able to reshape the iron at all; I can only unbind the carbon from the steel and create a melted slurry inside that becomes a useless, cold slag. It is not challenging and does nothing to undo the damage the company's already done; it's simply time-consuming. But the constant shifting, running, and unbinding is mentally taxing, and all that keeps me going is anticipating the look on my step-father's face when I appear and tell him it was me. I can see, however, why Atticus never dedicated himself to this sort of work. Cleaning up messes would be more immediately rewarding but would do nothing to prevent it happening again. Sabotaging equipment stops the abuse of the earth but gives very little emotional payoff, apart from a grim satisfaction that I have taken one tiny step in a journey of many millions.

At the end of a very long day, Orlaith wants to see llamas for some reason, so we spend the night in Ecuador, in a meadow in the foothills of the Andes, where it's summertime and the evening is mild. Orlaith stretches out in the grass with me and watches a wild herd of llamas sip from a small lake filled with runoff water.

<They kind of look like sheep except someone stretched out their necks and legs.>

Or maybe someone took llamas and squished them to make sheep.

<Oh, yeah! What came first, the llama or the sheep?>

That's an excellent question. Perhaps I'll ask Gaia sometime.

It's relaxing there, and I take the time to meditate a bit after I build a fire for us. Tomorrow will be an important day for me, and I want it to go well. I vocalize with Orlaith what I want to happen, because it helps to say it out loud.

"I want Thatcher Oil and Gas shut down, and though I know it will be difficult to confront my stepfather, I want to maintain control and not resort to violence."

<Okay! But remind me why that matters again? Sometimes you have to break a neck if you want to eat.>

"It matters because violence—or the threat of it—is how men tend to solve problems. Like right now Atticus is feeling pushed around by this vampire Theophilus, so he's pushing back just as hard, if not harder. I'm not sure if there's any other way to handle the situation, but I don't think he's looking especially hard for one. And I admit that sometimes violence *is* the only option, and for that reason I'm glad I'm quite good at it, but I don't want to make that my default solution. Whenever I can, I want to win with Druidry rather than asskicking."

<I know what you mean about violence being the only option sometimes. You just can't talk to squirrels, you know?>

"I probably could. And that's something I need to keep in mind. I have a lot of options. Violence is a well-traveled road, and I'd rather take the one less traveled."

Orlaith is not up to speed on her Robert Frost poetry, so she misses the reference. <I like well-traveled roads, though. Lots of smells to enjoy.>

"They do have their charms. Let's dream about them."

We snuggle up together in the grass, and I try counting llamas instead of sheep to get to sleep and continue healing my muscles from that encounter in Germany. When the morning comes, I shape-shift into a jaguar and give the llamas a friendly chase with Orlaith, just to get everyone's blood pumping. Then I change back, get dressed, and we travel through Tír na nÓg to get to Wichita, Kansas, where the offices of Beau Thatcher, my stepfather, can be found.

I charge up the silver storage of Scáthmhaide and use the bindings carved into it at Flidais's instruction to make Orlaith and myself completely invisible. Then we enter the steel-and-glass tower of Thatcher Oil & Gas, travel up to the tenth floor, and stroll right past his secretary's desk.

When I open the door to his office, he's on the phone, red-faced and angry, practically shouting into the receiver. He's hearing that his entire oil production is at a standstill and can't be fixed. Customers will begin to get their oil elsewhere when they can't fill orders. Good: He's already having a bad day.

I haven't seen him in the flesh for more than twelve years, and his flesh has suffered the ravages of time. He used to have very sharp features—bladed cheeks and a keen edge to the ridge of his nose—but the lines have softened and swelled now, there's heavy luggage under his eyes, and his hair clings to his scalp like thin wavy patches of pond moss, if the moss were pale gray. His mouth still has the same cruel curl to it, though, and it frowns at the door when we walk through and close it behind us. His eyes drop away, seeing nothing, and he resumes his bilious shouting into the phone.

"Right now I don't fucking care how it happened; I care about getting it fixed, God damn it! Tell me when you'll have it fixed!" He pauses to listen briefly and then interrupts. "Hey, are you a fucking engineer or aren't you? You're supposed to know how shit works. You can't tell me you don't know how to fix it without me suspecting that you're incompetent, you understand? Now, you'd better know how to fix it and tell me when it'll be fixed before the hour's up! Call me then!"

He slams down the phone and growls, "Shhhhit!" in

his frustration. It makes all of yesterday's work well worth it, and I smile.

That's when I drop my invisibility and Orlaith's and say, "Hello, Beau."

He startles, his eyes going wide, and says, "Who the hell are you?"

"I'm Granuaile. Don't you remember? The step-daughter you sent off to college in Arizona oh so long ago?"

"Bullshit. She's dead. Tell me who you really are and how you got that big damn dog in here."

I walk forward and seat myself in the plush leather chair opposite his mahogany desk. Orlaith sits next to me on the left.

"Come on, Beau. Believe your eyes. I'm Granuaile and I'm not dead. And, no, Mom doesn't know. I'd appreciate it if you kept this between us."

He takes a good long look at me and shakes his head. "I don't believe it. Where the hell you been? Why'd you let us think you were dead?"

"That's all secret stuff. The kind of thing where if I told you I'd have to kill you."

"Whatever," he says, waving my answer away. His hands drop below the desk after that and I almost comment but he continues to say, "I'm not really interested."

"Oh, I know. You never were." There would be no "Welcome home, Granuaile, I'm so glad you're not dead!" coming from him.

He scowls at me. "What do you want? I'm busy."

"No, you're not. You have an oil empire that's producing no oil right now, so you're not busy at all. You have me to thank for that."

"What?"

"Every well and refinery owned by TO and G stopped working yesterday, am I right?"

"How do you know that?"

"Because I made it happen."

"How?"

"*How* is not the question you should be asking. You should be asking *why*. And it's because enough is enough, or because of karma, or whatever you want to call it. I want you to stop. Reinvest in solar and wind, open a chain of hardware stores, I don't care. Just stop being a blight on the earth."

He sneers at me in disgust. "Oh, you're a goddamn hippie, aren't you?"

"I'm a Druid."

"What you are is full of shit and about to be arrested," he says.

The office doors burst open behind me, and four security guards rush in, presumably in response to a silent alarm he triggered behind his desk. They're fit and well-paid professionals, not the slow and soggy kind. Orlaith spins and growls at them, and that makes them pull up for a second. I have Scáthmhaide in hand, and when they see that, along with the tomahawk I have at my hip, they pull out those hard-plastic police batons. The one closest to Orlaith looks like he's going to use it on her, so I slide over there and poke him gently in the gut, forcing him back a couple of steps. "Let's be kind to animals, sir."

They start shouting at me to drop my weapon, Orlaith barks at them, Beau yells at them to stop fucking around and take me down, and I grin. Their uniforms are awful polyester blends and I can't mess with them, but their shoes are made of leather. Natural material there, even if treated with chemicals. Almost identical to the leather of the chair I was just sitting in. I bind the closest guy's right foot to the back of the chair, high up, and the binding simultaneously yanks his foot up in the air and the back of the chair down. They rush to meet, both toppling over and dragging across the floor toward each other, effectively blocking the other guards from getting to me. I repeat the binding on the others, and soon they're all immobilized and cursing, kicking at the chair. They won't stay that way forever—eventually they'll slip out of their shoes, but I plan to be gone by then. I turn around to bid Beau a mocking farewell, since I've delivered my message, and discover that he's pulled a gun out of his desk and he's pointing it at me. My amusement at the guards disappears.

"Aha! Not so funny now, is it?" he says. "You shoulda stayed dead, Granuaile. Pretty thing like you is gonna hate what's left of your life in prison. Now, put that fucking stick down slow or I'll pop you in the knee. My boys there will testify I had no choice. And drop that axe too; then we'll talk about what you've done to the wells."

His condescending sneer—a frequent nightmare from my youth—sets off a rumbling quake of rage inside me, and the careful admonitions I had made to myself last night float down the River Lethe.

"Okay, okay," I say, and slowly begin to sink to my knees, seeming to comply. Then I mutter the words to trigger invisibility, and as soon as I wink out of his sight I drop down behind the desk and roll out of the gun's line of fire, moving to my right and his left, away from my hound.

"Hey, now," he says, standing up and waving that gun around, searching for me. Orlaith is growling at him, and through our mental link I tell her not to move.

"Don't fuck with me. No telling who could get hurt," he says, the gun barrel drifting in Orlaith's direction.

It's not a direct threat, but it's not subtle either, and if I was angry before, now I'm ready to erupt. I come up on his left, raise Scáthmhaide, and bring it down hard on his extended right wrist. It's a blow across his body, but that's why long staffs are handy. He shoots a round into the top of his desk before letting go, at the same time making a high squeal of pain because I've shattered the bones in his wrist. He clutches it, takes a step back, and I drop Scáthmhaide to lay into him with my fists. Doing so makes me visible and he sees me coming but not in time to do anything about it except reflexively widen his eyes. I crunch my fist into his face, and he lets out another cry as he collapses. I follow him to the ground and keep punching him in the body as I shout.

"No!" *Whud.* "Telling!" *Fump.* "Who!" *Thud.* "Could!" *Smack.* "Get hurt!" *Whump.*

<Granuaile!> Orlaith's voice intrudes, and I look up at her. <You said you didn't want to be violent!>

"Oh," I say in a tiny voice, rearing back and realizing that Beau has curled up into a defensive fetal position. I have just beaten the hell out of an old man. An evil old man, to be sure, but I've failed miserably at keeping the moral high ground. Now the entire confrontation will be about my violence instead of his decades of ruining the earth for profit. I'm torn, because it felt so good to lay into him like I've always wanted to, but I also wanted to be better than that.

<Also, watch out for the dudes.>

Looking up, I see that a couple of the guards have won free of their shoes and one is circling around the desk to get behind me while the other is moving to the door. He opens it a crack, shouts to the secretary to call for backup, and closes it again. The other two guards will be free in another couple of seconds. I need to leave.

The guy who's trying to pounce on me from behind moves too slowly; his body language screams that I spooked him with the shoe thing. He can't explain that shit with science so he's got a clenched-teeth aggro face and nostrils flaring like a bull. Still, when I scramble to my feet, retrieving Scáthmhaide, he somehow summons the courage to try to bash me in the head with his baton.

I knock it aside and then before he can swing it back around I whip the bottom end of my staff up into his unprotected groin. He goes down with a whimper, all the aggro gone and the totality of his existence now consumed with the throbbing of his bruised balls.

Movement in my peripheral vision alerts me that one of the guards is climbing over the chair and lunging for the desk. I get there a split second faster and snatch up Beau's dropped gun.

"Nuh-uh," I say, pointing it at him. "Back off. Drop the batons. All of you, away from the door. Move fast, now, or I'll drop you with a bullet to the knee."

I gesture, they scoot, and I mentally tell Orlaith to head for the door. She growls as she passes them, essentially exchanging positions with the guards, and stands in front of the door. The three guards—the last one finally free of the chair—keep their hands up and their eyes on me. Beau is still lying on the ground, moaning. With the guards disarmed and Orlaith out of danger, I take my eyes off the three guards just long enough to carefully step past the one I'd nutted. Couldn't have him tripping me up.

When I reach the door, I'm afraid Beau might not take the proper lesson from this. "You were right, Beau," I say, calling to him. "Granuaile is dead. I'm someone else. Someone you can't control." A line from Whitman floats up into my consciousness and I seize on it. "*I help myself to material and immaterial, No guard can shut me off, no law prevent me.* Bye now, Beau. Shut down Thatcher Oil and Gas and move on."

Out the door when it opens, Orlaith, I tell her. I take care to turn on the safety, shove the gun in my waistband, and open the door. Orlaith trots out smartly.

The secretary is on the phone, calling for reinforcements, but looks up at our exit.

"Oh. Oh god. She's here." The phone drops from her fingers and she raises her hands. "Please don't kill me."

"Nobody's dead. Just don't move," I say, closing the door and concentrating on the wood—a paneled composite, I realize, rather than the solid hardwood I was expecting. I'm still not good with binding the unseen, so I forget the lock and perform a different binding instead, fusing the wood of the door to the jamb. Beau and his minions will have to be hacked out of there to get out. My hand is still on the doorknob and someone tries to open it from the other side as I work. I maintain my hold on the knob until I complete my binding, and then he can rattle the doorknob all he wants after that.

"Call 911!" the guard shouts from behind the door. "We need an ambulance!" Binding complete, I let go of the door and turn to the secretary.

"Did you hear that?"

She nods at me, eyes huge like hardboiled eggs.

"Well, better get on it, then. Tell them to bring something to hack through the door."

I head for the stairwell, ruling out the elevator as a death trap. The secretary watches me go until I'm past her desk, then she grabs for her phone.

Move down these as fast as you can manage, Orlaith, I tell her as I open the door. *But stay in contact with my hand.* As soon as it clicks shut behind us, I speak the binding that will turn us invisible again, drawing on a dwindling reserve of energy. I'm still somewhat stiff from my encounter with Weles, despite my opportunities to heal, so I can't move as quickly as I would like. After a few flights down we hear the door above slam open and boots clomping after us. Additional security must have arrived via the elevator only to be told by the secretary that we went downstairs. On the third-floor landing, I hear a door open below and hold up, telling Orlaith to stop.

Squish yourself against the wall right here, away from the banister, I tell her. More boots pound upstairs and soon three black-clad security guards round the banister, stick to the rail, and hurry right past us on the landing, soon to meet the other guys coming down. I wait for them to round the next flight before giving Orlaith the all-clear. *Let's keep going down, but try to go quietly.*

<My toenails click,> Orlaith mourns.

I think it will be okay. Their boots are loud. Plus they're shouting at one another now, wondering where we are.

We sneak out without incident after that, I toss Beau's gun into a public trash can—the kind with a lid on it, so people can't see it in there—and I keep a hand on the back of Orlaith's neck to guide her a couple of blocks away, out of the immediate vicinity of the building and security cameras. The invisibility melts away in an alleyway before I can dispel it, the energy completely drained from the silver reservoir of Scáthmhaide, and then, as sirens wail on their way to aid my stepfather, I shudder from the adrenaline comedown and wonder what I should be feeling.

I sink to my knees and wrap my arms around Orlaith's neck. "This is so strange," I tell her. "I feel terrible and awesome at the same time. Pretty sure that's wrong."

<Why?>

"I'm supposed to feel just terrible for utterly failing to be a good person up there."

<You're a good person! The best person.>

"But I didn't need to be violent. Even when he pulled that gun, I could have used Druidry instead of my weapon. Thrashing him felt good, but still I'm horrified at my lack of control. Thank you for stopping me from doing anything more." The fact that he needed an ambulance was bad enough.

<You're welcome. Maybe it was a mistake? Everyone

makes mistakes. That one time I chewed up your slippers was a mistake. It was fun to chew them, but once I knew it was wrong I didn't do it again.>

That makes me laugh. "You have a point there." I think, not for the first time, that Oberon and Orlaith are far more emotionally stable than humans. Hounds have much to teach us, as do all the creatures of the earth. I've made my share of mistakes, but thank all the gods that I have yet to regret choosing to become a Druid. I get to my feet and dust off my knees. "Okay, back to the park, and then we shift out of here."

We might be observed by traffic cameras on the way, and authorities might trace my path later, but there is no helping it. I have nothing left to keep us camouflaged across the city.

During the jog to the park, I continue to ping back and forth between elation and guilt. I'd undeniably done a good thing for Gaia by shutting down the operations of TO & G, but in hindsight my visit with Beau was definitely a mistake. He doesn't feel remorse over what he's done. He doesn't see that I'm right, only that I can punch him whenever I want and get away with it—and that I can make leather shoes stick to his upholstery. Maybe my leaving that binding in place, along with sealing his office door, will be a nice reminder that I'm not playing by the rules he's used to. That might be the only thing that gets through to him, short of driving his company bankrupt. I do hope that he decides to get out of oil without further prompting, but it's more likely that I will have to slowly choke his company to death. And no one should doubt that I will do it, with purpose and vigor and justice for Gaia.

What truly worries me is the idea that the elementals' habit of calling me "Fierce Druid" isn't merely a badass honorific. Maybe it points to something darker in my makeup, something latent that I didn't realize lurked

within me until events conspired to yank it to the surface.

The thing to do, if I must be fierce, is to channel it into
virtuous channels. I need to study Polish and memorize
Szymborska to improve my Druidry, and I have to fight
Gaia's battles until I can't fight anymore.

Orlaith and I return to the same peaceful meadow in
Ecuador to seek some balance after the violence of
Wichita. The runoff lake is cold, but I feel cleaner after
a swim. And after whiling the day away under a tree in
meditation, I open my eyes at dusk and smile, having
come to an emotional mountaintop where I can breathe
easy.

It was ugly work, dealing with Beau, and I certainly
could have controlled myself better. But confronting
him was a wall I had to climb to see the splendor of the
other side. I think I'll take Orlaith's wise advice and not
dwell on the mistakes I made while scaling that wall. I
will focus instead on not repeating them.

I suspect most people have someone like Beau
Thatcher in their lives—a person standing in between
who you used to be and who you want to be, guarding
the wall and proclaiming that you shall forever be imprisoned by their expectations and obligations. Crossing
to the other side will always be a struggle and fraught
with dangers that may leave scars. But, oh, the reward
when you leap over that wall or break through it and
shed the burdens of the past! I am light and free and my
path ahead is smooth and wide through a land of bur-
geoning promise.

CHAPTER 19

Sometimes you get an idea so simple that you wonder why you never thought of it before. What is the point, I asked myself, of having your own goddess of the hunt if you don't ask her to show off once in a while? Flidais was unlikely to do anything but follow her own whimsy, but since Brighid was on record as wanting the vampire threat eliminated and it was a genuine challenge, I figured it wouldn't hurt to ask for Flidais's help in tracking down Theophilus. A quick trip to Tír na nÓg to present the problem to her was in order. Instead of asking her to help, I challenged her to beat me.

"I haven't been able to find an ancient vampire for months now," I said. "I wondered if you could succeed where I failed."

And, as it turned out, Flidais was longing for something to occupy her attention. She was prone to ennui after hunting everything on the earth over a couple thousand years, and she needed something to distract her from dwelling on Fand's betrayal of Brighid anyway. She accepted my challenge straightaway and accompanied me back to Prague, bringing a rather moody Perun along.

I worried at first that she was breaking Brighid's offer of sanctuary by having him leave Tír na nÓg—he was supposed to stay there, and sanctuary was forfeit if he left—but she said not to worry about it, so I didn't.

I took her to the Grand Hotel Bohemia and said we'd be looking for the oldest vampire there, if that was a trail she could isolate somehow. She brought a couple of scent hounds with her, cast invisibility on them, and entered the hotel with the admonition to give her a few hours. She'd bind with them and coach them on what to search for. I might be able to do something similar but could never achieve the same link she could and be certain they had picked up the right scent; her hunting experience and skill with animals put her in a completely different league from me. I took Perun and Oberon to the Grand Café Orient, near the hotel. The café was determined to take advantage of the sunny weather in winter and offer outdoor seating. They had umbrellas over the tables to protect against sunburns or sudden rain, but I thought the latter was more likely, considering Perun's sour disposition. Clouds began to form and whirl directly above us. Tourists walking down the cobbled street looked up at them, a bit worried, and then looked at Perun as if the huge man wearing a blue sleeveless shirt on a chilly day was responsible. He was, of course: If there's some odd weather rolling in, you can almost always blame it on the big guy flaunting his hairy shoulders. People were trying to be cool about it and not stare, but they couldn't help themselves. They spotted him dwarfing his chair, looking as out of place as one might expect a thunder god in an outdoor café to look, and smiled or laughed at him. A pair of Spanish tourists thought he was an eccentric local and wanted to take a picture with him, and he obliged, grateful for the attention. It cheered him up a bit, I think.

After they left and we had Czech pilsners in front of us, Perun began to speak of what troubled him. He had seen Granuaile recently and she had suggested that Weles was working with Loki. Apparently Perun's old enemy had squirreled away another god of his pantheon and a horse used to divine the outcomes of battles. Perun and Granuaile had found the horse—and Weles had found them, and then later Loki appeared briefly, proving the link—but they had not found the god, Świętowit.

"I am thinking I go looking for Świętowit," Perun said. "Others of my peoples too. I thought all were burn by Loki, but maybe they live. The Zoryas do. Flidais may help with looking for others if Brighid does not need her in Tír na nÓg."

"I wish you luck with that. But if you don't mind backtracking a bit: Do you know why Granuaile would concern herself with the horse?"

"She is wanting cloak of divination. Witches in Poland give to her if she give to them horse. Good witches who worship Zoryas."

Interesting. Either she'd removed Loki's mark and wanted a cloak until she completed binding cold iron to her aura, or she hadn't and was hoping the cloak on top of the mark would shield her from Loki's sight. It was all news to me, and I felt a physical ache in my chest at the thought that I should be with the one I love rather than chasing down vampires. And there was a dollop of guilt on top of it, melting like whipped cream on hot pie, for not thinking of her earlier. I could smell that strawberry lip gloss of hers—or at least the memory of it was so strong that it seemed to be in my nose right then. Oberon was thinking similar thoughts, presumably because the mention of Granuaile reminded him of her hound.

<I miss Orlaith,> he said, and sighed heavily next to us.

Hopefully we'll get to see her soon, I told him privately, and it meant Granuaile for me as much as it meant Orlaith for him. But it was good to hear that she was taking measures to protect herself. I was doing much the same. Removing Theophilus would theoretically remove his death sentence on Druids—which would never have happened if I had kept running when I should have. I shook my head at the realization that all I did anymore was fight to get back to that place where I had only one Irish god after my ass. Aenghus Óg was long gone now, his spirit trapped in hell, but I supposed Fand could fill the role of Irish antagonist quite admirably from her prison.

Perun and I waited at that café for more than a few hours, downing schooners of pilsner and trading stories of older days while Oberon napped, but eventually I was too cold to stand it anymore. The clouds had moved off as Perun's mood lightened, but the temperature was trending toward icy. "You know what?" I said. "Let's go shopping. Flidais will find us wherever we are, right?"

"Is right. She does this to me before."

"Good. Let's go."

"What do we buy?"

"I need a jacket," I said, quite nearly shivering. I didn't want to employ the earth's energy to raise my temperature when there was a simpler fix. "Maybe we'll find one for you too."

Perun looked up at the sky and twisted his lips. "Eh. Okay. Is little cold maybe."

"No maybe about it." A couple of queries on the street led us a few blocks south to a square full of fashion shops and sausage vendors. Oberon's tail sawed the air when he saw sausages just dangling from the ceiling of the kiosks. We paused to buy him a couple and then entered a store promising that there was "couture" inside, which meant I'd be paying for that word more than practicality, but I did manage to find a selection of leather jackets that would keep my core warm and also provide a handy inner pocket for Luchta's stake. I picked a brown one and hoped Granuaile would like it. Just

like a seasoned shopping companion, Perun assured me
that I had made a good choice.

"Is very handsome. Too bad they no have jacket like
this for my size. Flidais would love. She would be very
excited and then tear from my body. Ehh . . . Now that
I think this, maybe is good they no have my size."

"It's too late," Flidais said from behind us, smiling at
Perun as she walked up to him. "Now that you've put
the idea into my head, nothing will do but I must have
you in leather."

<I don't understand why humans like to wear dead
cows,> Oberon grumbled while Perun and Flidais made
happy reuniting noises. <Cows are for eating.> Once
Flidais pointed out that we were far easier to track from
the Grand Bohemia than Theophilus, she let me know
where to find my quarry.

"He's in Berlin," she said, "and he has a significant
entourage. He's staying at the Monbijou Hotel, in that
neighborhood with all the museums and fancy restaurants."

I knew exactly where that was. There were some outstanding works of art in those museums—mostly on
Museum Island, formed by the Spree River forking and
reuniting—and I had visited them several times in the
past decades. "Your skills remain unparalleled," I said
to Flidais by way of thanks. "I'll leave you to your
search for suitable leathers."

I said farewell, returned to the trees of Petřín Hill,
and shifted through Tír na nÓg to Tiergarten in Berlin, a
pleasant and rather large wooded park with paths that
radiated out from the famous Victory Column. The old
tree bound there was a knotted, lichen-covered syca-
more, currently occupied by an alarmed red squirrel,
which Oberon saw immediately and lunged after, nearly
catching it by the tail before it scampered up the trunk,
out of reach.

<Aw! Dang it! Almost got him! And I would have too, if he weren't so squirrely.>

"Maybe next time, Oberon."

<That's right!> Oberon said, more to the squirrel than to me. He still had his front paws on the tree trunk, and his eyes tracked the one that got away. He barked for emphasis. <You just wait for next time, pal! Your doom approaches! Say goodbye to your nuts!>

There was an efficient train system nearby called the S-Bahn, which would take us to Hackescher Markt in only four stops, but since it was the evening rush hour and everyone was returning home from work, the cars were far too crowded to sneak Oberon on board. We had to go on foot, and that was all right. We needed time for full darkness to fall anyway.

We jogged in gray twilight through the outskirts of Tiergarten, with only a brief pause while Oberon tried and failed to catch a couple of rabbits, and then past blocks of flats and office buildings covered in unimaginative graffiti. Halfway to our destination it began to rain, the sort that couldn't decide if it wanted to be sleet or not. It was more piercingly cold than refreshing, and I was grateful for the jacket. I distracted Oberon from the weather with the memory that somewhere nearby, there was a road whose name—Große Hamburger Straße—translated to *Big Hamburger Street*.

<Really? What's the story behind that?>

"I don't know if there's a story," I said. It most likely meant that road was a fairly wide one that led to the city of Hamburg, but Oberon wouldn't find that interesting. "If there isn't, we should make one."

<Can you at least buy a big hamburger there?>

"I believe so. It would be a tragic waste of natural marketing if not."

It was dismal, cold, and dark when we arrived at the Monbijou Hotel, a modern building in cream and sporting a cool gray logo above the revolving glass door. I peeked into the interior from outside: Directly opposite the door was a lift, one of the narrow but deep elevators more commonly found in Europe. The reception area was to the left, complete with a primly uniformed employee, and to the right a fireplace beckoned, inviting people to sit at the small round tables scattered about. It was a lounge area, with the bar no doubt secreted out of sight from the street, and several people were already busy lounging in it. They were lounging, in fact, in an almost ostentatious manner, as if to say to passersby like myself, "Look uponst my exquisite lounging, foolish mortal, and mourn that you will never lounge with such cosmopolitan savoir faire." I flipped my vision to the magical spectrum and saw that three of the four people were not human. They had gray auras around their heads and hearts with a fiery red center, which meant they were vampires. None wore infrared goggles, so that was encouraging. The only human I could see appeared nervous, with ample justification. I thought at first that I would enter in camouflage and simply go to work, but that wouldn't be wise. They'd be warned by a revolving door moving by itself.

I camouflaged only Oberon instead and had him follow me inside. Once I got to the lobby, I veered left toward the reception area so as not to invite a closer look. They might smell my old blood anyway, but if I gave them no cause to examine the air I might buy myself a few more seconds of surprise.

Oberon, I want you to stay over here and dry off, I said, pointing to the couches in the reception area. No one was there except for the single employee behind the reception half-circle desk. Untouched German newspapers and magazines waited to be perused on an expansive black leather ottoman. *Be quiet and don't come*

*after me. I'm going to pick a fight and don't want you in
danger. These are very strong vampires.*

<But I can help! Remember that one time I helped you
against that vampire?>

*Yes, you did help, but you also got hurt. This is differ-
ent. That time before, the vampires ambushed me and I
needed your help. This time I'm ambushing them. If
I don't have to worry about your safety, that will be a
tremendous help to me.*

<Okay. I could use a nap anyway. That way I'd be
helping both of us.>

I think that's an excellent plan, I replied, though I
didn't think he'd feel like napping once the fighting
started. *Let's get you hidden behind this furniture here,
so the guy at the front desk doesn't see you. Then I can
drop your camouflage and use that energy for kicking
ass.*

<Sounds like a plan!>

I waved casually to the receptionist and pretended to
be interested in a newspaper while Oberon got himself
stretched out on the floor, out of sight. Once the receptionist lost interest in me and dropped his eyes, I dispelled the camouflage on Oberon and cast it on myself
instead.

Nap well, I told him. *But guard my jacket.* I kind of
liked it and it was sure to get messy in a few minutes. I
took it off and laid it on the ottoman. As soon as it left
my hands I dropped its camouflage, but the receptionist
didn't notice its sudden appearance. I took Luchta's
stake out of the inside pocket.

<I can nap and guard at the same time. If somebody
comes around here, they will see me and decide to let
that sleeping dog and your jacket lie.>

I returned my sight to the magical spectrum and
crossed the lobby to the lounge on the other side.
Through the open doorway, the lounge continued quite

far back to a bar and then to an area with restaurant seating, where the hotel served its breakfast. In the lounge, round tables rested in front of couches built into the wall, and on the opposite side of those tables were a few modern armless chairs right out of a Copenhagen design haus. Ten tables, seating three or four each, and they were all full. Thirty vampires and one very nervous human serving them drinks they did not touch—though I had serious doubts that she knew who or what she was serving. She only knew that something about this group seemed wrong.

Up to this point I had slain very few vampires myself; most of the war had been conducted for me by the yew-men or the Hammers of God. Unless these vampires were all very old, they had yet to see why vampires of early days had cause to fear Druids. Except perhaps for Theophilus. I did hope that he was there; I had no idea what he looked like, and their auras all appeared the same to me—so I had no way to identify which one was measurably older or more powerful than another.

I shifted my grip on the stake, carved with the unbinding that would undo the vampires' magic and then forcibly separate their component elements. I was anxious to try it out here, since it never got a test run in Prague. I'd examined the bindings earlier, and it was a clever execution. If there was no vampirism to unbind, it would do nothing to a human but hurt every bit as much as a normal stabbing would. But for a vampire, stabbing it anywhere with this stake would end its undead existence.

Murmuring the bindings to increase my strength and speed, drawing all the energy from the pool stored in my bear charm, I hoped I'd be able to either end this quickly or else lure them outside, where I could tap into more power from the earth. But I had my semi-effective unbinding charm, my ability to verbally unbind them, my stake, and at least a temporary visual advantage.

I really wished I knew how to tell the older vampires from the younger ones. Cosmetically, they were all frozen at the age they were when they died, and their clothing didn't give any clues either: They all wore bespoke Italian suits and expensive shoes. I would not be surprised if each vampire's ensemble was worth a year's salary to the average worker. And "younger" was a relative term. I thought of it as "younger than Theophilus and myself," but I had no doubt that every one of those vampires was a few hundred years old. Age equaled prestige in the vampire world, and truly young vampires would not be allowed to accompany Theophilus.

They spoke Italian too—a good clue that this crew had spent at least some time near the vampire power center of Rome, from which the campaign against the Druids had originated millennia ago. So when one vampire seated against the wall and facing the door lifted his nose and said, *"Sentite l'odore di quel sangue? E veramente strano,"* that was my cue to get the slaughter started, because they had smelled me.

I mentally targeted that vampire and surged forward, coming up behind the seated vamp and plunging the stake down over the back of the chair and into his right shoulder, puncturing the suit and his flesh. He made a short gurgling noise before his body liquefied and squirted in five directions—out his pant legs, his shirtsleeves, and his collar. I repeated the exercise with the vampire next to him and then completed the verbal unbinding on the third, taking out three vampires in a little more than three seconds.

And then, while the rest of the room was figuring out that, hey, maybe something ugly was going on, I staked another two and unbound three more verbally, using a macro-binding and simply changing the target. It was six or seven seconds, therefore, before the back of the room figured out that something was taking them apart and the champion lounging session was over. They all sprang to their feet, in some cases knocking over tables and chairs, and in one specific case throwing a chair in my general direction. It moved fast and I wasn't expecting it and it took me down, though it did no real damage apart from giving them more time to set themselves in defense. I gave zero fucks about that: Vampires had no true defense against Druidry, and I was going to thunderdome every single one of them.

I kept re-targeting and unbinding the vampires closest to me. The nearest two lunged in my direction, came apart, and showered me in blood. My camouflage was then useless, because I was silhouetted in red, so I dispelled it and kept unbinding as I climbed to my feet. I'd ended ten vampires in fifteen seconds; perhaps I could get the rest in under a minute.

A whole furniture set sailed through the air at my head, the vampires figuring that if it had worked once, perhaps it would work again. And it did, because dodging that many chairs and tables is impossible.

I crumpled underneath them, making sure to hold on to the stake, and the twenty remaining vampires charged for the exit. Most of them flowed around me, but a pair landed on top of the chairs, pinning me to the floor and allowing the others time to escape. Or at least that was their plan. I targeted each one in turn and unbound them; the weight lifted off me, and their entrails glopped onto the floor. I threw off the chairs just in time to see that there were only five or so vampires remaining in the room: The rest had scarpered off, but one landed on me with his knee in my gut, one hand around my throat and the other pinning down my stake hand. He was strong and would crush my larynx if I let him get comfortable; his nails were already drawing blood. I triggered the unbinding charm on my necklace, imperfect as it was, and let it do its thing: It affected the vampire like a punch to the solar plexus and he wheezed, the strength temporarily gone from his limbs. I wrenched the stake hand free and slammed it into his side beneath the ribs as his buddies scrambled past. He turned into something like melted raspberry gelato right on top of me, and I was so glad that I'd left my jacket with Oberon.

I gasped and coughed to get my breath back, then scrambled to my feet, even though without oxygen my muscles felt like Jell-O. The time I'd spent on the ground had let the vampires crash through the front floor-to-ceiling windows—they didn't bother with the revolving door—meaning that almost half of them were getting away.

A faintly heard *"Sheiße"* from behind the bar was my only clue that the human server had survived.

<Atticus? You all right?> Oberon's voice asked in my head.

Yep! I'll be back. Take your nap.

Jumping through the jagged portal of glass, I saw that the vampires had split into two groups. One had gone left at a diagonal angle toward the S-Bahn station at Hackescher Markt, and another had gone right toward Monbijou Park and the Spree River.

Considering my low reserves of energy, I hauled off after the group to the right, since chasing them through the park would allow me to reconnect with Gaia and replenish. There was a flower bed, now sad and brown for the winter, surrounding a pedestal with a bust of somebody on top staring with blank bronze eyes at me. The straggling vampire in the back was approaching it as I unbound him. He exploded and covered the statue in gore.

It said CHAMISSO underneath the bust, and I recognized it as I passed. "Hey! Adelbert von Chamisso! 'Sup,

Bert?" I'd helped him back in the day to "discover" and classify some flower species. He was a good guy; I didn't realize he'd been so well thought of in Berlin, and it's not every botanist who gets a statue made of him. "Sorry about the vampire guts, big guy."

I caught five more, able to move faster than them, with Gaia's aid. Four in the park, and the last one in the Spree River. He jumped in out of desperation and disappeared underwater; since he didn't need to breathe, he wouldn't come up until he was good and ready. But that same lack of buoyancy made vampires terrible swimmers. They sank to the bottom and had to walk instead of swim, much slower than anything else. He couldn't float up; he'd have to claw and crawl his way out, if I ever let him get that far. I splashed after him, shapeshifted to a sea otter, swam right out of my clothes, and held the stake between my wee front paws until I was able to close the gap between us. Then I shifted back to human and sank the stake into the vampire's calf. He dissolved in the river beneath the Bode Museum and got washed away by the current.

That left me naked in the Spree River, and I'm not ashamed to say the temperature led to some shrinkage.

That was nineteen very old vampires erased from the world, however, and all I got was naked and some bruising. Not bad. Quite good, in fact. And if one of the unbound had been Theophilus, then I would count it as a perfect ambush. But eleven of them had escaped cleanly to the S-Bahn, and there was no telling where they had gone.

I returned to the Monbijou Hotel in shivering camouflage to avoid alarming the local populace. My priorities amused me and I snorted into the darkness. I had no problem disassembling vampires in plain view but didn't want to truly terrify anyone with my full frontal nudity.

Once outside the hotel, I called Oberon to come join me outside. *And bring my jacket, will you, please?* I asked.

<Okay. Ha! The man working at the desk just saw me get up and he freaked out. I don't know what he's saying, but he's got those terrified *Twilight Zone* eyes.>

Sirens began to wail and grow closer. *Yes, I imagine so. He just saw men crash through the window, and if he's been into the lounge he's seen an awful lot of blood. The sudden appearance of a huge hound after all that probably made him lose bladder control.*

We scooted around the corner to a Nike store on Hackescher Markt, where I was able to discreetly snatch a pair of sweatpants and a shirt. I didn't bother with shoes, and the leather jacket didn't exactly match, but it was better than bare skin in this weather. I made a mental note to come back and pay for them later.

Let's head back to the park, Oberon. You have a fateful date with a squirrel.

<Yeah! That's right!>

I wondered how the hotel staff would explain to the police what had happened. I wondered if maybe I'd been caught on a security video, unbinding vampires—a distinct possibility and one I hadn't worried about as I had in the past. If that encounter was recorded, it could prove problematic, but I doubted it would make the news. There were too many uncomfortable questions for police to answer: Did I have a new, horrifying weapon that liquefied or exploded people on contact, or were those victims not exactly human? Or both? They couldn't let that get out until they had the answers. Governments have been in the habit of suppressing information "for the population's own protection" for centuries now; it's how gods and monsters can still walk the earth and the mass of humanity thinks of them as mere stories for their entertainment, an escape from a lifetime of toil to pay the bills. Maybe they would call in the real-life equivalent of Fox Mulder to investigate this. Or the authorities might be so desperate to catch me that I would find a screen cap of my face on every television in Germany.

Either way, the vampires who escaped wouldn't remain in Berlin for long, and I figured I shouldn't either. A hot shower, a real change of clothes, and a few hours of blissful slumber far away from sirens were what I needed. A reunion with Granuaile would be perfect, if I could catch up with her, but we had no home base until the place in Oregon was ready, and I doubted I'd be able to divine her location now if she'd secured a divination cloak from the Polish coven, as Perun had suggested. Not that I had my divination wands on me anyway.

"I'm up for sleeping someplace warm," I told Oberon as we jogged back to Tiergarten in the rain. "We need to visit the Southern Hemisphere."

<Fine by me. How about someplace dry in Australia? Alice Springs?>

"That sounds perfect right now."

CHAPTER 20

Knowing that there's something ye should be doing but can't is like having an itchy arsehole ye want to scour clean but you're at Court and that sort of thing is frowned upon. I should be helping Brighid hunt down Fand and Manannan Mac Lir, but I have apprentices to protect and teach. I suppose I should take comfort in the fact that this is something I can and should do. It should be fecking joyous. I think it would be, except for me itching.

I tried to tell Brighid what happened, but her gaggle of Fae chamberlains wouldn't rouse her. She was excessively wearied after some trip to Svartálfheim, they said. She left explicit instructions not to be disturbed unless an actual physical attack was under way, and me wishing to speak to her didn't qualify. So I wrote a note.

And I don't try to see Flidais about the problem, because what if it really isn't Flidais I'm talking to but Fand in a glamour? Best to let Brighid deal with it as she wishes, when she wishes, and bear the itching in the meantime.

Divination is no help. I cast wands, watch the birdies for some augury, and all I get is the vague idea that they're hiding in a swamp. But no indication of where that swamp might be, not even if it's on this plane or one of the Irish ones or somewhere else.

So it's work for me now, instead of worry.

I've started the kids on both Latin and English. Nouns for the earth and sky and sun and adjectives to describe them, things like that. Verbs for things you can do outside, and we do those things, like run and eat lunch and smell pine needles. And I start them using Latin to talk to Colorado—phrases that they repeat verbatim but backed by thoughts and images, to begin the process of separating headspaces. I'll start them on Irish in a couple of years.

The house has an unfinished basement, and the pack has been working on it during the day and I've begun working on it for a couple hours after dinner each night, warding it every way I know how. The promised help from Tír na nÓg hasn't arrived yet, but I hope it will soon. It's going to be a sanctuary for the kids during full moons and all other emergencies, like troops of trolls barging through your land, smelling like exactly the wrong cheese. We've already coached them in what the full-moon drill is, after that troll business.

Hal Hauk arrives around dinnertime with whiskey and the new identity that Siodhachan asked for. Ty and Sam are with him too, just being friendly and neighborly pack leaders but also because they're hoping for a finger of the bottle Hal brought. They get one as Greta pulls out glasses for everyone and Hal pours. It's Midleton, which I'm told is very fine, and we all raise our glasses as Hal proposes a toast.

"An impromptu wake for Sean Flanagan, a fine identity that got shot down in Toronto, and a welcome to the new Siodhachan, who will henceforth walk the world as Connor Molloy. As soon as he pays me for the trouble." There are wry chuckles at this, and I join in. "But mostly this is a rare, fine drink with rarer, finer friends. It's my privilege to call you such."

I say, "Aye, lad," but everyone else says, "Hear, hear,"

or maybe "Here, here," and I don't understand why they would say either one. English has way too many fecking homophones, and when you combine something like that with what might be a slang term or polite jargon, it's just not fair to lads like me trying to pick up the language. I'm getting much better with it already, but little things like that are probably going to keep me stepping on me own bollocks for years.

Midleton is as fine as reported, and then I offer everyone a spot of lamb stew and soda bread. It's fortunate that I made a great big batch, thinking we'd have leftovers, but with extra guests it's just as well I erred on the side of generosity. And it's also a good thing, I decide, that Greta found a place much bigger than I thought we'd need. It has a huge dining room and extra seating in the kitchen area, so it's already a place people like to visit.

We're all there—the apprentices, their parents, the translators, the pack leaders—having a laugh and being happy, when all the wolves freeze or put down their spoons and cock their heads, listening. Some of them look toward the big bay window leading to the backyard.

"No—" Sam says, the instant before the glass shatters and bullets riddle the room. The parents instinctively place themselves in the line of fire, protecting the children, and they take a few rounds as a result. That's going to trigger transformations for sure, and I'm not the only one to shout, "Full-moon drill! Go!"

It's only me and a few parents who aren't werewolves, so it's our job to make sure the kids get safely down to the basement. The wee ones move fast and stay low to the ground; they already know they don't want to be anywhere around when their parents' bones start snapping and the teeth come out. We hear the snarls and cracks and howls of pain begin before we're out of the room, though. They're all turning, including Greta, and the gunfire continues and just accelerates the transformations, so they don't have time to tear off their clothes first. They're going to rip right through them as they transform, and that will increase the pain of it. The pack is going to be fecking irate, and I almost feel sorry for whoever's doing this.

I leave the kids in the basement with Tuya's mother, Meg, and she locks the silver-lined gate we installed at the bottom of the stairs. They have food and water down here and emergency buckets; they can last for days if need be, by which point the danger should be long over. Then I slip on me knuckles, cast camouflage, and exit out the front door while I'm hearing all kinds of ruckus going on in the back.

The camouflage turns out to be a good idea, since some fecking arse almost takes me head off with a bullet as soon as the door opens. I duck down and scramble to the side and search for who's responsible. There's a tall figure with a handgun maybe forty yards away, and his hearing must be stellar, because he fires two more rounds that come damn close—one grazes the back of me calf as I'm running. Balls to that: I need to change the rules on him. I tumble onto the front lawn and shuck off me shirt before shape-shifting to a kite, which lets me fall out of the pants. Another round hits the turf where me body was a second before the shift, and I hop away from there as quietly as I can. Me torn shoulder muscles won't let me fly yet, but of all my forms this is also the quietest one on the ground. I make little bird-hops in his direction, and he hears even that. But since he has no idea what's making the sound, he's aiming too high. A dart to the left and then a leap up, extending me talons to latch on his right wrist, since he's left his whole arm out there for me to perch on, but it's not a gentle landing. I clutch as hard as I can and that hand shears clean off, dropping onto the ground along with the gun. I'm expecting a scream or some cursing as I drop with it, but instead the spooky lad *hisses,* and the blood pumping out of him is dark, like it would be when it's starved for oxygen. I hop away—not caring about the noise I'm making now, because he can't shoot me—and see him bend down to snatch up his right hand with his left. He doesn't give a damn about the gun anymore: He just jams that hand back onto his stump like it will help, and then he turns and runs down the road leading to town—*fast.*

That's not a man, I realize. That's a damn vampire. We're being attacked by vampires. Fecking Siodhachan!

I shift back to human, take off after him, and then I recite the words of unbinding before he can get out of range. The vampire comes apart with a wet sound as the elements of his body forcibly separate, and I pivot immediately to give the wolf pack some help behind the house.

Siodhachan said that we might get some vampire blowback from whatever he was doing, but I didn't expect anything like this. Guns, I mean. I haven't figured out how to ward against those. Or people with a basic understanding of tactics. You don't have to get into the house and pass my wards when you can shoot from outside them and get everyone to come to you. It's not in the nature of werewolves to sit behind walls: You poke them and they're going to hit back. Shoot them and they won't rest until they have your entrails in their teeth.

By the time I round the corner of the house, most of the gunfire has died down: It's close quarters fighting now, because the pack has streamed out of the house to make a meal out of whoever ruined dinner. Magical sight tells me there are six vampires and one human against fourteen werewolves all told, when you count the parents and translators and the visiting pack leaders. I don't think they expected to be outnumbered two to one; you'd have to be daft to think that would work out well. I think they were expecting just me and Greta, maybe a couple more.

The werewolves are all bleeding and completely savage. The vampires didn't use silver bullets, so all they did was make the wolves crazy. The only way to beat them is through silver or to tear them up physically. It *can* be done, and it already has: One wolf is down and not moving, two legs ripped completely off and its lower jaw missing. He's undergoing his final shift, what Greta calls the "termination clause" of lycanthropy—for all the shit ye have to endure while ye live, at the end it at least gives ye back your humanity. It's Nergüi, Tuya's father, lying there. Damn it.

Two vampires are down and the rest are surrounded. I recognize the wolf forms of Sam, Ty, and Greta, but the rest are a mystery to me since I've never sparred or run with them before. There was just that one brief time with the trolls, and I never figured out who was who.

Sam, Ty, and Greta have formed a hunting group with a fourth wolf that might be Hal Hauk—he's the biggest of the big dogs. They're masterful, surrounding, nipping, timing their springs at the vampire so that he hardly has a chance to land a blow before he loses a chunk of flesh somewhere else. Once he goes down, he doesn't get up; teeth lock on the throat and tear it. Then it's on to the next target. The three other vampires are surrounded by less-experienced wolves; they might take longer to go down, but it's inevitable. The human is backpedaling away, shouting at the vampires in some sort of spitting language, and it's him the leaders target next.

Something's dodgy about him. He's acting like he's the boss of their party, but I see nothing in the magical spectrum that would explain why six vampires were taking his orders. I turn off the sight as I get closer, and he's dressed strangely too. Not a commando outfit or any sort of modern warrior gear; he's wearing a suit with a brightly colored scarf thing around his neck.

I see the moment where he counts four wolves coming and understands that this is the end for him and in the next instant his grim determination to take somebody with him. I'm too far away to do anything; all I can do is pray he won't be successful. The first big wolf leaps at him; he raises that gun of his, crying out in defiance, and shoots it point-blank down the wolf's throat. The bullet explodes through the back of the head and the big wolf goes down, completely still. In the next instant Greta takes the man down and ends him before he can take another shot. Sam and Ty get in there and help tear him apart, even though he's dead now and there are still three vampires standing.

I can help with that part, so I do, not wanting any other wolves to get hurt. One by one, I unbind the surrounded vampires, then finish off the fallen ones. None of them will rise again. But this doesn't calm those younger werewolves down like I think it will. They are still far beyond the horizon of calm, and when they spot me standing there naked with a pumping heart and meat on my bones, they come after me to have a bite.

"Bollocks," I say. I could handle a few of them, maybe, but not nine, and not without hurting them seriously. I can't fly away as a kite with me torn shoulder muscles, but bears can climb trees much better than wolves. Maybe I can climb high enough to keep me out of reach of their jaws. I shape-shift and muster what speed I can for the nearest ponderosa. The brass on me claws should help me climb three-legged.

Once I reach the tree, it's grand for a couple of seconds. I get up maybe five feet off the ground, but me arse is still low-hanging fruit for the pack. Claws and teeth sink in; I shake a couple loose, but one will simply not let go, and I have to haul him or her up with me. Without the claws anchoring me to the tree and the strength it lends, I wouldn't have been able to do it, and I make a mental note to buy Creidhne a beer.

Once I get me arms and chest around a branch high enough off the ground to be safe, I have to figure out how to get rid of the wolf attached to me arse. The simplest solution, which I use, is to shape-shift back to human. Part of that expansive backside just flows right over and between those teeth, and suddenly there's not enough purchase for him to hold on. The wolf falls but takes a mouthful of me backside with him. The wee pack of young wolves collects around the base. They leap up to reach me but can't quite make it.

Safe for the moment—if ye don't count me chewed arse—I call to them.

"Greta! Sam! Ty! It's Owen! Can ye get everybody calmed down so we can talk?"

I'm not sure how much of that penetrates, if anything. Greta says it's tough to process spoken language when she's a wolf—the pack tends to communicate via their own link. And when they're far gone into the animal side, like during a full moon or when the anger is running high, the human is pretty much gone. Right now we're at a half moon, so we should be fine, except the anger is about as raw as a wound ye rub with salt and lemon juice. Looking over at where the big wolf fell, I understand why. The final shift is over, and that is indeed Hal Hauk lying there with the back of his head missing. Maybe that was a silver bullet the human used and maybe not. Tough to survive a head wound like that, either way.

The rest of the wolves all race to the bottom of the tree and surround the base, snarling and snapping at me. I just keep hollerin' at Greta, Sam, and Ty, hoping something will get through. It's grim and desperate shite, yelling at them and getting barks and growls in return, but keeping their attention here is better than letting them tear off through the woods so close to the city. They could wind up killing people out for an evening stroll—or, worse, go back into the house and see if they can get after what's in the basement. And me heart drops down to me guts as I realize how Greta's going to take this: Hal will be the second pack leader she's lost because of something Siodhachan did. Gunnar Magnusson was the one who turned her, but Hal was there when he did; she's known him since her old days in Iceland. I have little doubt that were Siodhachan here right now, she would try to kill him. And I fear that may be where she stands regarding him from now on, nothing to be done about it.

It's Sam who gets control first. His form begins to shudder, and then his bones slide and pop under the skin and most of the hair falls out, and his howls turn into hoarse screaming as his vocal tissues transform. Ty goes next, and the two of them start to exert their influence on the rest of the pack, calming them down. But Greta is having none of it. She leaves the tree and returns to Hal's body, snuffles a couple of times, and then throws back her head and howls. Maybe if it was just an ordinary wolf doing its ordinary thing I wouldn't care, but because I know who it is and why she's howling it's the most terrible, lonely thing I've ever heard in me life. Part of me wants to join in, because we'd been having a laugh together not ten minutes ago. This had gotten so cocked up so fecking fast.

Sam and Ty let her do her thing while they get all the other wolves either shifted or in the process of shifting—it's rough, because they're riled and haven't all torn into something, but the leaders' commands have a powerful influence on them. Then they turn their attention to Greta, calling her name and no doubt trying to reach her on the pack level too. But she shakes her head, rips out a few ragged barks, and takes off uphill, disappearing into the trees.

I could chase after her, but I don't see the point. She has a lot of anger to work out, and she's going in the right direction to do it without hurting anyone. Putting meself forward as a target for that anger would be dangerous as well as foolish. She'll come back when she's ready—and I'm aware that it might not be for days.

In the meantime, we have a fecking mess to manage. I drop down from the tree and nod at Sam and Ty, who have blood on their faces. We walk together to where the human's body lays sprawled and mutilated. If Sam and Ty feel sick at being responsible for the torn flesh and the blood on their mouths—*in* their mouths—they make no indication of it.

Ty asks, "Are the kids safe in the basement?"

"Aye. None of them were hurt."

"Good," Sam says. "So who the hell was this?"

"I have an idea," I reply, "but I don't know for sure. He looks like someone Siodhachan told me about. Might be the guy who put him in the hospital in Toronto."

I squat down and pat through the shreds of his coat until I discover an Austrian passport. "Werner Drasche," I read aloud. "Yeah. This is the guy. Supposed to be the lover of the really old vampire, Theophilus."

"Why is he here?"

"I don't think he'll be fecking telling us."

"He lost the privilege of conversation when he started shooting." Sam crouches down and picks up Drasche's gun, checking the ammo. "Damn." He drops it as if stung. "He's got silver. The others don't."

He'd know, I suppose. I see a hole in Sam's side, and if that was a silver bullet he'd be at death's door himself instead of walking around. Someone would have to dig that out of him before his skin closed over it; accelerated healing can have that drawback against these modern weapons.

"Doesn't make sense to come in here with only one clip of silver rounds," Ty says.

"It does if you're traveling in a hurry and expecting only one werewolf instead of fourteen," I tell him. "I don't think ye were the target. I think they were after me and knew that Greta would be here."

"Oh. You think this is that vampire war against Druidry?"

"Aye, that's what I figure. Siodhachan told me he was going to go around blowing shite up and something like this might happen. I have wards on the house, but they never got close enough to trip them. And I didn't expect firearms. I'm sorry."

"Ffffuck," Sam swears. "I have phone calls to make and a memorial service to arrange. And this isn't over. Killing a well-loved pack leader like that is going to have consequences."

"Wait," I says. "Let me help you with that bullet, at least. And anyone else who got shot. I can maybe pull it out of there without digging around too much."

The iron content makes it a challenge to bind those bullets to me palm, but not an insurmountable one, and it's better and faster than going in with tweezers. Nobody was facing the window directly when the bullets started flying, so most of the wounds are in the sides, arms, and legs, and a few glanced off ribs.

They'll all be fine in a few days, but no one's worried about that. We have to get dressed and look presentable before we bring the kids up out of the basement. And it falls to me and Ty to tell Meg and Tuya—through a translator—that Nergüi got killed. It's really on me, but Ty feels some responsibility too. The pack, he says, should be represented and reassure them that they are still welcome and will be taken care of.

I expect I'll lose Tuya as an apprentice; even if she wants to continue, I'm not sure that's something Meg would want. People understandably want to avoid pain, and I think this house—especially the basement—will always be a source of pain for them. They might decide to forgo the company of wolves and Druids from now on, and I would not blame them. And Greta, when she comes back, might not be too fond of Druids either. I've failed them all so miserably, I'm not sure I want to keep me own company anymore.

CHAPTER 21

I'm not even a quarter of the tracker that Flidais is, and I didn't want to ask for her help finding Theophilus again but I saw no other choice. She flatly refused to help, however, for the very good reason that, shortly after helping me earlier, she heard that Fand had escaped her prison and Manannan Mac Lir was most likely responsible.

"Oh," I said. "That's not good at all."

"No. Finding her is my priority now." It would be Brighid's priority too, no doubt, and most likely Owen's, since he had a hand in imprisoning her. If I knew him at all, he was incandescently pissed at himself right now. He couldn't go around calling other people cock-ups if he made such a huge one himself.

Perhaps Fand's escape and Manannan's disappearance would wind up becoming a priority of mine soon enough, but for the moment I needed to end the vampire threat. Three Druids against tens of thousands of vampires was terrible odds, no matter our advantages. I was on my own again and out of options—except for a more personal one. Leif Helgarson had sent me into a death trap in Prague. It wasn't the first time he'd played me and I doubted it would be the last, because I had a blind spot where he was concerned—or maybe a stubborn resistance to thinking he really cared nothing for me during all those years he was my attorney and friend. The cold, rational thing to do would be to track him down and unbind him, to eliminate his ability to mess up my life anymore, but instead I wanted to track him down and just beat the hell out of him. If there was, in fact, any hell at all to be beaten out.

I was still not clear on the true nature of vampires but had serious doubts that they were the creatures of hell that the Hammers of God and popular culture thought they were. To my knowledge, they were not truly repelled by crosses or holy water. To inflict real damage you had to assault their centers of power, around the heart or head, or else burn them. Actual fire was best, but the sun would do. A nice, old-fashioned smackdown, though? Leif would shrug that off in a day and I'd feel a whole lot better.

But how to find him? He claimed to be in Normandy, which might or might not be true, but even if it was true, that didn't exactly give me his address. I couldn't find him via divination, but if he was in Normandy, perhaps I could find who would be his next meal: someone staggering alone at night, drunk on pinot noir. And maybe if I asked Mekera to help—she was far better at divination than I—she could track down Manannan and Fand in the bargain.

I'd left Mekera, the world's greatest tyromancer and infamous hermit, on Emhain Ablach, the Isle of Apples, just before shifting to Toronto. She'd been the one to help me find that vampire directory, in return for removing her to a safe place where she wouldn't be bothered. I'd promised to tell Manannan she was there and ask him to take care of her, but I realized that I hadn't ever gotten around to that and now he was missing. That gave me excuse enough to interrupt her solitude. She might actually need something. Or Manannan might be there.

Shifting to Emhain Ablach meant that Oberon was reminded of his determination to make chicken apple sausage out of the rare apple varieties there and the legendary Vicious Chicken of Bristol. He was trying to pin me down on where to find the best fennel and other spices for *The Book of Five Meats* as I called out for Mekera. We had to circle halfway around the island before we got a response.

"Hello, Siodhachan," she said, coming out of the trees. "Back for another cheese?"

"Yep. Did you see me coming in advance?"

"No. Haven't been able to make a cheese since I got here, so no divination. Haven't seen this god you told me would be dropping by either."

"Oh. I was going to ask."

"What is it you want?"

"I'd like to know where that god is, where a vampire will dine in Normandy tonight, and where to find an escaped goddess."

"Location, location, location. Three questions, three cheeses. All right. Go shopping for me, and that'll be payment enough."

"What do you need?"

"Only everything. I got out of Ethiopia with some vegetable rennet, but I lack dairy here and all my other supplies. I'll make you a list."

"All right."

"I mean as soon as you bring me paper and pen. I'm really starved for resources here, except apples. Unless it's safe for me to return to my home?"

"Not yet. Just tell me what you need and I'll remember."

It was a very long list. "That's going to be a lot of shoplifting," I muttered, but she heard me.

"You don't have any money?" Mekera said. "I find that hard to believe."

"If you go with me, I'll pay you back."

She rolled her eyes. "You're determined to get me back into the world."

"No, it's not that. I want to help, but I don't want to steal if I don't have to."

"Let's go, then. I'll reintroduce myself to my bank."

It was hours of errands after that, but Mekera was efficient and knew what she wanted and where to get it. In addition to cheese-making paraphernalia, she picked up a few more outfits and plenty of food that wasn't apples. When she finally got started on her tyromancy, most of the day had burned away.

In the pattern of the curdling cheese she divined the future, the complex patterns revealing truth to her far more clearly than my wands ever could.

She began with Fand: "She's not on earth. A different plane. A castle surrounded by a fen. Lots of yew trees. Creepy."

She'd taken up residence in the Morrigan's Fen? At first I was surprised that the Fae living there would permit it. Those loyal to the Morrigan tended to attack first and never question it later. Then I thought of a reason why they might and privately bet that Manannan was there with her. Mekera confirmed it with the next cheese.

"He's in the same place." It made sense; now that the Morrigan was dead, Manannan had taken over her primary role as psychopomp, escorting the dead to whatever afterlife they had earned. The Fae there would accept him as the heir to the plane and protect him—and Fand as well, which I'm sure was her intention.

The last cheese was a longer process, since we didn't have a name to look for. We instead needed to find a place in Normandy where someone would fall victim to sudden blood loss via the neck. That could mean we'd get a false positive—someone getting their throat slashed—but I was hoping slasher crimes weren't all that common in Normandy. Or that there weren't a large number of vampires there.

"It'll happen in Le Havre," Mekera said, after studying the curds. "I can get an address: Seven Rue de Bretagne. It's not a house—some kind of business. But I don't have a name for it."

"When?"

"Very soon. Within the hour."

"Anything about the victim? Male or female?"

"Male. Middle-aged."

"Thanks! You're amazing, Mekera. But I gotta go. I'll be in touch. I hope."

"What?"

"You'll be fine. And I'll pay you back!"

It was an abrupt leave-taking, but I didn't want to miss Leif. I'd have to shift to someplace outside the city and jog in, no doubt, and when I checked the bound trees nearby, sure enough the closest one was miles out of town to the north.

"We have to move fast, Oberon," I said once we arrived. "Stick with me and watch for cars when we cross streets."

<What are you going to do?> he asked. <Is this going to be a duel?>

"I honestly don't know," I answered. "Maybe. It'll be a reckoning."

It took twenty minutes to get there, with a couple of quick stops to ask directions. The address turned out to belong to a restaurant that didn't cater to tourists; one either spoke French there or pointed at the menu.

I walked right in with Oberon, shocking the sophisticants dabbing at their lips with linen napkins. *"Mon Dieu!"* one man said, so startled by my hound's appearance that he dropped his fork into some delicate sauce, which splashed onto his lap. *"Qu'est-ce que ce foutu gros chien fait ici?"*

<Hey, did that guy just call me gross?> Oberon asked.

Yes, but that means big *in French, as it does in German.*

Leif wasn't in the restaurant—a fairly decent affair, with twenty tables—though there were several middle-aged men enjoying wine. I pushed past a waiter and ignored the exclamations of the staff as I entered the kitchen. No vampire at the sous station; not hiding in the freezer either. The saucier got saucy with me and demanded that I leave, and I told him I was leaving so that he didn't try to escalate any further. I made for the back door, shouty chefs with kitchen implements trailing after me, and burst through into a dank alley with a foul trash bin and a couple of scooters parked nearby. A thud on the cobbled stones drew my eyes to the right, where I spotted the blond-haired Leif Helgarson, who launched into a cover story in French upon being discovered: "Oh, thank God you're here, this man needs help! He just—" He stopped and switched to English. "Oh. Hello, Atticus."

"Is he still alive?"

"For the moment."

I flicked my eyes to the trash bin. Behind a restaurant like this, they got emptied often and people expected a terrible smell. Great place to dump a body.

"A little fast food, easily disposable?"

He ignored the question and asked, "How did you find me?"

I ignored his question right back. "Let's talk about why I went to the trouble."

We were interrupted by the saucier coming outside to make sure I was gone. I shoved him back into the kitchen and slammed the door closed. "But let's talk elsewhere. I've drawn attention to myself, and that's not good for either of us."

"Agreed. There is a quay along the Bassin du Commerce. We should find privacy there."

"All right." Switching to my mental link, I said, *Keep me between you and Leif, Oberon. I don't want him deciding to take a swipe at you.*

<Whoa. You think he might?>

I don't know. Let's be cautious.

We walked in silence out of the area and to Quai Lamblardie, where pedestrian traffic was light as long as we stayed away from the bridge spanning the basin. Sirens announced that Leif's victim had been discovered—most likely by the kitchen staff. And since they hadn't seen Leif, they would probably pin it on me, unless the wine-soaked man could tell them anything about Leif. I doubted he would; Leif had probably charmed him.

The skies above Le Havre were clear as we walked along the quay, and in truth it was a beautiful night there. The Bassin du Commerce was a long and rectangular stretch of water designed to provide attractive reflections during the night and add value to the real estate ringing it, and perhaps to inspire romance between couples walking along it. Leif and I were not that kind of couple. I was inspired to punch him in the mouth, and he sensed it.

"Your heart rate is elevated and you are giving off many other signals of aggression, Atticus. Should I be worried?"

"Not terribly. I don't mean to unbind you, anyway. Don't give me a reason."

"Never fear. Continuing this existence is my primary goal."

"And what are your other goals? Do you wish to see me dead?"

"Of course not. As the famous Vulcan said on more than one occasion, I wish for you to enjoy extreme old age and economic bounty."

"What? That's not even close to how he said it."

"Oh, I may have paraphrased. Does it matter?"

"Gods below, yes. You can't go around messing up Spock like that."

"A pity. I thought I had finally caught on to something 'cool' there, in the sense that beans are cool in the phrase 'cool beans.'"

"Gah, just shut up."

"But the sentiment is true. I wish you only happiness."

"I sincerely doubt it. That's just a phrase you stole out of the Machiavellian playbook."

"I do beg your pardon, old friend, but I do not think you can judge me. Do you not have your own agenda? Do you not manipulate others to further your own ends?"

"I'm not even close to you in that regard. I don't betray people like you did me."

"I am surprised you still harbor a grudge over a necessary step. Removing Zdenik was the only way to get where I am now, and you were the only way to remove him."

"What? Where are you now? Feasting on winos in Le Havre—that's a step up for you?"

"I was not referring to my dining preferences. I meant I am in a position to remove Theophilus from power."

"Oh, so that's what it was all about? You can frame it like you're doing the world a favor, but cut the shit: This is all about you."

"Fair enough, but again, I must ask: How are you different? Are you not even now acting in your own self-interest? You can claim to be fighting the scourge of vampires on Gaia's behalf, but let us be honest: This is all about you. Gaia cares not whether we graze on the humans. We are no threat to her existence. So what you are doing is pursuing a personal vendetta against Theophilus. And I thought you would have learned a thing or two about revenge when we visited Asgard together."

Aaaaaand *that's* when I punched him. Knocked him right off the Quai Lamblardie and into the water, not caring whether anybody saw and reported a public brawl or attempted drowning. When Leif fought his way to the surface and climbed the brick walls of the man-made basin, I lost control and shouted at him.

"You arrogant fuck! I was only there because of you! The mountains of shit I'm dealing with regarding the Norse are all due to that trip, and I only made it because I was trying to be loyal to *you*! Gods below, I put you back together after Thor pounded your head to gelatin! And then you betrayed me and got me involved in this vampire business!"

"You cannot pretend you had no hand in escalating it," Leif said, scaling the wall.

"What does that have to do with your betrayal? When someone hits me, I hit back."

"So do I." He coiled and sprang vertically over my head, tumbling once in the air and landing within striking distance. I hadn't enhanced my strength or speed, so I wasn't able to dodge or block his blow to my midsection. The air whuffed out of me and I staggered back, gasping for oxygen. He didn't follow up but rather stripped off his jacket with disgust and whipped the sodden mess to the ground.

"You have ruined this suit. Salt water contaminated with motor oil and the remains of many unlucky fish. Disgusting. Not that you care."

"No, I don't," I managed to say between gulps for air. With my breath returning, I said the words to increase my strength and speed. Enhanced by those bindings, I would be his physical equal—at least while the energy in my bear charm lasted. Leif knew from experience what

I was doing and smiled faintly, setting himself in a defensive position.

"Theophilus was in Berlin, not Prague," I said, settling into a kung fu opening stance.

"Yes, I heard."

"Did I get him?"

"No. He yet lives. But you got some very old ones there, some older than me. Well done." He gave a few polite golf claps and smirked.

And then we had us a fight. Fast and brutal and skilled, like our old sparring sessions back in Arizona, except that now I was genuinely angry and had limited resources available. I could neither afford to take my time or make costly sacrifices that I might make with the knowledge that I could heal it quickly.

One thing I had learned from my old sessions with Leif was that it was useless to deliver body blows to a creature that did not depend on oxygen for energy. He never ran out of breath or stamina in the human sense, so those were a waste of time. Blows to the head could disorient him, however, and opening cuts above the eyes could blind him and make him more vulnerable. Though most of my blows got blocked or redirected, I did manage to plant a fist into his nose, and my elbow shattered a cheek.

But he also knew my weakness: Body blows would drain me until I had to slow down, and then it would be over. I suffered a couple of cracked ribs from his hammer fists and lost my breath again to a knee in my gut.

A lucky uppercut surprised him and he lost his feet, landing heavily on his backside, shaking his head to clear it. I had almost nothing left in my tank, so I collapsed across from him and dispelled my bindings, ending it.

I breathed heavily and bled on the quay, and Leif sat still except for his face, which was noisily reconstructing itself. Since he had recently dined he had plenty of energy for it. He wiped at the blood underneath his nose, looked surprised at how much there was on his sleeve, and then folded his legs underneath him. He dropped his head and shook it slowly as he spoke: "I know you will not believe me, but I have to say it anyway: In regard to Theophilus, I did not betray you."

"Bullshit."

"Drasche had me under surveillance. I thought my phone was secure but obviously I was overconfident. Theophilus really *was* in Prague, but once Drasche heard you might be coming, he sent his lover to Berlin and set up an ambush for you at the Grand Bohemia."

"How could you possibly know that?"

"Because I am not completely cut off from information. Nothing is volunteered to me anymore, but I do have several people under surveillance myself, and one of them happens to be working for Drasche. My people intercepted a call from Drasche to this individual, telling him to get his undead ass over to the hotel because you were on the way. Unfortunately, I was unable to warn you. Your old number did not work and I left a voice mail with Hal Hauk since he did not answer. Please confirm with him."

I would do that, but his excuse at least had the whiff of plausibility. I had called Leif using Ty's phone, so he didn't have my new number.

"And now? Where is Theophilus *now*, Leif?"

"At this precise instant, I cannot tell you. But I know where he will be soon enough."

"Where?"

"What is that expression? 'All roads lead to Rome,' I believe?"

"He'll be in Rome, where I've practically eliminated all the other old vampires? Why should I believe you this time when you've lied to me so often?"

"I did not lie about Prague. I guessed that he was there—which I made clear to you and which also turned out to be a correct guess—and I am not lying about this. He must go and reclaim the city to have any legitimacy with the rest of the world's vampires. He considers the planet his empire, you know. But your guerrilla tactics have scattered us from our strongholds, driven us to hiding like rats in sewers, and, as you saw, feeding on drunkards in alleys. I do not particularly mind, but he cannot countenance that."

"I don't know. He ran away pretty quickly in Berlin. What makes you think he wants another confrontation?"

Leif chuckled. "I am sure that running away stung him, and now he is working himself up to a real fight. He has had it too easy for too long, has he not? All vampires have. Remember *Cymbeline*? *Plenty and peace breed cowards—*"

"And *hardness ever of hardiness is mother*. Of course I remember it. But it doesn't follow that he'll go straight to Rome."

"I think it does. I think he imagines all sorts of scenarios where he crushes you in Rome and finally frees the undead from the Druidic threat. He must be the hero of all vampires, you see. His ego requires it. And my sources say it has been a couple of days, has it not, since your yewmen have staked any vampires?"

"Yeah. Cash-flow issues. Drasche's plan worked in that regard."

"Then the proverbial coast is clear. He will retake Rome and he will be bringing a small army with him to do it. He will wait for you to come get him, and this time he will be ready for yewmen. He will have a plan."

"All right, Leif," I said. "Let's make a deal."

CHAPTER 22

I have slept the slumber of the peaceful victor. And while a portion of my guilt remains, I believe I'm in a happy place. Even if I did it wrong, at least I finally did *something* about Beau Thatcher. Now it's in the past, and maybe I can leave it there and simply enjoy my cup of fulfillment; I'd like to think that I delivered some karma to my stepfather rather than earned any bad karma of my own. It might be worthwhile to discuss it with Laksha; she seems to have a heightened sensitivity to actions and their consequences now.

Still, I cannot deny that I feel good. I've crossed off the biggest item on my life's to-do list, and now I feel like sharing it with someone. But I haven't heard from Atticus in a while. I text both him and Hal Hauk but receive no answer. If Atticus got into any sort of trouble over the past couple of weeks—and he almost certainly did— he's probably switched to a new phone and I'll need to wait for him to text me. And he won't unless he's truly worried; he's sweet about giving me my space. But now that I can be with him without worrying that I'm showing Loki precisely where to find him and Oberon, I'd love to hook up again. The thing is that if I can't reach him via cell phone and also have no ability to divine him, thanks to cold iron, he can be pretty difficult to find. Perhaps the Sisters of the Three Auroras might have ideas. If I ask them where the crazy magical stuff is happening in the world, they might be able to pin that down, and wherever that is, I'll probably find Atticus. And if not, maybe it will turn out to be something that requires a Druid's attention anyway.

There's another reason to visit Warsaw: I've read a few of those poems by Wisława Szymborska now. "Nothing Twice" is fabulous, and so is "Theatre Impressions." She's definitely my kind of poet, and I think it's time to learn Polish. Delivering that news will be welcome to the sisters, I'm sure, and make the trip worthwhile even if they're not able to help otherwise. I will most likely spend quite a bit of time with the sisters in the near future, if they're comfortable with it.

I discover, once we're in Tír na nÓg and searching for spots, that there are no bound trees closer to Malina Sokołowska's house than the black poplar in Pole Mokotowskie. I might need to fix that if I'm going to visit them more frequently. They have stands of pine trees nearby that would work just fine.

The jog to Radość is pleasant, though. It's early afternoon in Warsaw when we arrive, and the streets are not terribly crowded between lunch and the rush hour home. The gate to Malina's property is open, and Ewelina is sitting cross-legged on the ground outside the gate, smoking a cigarette. She flicks it into the hard-packed gravel of the street and rises, grinning, when she sees me. "Hello, Granuaile." Devil horns. "Rock on." She pushes the gate open wider and invites Orlaith and me to enter. Dominika immediately bounds out of the house and almost slips on the mossy steps as Ewelina closes the gate behind us.

"Whoops! Granuaile! You're here! Come with me and talk to Miłosz!" She grabs my arm and yanks me around the side of the house.

"Oh ... Okay. What's the hurry? Is something wrong?"

"I think he's sad. Will you talk to him for me?"

"Sure." I smile faintly behind Dominika's back. While I hope it's nothing serious, I also doubt it's anything but her imagination; it's wonderful to see that Miłosz has someone to worry about him, though. He will be pampered instead of neglected now. He has his nose in a bag of oats when we clear the corner of the house.

Switching over my vision and binding my mind to his, I greet him and ask if he is well. He lifts his head out of the bag and nickers at me in recognition. He answers that he is mostly content.

Is anything wrong?

His reply is that he'd like to go for walks instead of being in this same area all the time—a request that sounds simple enough and certainly understandable but somewhat fraught with risk since Loki wants him back. The mark on his hide hasn't been burned away, and I don't think I could bear to hurt him to get rid of it with the Rune of Ashes. Besides, I think the sisters are almost hoping Loki makes a move to get him—but I think they want him to make that move here, where they have all their wards in place.

I tell Miłosz I'll see what I can do about that and then relay his wishes to Dominika. "He just wants to go for walks."

"Oh!" She bites her lip. "We won't be able to protect him as well."

"What if all of you accompanied him? The entire coven as opposed to simply you? Change up the times and routes so they're not predictable, but be aware that an attack could come at any time?"

"Yeah. Tell him we'll figure something out."

Dominika's and Miłosz's worries temporarily relieved, I accept the invitation to baked goods this time and enter Malina's house. There's no old-world kitsch inside; it's spare, modern, and minimalist, with a focus on large oil canvases and small bronze sculptures celebrating femininity.

I'm given tea and cake and chitchat from the witches in attendance. Only half the coven is here. The news that I'd like to tackle Szymborska and the Polish language is well received, and after that I judge it would be a good time to ask for a wee favor couched as an effort to help the coven. I address the leader.

"Listen, Malina, I'd like to find Atticus and ask him about the vampire situation, among other things. But he's been out of touch and I'm not sure how to locate him at the moment. Might you have any idea how to do that?"

She blinks at me and says, "His cold iron aura shields him from our sight. He's cloaked every bit as much as you are."

"Oh, I know. But I thought we could be clever about it and search for where the ruckus is."

"What do you . . . ? Are you talking about something specific? If so, maybe we could find it. Could you describe the ruckus?"

"No, it's not specific. I simply think that whatever you find will be vampire-related."

"We have trouble divining the undead as well."

"Yes, but I thought that by now they would have recruited a few magical allies. Atticus has been paying some Fae to assassinate them, and they've been quite effective. I think the vampires might start paying magic users of their own for protection. So I suppose what I'm saying is, wherever you detect that a large magical signature has flared up recently, that's where Atticus will be. And if he's not, well, maybe a large magical signature deserves my attention anyway."

"Hmm." Malina taps her index finger on the granite

kitchen countertop a few times, considering. Her eyes travel around the room, taking in the witches present. There are six in all, and she nods. "Okay, it's worth a try if it gets us closer to a vampire-free Poland. There are some here in Warsaw and a few others preying on students in Poznań that we particularly do not enjoy. Anna, will you remain here and give Granuaile her first Polish lesson? The rest of us will try to find the equivalent of a magical ruckus."

As the other sisters file out to the back acreage, Anna does a little Muppet flail in her excitement to teach me her language. She grabs a pad and pen and starts with the alphabet and sounds. I've always liked the letter z, so discovering that Polish has three versions—z, ź, and ż—confirms that I have made the right choice. Time slips by in language acquisition over tea until Malina and the others return. I notice they have little moonshine yarrow blossoms in their hair.

"Rome," Malina says without preamble. "You need to go to Rome."

"Why? What's happening there?"

"Something very strange is going on in the Piazza di Spagna. I'd say it's almost Rosicrucian, except it feels a bit off."

"I don't know what you mean by that."

"The short version is that there are powerful wards around some of the buildings there, but they're unusually constructed. They're probably traps. I wouldn't simply walk in there to see what happens."

"And these are recent?"

"Yes. We haven't sensed anything like this before."

"Okay," I say, getting up. Orlaith rises with me and wags her tail. "I'm on it."

"Be extremely careful, Granuaile. Call us if you want to talk about it once you take a closer look."

"All right, will do." I thank Anna for the language

lesson and take my leave, jogging back to Pole Mokotowskie with Orlaith. I teach her the names for Italian
charcuterie on the way, with the result that she can't
wait to try prosciutto and culatello and salama da sugo
ferrarese.

"We'll see what we find first once we get to Rome: a
deli or Atticus and Oberon."

CHAPTER 23

Funerals are a bit fancy now, I notice, since everyone dresses in the best black clothing they have. In me own day ye had one set of clothes, two if ye were doing well, and ye washed them when ye got tired of the dirt and the bugs on your balls, not because somebody died. But Greta gets me some proper mourning clothes, because that's a sign of respect, she says, so I go along because Hal fecking deserves all the respect I can give—Nergüi too, of course, who entrusted his family to me.

It's really a hastily arranged memorial service instead of a funeral. Hal left instructions to be buried in Iceland, and Nergüi is to be returned to Mongolia. But the idea is the same: Ye remember the fallen and share why they were important to ye and give what comfort ye can to the family, even if it's fecking useless and your words can't possibly mend the hole torn open in their world and the yawning abyss of the future without their loved one. People still need to know that ye would fix everything if ye could.

Since Greta came back, she hasn't said very much beyond "We'll talk later" and a few grunts. I don't have to cast wands to guess that it won't be a pleasant talk, and I admit me guts are in a twist about it. Since I got pulled back into this time, the only thing that's kept me from throwing shite at people is Greta. I know that when ye think o' love you're supposed to think o' kissy faces and scented soap and hummin' happy songs together, but there's another vital part to it that people rarely admit to themselves: We want somebody to rescue us from other people. From talking to them, I mean, or from the burden of giving a damn about what they say. We don't want to be polite and stifle our farts, now, do we? We want to let 'em rip and we want to be with someone who won't care if we do, who will love us regardless and fart right back besides. I'm thinkin' that maybe Greta could be that person for me. Or she could have been, until the fecking vampires showed up.

The entire Tempe Pack has driven up for the memorial on Greta's land, and I think the plan is they're going to do a run in the mountains later tonight for Hal, with most if not all the Flagstaff Pack joining them for Nergüi, and the next full moon will be dedicated to them as well. I hear dark mutterings that the vampires will be paying for this.

Meg and Tuya are going to stay, which surprises me. Nergüi and Meg both wanted their daughter to be a Druid, and Meg hasn't changed her mind about it. They're going to take care of things in Mongolia for a while and then they'll be back.

I keep me face shut during the memorial; I didn't know Hal or Nergüi half so well as the rest, and this is a pack thing if anything is. There are some interesting noises made at werewolf memorials: half barks and yips and growls, plus faces sliding around as they fight to keep hold of their emotions and their human forms. Nobody completely loses it, though. Afterward, Greta crooks a finger at me and we walk off some distance into the trees before she speaks. She has a black veil over her eyes, but the cold blue of them still seizes me when she looks up. Her voice is tight and controlled and distant. She's wearing a man's suit and tie in silver, which has some kind of symbolism to the pack. Out of the inside jacket pocket she withdraws the plastic bag that Hal brought with Siodhachan's new documents in it. She tosses it to me and then spits to the side.

"I want you to find him and tell him he's not welcome here anymore. He's not welcome among any members of the Tempe or Flagstaff packs, and, yes, I speak for Sam and Ty in this."

She waits for me to say something, but if she's expecting an argument she's going to be disappointed. "Okay," I says.

"I wouldn't ask you to never speak to him again. But I cannot stress how much we are tired of his shit. No, no—*tired* isn't the word. Furious, enraged, ready to destroy him—that's closer. We do not want our pack to be collateral damage in his endless series of crises. So henceforth we will have no association with him whatsoever."

I don't know what *collateral damage* is, so I just nod and look it up later. Greta takes that as her cue to continue. "If you wish to meet with him, do so far away from here. How he gets in touch with you must be mundane as well. No Fae messengers. He needs to use either mail or social media. I will help you with that if you need it."

"All right." I'm so relieved that she's not sending me packing over this that I can't manage anything else.

"No favors. No more IDs. His legal relationship with Magnusson and Hauk is terminated, and they will serve papers to that effect. No watching his hound or his sword—which Sam and Ty brought to the service, by the way, and you're to take with you. It's waiting in the house, on the dining room table. So nothing from now on. He may live in peace outside our territory, but if he is stupid enough to enter it again, we will do whatever we can to end his very long life. Is that clear?"

"Absolutely."

Tension drains out of her shoulders, and she exhales slowly and closes her eyes. She'd said what she wanted to say.

"Good. Do you have any questions?"

"I don't suppose maybe the law firm has any idea where he is? Maybe I can get this over with quickly."

She shakes her head. "My guess would be Rome, but I don't know. Can't the Fae find him?"

"Nah, he made sure the Fae couldn't find him a long time ago. Why Rome?"

"If he's truly trying to break the vampires, then that's where he'll be. He might have done something there already, and that's why we got hit."

"All right, Rome it is. Worth a look. Any place specific in Rome?"

"Wherever the rich people are living now. Prestige, wealth, power—the old vampires like to let everyone know they have it."

"Right. I'll get a couple things together and go." I think about kissing her goodbye, but I'm not sure she would welcome it. I give her a tight nod instead and turn back to the house. After a few steps I hear her move, and it's fast. I don't get to turn around before her arms are around me, hugging me from behind. I stay still and she rests her head between me shoulder blades.

"Thank you, Owen," she says.

"No need for thanks," I reply. "I want the new Grove protected every bit as much as you want to protect the pack. And the solution is the same: Keep Siodhachan the feck away from here."

She doesn't respond to this except to squeeze a little harder.

"This could be fast, but it could also be days or weeks before I catch up with him. And I'm pretty sure I'll have to help him with the vampires if he has an endgame. So explain to the kids and the parents, will ye, why I'm gone and that I'll be back when it's finished. I don't want this to happen again."

"No. We definitely do not want that." She lets go, only to spin me around to face her and bring her hand up to the side of me face. Those eyes hold mine through the veil. "Be ruthless and thorough and don't worry about us. We'll be here."

"Good." I nod, she lets me go, and I return to the house. Greta stays in the trees. I grab me knuckles and Fragarach from the dining room table, and I also pick up those stakes that Luchta made for us—one for me and one for Granuaile, in case I find her with Siodhachan.

I don't know how the pack stands in regards to her, and I don't want to bring it up until it's necessary. Better to let her decide if she wants to have a separate status from Siodhachan or throw in her lot with him.

I know what I want: Greta and Owen's Grove, allowed to live in peace. There's harmony there to be found, and I'll fight for it, and damn the paradox of fighting for peace.

CHAPTER 24

It feels a bit like parachuting behind enemy lines, shifting into Rome. Here, Theophilus and his old nest of vampires manipulated Julius Caesar and the others that followed him into attacking the continental Druids, and their campaigns, combined with the spread of Christianity, effectively wiped us out. He thought he'd won. I suppose he did: When you wait two thousand years before launching a counterattack, you cannot truly say you're fighting the same war.

My visits to Rome throughout the centuries had always been brief affairs for art appreciation, just day trips, when the vampires would be asleep. But I made sure that I always kept the tether updated. It's located on the northern edge of Rome, in Villa Borghese, a large estate that was home to an old family with close ties to several popes. Today it's partially public land, with a zoo and expansive parks. It will be a reliable gateway to Rome for a long time to come, and it's conveniently located close to the Piazza di Spagna, where Leif suggested to me that I might find Theophilus.

"He had a flat right on the piazza, and so did several others of the leadership. Bought them for a song centuries ago, bequeathed them to their new identities once a generation, as you have no doubt done with your own assets, and now they are worth millions of euros each because the location has become so desirable."

"It wasn't always so?" I asked.

"No. When Keats and Shelley lived there, it was mocked as the 'English Ghetto'—so cheap that poor foreign poets could afford a room. I know for a fact that your Fae assassins dispatched a couple of the vampire leadership there. Theophilus will want to reclaim those flats for symbolic reasons."

"You mean he'll buy them?"

"Eventually. He and his entourage will charm their way in for the short term while they work on making everything legal. If they want a flat and find it occupied, they can kill the owner and make it available."

"He has the money to pay for these?"

"Oh, most certainly. Remember, in addition to his own considerable wealth, thanks to Werner Drasche he has all your money to play with now. He'll spend it quickly just to spite you."

When I arrived at the Piazza di Spagna—so named for its proximity to the Spanish embassy, not because the Spanish had anything to do with building or designing the plaza—it was not so crowded as one finds during the high tourist season. The unusually cold weather encouraged tourists to spend their time indoors at museums or churches. I walked with Oberon to the boat-shaped fountain designed by Bernini at the bottom of the Spanish Steps, enjoyed the beauty of it for a while, and thought seriously about going into Babington's Tea Rooms on the left side of the steps for some tea that would be ridiculously overpriced but would at least have the benefit of being hot. Bereft of euros, though, I'd have to wait.

First I wanted to test Leif's assertion that Theophilus and company had taken up residence in the flats ringing the piazza. The giveaway would be armed thralls standing guard outside the residences with firearms in shoulder holsters and earpieces in their ears. But I didn't want to announce my presence any earlier than necessary. I began with a casual scan of the buildings in the magical spectrum to see if anything jumped out at me. I expected nothing, but something most definitely jumped up and down for my attention.

Three buildings opposite Babington's were sheathed in wards of some kind. Those weren't something a vampire could do, so they must have been put in place by a paid magical contractor, and that contractor might well remain nearby.

They were all five or six stories high, with the bottom two floors devoted to high-end retail and the upper stories divided into flats. From left to right, they housed shopfronts for Pucci, Casadei, Jaeger-LeCoultre, and Dolce & Gabbana, though a large doorway allowed access to interior stairwells and elevators. To get to them I'd have to cross the threshold of those wards, and I wasn't ready to do that. Above the fashion shops, rows of windows checkered the façade, most of them shuttered closed but a few thrown open to let in the weak winter sun. The open windows provided a big clue to where the vampires were not. Looking up, I could see the green umbrellas of boxed trees and hints of rooftop gardens—lofty aeries for the obscenely rich to gaze down upon the hoi polloi.

Keeping my magical sight active, I urged Oberon to take a circuit of the block with me. I wanted to know if the wards protected all sides of the buildings. While the structures all shared walls, with no alleys between them, they were easily identifiable by the paint jobs. The Pucci building was a sort of sun-washed mauve, Casadei occupied a terra-cotta building, and the third and largest was a yellow cream color. And a circuit of the block down narrow cobbled streets confirmed that they were, in fact, warded on all sides. I was careful not to break the boundary of the wards or let Oberon stray too close. They were of unfamiliar origin and I wasn't sure what they would do. I shouldn't let my eagerness to slay Theophilus lead me into a foolish mistake.

Around the back side of the buildings, in a narrow street filled with glove shops, handbag hawkers, and jewelry stores, a pair of pickpockets made the foolish mistake of trying to work me. I didn't have a wallet, for one thing. They looked like brother and sister. The girl made appreciative noises over Oberon and tried to occupy my attention by leaning over him and letting her loose-fitting blouse fall away. It was impossible that she was unconscious of this—for one thing it was too cold for such clothing, so she was obviously trying to distract me. Meanwhile, her partner or brother kept moving past me and then circled back around. When I felt his fingers dip into my back pocket, I dropped and swept his legs. He landed on the cobbled stones, hard, and then I spun and pinned him, fishing a few bills out of his pocket. The girl shouted at me and then tried to discourage me by calling for help. I let the boy up and grinned at them both.

"You targeted the wrong man," I said in Italian. "Run along now. I know you don't truly want the police to look into this." Without being prompted, Oberon laid back his ears and growled at them. They took off but cursed me soundly. I thanked them for the lunch money.

The few passersby who had seen the altercation had no trouble with me. Apparently, pickpockets were common in the area, and they gave me a couple of "Bravos!"

We completed the circuit of the block, returned to the piazza, and I slipped into Babington's for some picnic food to go—they sold such things even in winter, because the days were usually much milder than this.

We sat on the Spanish Steps, a good distance above the tourists collected around Bernini's fountain, and Oberon wagged his tail at a steady stream of people who wanted to pet him as they passed.

<People cannot resist me, Atticus. Are you seeing this? I am the Most Interesting Hound in the World.>

That's indisputable, buddy.

<Hey, is that another hound down there?> He got to his feet and stared off toward the north end of the plaza. <It is! I think it's Orlaith! Yes! And there's Clever Girl!> I followed his gaze and saw a familiar red head and a staff. I grinned, stood, and called to get her attention. She waved back, and the hounds ran to meet each other in the middle.

<Atticus, I ate all my food already and don't have any to give Orlaith! What do I do?>

Don't worry, we'll get some for her.

"Hey. Nice jacket," Granuaile said, smiling at me as she climbed the steps, but then she halted, cocked her head, and the smile disappeared. Her arm raised and she pointed, waggling her finger around. "Whoa, what the hell? What happened to your little Mini Cooper beard?"

My hand drifted up to my chin. "Oh! I had to be Nigel in Toronto. Don't worry, I'll grow it back."

"You actually went to Toronto? Sounds like a story. I expect we have plenty to catch up on." She smiled once more and came up the steps, arms wide. "C'mere."

Gods, it was good to see her. It was a pretty joyful reunion, having her in my arms again. I hadn't seen her since Hal Hauk gave me the news about Kodiak Black's death, and we did indeed have plenty of catching up to do. I watched the hounds on the steps, while she visited Babington's to pick up some munchies for herself and Orlaith. Orlaith had been looking forward to charcuterie once she got to Rome, but since Oberon was there to play with and I promised she'd get the good stuff eventually, she wasn't too upset about settling for a picnic selection of salami and cheese.

Granuaile had been busy while we were apart. Fjalar had removed—or rather burned away—Loki's mark, and then she secured a divination cloak from the Sisters of the Three Auroras by fetching Świętowit's horse from under the guard of Weles.

"I'll be spending more time with the sisters," she said. "I'm going to learn Polish for my new headspace and memorize Szymborska's poetry."

That was surprising. "Wow. I'm envious, because I never learned Polish, but if you're wanting another headspace for plane-shifting . . ."

"Why not memorize something in Latin or Russian?" Granuaile finished.

"Yeah."

"Because I want beautiful stuff in my head. If I put the Russian lit I've read so far into permanent memory, I think it would sour my sunny disposition."

"Fair enough," I said. "But at risk of souring it now, I should tell you that Fjalar's dead."

"What? How did that happen?"

"Brighid killed him. He was leading an army against the dark elves and he wouldn't talk to us. Odin had told him to march on Svartálfheim and so he did, and Brighid made him an example."

"Damn. So that was what they were talking about. They hinted that they might be going to Svartálfheim while I was in Asgard."

"It's all under a happy treaty now. But I think that Odin—and maybe even Brighid, the more that I think about it—engineered the whole situation to make the dark elves come to the table. It was cold-blooded and Machiavellian but in retrospect probably necessary. They weren't very willing to talk at first. The Morrigan said we needed them on our side, and now they are. The bonus is that the dark elves promised never to take a contract out on us again."

"Hey, that's good news!"

"Especially since Fand escaped. Did you know about that?"

"No! When was this?"

"A few days ago. But hopefully that will be someone else's problem. We're both shielded from her divination now. And I know where she is. I'm going to tell Brighid and let her take care of it. I have enough on my plate as it is."

I told her about my run-ins with Werner Drasche and how my attempt on Theophilus in Berlin was a near miss. Also that Diana was free of her prison but still supremely pissed at us.

"She made an oath to leave us alone and broke it immediately. Jupiter said he'd keep her from pursuing us from now on, but we'll see."

"So what's on the agenda here?" Granuaile asked. "Did I catch you on a break, or have you even started any shit yet?"

"I was casing the joint," I explained, then pointed to the warded buildings. "Look at those buildings in the magical spectrum. They have some strange wards on them."

She did and then turned to me. "Yeah. Malina said there was something odd going on at the piazza. Said those wards are as much traps as they are for protection."

"Ah, I was wondering how you found me here."

"Yeah, I just asked where the weird was happening in the world, and she pointed me here. And look! You're right next to it!"

"Very clever. Did she say anything else about those wards?"

"Yes. She said they looked kind of Rosicrucian but different somehow."

"Rosicrucian? Shit."

"What? Why is there shit?"

<Hey, whoa! It wasn't me!> Oberon said, panic in his voice.

<Me neither!> Orlaith chimed in. Hounds never want to be blamed when shit happens.

We reassured them that we were speaking figuratively and did not suspect for an instant that they were to blame, and once they went back to nipping each other's ears and getting petted by passersby, I explained in a low voice to Granuaile why I was worried.

"Rosicrucians have a long and occasionally dark history—are you already familiar with them?"

"I've heard the term before but don't know very much about them."

"They're a secret society that began in the early fifteenth century. They influenced Freemasonry and plenty of other societies that pledged themselves on their face to the betterment of society but kept their methods for achieving that behind closed doors. Some of them—I should say many of them—were genuinely trying to make things better, and I think that they did in some cases. They had a philosophy and despised the corruption of the Catholic Church, and they thought their mucking about with the mysteries of the universe was entirely honorable. We still have some Rosicrucian orders scattered about today, or other secret societies that claim no formal ties but were clearly influenced by them. The thing is, some of these groups—or, rather, offshoots of them—were cauldrons of evil, you know? Dudes made up their own secret societies and wore the term *Rosicrucian* to give them respectability, but underneath that lurked horrors, like a syphilitic dick hidden under a blanket. They would say they were dedicated to the sciences, but that really meant that they were pursuing alchemy and trying to learn dark secrets. You remember that Werner Drasche's powers were given to him by an alchemist and that he later killed his creator, so to speak? Well, I got a good look at his tattoos back in Toronto. On the very top of his pate, in amongst the alchemical symbols, was a Rose Cross."

"Oh. So some kind of Rosicrucian bad seed created the arcane lifeleech."

"Yes. And it's a safe bet that these Rosicrucian wards are going to be nasty. In fact, given that they most likely exist to protect Theophilus and we know of his connection to Werner Drasche, we can practically guarantee it. Let me throw another name at you: Ever heard of the Hermetic Order of the Golden Dawn?"

"Golden Dawn—yeah. Wasn't that the group with Bram Stoker, William Butler Yeats, and Aleister Crowley?"

"Yes. They were influenced by Rosicrucian mysteries as well. Very much into that, as well as into Hermetic Qabalism."

"Hermetic Qabalah as opposed to Jewish Kabbalah?"

"Yes. A different system. More syncretic with other traditions. But their ceremonies still have the Tree of Life as their basis, so if you're going to do something major—like ward three buildings—you probably need more than one person working on it."

"Meaning there might be a bunch of Rosicrucians nearby."

"Exactly. Let's take a closer look at those wards."

We descended the steps and crossed the piazza to examine the wards, hounds trailing behind us. In the magical spectrum we saw points of light in what appeared to be a random distribution, but after our recent conversation I was able to spy a pattern.

"Look here, Granuaile," I said, pointing near the boundary of the ward but being careful not to touch it. I traced my finger in a lightning pattern. "See this? Ten points on the Tree of Life. And interlocking with it on all sides are more trees. It's a Qabalistic ward. The Hermetic kind, I'm guessing."

"Yes, I see. But what does it do?"

"That I do not know. We can see people going in and out of the stores here without a problem. I'm betting that it's a ward specifically to mess with Druids. And I'm nervous about it because I remember when the Hammers of God confronted me in Tempe and essentially cut off my ability to bind anything. So I'm not anxious to stick my finger into this particular socket."

"Well, you told me that you are on better terms with the Hammers of God now after Toronto. Why not give them a call and see if they can take this down? I mean, we don't absolutely have to go after the vampires today, right? We can wait for a bit of help?"

"Yes. That's an outstanding idea." I pulled out my new burner phone and punched in Rabbi Yosef Bialik's number from memory. He answered in a sleepy voice—it's not early afternoon in Toronto but rather closer to six in the morning. "Hello, Rabbi? Atticus here. How soon can you and your friends get to Rome?"

CHAPTER 25

After Atticus convinces the rabbi to fly to Rome as soon as he can, we have the rest of the day and a night to kill. It's just as well: Neither of us is 100 percent healthy, still recuperating after our assorted run-ins with gods and the undead. We decide to shift elsewhere before the vampires wake up for the night, but we take our time returning to the Villa Borghese. We make a date out of it, visiting a charcuterie to fulfill my promise to Orlaith and delight Oberon in the process. I'm not super-familiar with Rome; I had to get instructions to find the Piazza di Spagna—so Atticus shows me a few things and we get espressos at one of the ubiquitous *caffè* bars that pepper the city the way Starbucks peppers Seattle. I love the clink of saucers and cups and the gurgling hiss of steam wands frothing milk over the music of the Italian language. When we get to the Villa Borghese it's about an hour before dusk, and as we're walking to the tethered tree we see a familiar figure walking toward us.

"Oi! Well, at least findin' ye wasn't the nightmare I expected," a deep growly voice says. "Didn't have to take a single step onto that dead land."

"Hello, Owen," Atticus says. "We were just about to leave. What are you doing here?"

"Lookin' for you. I have news, good and bad, and

some of your bollocks." He tosses Fragarach to Atticus in its scabbard, and the leather strap flaps in the air. Then he tosses a plastic bag to him, which Atticus catches and examines.

"Oh! My new documents. Thanks. It'll be good to have a bank account again. Huh—Connor Molloy. Not bad."

The archdruid's face twists into an ugly sneer and he spits to one side. "The good news is that Werner Drasche is finally dead. Greta killed him."

"Oh, wow. That *is* good news! But wait—are you saying Werner Drasche was in Flagstaff?"

"That's exactly what I'm feckin' saying to ye, lad. And before Greta killed him, but very shortly after Hal Hauk brought your documents there and raised a toast to your bloody arse, Werner Drasche brought seven vampires with him and shot up our house. Now, why do ye suppose he'd do a thing like that?"

"Oh, no. I bet it was retaliation for Berlin."

"What's Berlin?"

"A city in Germany. I unbound nineteen old friends of Theophilus there, but he escaped. He must have told Drasche to strike back however he could."

"So he hopped on a plane and came straight for us."

"I guess so. Was anyone hurt?"

Owen's fists clench at his sides and he shouts, "Yes, someone got hurt! Hal Hauk is *dead,* ye fecking shite-heap! Because of you! He was there to deliver your new identity and then he took a silver bullet to the brain because of something you did in Berlin! And the father of one of me apprentices was killed too!"

Atticus shrinks back under the onslaught. It's awful, terrible news, and I see that it hits him hard. Especially since it was delivered with such a large load of blame.

"Oh, gods," he says. "What can I do? Is there a service to be held, or . . . ?"

"It's been held already. I just came from there. And I have a message to deliver from the pack—packs, I mean, both Tempe and Flagstaff. You're banished, lad. If ye enter their territory again, they'll try to kill ye. They're not going to hunt ye or set the world's packs on your tail. But ye can't ever go back. And Magnusson and Hauk won't be your firm anymore after they finish what business they have with ye. Time to get some new attorneys."

"What?" I say. "Wait, that's—"

"Completely deserved," Atticus says. "I understand their point of view on this. I don't blame them."

"Well, they shouldn't be blaming you either!" I said. "It's not like you pulled the trigger."

"No, but I gave Drasche a reason to go there. They're perfectly justified." His voice has gone cold and dead, and I know what he's doing: He's walling up his pain in a different headspace. But at least it's calming down Owen, who looked for a moment as if he would throw a punch. He looks up at his old archdruid and says, "Thanks for letting me know. And bringing me my sword."

Owen merely grunts in reply and turns to me. "Speaking of weapons, I have something for you too, Granuaile."

I immediately assume it's a parting gift and gasp, "What? Am I banished too?"

"Not that I've heard. I imagine they won't jump to do ye any favors, but I don't think they'd go after ye either. No, what I have is a stake carved by Luchta."

He's dressed in jeans and a soft brown leather coat lined with lamb's wool. He pulls out a hardwood stake, beautifully carved, and tells me it'll unbind a vampire no matter where you stab it.

"Siodhachan and I each have one as well."

"It works," Atticus assures me. "Luchta's a genius."

"Thank you," I say, taking it from Owen's hand. It's well balanced, and I might be able to throw it. I'd have to experiment first.

"Right," the archdruid says, clapping his hands together. "How can I help ye stop this vampire shite?"

Atticus is surprised at first but doesn't reject the offer. "We can't do anything until tomorrow. We need to catch up anyway. Let's shift to a place I know almost directly south of here. It'll be a warm night and keep us in the same time zone. Follow me."

He and Oberon shift planes, leaving a binding to trace him through Tír na nÓg and thence to a cliffside view of an ocean with a sandy beach below. The sun is low on the horizon and painting a bank of clouds orange and pink.

<Warm here!> Orlaith says, and she and Oberon immediately get involved in a game of chase now that there's room for them to stretch their legs.

"Ah, nice. Where's this, then?" Owen asks when he appears behind me at the tethered tree.

Atticus gives a tiny grin. "Welcome to Caotinha Beach in Benguela, Angola. No one is going to bother us here. We should be able to relax and recharge."

We pick our way down off the cliff, and the water in the bay is an attractive blue-green. A lonely fishing boat is parked so far offshore it appears to be little more than a flattened buoy. The sand is warm without scorching, and we have this isolated stretch of the beach to ourselves.

I don't think Atticus or Owen wants to continue talking about Hal or being banished, and it's probably too soon to battle-plan for tomorrow, so I flail about for a safe topic. The hounds splash into the ocean and play in the tide while we take seats in the sand.

"Let's think ahead for a minute, Atticus. Owen's going to be training his apprentices from now on. But what are we going to do if we get to the other side of this vampire problem?"

He squints at me in the sun. "Well, we'll live in Oregon, I suppose."

"I know that. But what will we *do*? Because I want to defend the earth."

He cocks his head to the side. "Aren't you already doing that?"

"I mean actively defend it from pollution. Clean it up. Tip the climate back toward something that won't kill us all. Restore balance after centuries of unsustainable exploitation."

"That sounds impossible to me. Like taking up the labor of Sisyphus and expecting the boulder to stay at the top of the hill for you when it never would for him. Just because you *can* do something doesn't mean that you should."

For a moment I'm taken aback, but then I recover. "No, Atticus, that argument is what you use when you're talking about crazy shit like eating brains or fucking a goat—"

Owen interrupts to say, "I tried to tell him that centuries ago, but he didn't listen." I don't want to go there, not least because it would distract me from making my point, so I continue as if the archdruid hadn't spoken.

"That's not a valid argument when you're a Druid talking about defending Gaia. The right thing for us to say is, *'I should fight despoiling the earth because I truly can.'* We should be trapping carbon and forcing the petroleum and coal industries to gasp out their final blackened breaths."

He appears genuinely perplexed by my reasoning. "But that's not why Gaia made Druids. She's going to be fine and continue to exist whether humans are here or not. She allowed humans to be bound to the earth to protect elementals from magical exploitation, not mundane wear-and-tear."

"The rising sea levels and mass extinctions are hardly mundane wear-and-tear. And industrial-level contamination didn't exist five thousand years ago, so of course that wasn't on Gaia's mind."

Atticus shrugs like it's not important. "I think it's a waste of time."

"Well, I think it's the best possible use of it."

"Ohhh, are ye going to get into a fight?" Owen says, a hopeful note in his voice. "Me nipples are getting hard already."

This clearly isn't the safe topic I'd been hoping for, but now that I'm in it I can't stop. "So you want to live in Oregon and just do nothing?"

"What I do isn't *nothing*. I've been on call for the world's elementals for two thousand years. I have plenty of tethers to mend, new ones to make, and a fortune to rebuild."

"But that's it? You don't want to do anything to help?"

"I help every time an elemental asks for it."

"I know, Atticus, but I'm talking about your love for the earth and the desire to help even when it's not asked for."

"It was never really an option for me before now," he says. "If I used magic I'd be sending a beacon to Aenghus Óg, telling him where to find me. That threat is gone now, but I'm still not in a place where I can think about this as a realistic occupation. I mean, you could spend your whole day at it, and then what would you do to buy your hound a steak?"

Owen interjects again, but this time he's not mocking but correcting. "That's poor thinking there, lad. Ye let your hound hunt. There's nobody who can live off the land better than Druids. Ye don't need these modern economic bollocks, and ye know it."

"That's true, Atticus. You'll own the Oregon property free and clear, and we won't require much else except maybe beer money."

"What is this, are you guys tag-teaming me?"

"I don't know what a tag team is, but we're not attacking ye, lad. Honest, now. Ye said it yourself: For too long it was just you, and ye couldn't do a damn thing but survive. But now it's different, and ye should consider how your duty might have changed with the times."

"It's not that different yet," Atticus replies. "I'm still just trying to survive."

"As are we all. Perhaps it's premature to be thinkin' of the future. I can't be speakin' for Granuaile, so I'll say me own advice is to avoid falling into your old patterns if we get past this vampire bit. Give the options a good think. As for me, I know what I'll be doing: making more Druids."

"And I'll be doing everything I can to make dirty energy so expensive that people will flock to solar and wind. But I'll also get a day job in Poland, I think."

"Really?" Atticus asks. "Why there?"

"To immerse myself in the language. And besides," I say, brightening at the thought, "I like having beer money. I might even bartend again."

Atticus drops his head, draws his knees up, and wraps his arms around them. His voice is low and muffled. "I remember going to Rúla Búla with Hal when you worked there. He was truly one of the good guys. Gods, I miss him already."

I should go ahead and admit it to myself: I'm terrible at choosing safe conversation topics.

CHAPTER 26

When I woke up on the beach in Angola, Oberon curled against my side, I felt physically healed but afflicted with an emotional malaise. Or, to be more specific, an unholy horde of Guilt Ferrets. They're bastards.

The Jewish tradition has a day of atonement, and right then it sounded like a great idea to me. Except that a single day might not be enough in my case. I might need something like a year of atonement. I know that I did not kill Hal myself—or Kodiak Black, or Gunnar Magnusson, or the Morrigan, or innumerable others— but that's not how guilt works on a mind. It points out a string of cause and effect to saddle you with responsibility that isn't yours, and then it hops into that saddle, rakes you with spurs, and rides you until you collapse.

Unless you can find some redemption along the way.

Owen hasn't said anything, but I'm sure he's feeling the bite of guilt about Fand and Manannan Mac Lir. I shared with him what Mekera told me, in hopes it would help him on his own journey.

"Owen, listen: I know where Fand is," I said. An odd way to begin a conversation at sunrise, but my archdruid has never cared for niceties. "She's holed up at the Morrigan's Fen with Manannan. They're going to be tough to peel out of there, but I imagine the sooner you move against them the easier it'll be."

"How d'ye know that?"

"I talked with a seer who's quite a sight better than you or me. She told me."

"Well, it fits. I could see that they were in a swamp, and the Morrigan's Fen certainly qualifies. Damn good hiding place. I never would have thought to look there. Thank ye, lad."

I caught a couple of pensive expressions on Granuaile's face last night, which she claimed represented nothing when I asked. I didn't know if she was wrestling with Guilt Ferrets of her own but speculated that her renewed fervor to battle the slow poisoning of the earth might be her own method of atonement. Few things shape our lives so strongly as guilt.

Or perhaps she was worried about Loki, with good cause. I'd already known that Loki had found her at our cabin in Colorado, but over last night's campfire she told Owen and me for the first time the details of what had happened there. Inside the fire ward we'd placed around our cabin, she had beaten him up, put a tomahawk in his back, and pronounced that he was now living under the death sentence of a Druid. There was no doubt that the reverse was also true—he would kill her on sight, if he could. And the same was probably true for us.

I'm sure he had something to do with her worry. When she first asked to become my apprentice, I did all I could to warn her: Magic users sometimes lived very long lives, but they very often died violent deaths. And I showed her that stinking carnage at Tony Cabin, had her look upon the chewed-up head of Emily the corrupt sister, all of which was more powerful than simply telling her, and she still chose to be a Druid. But even being shown rather than told about violence is nothing compared to experiencing it yourself, and I think she was changed by her encounter with Loki in India. How could she not be? I hoped that striking back at him, coupled with the protection of her divination cloak, gave her a measure of therapeutic satisfaction. But the insouciance she possessed when she was first bound and flush with the wonder of Gaia—that might have been crushed like her bones, and she couldn't bind those feelings together again.

"Before we get into this today," I said to her, "we should probably think of where to keep the hounds safe. This place is nice, but there isn't much in the way of fresh water or game. Pretty much a desert up on top of those cliffs."

"I know a good place," she said. "Foothills of the Andes. Mild temperatures right now. Nice freshwater lake. Fat, slow llamas nearby if they get hungry."

"We should feed them first, but, yes, that sounds good."

When we asked the hounds what they wanted to eat, Oberon had an immediate answer: <Poutine!>

We got them both to Toronto, where it was just past midnight, but Poutini's House of Poutine on Queen Street West was open late and we scored some huge containers of the good stuff. Then we took them to the spot in Ecuador that Granuaile knew about. Even though they'd slept all night in Angola, they assured us that they would have no trouble sleeping some more after the glories of full bellies.

The bitter cold of Rome contrasted starkly with the warmth of the Southern Hemisphere, and Owen noted aloud he was thankful for his coat.

"Me tits would be all in an uproar if I didn't have it," he said.

We all filled up our reservoirs of energy before we left the Villa Borghese. Rome was one of the oldest and most continuously paved cities in the world. Even beneath the pavement there is more pavement, a city built on centuries of older cities. We wouldn't have endless energy to spend against the vampires should it come to a fight. Our best hope was to break through their wards and take them out before nightfall.

" 'Tis a dead, frigid hellscape for a Druid, an' that's no lie," Owen commented as soon as he hit the city proper and the touch of Gaia was lost.

"It's really unusual, though, for it to be this cold here," I said. It was midmorning, and the city was covered by the sort of low dark clouds one would expect to boil out of Mordor. "Looks like it might snow, and that happens maybe once every twenty years. I bet you the Romans will freak out and stay at home."

"Good," Granuaile said. "The fewer people we have to worry about, the better."

Tourist traffic in the Piazza di Spagna was almost nil. Even the vendors selling selfie sticks and other nonsense had written the day off and stayed home. We'd told the rabbi to meet us in Babington's, a decision that at least kept us cozy while we waited.

He in turn spread the word to the other Hammers, and we saw them begin to trickle in after noon. We didn't hail them and invite them to pull up a table but rather let them find each other and wait for Rabbi Yosef. I was worried that some of them might possess the extremist views that Yosef had in his youth, and I'd rather wait for him to arrive before introducing ourselves to devout monotheists as pagans adept in the practice of magic.

Rabbi Yosef arrived last, in the midafternoon, since he had the farthest to travel. He first greeted his comrades with hugs and a wide smile, then he spied us in the far corner and waved us over. He introduced us as the fine individuals who allowed the Hammers to do such wonderful work in the Western Hemisphere recently, and now,

Lord willing, we would help strike another mighty blow against the oldest of evil's minions on earth.

We got polite nods but no names from the rest of the Hammers. They were not anxious to make our acquaintance. We were to be useful creatures rather than friends.

"Shall we look at our target, then?" I asked. We settled our bills and bundled up against the chill outside. A few hardy tourists determined to get their money's worth for their air tickets to Rome tried to look cheerful in the gloom. The surface of Bernini's fountain, I noticed, had a thin coating of ice at the edges.

Once in front of the buildings in question, Rabbi Yosef Bialik squinted at the wards and muttered in Hebrew to his companions. They nodded and exchanged some words, and then he addressed us. "You are right. These are interlocking trees of the Hermetic Qabalah. But they are collapsible triggers."

"What do you mean?"

"Upon any tree being dispelled with cold iron—or anything else—the rest are able to isolate themselves and remain intact. You cannot dispel the entire ward, in other words, only the portion of it you walk through with your cold iron. The remaining trees are supposed to note the absence of any around them and trigger a response."

"What response?" Granuaile asked.

"That I do not know. It could be an attack. Or it could merely be an alarm, letting the casters know that the ward has been broken."

"Normal folks pass in and out without consequence, then," I said. "Clever."

"I'm normal folks," Owen said. "No cold iron on me."

"They will, however, like us, be able to detect the use of magic nearby," Yosef said. "If you were to use any magic at all, they would know it."

"Fair enough. I should be able to take a look inside, though, to scout. Or any of you lot could do it."

"You go," I said. "But keep your right hand in your pocket so no one spots your tattoos."

Owen scanned the three buildings and chose the yellow cream one on the right, with Dolce & Gabbana on the bottom floors.

"I like that it has a green door," he said, explaining his choice.

He walked through the ward without trouble, disappeared into the building, and returned not five minutes later.

"There's a hallway that goes back a ways. No place to hide. Elevator and stairs at the back with a man there asking if I was a resident. Both the elevator and the stairs are fecking narrow and I wouldn't want to go up either one. Anyone at the top would have one hell of an advantage."

"What was the man like?" Granuaile asked.

"Big bastard. Had one of those modern suits and a curly thing coming out of his ear. Clearly security. But there was someone else too. Not a guard exactly, and he said nothing, but he looked at me closely. He was sitting on the stairs, had these loose white clothes on him and an orange sash with symbols sewn on it in gold. And the weirdest hair I've ever fecking seen."

"How so?"

"Shaved on the top and above the ears except for a greasy strip all the way around, like a hairy ring."

"A tonsure?" I asked.

"If I knew what a tonsure was, maybe I could fecking answer ye."

"So we have bodyguards and spooky cultist types," Granuaile said.

"Any other wards inside, Owen?"

"I'm sure there's plenty more upstairs, but I didn't get

there. Didn't want to start a fight without knowing the odds."

I turned to the rabbi. "If you have kinetic wards, I'd start with that. If they're expecting me, then they might come out with guns blazing. Or they'll use something else mundane that cold iron can't dispel."

"Of course. And then a cloak of indifference. Innocent people will not care about what we're doing. Not that there are many people out here on a day like this."

"All right. We're going to withdraw out of sight, and then we'll swoop in if needed."

The rabbi had no problem with this and immediately resumed his conversation in Hebrew with the other Hammers of God. Owen, however, had an objection.

"Why are we hiding? Let's kick some arses already and go home."

"We need to draw them out first," I said. "The Hammers can ward themselves on the dead land, and their ward moves with them. We can't do either, and we also can't afford the energy. If we stay in the open when this begins, the most likely result is we'll get shot. If we charge in there, the likelihood of getting shot is even higher—that guy with the crinkly thing in his ear probably had a gun underneath his jacket, and there are, without doubt, many more men like him upstairs. You taught me yourself, Owen: Never give the enemy what he wants. They want Druids to walk into that trap, so we'll give them Kabbalists instead."

Owen bared his teeth and growled in frustration. He hated it when I was right.

With a little bravado and a little luck, we ascended to the rooftop room in Babington's with a view of the piazza. It was almost like a picnic pavilion, with a low wall, wide-open windows, and fantastic views. Down to our left and proceeding up behind us, the Spanish Steps rose to the church at the top. The piazza in front of us showed the ten Hammers of God aligning themselves in a Tree of Life formation, with Rabbi Yosef at the top, facing the green door near the entrance to Dolce & Gabbana.

"You're in for a show," I said to Granuaile and Owen. "You've never seen this kind of magic before. Those beards are going to throw down at some point."

"What? Their actual beards?" Granuaile said.

"You'll see."

The Hammers of God began to chant and move in ritualistic sequence. We didn't see all of it very well, since we were above and behind them to the left, but we had an excellent view of the three warded buildings. I was watching them more than the Kabbalists, to see what sort of reaction they provoked.

Part of me wanted to watch in the magical spectrum, but I didn't want to waste the energy. Within a minute of the Hammers' chanting, a couple of windows in the buildings flew open and pale, white-clad men with tonsures leaned out to lay eyes on the Kabbalists. They watched for a moment and withdrew, closing the shutters behind them.

"Okay, they're aware of the Hammers. Response should come soon."

Two men appeared on the rooftop garden of the terracotta building and pointed guns down at the Hammers of God. They had large, bulky silencers or mufflers or whatever screwed on to the end of the barrels. I am not a munitions expert. They popped off a few rounds, which ricocheted off the Hammers' kinetic ward, taking out a window to the north in one case but otherwise embedding themselves in the ancient brick and plaster of the buildings surrounding the piazza. The Kabbalists continued whatever they were doing. And, remarkably, so did the sparse dozen or so tourists in the piazza, who gave no sign that they had heard gunfire. The would-be assassins looked at each other and shrugged, then one held a finger to his earpiece and spoke, obviously reporting to someone via Bluetooth that guns weren't going to work. They disappeared after a moment.

"Okay, we're going to get a different sort of attack next," I said. That's when it began to snow in Rome. Big fat snowflakes eager to blanket the Eternal City and paralyze it.

Tonsured men of assorted backgrounds, dressed in the billowy white clothing Owen had described, with an orange sash crossing from their right shoulders to their left hips, streamed out of the three buildings. They were heading for a spot opposite the Hammers of God, presumably to form their own Tree of Life. Seeing this, the Hammers of God formation flattened into two lines, staggered so that the line in back could see between the shoulders of the front line, and then in sync they drew silver knives out of their coats and threw them at a single target. Some missed, but most didn't. The targeted man went down with seven knives buried in his torso and one in his throat.

"Holy shite!" Owen said. "Why did they go after that one?"

"Align yourself with the forces of hell and you're fair game in their eyes," I said.

"No, I mean, why that one particular man?"

I shrugged. "Random target of opportunity. It was smart, because they disrupted their formation before it got started. The Hammers didn't want them to get their own kinetic ward, or anything else, going. They need ten dudes to do anything major."

"Well, I think they have ten anyway," Granuaile said. "Another one just appeared—yep. That's ten. They might have more waiting."

"Oh, damn." The Hammers didn't have additional guys in reserve. If one or more of them went down, they could maintain what they'd already cast but not do anything in addition. Their strength in formation was impressive, but their weakness was needing to maintain that formation.

Their cloak of indifference—or whatever they were using to distract passersby—worked astoundingly well. A woman in heels clicked across the piazza, right by the body of the dead Qabalist—who was an obvious murder victim and could not be mistaken for a sleeping vagrant—and walked into Dolce & Gabbana as if she had seen nothing amiss. I wondered what its range was because while Granuaile and I had the protection of cold iron, Owen did not and he had clearly seen that man sprout steel in his body and go down.

The Hermetic Qabalists began their own chanting and synchronized moves, but the Hammers of God wanted to disrupt them before they completed anything. So Rabbi Yosef Bialik's beard got unleashed like some hairy nightmare elder god, puffing and expanding and then twisting into thick tentacles, three on either side of his chin. They began to stretch out for the point man of the other formation, and Granuaile gasped while Owen pointed a shaky finger at him.

"What kind of extra-special batshite is that right there? Gods below, Siodhachan, if Brighid was here I'd tell her to kill it with fire!"

"Haha. Told you."

"I'm gonna have nightmares." He pawed at his face. "I need to shave."

The Hermetic Qabalist had a response to the hairy cables coming his way: His tonsure came alive in much the same way, and a halo of tentacles formed around his skull before rushing to meet the rabbi's.

"Oh, yuck!" Granuaile said. The two sets of hairy ropes met in the middle, struggled to get past each other, failed, then entwined and tore at the enemy in an attempt to pull the other out of formation.

"Are you kidding? This is awesome," I said.

"Since I've become a Druid, I've seen some pretty weird shit, Atticus," Granuaile said, "but Beardy Baggins there squaring off against Squid Head McGee in the snow might be the weirdest."

"Hold up, now, who's that lad coming out of the building on the left?" Owen pointed to a slim, pale figure wearing sunglasses and a bespoke Italian suit. I recognized him from Berlin; he was one of the gang that got away.

"That's a vampire."

"How? It's not night yet," Granuaile said.

"Might as well be. No sun's getting through that cloud cover except the weakest kind."

"Easy way to find out," Owen said, and he began to roll out the words for unbinding. Meanwhile, the vampire moved briskly—not running, just a late-for-a-meeting walk—to position himself behind the rearmost Hammer of God. He was moving too slowly to trigger the kinetic ward, and so he encountered no difficulty. He reached over the shoulder with one hand to grab the Hammer's bearded chin, placed the other on top of the head, and twisted savagely, snapping his neck. The Hammer's body went slack and he tumbled to the cobblestones. Just as the rest of the Hammers were becoming aware that their formation had been disrupted and the vampire was moving to take out yet another of them, Owen completed his unbinding, and the contents of that fine Italian suit popped like a swollen tick before collapsing into a dark red puddle on the piazza.

This caused one of the boys in white to cry out in Italian, "A Druid is here!"

A window in the terra-cotta building flew open and a voice boomed, "Do not let him escape." More windows

flew open—probably half of the total available flats—
and vampires leapt out of them, regardless of how high
off the ground they were. This was far more than the
eleven who'd escaped in Berlin. I honestly could not
count them all because they kept coming. They began
to fan out around the plaza to find me, and using camouflage wouldn't matter. They'd locate me via smell,
because my blood and presumably Owen's were two-
thousand-year-old vintages.

"Shit. Hey, wait: They think there's only one of us. I'll
be the bait down there on the steps and let them come
after me. You guys stay here and pick off all you can."

Their protests followed after me as I dashed down the
stairs. "If ye cock this up, you'll be dead!" Owen pointed
out helpfully.

When I plowed through the front door, the first thing
I did was slip on the icy steps and fall on my ass. An
inauspicious beginning to battle. But I got up and noticed that the Hammers of God and their tonsured op-
ponents had fallen to hand-to-hand—or rather to beards
vs. scalp squids. Both formations were broken up now,
and it was a brutal hairy mêlée that I might have enjoyed watching under other circumstances. But there
were many speedy vampires spreading out over the
piazza and I needed to get myself in position to lure
them, hoping that Theophilus himself would come out
to play eventually. Beginning to draw on the reserves of
my bear charm, I increased my speed and drew out my
stake, keeping Fragarach sheathed. Then I chose a vamp
as I ran over to the bottom of the Spanish Steps and kept
my eyes on him as I mouthed the words of unbinding.
He was circling around toward the Keats-Shelley House
on the other side of the steps from Babington's, and just
as I completed the unbinding, he realized that I wasn't
admiring Bernini's fountain like a tourist. His mouth

formed a tiny *o* of surprise, and then he turned into mobile slush.

"He's there, at the steps!" that same stentorian voice called from the terra-cotta building.

The vampires began to converge from all sides—some had moved fast enough to run to the top of the steps and cut off escape to the road that snaked beneath the Trinità dei Monti church. Not that I wished to escape.

I scooted over to the large block pillar of marble at one end of the steps and put myself on the other side of it, facing the stairs, in case they decided to direct sniper fire in my direction from those buildings. Unlike the Hammers, I had no kinetic ward. I'd handle the vampires coming from above and behind Babington's and trust Granuaile and Owen to take care of threats coming at me from the piazza.

It was an excellent plan for about ninety seconds. A lot can happen in ninety seconds. I unbound just as many vampires as I did in Berlin, probably more—all their fine clothing ruined by the juicy sounds of their owners' elements being forcibly separated. Splortches and splashes and gushes ahead of me, even more behind me. So much blood on the steps, splashes of black and sometimes red in the white snow, if the vampire had fed recently. A few vampires got past Owen and Granuaile and rounded the pillar on me, but I staked them and wondered how many Theophilus had brought with him. He was sacrificing a lot of soldiers to get to me. Did he have the guts to fight himself, I wondered? Had he emerged from the warded building, or was he still coldly issuing directions from the safety of his darkened room?

The vampires figured out that Granuaile and Owen were doing most of the damage, and they sent a few of their soldiers over the rooftops to land on Babington's and deal with them. Not that I saw that happening from down on the steps—I pieced that together later. The first

I realized that something was wrong was when I heard Granuaile cry out in surprise. I looked up at the Babington's rooftop and saw her twist in midair and just barely catch the tiled edge with her hands. She and Owen had been facing in my direction and leaning out the wide window of the pavilion to target the vampires coming my way, so they hadn't seen the ones sneaking up behind them, and Granuaile got defenestrated. To keep from falling, she'd had to drop Scáthmhaide—the only source of energy available to her. A vampire danced down the slope of the roof to finish her off, while Owen made the inexplicable decision to shape-shift into a bear to fight the remaining two in the room. He couldn't unbind any vampires that way, either by unbinding or by stake. I targeted the one coming after Granuaile and spoke two whole words of Old Irish before an unseen fist slammed into the side of my jaw, both breaking and dislocating it and causing me to bite off the tip of my tongue. It spun me around and I tried to face my attacker, but my balance was a mess, my ears were ringing, and the pain was occupying all my headspaces until I could get it shunted into a tidy screaming box. The result was that I slipped on the icy steps and fell on my ass again. I let go of the bloodied stake in my left hand when a booted heel stomped down on my fingers and broke most of them. The stake got kicked away, and I blinked furiously and triggered my healing charm, trying to focus enough to have a chance at saving my life. A ball of dough sitting atop a pickle laughed at me, and I blinked again. Now it was a pale, bloodless face laughing at me, and the torso was dressed in a hunter green turtleneck underneath a long olive trench coat. Dark eyes and a douchelord's haircut up top, clean shaven, and a scar that began on his upper lip and continued underneath the bottom one.

"Thfff."

He cupped his right ear and mocked me. "I'm sorry,

what was that? Theophilus? Yes. We meet at last, Mr. O'Sullivan. For a very brief time, at the end of your life. You were better than all the rest of the Druids, at least—congratulations on presenting a genuine challenge. Thought I should say farewell in person."

I scrambled back and up in a crabwalk to put some distance between us. Pointless, really, when he could close it very quickly. I stole a glance at Granuaile. She was still hanging from the roof, and a vampire was trying to stomp on her hands to make her fall. It wasn't necessarily a fatal drop—three stories—but there was nothing save unforgiving stone waiting below.

Theophilus followed my gaze and didn't like what he saw any more than I did. "Karl!" he shouted. "Hurry up and help Hans with the other one!" Karl turned his head to confirm that, yes, Hans was still having difficulty subduing Owen in the little rooftop pavilion. And that's when Granuaile lunged up, grabbed Karl's pant leg, and yanked mightily to pull him off his feet. He hit the edge of the tiles with his ass next to her handhold, she latched on to his torso, and then they were locked in a horrible embrace and fighting as they fell, tumbling so that when they disappeared behind the raised blocks of stone partitioning the steps, they were falling horizontally, the vampire's back to me and Granuaile almost invisible except for the trailing flame of her hair. The crunch of their impact and their joint, choked cry of pain caused Theophilus to wince.

"Ouch," he said, and my inarticulate attempt at shouting Granuaile's name sounded as if I were trying to talk through duct tape. I reached behind my right shoulder and drew out Fragarach, pointing it in the general direction of Theophilus. His eyes returned to me and he snorted. "What do you think you're going to accomplish with that? Steel won't do anything except make me hungry later for any blood you manage to spill with it now."

He was right. Steel wouldn't do anything significant to him unless I could manage to decapitate him. But Fragarach was more than simple steel. It could cut through any armor, or make people tell the truth, or summon winds. Down the steps to the west, past the fountain and beyond the plaza, the narrow Via dei Condotti descended in a straight line to the Tiber River, which I'd be able to see on a clear day. But it was all dark and gloomy now. It was a long shot, but I had to try. Summoning wind didn't require a verbal command, just an effort of will and a source of energy. I pointed Fragarach down the Via dei Condotti and gave it all the juice remaining in my bear charm and a little bit of me as well. I groaned from the effort, drained, and fell back against the steps.

"What the hell was that?" Theophilus said. I gave a little bit more of myself to target him and trigger my unbinding charm. He clutched his chest and said, "Hrrk," so I hit him with it again. He took a step back, but that was all I had left. I listened to Owen bellow upstairs, out of my sight, heard people finally screaming about the blood-soaked snow, and realized that the Hammers of God must have either suffered mightily and their cloak was no more or at some point the carnage became too great to ignore under any spell. I heard nothing from Granuaile. And Theophilus, when he recovered, finally looked annoyed. If nothing else, I'd defeated his smug expression. And maybe I'd get a small result for my efforts after all. The dirty-dishwater clouds in the west swirled and tore apart as Theophilus said, "I think that's enough," and a few weak rays of late-afternoon sun pierced the snowfall and set his head to smoking as he lunged for me. He felt the burn and halted, turned, and shot away into the plaza, behind the buildings, where there was plenty of shade. His entire face sizzled and vented steam, and now he looked satisfactorily pissed.

I heard a scream from up at the top of Babington's and saw a human form engulfed in flames, flailing in the pavilion. Owen's troublesome opponent had caught much more of the sun up there. Pointing at me, Theophilus turned his head to call over his shoulder, "Marko! Shoot him!"

The steel barrel of a rifle peeked out a window in the terra-cotta building, and I scrambled to hide myself behind the stone pillar. A bullet cracked off the steps and shattered some marble quarried hundreds of years ago. I was effectively pinned down now, unable to speak any more unbindings through my broken jaw, and my stake was nearby but in the line of sight of a sniper. I couldn't bind it to my palm without the ability to craft the binding. At least the sun had placed me in a no-vamp land. Any vampire who wanted to get to me would have to get through the sun first.

I allowed myself a tiny sniff of hope: I'd figure something out in the next minute or so. A minute without someone in your face was all you needed sometimes. And then the lovely yellow patches of light on the steps faded as the storm clouds boiled back together in the absence of continued influence from Fragarach.

The literal dimming of my prospects gave me new and very serious doubts about whether any of us would survive this. I had a painful and debilitating injury, no juice left, and no way to get any more. I hadn't seen Granuaile get up from where she'd fallen, and as soon as the sun disappeared, more vampires leapt onto Babington's roof to bait Owen's great big bear. A stolen peek into the plaza allowed me a glimpse of the Hammers of God still battling the twisted Rosicrucians. There were fewer of them on both sides now, attrition taking its toll, but the vampires were leaving them alone, focusing on eliminating the Druids instead. They were coming; Theophilus was coming. I wasn't going to get that minute to think.

Maybe, instead, a quick observation: Theophilus had used only two methods of attack so far, and, unless I was mistaken, he had rarely deviated from them his entire life. He either ambushed victims or sent overwhelming numbers at them. And I can't fault either strategy, because both are likely to lead to victory, and victory is what it's all about. Winning is the difference between old guys and dead guys.

But when your opponent *knows* you'll try to ambush him, some of your advantage disappears. Theophilus had already sucker-punched me once, and if his sniper could get a clear shot he'd take it. So his move would be to have his lads rush my position and flush me from cover. He wouldn't square off against me except as a last resort. I'd be willing to bet that he was a terrible fighter. Fast and strong and invulnerable to most attacks, but untrained. Which meant that Leif could probably take him, despite being younger and relatively weaker. Which meant that I could probably take him. If I had any access to Gaia's energy, that is.

Drawing on old knowledge that these European vampires would never have bothered to acquire themselves, I set myself in a crouching stance behind the pillar, right foot forward, still sheltered from sniper fire. And then I began a series of forms with Fragarach that I had learned in China; when combined at speed, they formed a whirling defensive guard about my head and torso. I didn't know from which direction the attack would come, so I had to give myself some chance of slowing them down, since they would be coming with a significant speed advantage.

The first one came from behind the pillar on my right and led with his face, fangs bared. He expected to find a stationary target, not a steel blade whipping through the air that he wasn't breathing. Fragarach sliced through his head from top to bottom in front of his ears. His body's momentum carried into me and knocked me a bit to the left, and I was already thrusting in that direction, expecting another vampire to appear from there, the old one-two. And, sure enough, one did. He ran right onto Fragarach's point, which missed his heart and punctured the lung he didn't need. Still, it hurt, and he stopped, though he hissed and hit me with his dead-body breath. Feeling exposed, I twisted the blade and darted back behind the pillar, yanking Fragarach and the vampire with me. It was therefore his head instead of mine that got exploded by sniper fire from Marko.

I re-centered myself between the bodies and resumed my defensive forms. Neither vampire was completely toast, but they were down for now, until they could be unbound. In the meantime, I needed to be ready for the second wave. It would be any second now—I was sure I'd feel the impact before I saw anything coming.

But no more undead minions materialized. I just got a good workout when I was already exhausted and in pain. Maybe that was the plan: Wait until I couldn't maintain my defenses and then swoop in. As soon as I considered it, though, I realized Theophilus didn't really have that luxury; when and if Owen dispatched the vampires that currently occupied him, he'd be able to unbind any that were left, provided he could talk. I was starting to think that perhaps he had shape-shifted because of a similar injury to mine. If his jaw had also been broken—a tactical move on the vampires' part—then bulking up as a bear and fighting it out would make sense for him.

Maybe we had truly fought through most of the vampires. Or maybe there was some other skullduggery going on—time being taken to reevaluate strategy, given that I had demonstrated you *can* take out a vampire with a sword, albeit not permanently.

A blur zipped past me to the left up the central flight of the steps and then stilled well out of reach of my sword. It was Theophilus, face crispy and wizened and bereft of the smug confidence he'd displayed earlier. I kept my eye on him but didn't stop moving Fragarach through my defensive forms; his appearance was most likely intended as a distraction and I'd be hit from the sides or even up top—

Flicking my eyes upward, I saw a dark shape descending from over the top of the pillar, and I pivoted to my right and hacked through it, splitting the body in two. But the gambit served its purpose. During that crucial second or so, Theophilus moved with blinding speed and bowled me over, tackling me to the cobbled plaza stones and trapping my sword arm against my body. As soon as we hit the ground on my left side, he reared back, grabbed Fragarach by the blade, and ripped it out of my hand, uncaring about the deep cuts he received as a result. He tossed it away onto the steps of the Keats-Shelley House. I was unarmed, drained of energy, and unable to speak—he had me and he knew it. He grinned, feeling confident again, and held me down with a grip stronger than any iron bands I've seen.

Just to make that smile disappear again, I wanted to tell him Werner Drasche was dead, but I couldn't.

"Well done, sir, well done," he cooed at me. "Not good enough, but definitely a fine challenge. A worthy opponent. When the world's nests hear that you killed so many but failed to kill me—even with the sun!—that will only add to my prestige. You've done me a favor in a way. But that doesn't mean I won't ram my fist through your skull right now."

I didn't have the strength to break free. When he lifted his hand away I wouldn't be able to block his blow in time, or even if I did manage to get in the way it would be an utterly feeble attempt. So I drained my own energy to trigger the unbinding charm on my necklace once more, having no other weapons at my disposal. I nearly blacked out at the drain, but he did let go of my left arm to clutch at his precious turtleneck. He hissed, and then when the pain faded he raised his fist high and said, "Good night—hunh!"

His eyes bulged and he looked down at his right side, where a familiar stake had embedded itself underneath his arm. He dropped his fist to pull it out, but the unbinding had already begun, shredding him from the center out. The world's oldest vampire gave a wet gurgling scream before he liquefied and splurted out through his fine clothing. The turtleneck didn't save me from an overdose of gules but perhaps made it look like I had died too. I followed the path of where that stake must have come from and saw Granuaile standing off to the left, behind the pillar opposite mine, leaning heavily on her staff. Her clothes were covered in gore and she was favoring her left side, but apart from either deep bruising or perhaps some small fractures, she was all right. She gave me a lopsided grin. "Hey. You look like I feel. Don't let me forget: We need to buy Luchta, like, *all* the beer for giving us those stakes."

I wanted to shout at her to beware of the sniper, but I think she knew about him anyway, judging by the fact that she was already behind cover. I, however, wasn't.

But the disadvantage to peering through one of those scopes is the very small field of vision. The sniper hadn't seen Granuaile coming, and now he had taken his sights off me to search for who had just killed the boss. Or at least I surmised as much by the fact that I didn't immediately die of a bullet to the brain. Flailing for a second in ancient vampire goo, I sat up with an effort and crawled back behind the pillar.

Owen wasn't finished making a ruckus. Babington's rooftop pavilion was on fire now—presumably ignited by the smoking corpses of the vampires caught in the brief rays of sunlight—and he used his brass-covered claws to burst through the wall as a bear and slide to the edge of the roof, where he shape-shifted to a red kite. I followed his progress as he arrowed across the piazza to a window in the terra-cotta building where Marko's rifle muzzle poked out. He didn't get there before Marko fired but rather just as he fired, knocking the muzzle down with his talons so that the bullet went *spaff* into Bernini's fountain. I don't know if Marko was aiming at Granuaile or me. He didn't get a chance to shoot again after that. Owen disappeared into the building and I presume he took out all the gun-wielding lads one way or another, because he eventually emerged from the front entrance, dressed in one of their suits.

In the meantime, authorities were pouring into the piazza, trying to reestablish order as a precursor to figuring out what had happened. The wail of sirens heralded the arrival of firemen and paramedics. Granuaile and I had no difficulty pretending to be traumatized victims, and neither did the Rabbi Yosef Bialik. Only five of the Hammers of God survived, but they had defeated the Hermetic Qabalists completely, and their beards looked like normal facial hair again. I noticed that all the silver knives had been removed from the body of the first Rosicrucian the Hammers had taken out. The rabbi floated the idea that maybe we should blame everything on the guys with the funny haircuts, and I nodded my approval.

"I have lost good friends tonight, but this was a true triumph over evil, yes? We will talk later. When you can talk." Yes, we would. I owed him some Immortali-Tea for sure.

When Owen emerged from the building, he still had

enough juice left in his brass knuckles to cast camouflage on the three of us and get us out of there. His jaw, I noticed, was misshapen, as I'd suspected. It was dislocated for sure and possibly broken like mine. We limped and grunted our way back to the grounds of the Villa Borghese and fell onto the grass once we felt Gaia's presence again. I numbed the pain first so I could keep my head clear, then set about getting my jaw back into place and the bones and teeth bound together like old friends. Owen's jaw was merely dislocated, and once he popped it back into place with an audible crunch, a river of profanity that had been dammed up all during the fight spewed forth. Granuaile likewise worked on her wounds, and once Owen wound down, we rested in silence and healed. After an hour I could talk again, albeit with a thick slur.

"Yay team," I said.

"Damn," Owen said. "I knew it wouldn't last forever. But it was right peaceful there for a while, not having to listen to your yapping."

CHAPTER 27

Fishing out my burner phone, I made a call and spoke past my bloodied lips and tongue. "Meet ush now at the Antico Caffè Greco by the piazza." I thumbed off the call once I got an affirmative response.

"Who was that?" Granuaile asked.

"The ansher to what happensh next. Hungry?"

"Not while covered in blood. Maybe afterward."

"I'm sure they will have a washroom."

Charged up again, we camouflaged ourselves and walked back through the piazza, ignoring the barriers and surveying the damage. Babington's suffered damage only to the rooftop pavilion; someone got up there with a fire extinguisher and saved the building. There was nothing but oily stains and empty clothes to mark the final deaths of the vampires—Owen confirmed that we had gotten them all. He hadn't killed all the thralls but left them broken and, in one case, naked. He'd lost his stake on top of Babington's somewhere and would have to look for it later. Mine had been found by the police on the steps and was being bagged as evidence. As soon as the officer put it down, I snatched it up, unseen, and shoved it underneath my jacket.

Normally there would be something of a wait to get into Caffè Greco, the legendary establishment where Keats and Shelley and many other artists and poets

dined over the centuries. Its red and gold interior with
vaulted ceilings fairly teemed with the ghosts of creative
minds, and people lined up to park their buttocks where
famous buttocks had lounged in days of yore. But on a
freezing, snowy evening in Rome, it was almost de-
serted. We kept the camouflage on when we entered and
shambled past the maître d' to the restrooms, where we
could attempt to clean ourselves up somewhat. We could
get our faces and hair clean, and Owen had stolen his
clothing so he was in good shape there, but my clothes
weren't going to look decent again before they had gone
a few rounds with industrial-sized containers of bleach.
Better to unbind them and let them feed the earth.

"Ye look like ye killed a bus full o' people, lad," Owen
said.

"Yesh, I do. But it'll be okay. I think."

We walked out together in camouflage, dropped it,
then walked right back in again, entirely visible. Granuaile didn't look bad at all, having managed to either
clean or conceal most of the blood on her. I was the one
who had to talk my way in. I explained in broken Italian
to the alarmed maître d' that my clothes weren't stained
with actual blood; it was corn syrup and food dye,
thrown upon me by some damn animal-rights activists
who'd targeted me for my leather jacket. I gave him fifty
euros, courtesy of the pickpockets I'd run into yesterday,
and we were seated with alacrity at a table for four.

"Our friend will be joining us shortly," I explained.

We ordered espressos and sat in silence. We were exhausted, cut off from Gaia, and quietly trying to manage
our pain. There was little else to say until our guest
showed up.

When he did, Owen was the first to spot him. "Fecking hell?" he said, then he began to speak the unbinding
for vampires. I saw that a tall, pale Viking with straight
blond hair approached, dressed in a modern Italian suit.

"No, no!" I said, clapping a hand over his mouth. "Thash who we're waiting for!"

Leif Helgarson halted, because he'd heard what I said, and held up his hands to show that he was harmless, but Owen slapped my hand away and growled, "Gerroff me, ye poxy cock!"

"All right, jush lisshen to him. He'sh gonna keep your Grove shafe."

"Fine. But give me your stake just in case," he said. "He'd better fecking behave." I handed it over, and he laid it on the table in plain view as a warning.

"Atticus, what's going on?" Granuaile said. "I thought you hated him."

"Not as much as I hate the thought of a never-ending war." I waved Leif over. "Shometimes a deal with the devil is better than an eternity of righteous shuffering."

"Good evening to you all," he said formally, pulling out his chair and seating himself. "I am grateful for the invitation to join you. Congratulations on your victory against the Druids' oldest enemy."

"Thank you," I said. Granuaile and Owen just stared at him in silence, their muscles tense and ready to lash out.

"I have the document you requested, Atticus," Leif said. "It is in my coat pocket." His eyes latched on to Owen. "I am going to remove it very slowly."

"Aye. Ye take your fecking time with that," Owen said.

Leif's pale hand crept slowly toward his jacket pocket, and Owen's grip on the stake tightened. The hand disappeared, the faint rasp of fingers against paper could be heard, and then a single folded sheet emerged in his hand. He extended it to me.

"If you will, Atticus."

I took it from him and unfolded it, as Leif crossed his

arms across his body, where Granuaile and Owen could see them. They relaxed infinitesimally.

"Thish ish a treaty," I told them. "To be shigned by the four of ush if you are willing."

"I'll donate me bollocks to charity first," Owen said.

"You're not required to shign it," I said. "Just lisshen." Looking at the text, I became daunted. My jaw and tongue were in no shape to read this well. "Granuaile? Would you mind?" I offered the paper to her and she snatched it from me without looking, keeping her eyes on Leif.

"You stay super fucking still," she told him.

"As you command," he said.

Her eyes dropped to the contract and scanned it while Owen remained on guard.

"It says we're to help him eliminate competitors among the vampire leadership," she said.

"We will give addreshes to the Hammersh of God," I explained. "We don't have to do it ourshelves."

"And you have already completed most of the work with your efforts to date," Leif added. "I anticipate few if any obstacles at this point. I am, to the best of my knowledge, the oldest vampire in the world now."

Granuaile continued, "It says that from now on, vampires may not occupy any part of North America west of the Rocky Mountains."

"And?" I prompted.

". . . And Poland." Granuaile looked up at me.

"I do try to keep my promishesh."

Leif pointed out, "The detailed language beneath says that vampires are to be given a month to evacuate those territories. After that, they may be unbound or staked on sight."

Owen growled, "What do we have to give up for that?"

Granuaile dropped her eyes back down to the paper.

"Everywhere else we have a truce. Live and let be undead, I guess. We don't unbind vampires on sight; they
don't attack us. The war is over. Each side is allowed
to defend itself in the case of physical attack."

"Bah. That's ripe for abuse. Kill a lad and then say he
attacked ye and it was self-defense."

Granuaile nodded once to acknowledge that and kept
reading. "The vampires agree to maintain their population in the allowed territories in keeping with the
Accords of Rome, which specifies one vampire per one
hundred thousand humans." She looked up at the ceiling, considering. "If you subtract the population of just
Poland and the West Coast, that means a significant net
reduction of vampires worldwide."

"It's all shite," Owen said.

"Your Grove will be shafe, Owen," I said. "Even
when they are bound someday."

He glares at me, but I know from experience that it
means I've gotten through to him. If he isn't yelling at
me, at least he's thinking about it.

Granuaile cocks her head to the side and points at
the treaty. "If I'm going to sign this, I want additional
clauses."

"What did you have in mind?" Leif asked.

"Vampires agree to immediately divest their significant financial holdings from fossil fuel investments.
Any energy investments will be in renewable, sustain-
able sources."

"I see. What do we get in return?"

"The gigantic hint that fossil fuel investments are going
to pay terrible dividends from now on." She smiled at
him. "I guarantee it. Sell while the selling's good."

"Done," Leif said.

"And I want regular updates on the progress of Poland's evacuation until it's complete. Names of the vampires who leave and the cities they used to occupy." She

turned to me. "I'm going to see the sisters often, Atticus, and they'll want to know."

"The contract already specifies that you will get a full report at the end of the one-month grace period," Leif replied. "After thirty days I will verify that every vampire has left Poland or else give you their location so that they may be unbound in accordance with this contract."

"Ah. Good enough." She set down the contract and drained her espresso. "Well, I'm satisfied. I'll sign it."

"Me too." We both turned to Owen, who shifted his eyes between us.

"Ye really think this shite is worth signing?" he asked.

"I do. Join ush, and with our combined shtrength, we can end this deshtructive conflict."

I did not add that we would "bring order to the galaxy," but Granuaile put her hand up to her mouth to cover a smile anyway.

Owen missed it entirely. He said to Leif, "Add Ireland to the list of vampire-free zones and I'll sign it. If there's any arse-kicking to be done in Ireland, I want to be doing it meself, not leave it to some dead lad."

"Done."

"Good," Owen said. "Let's get this over with and start staying far away from each other."

"Wait! One more thing!" Granuaile said. "A condition of my signature is that you have to finally answer this question, because I've been so curious: Do vampires poop?"

Leif slumped in his chair and rolled his eyes at the ceiling. "Please, no. Leave me with some dignity."

"You can be as dignified as you wish when you're leading the vampire world. We want to know."

He gave a dramatic sigh and covered his eyes with one hand while he spoke so he didn't have to look at us. There was pain in his voice as he explained, "There is not really any excrement *per se*, nor any contraction of the bowel. There is just . . . this . . ." The fingers of one hand flailed about like lost moths, as if in search for the proper words, and then clenched upon finding them. He nearly wept: ". . . *unseemly* discharge."

Granuaile promptly threw her head back to laugh and fell backward in her chair. She rolled over and slapped the floor with her palm, carried away not so much by the content but by Leif's evident disgust at speaking the truth aloud.

Owen and I had a good chuckle out of it too, and I was glad Granuaile had remembered to ask him. He would never have answered except at that very moment.

Leif produced a pen and wrote in the addendums to the contract, while we tried to get control of ourselves. We all signed and he countersigned and then we schooled our expressions to look dignified, though for our parts it may have come across as three parts pain and two parts weariness.

"Thank you all," he said, folding the contract. His gaze turned to me and he smirked. "We should not part without a few words from the Bard. *Now breathe we, lords: good fortune bids us pause, and smooth the frowns of war with peaceful looks.* Who said it?"

"King Edward IV in *Henry VI, Part III*." I spoke the next words slowly, making a special effort to enunciate clearly in spite of my injuries. "I will raise you a quote from *Cymbeline: Laud we the gods; and let our crooked smokes climb to their nostrils from our blest altars. Publish we this peace to all our subjects.*"

"Well spoken," Leif said, his smirk widening to a broad smile. Waggling the contract, he said, "I will send you copies of this wherever you wish. For now I have much to do. A publishing of the peace, as you said." He rose slowly from his chair, so as not to alarm Owen or Granuaile, and bowed. "Do keep in touch. Farewell."

Once he was out of sight we all visibly relaxed, but we

didn't say anything until we were sure he couldn't overhear us. I closed my eyes and gave silent thanks to Brighid, the Morrigan, and all the gods below for this moment of peace that was centuries in the making—not that they had anything to do with it, apart from Brighid's idea about the stakes. Sometimes you simply need to say thank you to someone, to be grateful for the road behind and the road ahead and the place you're at, and gods are very good at accepting those feelings. And for all that humanity asks them for intercession with this crisis or that, it's important when things go well to be thankful or at least conscious of your good fortune, whether the gods deserve the gratitude or not. We strive so much to achieve these small slivers of balance that it would be a shame not to look around and appreciate them when they happen.

"We did it," I said, a tinge of wonder in my voice. "Three Druids againsht the vampire who nearly wiped ush out and we finally got to him. Two thoushand years of hiding and waiting and then a lot of maneuvering and blood, but we got him." I turned to the others. "Thank you both for your help."

"Right. Can we fecking leave this festering shite of a city now?" Owen asked.

"Yeah," Granuaile said. "Let's get our bruised and battered asses to a green place and stay there for a while."

Well, maybe it wasn't such a great moment for them. They didn't have to live through the two thousand years to get here. They also couldn't grasp the sheer number of lives lost to Theophilus's war—only Hal Hauk, I suspect, mattered to them, as he mattered to me. Yet so many others had fallen and they deserved to be remembered too, so I would do it. And I still had a huge debt to work off for the yewmen's aid, and the Rabbi Yosef Bialik was due some remuneration. But I will pay it all gladly and be rid of this old fear. It had shackled my consciousness for so long that I didn't realize how much it weighed until I won free of it.

"Good idea," I said, a painful grin spreading my smashed lips. "I think I'd like nothing sho much as to play with my hound right now."

epiLogue

Three weeks later, after the winter solstice and the New Year, it was such a clear blue day in the Pacific Northwest that I didn't mind the winter chill. Thanks to the new treaty with Leif, Owen would be able to get to the serious business of training apprentices in peace—which included the peace that came with my absence. And since Granuaile, like me, was effectively shielded from divination, Fand and Manannan Mac Lir wouldn't be able to find us at the new place in Oregon, if that was on their list of things to do. I hadn't heard anything about their recapture and didn't plan to inquire. My plan was to ignore them until I couldn't.

Magnusson and Hauk finalized the closing of the property for us and then gave me papers terminating me as a client. The termination saddened me, as did the cause for it; since I'd never gotten a chance to attend a memorial for Hal I held my own private one in the woods, shed tears at his passing, and hoped that wherever his spirit was he would forgive me.

But the property, at least, was worth the wait: an isolated spot in the Willamette National Forest, a legacy homestead with a wraparound porch and one of those steep green roofs. There was even a greenhouse for growing herbs in the winter, a new addition to the property that was Granuaile's idea. She had paid for it out of her own funds and said I should consider it a house-warming present. And an investment.

"I think you should get back into the tea business," she said upon revealing it to me, draping her arms around my shoulders and kissing my cheek. "But do it online this time. Sell your Mobili-Tea and so on and we'll ship it." It made me happy that she was thinking about the long term. The first-person plural made me happier.

Maybe my worries about us as a couple were un-founded, but ... well. Doubt is a pernicious, invasive weed in the mind that is nigh impossible to destroy once it germinates. You can pull it out and think it's gone, only to find it growing again after weeks or even days. Not that Granuaile had given me doubts about her fidelity; I'm not particularly jealous in that regard anyway—we are made to enjoy the bodies of other people, and I've long thought it silly to condemn another for acting according to their nature. Passion, though: That's entirely separate from lust. Granuaile is still in her thirties and hasn't lived long enough to know what a slow burn is. So when we first made love after Rome and it was different than before, damn if doubt didn't sprout in my mind with the speed of a time-lapse video and wave hello like an improbably cheerful hostess at a steak house. The last thing I wanted was Friar Laurence from *Romeo and Juliet* in my head, reminding me that *These violent delights have violent ends and in their triumph die, like fire and powder, which, as they kiss, consume,* but there the bastard was, schooling me as if I were a horny young Montague instead of someone far older than he was. And he kept at it too, into the next day, until I said aloud, "Hey, fuck you, Friar Laurence, okay?" and Oberon heard me through our mental link.

<Who are you talking to, Atticus? Do you need me to chew on him?>

No, I was just worried because it was different and I've had more than my fair share of relationships. I can read the signs, and I'm not ready for it to end. But I also know from a surfeit of experience that people outgrow each other, and she still has plenty of growing to do. I can't teach her Polish, so she's been spending lots of time in Poland with the Sisters of the Three Auroras. She already scored a bartending job in Warsaw to get the immersion she needs, and she also spent time monitoring the activities of Thatcher Oil and Gas. I only see her now when she comes home to sleep and on her weekends, which are Mondays and Tuesdays.

But it was entirely possible—even probable—that my worries were unfounded and magnified out of proportion by the infamously fragile male ego. Apart from my imagination, she had given me no cause to fear. What I should be doing was the same thing everyone should be doing: enjoying the blessings I have while I have them, instead of worrying that one day they will be gone. I fought to keep that thought foremost in mind rather than the poisonous words of that fucker Friar Laurence.

The pine and Douglas fir lent a crisp scent to the air on a January Monday, and down by the McKenzie River the air was especially fresh. We took a walk down there with the hounds for what we assured them would be a memorable occasion.

"Granuaile and I would like to try something," I said to the hounds. My tongue, jaw, and lips had healed to the point where I could speak without impediment. "A new kind of binding. But we need you to be still for a few minutes while we do it."

<No tail wags?> Orlaith asked. <Hard to stop when I am happy, and I am happy now.>

Granuaile answered her, "Wagging your tail will not be a problem. But if you could keep the rest still, that would be great."

<Hey, wait a minute,> Oberon said. <Is this some kind of trick? Are you guys going to drop some sausage in front of us and tell us not to move?>

"No, Oberon," I said. "There is no food involved here at all. But we're pretty sure you're going to like this. Just be patient and enjoy the sun while it lasts, okay?" It was a rare clear day for an Oregon early winter, but in a few hours a storm system would roll in from the Pacific and it would get even colder.

Oberon and Orlaith sat down side by side in the grass, tongues lolling out and tails wagging like the happy hounds they were. Granuaile and I sat down facing them, legs crossed beneath us. I nodded at her and we both flipped our vision to the magical spectrum, where we could see the hounds' auras and the bindings that linked their minds to ours. We had long promised the hounds that we would bind them together eventually so that they could hear each other, but since we had never actually done it before, we didn't tell them what we were planning, in case it didn't succeed.

We began to work on the new binding in tandem, Old Irish streaming out of our mouths in almost identical patterns. The only difference was in our targets: I was starting with Oberon and binding his thoughts to Orlaith, and Granuaile was binding Orlaith to Oberon in turn. For now they were also connected to us: We'd be able to hear both sides of their conversation, but out of necessity we would soon give them the equivalent of their own private line, or else we'd constantly hear them chattering when we were trying to sleep or concentrate on something else. When the bindings were complete, no chimes or sirens went off in their heads. They would have to be told the link was there and then discover that they could use it. We had agreed to tell Oberon first and let him be the uncertain one.

"Okay, Oberon," I said aloud. "You should be able to

talk to Orlaith now. Go ahead and try it. Think something at her rather than at me."

<What? Like, now? I mean . . . do I just say hello? Hello?>

Granuaile's hound replied and got to her feet, her entire rear end shaking back and forth in her excitement. <Hey! It's Oberon! I can hear your words! Can you hear me? Hi, Oberon!>

Oberon got to his feet too, every bit as excited. <Oh, yeah! Wow! Hi, Orlaith!>

<Hi! This is great!>

<Yeah, finally! I've been wanting to tell you that I think you're an amazing hound. I knew from the moment I first sniffed your ass that we would get along!>

<Aw, that's so nice of you to say! I thought the same thing about you!>

Oberon reared up on his hind legs and pawed at the air in Orlaith's direction, and she mirrored his action, as if they were boxers instead of wolfhounds. Then they jumped around in tight little circles. <Oh, wow, three kinds of cat shit, Orlaith!> my hound said. <I know I should be saying very impressive things right now, but I'm too happy to think! I just want to run in circles!>

<Me too! Let's do it!>

<Really? Okay! You're so perfect!>

And then the two of them tore off through the forest, carried away by their joy, leaving Granuaile and me behind, facing the river. We exchanged a glance and laughed at our hounds for a few seconds, and then Granuaile leaned over and kissed me. She pulled away an inch and murmured in a low voice, "I knew we'd get along too, you know."

"Wait, what? Like Oberon knew?"

"Ha! No. But the first time you walked in to Rúla Búla, I just knew. I was attracted on first sight, not first sniff."

"Because Laksha was in your head and told you I was a Druid?"

"No, no. I saw you first. Laksha didn't tell me about what you were until later."

"Ah, that's a fine salve for my ego." Her lips remained close to mine and I could smell her strawberry lip gloss. It felt the way it used to again. "You still drive me crazy, you know."

"Yeah," she said, smiling. "I know." And then we broke our eavesdropping link to our hounds so that they could enjoy their privacy, and we enjoyed some privacy of our own right there on the riverbank, not caring in the least how chilly it was outside.

•

There was bliss for a few days. They were the kind of carefree days you dream of having someday, the kind of days you spend most of your life working and suffering for. And then Orlaith came into heat and the hounds disappeared into the woods for long periods, until one night they sat us down by the fireplace for a Very Serious Talk.

<Atticus and Clever Girl, we have been discussing this for a while, and we think you should know something,> Oberon said.

<Yes,> Orlaith added. <This is a very important thing. Are you paying attention?>

Granuaile and I assured them that they had our full attention.

<I'm pregnant!> Orlaith gushed.

<That means you're going to need to buy a lot more sausage,> Oberon explained.

We both clapped and squeed and gave them hugs. "This is fabulous news!" Granuaile said.

"Yes, indeed! I think we should celebrate," I said. "Oberon, I never did goulash you when we were in

Prague. Let's all go get goulashed!" Granuaile and Orlaith didn't know what that was all about, but they got
on board with the idea quickly enough.

I've decided that, apart from the herb greenhouse, I'm
going to plant a flower garden around the cabin and
keep some bees. The puppies should be here in time to
play around in the spring blossoms. They'll be simply
adorable, and harmony will have found us.

Read on for an excerpt from the first book
in a new epic fantasy series
by Kevin Hearne.

A PLAGUE OF GIANTS

KEVIN HEARNE

Published by Del Rey Books

Coming in 2017

The only reason I didn't kill the lad who woke me was because he did it from the door and closed it on the dagger I whipped from under my pillow and threw at his face. I am prone to violence beyond reason when I am woken from a sound sleep. The rest of the time I like to think I have a reason for my violence.

"Hearthfire, you have urgent matters of state to attend," he shouted through the door. My dagger still quivered in the wood. Real Fornish wood, not glass or steel. The damn door to my bedchamber was worth more than much of my Crucible.

"The matters of state can urgently hump a sand badger until the morning," I growled, and my hearth stirred beside me, sensuously stretching and curving in ways that soothed my sharp edges. I did not want to leave her.

"We would not wake you if it were not dire."

Since Sefir hadn't yet been fully roused, there was no reason to continue the argument and risk waking her, too. I slid out of the sheets, cursed silently, and allowed the moonglow streaming through the skylight to guide me to a chest, on which was folded my favorite ice howler fur. Draping it about me, I opened the door and glowered at the lad who'd been sent to fetch me. I didn't know his name, but he knew enough about the expression on my face to skitter out of throttling distance.

"Your advisers await in the Crucible, Hearthfire."

"Understood. Begone."

He scampered away and I stalked down the halls to the Crucible. Rumblings from Mount Thayil vibrated through the walls of glass and rock.

My advisers were there as the boy had promised, but none would meet my eyes. My feet must have been in a sorry state, judging by the mournful gazes directed there. These men would plunge their hands into lava for me, charge a wall bristling with archers at my command, but they would not look me in the eye. I sighed and wondered if I would ever meet another again—apart from my hearth—who could match my stare for more than a heartbeat.

"Well? What is it? Report." They shuffled their feet and made throat-clearing noises, and one or two ventured a mumble, but spectacularly failed to say anything intelligible. The news must be dire indeed for them to remain so taciturn—especially when they were in full armor and I was wearing nothing but a fur.

"I have never punished anyone for speaking truth," I said quietly. "Nor will I now." I paused, and after none of them took their cue to speak, I continued in the same low tone. "I have never punished anyone for remaining silent, either. But if you don't tell me why I'm not in bed with my hearth, I'll let you all take a swim on the Rift side of the island, is that clear?"

Their very beards trembled. It was Halsten who managed to speak first, an orange-haired, over-muscled houndmaster who braided his mustaches with silver thread. He was openly mocked for his vanity but secretly envied, if I guessed correctly.

"Hearthfire, it's the volcano . . ."

"Has it blown?" I snapped, my eyes narrowing.

"No, no, not yet," Roffe assured me. No one would ever confuse him with Halsten. Roffe's beard was brown and curly and spread like a fan to cover his chest. "But the firelords assure us of an eruption today."

"A huge one," Volund added, somehow managing to convey that this tiny fact was the most important ever uttered.

"I see." If I had leisure, I would make sure to ask the firelords monitoring Thayil why I got less than a day's notice of the end of my realm. "Our crops?"

"Total loss," Halsten said. And with less than a day to work at it, there would not be time to transplant anything. "The city?"

"The same. We must abandon it if we wish to survive."

"Teldwen's tits!" I cursed, and as if in reply, the ground quaked beneath us and the sky boomed with a thunderous explosion, shattering the skylights in the Crucible. The stone pedestals set throughout the Crucible shook, toppling the priceless glass sculptures to the floor and exploding the heirlooms of my line. My sire's works, his sire's, and my own exploded into slivers and shards across the polished marble. "Apparently I am not to be given enough time to get dressed."

They didn't hear me over the cacophony rolling through the sky. My father had warned me this day might come, and his father before him. And the firelords had warned my sires just as they had warned me: Mount Thayil would erupt again, violently, and when it did, there would be little hope of saving the city. So my grandsire had been the first hearthfire to commission the building of transport ships, a fleet to be used for nothing except evacuating the entire population of Harthrad on short notice. The project had consumed plenty of treasure, and there were those who showered the family name of Mogen with ridicule because of it. Why do we have a functional port and a fleet of glass boats that generates no revenue whatsoever? Why are we paying men to build and maintain empty ships that are in some cases older than anyone alive? Why are we storing perfectly good food and water when we could sell it or consume it? I expected that the owners of those sneering voices would be eager to board the ships now, and a small part of me wanted to make them grovel first. But that was truly the small part of me; I knew that some of those giants would be my staunchest defenders once I saved their lives.

"Give the evacuation order," I shouted in order to be heard. "Bring only tools, weapons, armor, coin, and family members. Leave everything else behind. People who refuse to leave everything else behind will be left behind."

"Yes, Hearthfire!" my men chorused, and then Roffe followed up. "Where are we going? Tharsif or Narvik?"

For the first time, I had cause to smile. "We're not staying in Hathrir, brothers. You know very well none of the other Hearthfires will welcome us—especially Winthir Kanek. My very presence in Tharsif would be a challenge to him. And the other islands in this blasted archipelago cannot sustain us. So we're going to Ghurana Nent, north of the Godsteeth bordering Forn but south of Hashan Khek."

"We're invading?" Volund's voice was strangled with surprise and a note of hope.

"No, Volund, armies invade and they attack the native populace. We're refugees, you see, so we're settling. Settling in a land with bountiful natural resources we won't have to import anymore. Close to a mountain that won't explode on us and full of metals, and close to our Fornish trading partners in Pont. Closer still to forests we can harvest ourselves. We will all build new hearths and prosper. And our excuse for all is the eruption of Mount Thayil. Thus we turn a disaster for our generation into a boon for our heirs. We plead inno-

cence and beg for charity and all the while we build defenses, and by the time the Nentians realize we don't
plan to ever leave, they'll discover that they have a hare's
chance in a falcon heath of making us. This was my
grandsire's plan, passed on to my sire and passed on to
me. Think on it," I admonished, waggling a finger, "but
say nothing. Have everyone get safely in the sea and
then follow my ship, telling them only that I'm leading
them to safe harbor. Is that clear?"

"As glass, Hearthfire," Volund said. He was smiling
now, and so were Roffe and Halsten. They finally saw
what my grandsire had seen—that this eruption, long
expected, wasn't the end for us but the beginning. Indeed, it was a much-needed spur to our withers, urging
our people off this blasted rock to a land large and rich
enough for the Hathrim.

The air boomed and I had to shout to be heard. "We
will speak more in private once we arrive. I must retrieve
my armor and tell Sefir we're leaving. Halsten, don't forget the damn hounds and some livestock. We will need
them eventually. See you at the docks." My advisers
turned to relay my orders to the city, moving in a strange
sort of pantomime. Normally I would hear the click and
clatter of their armor as they moved, but all was lost to
the boneshaking roar of Mount Thayil.

Roffe never made it out. A black boulder of volcanic
basalt plowed through the ceiling and obliterated him,
and the impact vaulted Halsten and Volund a good distance away. Had my grandsire not built so well, the entire structure might have collapsed on us. As it was, we
had no time to bid Roffe a proper farewell; not if we
wished to survive ourselves. We needed to get out fast
and hope that everyone with some kind of kenning made
it to the boats.

Harthrad has a goodly measure of firelords like myself
and a number of lesser lavaborn but no furies like some

of the southern cities. In Ghurana Nent there will be few opportunities for our young giants to visit the fires of Olenik, to burn away the child and be reborn immune to flame and heat. I have not spoken of it yet to anyone, but I think it is vital for our long-term survival that we find the Sixth Kenning, which some believe is a fable but which logic insists must be there. For without it—or at least reliable access to the First Kenning in Olenik—we will flicker and wane as a people until we are snuffed. Better that we find the Sixth Kenning and gain dominion over animals. Think what we could do then with our hounds! Discovering it would be a great gift to my people and a fine legacy.

I gave the Crucible one last look as Halsten and Volund got to their feet. All the beautiful glass blown by the Mogen line was destroyed, and the stained windows cracked and slid out of their iron frames, shards tinkling in silence compared to the thunder in the sky above. The gold-and-glass throne would melt in a lava flow, the stone of my hearth would crack from the quaking earth, and all my material wealth would burn, except for the large sack of gems I would take to finance the building of a new city. Raelech stonecutters weren't cheap, but they worked fast and loved nothing so well as riches from the earth. Even with their help, my people faced a trial of fire ahead. As my kingdom fell about me and I ran to my bedchamber, I laughed as I realized that I was looking forward to it.